THE MADONNA LIST

The Madonna List

MAX FORAN

Max Foran

To Dianne
With hopes for some
satisfying reading

Max
13/9/05

BRINDLE
& GLASS

Library and Archives Canada Cataloguing in Publication
Foran, Max
The Madonna list / Max Foran.

ISBN 0-9732481-8-1

I. Title.
PS8611.O62M33 2004   C813'.6   C2004-904963-1

Cover image: Jeff Playford, designlogic australia
www.designlogic.com.au • www.istockphoto.com

Brindle & Glass is pleased to thank the Canada Council for the Arts and
the Alberta Foundation for the Arts for their contributions to our publishing program.

Brindle & Glass Publishing
www.brindleandglass.com

1   2   3   4   5   08 07   06   05

PRINTED AND BOUND IN CANADA

To Heather who has always been there with and for me.

Part 1

Rome, May, 1218

It was dark in the room, and the air was dry with the dust of the streets. Reginald of Orleans lay on the hard wooden pallet, sweat glistening on his chest and arms, and his throat dry with fever.

Two maidens suddenly appeared beside his bed and everything seemed shrouded in a misty glow. They were beautiful and clothed in white. No words did they speak, although their lips moved in silent prayer. Then he saw her: a third maiden, rapturous and beautiful beyond all imagining. Reginald recognized her immediately: The Blessed Virgin Mary, Mother of God and Mistress of the World. Transfixed, he saw her virginal hand reaching towards him, anointing his hands and feet even as she thrilled him with her golden words.

"Let thy loins be girt with the girdle of chastity. Let thy feet be shod for the preaching of the Gospel of Peace."

From out of the folds of the night air, the Vision produced a snow-white scapular which she lay in front of Reginald.

"Behold the habit of thy Order."

Three names were clearly emblazoned in gold on the scapular. Reginald leaned forward but the Vision was gone.

He touched his forehead. It was cool; the fever had left him. Quickly he threw himself to his feet. He found parchment and wrote down those words in gold that still burned in his mind, and afterwards fell to thankful prayer. The Blessed Dominic himself was coming on the morrow. He would share this miracle with him, and afterwards they would pray.

Toulouse, February, 1219

The white-robed figure kneeling before the crucifix at the end of the long room appeared frozen like a statue. Only the wispy vapour from soundless words hanging in the cold air gave him life. Dominic Guzman was praying, oblivious to the chill that made his companion friars on the stone floor curl protectively under their thin blankets.

Suddenly a whitish glow broke the darkness, and three maidens appeared at the far end of the dormitory, the one in the middle shimmering in a sapphire-blue gown. Slowly they came towards him, blessing the prostrate forms on either side with a long silver sprinkler and water from a magnificent golden vessel. They stood before him. As Dominic fell to the floor in supplication, the beautiful one spoke.

"I am She whom you invoke every evening, and when you say, 'Eia ergo advocata nostra,' I prostrate before my Son for the preservation of the Order."

Then she opened her mantle and revealed a legion of friars and sisters from many orders. Dominic recognized many of his own departed. The three in front, smiling at him, he did not know. He opened his mouth to speak, but the vision had disappeared.

For the first time, Dominic noticed the cold. He shivered in his thin robe. For a moment he fumbled at his waist and thought of Reginald. Then, rising, he rang the bell for Matins.

CHAPTER I

Genoa, Spring, 1832.

Bernard's first stop was at a dingy tavern at the water's edge. The windowless interior reeked of smoke, sweat and residual vomit. A couple of Greek sailors, very drunk on cheap red wine, argued in one corner.

A more sober foursome playing cards eyed Bernard curiously as he made his way towards a small, swarthy man in a filthy apron trying to manoeuvre a keg of ale into position under the low wooden counter that served as a bar for pulling beer. He greeted Bernard amiably in a Sardinian dialect that brought a smirk to the face of one of the card players. Bernard watched him guide the greasy keg into place. Then, in a flawless imitation of the barman's thick Sardinian tones, he engaged him in familiar conversation.

Their heads had been close together for about five minutes when Bernard handed him a jangling money pouch and a small vial. The barman deftly pocketed the coins and the vial, bared his gums in a leer that passed for a grin, and slapped Bernard on the back. He then shuffled over to the counter, and poured them each a glass of wine.

"Remember, friend," said Bernard, "no more than half. He's no good to me dead." Then one of the Greeks in the corner threw up. The barman swirled a mouthful of wine through his teeth, then, with his drink still in hand, he took a pail of sawdust over to the flecky mess.

Bernard left the tavern, his drink untouched. Outside, he inhaled heavily at the sea, and began walking along the quay.

~ ~ ~

Vincent Birous sat in his lyre-backed chair, alternately reflecting and dozing, an afternoon's work of cargo consignments lying on the walnut desk. He acknowledged the weight of his fifty-three years with the lassitude of one who could afford the luxury. He had done well. Vincent Birous, born a fisherman's son, a barefoot uneducated boy learning the ways of the world amid the reek of fish and poverty on the docks of Marseilles.

At twenty-five, he had rented a leaky old tub, and through wheedling and bluster parleyed his way to a slice of the supply contracts for Napoleon's armies in the Mediterranean. Now he was the owner of one of the largest shipping companies between Marseilles and Naples. He had achieved success through burning ambition, sound business instincts, a fear of privation, and – when the need warranted – an absence of scruples. Like most self-made men, he measured his success simplistically: through his possessions and the respect they engendered. This beautiful villa, perched on a hillside by the sea, represented wealth and status.

The Birous library was reputed to be one of the best in Genoa. In front of the magnificent desk at which Vincent sat was a century-old, ornately finished harpsichord. Vincent's son Bernard played it superbly, and, according to his private tutor, had enormous potential – if he ever decided to take his music seriously. To the right was a reading table on which sat a priceless copy of Tasso's "Gerusalemme," which Bernard was currently translating into English for a professor at the university. Then there were the books. They sat in deep, elaborate bookshelves that occupied three walls; the fourth was dominated by balcony doors which opened to the sea. The two-thousand-volume collection contained works in half a dozen languages on subjects ranging from philosophy to satirical poetry, the Sciences to mythology, and Greek tragedies to English comedies, all gazing down at Vincent from the shelves through covers that he never would open. Vincent looked out the window to the sails of a ship approaching Genoa Harbour. That, out there, was his domain: the sweat of work, the excitement of the elements and the profanity of camaraderie. The library was his favourite room and he considered it his private retreat, but spiritually it belonged to Bernard.

Vincent thought about Bernard often these days. After all, the boy was twenty-two and ready to assume his proper place in the family business. He had inherited his father's business sense, and he could handle people – ruthlessly, if the mood took him. At age ten, Bernard had bought a peasant woman's proudly displayed tomato crop for a little more than half its market value, softening her heart with a story about his sick mother and crippled father.

Most significantly for the family business, the boy's astonishing facility with languages would prove indispensable in Vincent's plans to expand his markets beyond the Mediterranean and the Baltic to the British Isles, and across the Atlantic to the New World. Bernard had the rare ability to absorb a language after brief exposure, something he experienced often on the Genoan docks. At twelve, he could speak half a dozen languages. At twenty, he could write them as well. Vincent glared at the unfinished work.

Why then, did he have this sense of unease over a son who had excelled in everything he attempted? A barrier existed between the two men. Lacking the insight and patience to probe the labyrinths of his son's complex personality, Vincent relied instead on taking it at face value. The result was enjoyment without fellowship, conversation without intimacy, and dialogue without understanding. In short, a son he didn't know. Bernard seemed to care deeply about nothing, not even the business Vincent was about to give him. The ability was there but the passion wasn't. Vincent didn't know about his son's headaches and the blinding lights that accompanied them. Things might have turned out differently if he had.

~ ~ ~

In her small stone house, set a couple of hundred yards back from the Molo Veccio, Gina Patrone was painting her nails. She sat cross-legged on her big brass bed, a faded robe wrapped around her naked body. Gina was proud of her bed. It had cost her a great deal: three months, years ago, ceaselessly pleasing a fat, bald count. Then for a time she had been queen on this bed. She had had her pick while the other girls got her leavings. But now!

She got up, and facing the mirror, let the robe fall to her feet. For a second, her eyes formed a kind judgement. Yes, she still had the wild, exotic look that inflamed men. But she knew full well that what she saw was the twilight of overripeness before decay. She put the robe back on and returned to her nails. A knock came at the door. Gina frowned. She was not expecting the oafish, drunken Pasqual Cordoba until after dark. Irritably she went to the door to usher in – not Cordoba, but a tall, fine-featured young man with black hair and piercing dark brown eyes.

She studied the young man in front of her. She had known Bernard Birous at once, having seen him several times from a distance. She liked what she saw then, and she liked it now, up close. The easy bearing, the fine clothes, the handsome face, and most of all, the eyes. They looked into hers with an intensity that made her tremble inside. But like the professional she was, Gina calmly returned his gaze. It would be interesting to see how this one got around to business.

He leaned forward, looked into her eyes, and murmured. "You must wonder why I am here, Miss Patrone."

Gina decided that she would make it easy for him. She reached forward and took his face in her hands. She kissed him softly, and began guiding his hand inside her robe. She was surprised when his hand suddenly froze, turned, and grabbed her wrist. For a second, they faced each other. Gina was flushed. When he broke the strained silence, Bernard's face was white, but his voice was calm and controlled. "Miss Patrone. May I speak to you on a matter of . . . mutual interest?"

Bernard went on. "Captain Pasqual Cordoba is, I understand, a regular visitor?"

"What business is that of yours, sir?"

"None, unless I am incorrect in assuming that you consider him – as I do – a boorish fool."

Gina's look told Bernard he was right, so he went on confidently.

"The swine has offended my family and, with your help, will be made to pay. The reward for you will not be insignificant."

He laid seven gold coins in a row on the small table in front of the divan.

Gina's eyes betrayed nothing, but her mind raced. The equivalent of six months' bitter labour glinted up at her. *To do what?* she wondered.

As if reading her thoughts, Bernard smiled and produced a leather bag from his pocket. He extracted a small jar, unscrewed the top, and dipped his finger in the colourless ointment.

"Innocent-looking and harmless, but extremely painful when applied to certain organs."

He paused to see whether Gina understood, then continued. "I think our ignorant captain will consider his burning member but a prelude to blindness, insanity and an early grave."

Gina opened her mouth to protest, but Bernard raised his hand. "Please allow me to continue. No danger is in store for you, Miss Patrone. I desire only to teach the scum a painful lesson, one that will last months before recovery – although I vouch I'd sooner inflict the wretch with the genuine scourge. The ointment needs time to do its mischief. Indeed, all will be in vain should Cordoba practise even modest hygiene. Cleanse immediately after use, and you will have no hint of pain."

Gina's eyes flicked from the jar to the gold coins on the table.

Without speaking, Bernard extracted seven more coins, which he counted into the palm of his hand. "Seven now, and these seven more when I know you have succeeded. A handsome reward for such a small task. Be assured, my dear lady, no harm will come to you. You have my word as a gentleman."

But Gina scarcely heard his words. She thought of Cordoba thrashing about on top of her, stinking of wine, and afterwards, belching and breaking wind like some bloated toad. Gina almost snatched the jar from his hand. "I'll do it. He'll be here soon."

"Good. The consequences will be manifest by tomorrow, and so then will be your seven additional coins."

Now feeling euphoric at the thought of Cordoba's discomfort and her instant riches, she moved again towards Bernard. She dropped her robe to the floor and put her arms around his neck. Then her open mouth was on his and her hand moved towards his belt. Abruptly he shoved her away.

"Your ardour is misplaced, Miss Patrone," rasped Bernard, backing toward the door. He cleared his throat and said, with a mocking smile, "Save it for Captain Cordoba. Doubtless he will appreciate it far more than I."

Gina, too, was gathering herself. "As you wish." Her voice was controlled.

Bernard's hand was on the doorknob before he turned once more to face her. "You will go through with our arrangement, won't you? You can't afford not to, really. I should think that fourteen gold coins is a great deal for a lady whose business prospects are so visibly limited."

Then he was gone into the gathering dusk. Behind a mottled hedge a hundred yards away, he bent double, holding his head to quiet the noises and blunt the pain that stabbed at his eyes.

~ ~ ~

Inside the Amerigo Vespucci Inn, the air was thick with animated talk. University students had piled their books on hardwood tables under the convivial glow of ships' lanterns. At one table, a young man pounded the table with his fist before an enraptured audience. The Italian states were like whores, he was shouting, passed from the Sardinians to the French, to the Austrians, and the meddling British. With a flourish he cried out for unification, the Republic of Italy.

A moment's silence hung like a dam about to break. Then yells and noisy toasts told the barman to bring more wine. He grimaced. It would be a long night.

Another crowded table shook with broad laughter. Renato Santini was demonstrating the best way to bring a ship into the wind during a storm. He stood with his feet planted well apart, wineglass in hand, yelling orders and simulating the sounds of storm and ship. His half-dozen companions acted out the orders between guffaws. "Corsica on the yardarm," he screamed.

"Aye, aye, Captain," chorused the rest. "Lock up your daughters, Bastia mothers."

Renato sat down, swallowed a gulp of wine, and surveyed his friends. They were all looking forward to their summer voyage to Corsica. It had taken Renato several months to convince his father that he and Bernard Birous could manage the Santini family's handsome sloop without the older man's aid. His father had only yielded on the condition that Bernard be in charge. At the time, Renato had been happy; it meant they could go. Now, suddenly, it bothered him.

The conversation at the table veered into bawdy forecasts about the sexual proclivities of Corsican women. Renato poured himself more wine from the decanter. Heedless of the babble around him, he stared at his glass. Why should Bernard be Captain? It should be his by family right. Besides, he knew as much about sailing as Bernard did. He dipped his finger into the wine and morosely flicked pink spots across the unfinished church on his sketchpad. No damn inspiration! That's why he had come here early. He couldn't sketch properly today because he had been too upset, and it was all Bernard's fault.

Renato suddenly pushed his chair from the table, rose dramatically to his feet, and thrust his brimming glass towards his friends, interrupting their exchanges. His voice was loud and challenging. "To the captain of the *Half Moon*."

His glass stayed in the air, demanding. He waited. Then, six glasses touched his, answering the call. "To Renato Santini, Captain of the *Half Moon*."

Bernard, unnoticed, watched from the door. When the revellers were seated, he drew up a chair.

"You're late, Bernard," Renato slurred.

"I had something to take care of. Were we discussing Corsica?" Bernard said affably.

A babble greeted him as he was informed all at once about sailing dates; who was bringing what; the quality of Corsican wine; the doubtful morality of Bastia girls; and how Antonio's distant relatives had promised them the use of an old farm house for the duration of their stay.

Suddenly, Renato was on his feet, swaying slightly. His eyes were on Bernard. "To my crew," he shouted, and drank noisily. As the group of friends cheered and drank, Bernard gazed disinterestedly at the fire.

~ ~ ~

An hour later, only Bernard and Renato remained at the table, discussing how fine it would be to kick the Sardinians out of Genoa. Renato was now quite drunk. Bernard was not sober, either; a few glasses of wine were enough to make the room spin pleasantly for him. Too bad, Renato noted, that the radical group had left. They could have joined them.

There was a long pause in the conversation, and Bernard could tell that Renato was gathering himself. He looked more at his glass than at Bernard, and his voice was edged defensively. "My father is sometimes a conservative fool. I should captain the *Half Moon* and you know it, eh?" His eyes rose to Bernard's, and he licked his lips. He went on. "I told them too. You heard me."

"I know," replied Bernard casually. "Your tongue became loose, and you said too much. Your father may be conservative, but he is also right. I am the better sailor. It's as simple as that, Renato."

"We're not children any more, when you were always best," Renato said agitatedly. "It's going to be different now. My lackey days are over." He grabbed his sketchbook from on the table and thrust it at Bernard. "Could you do that, Michelangelo? I think not. I can sail the *Half Moon* as well as you can, too. No, better. And I set people adrift who don't know their place at sea."

Across the table, Bernard's eyes blazed. "You don't know what you're talking about. It's not your decision. Shall we just go along to your father and tell him that Captain Renato is now at the helm?"

Renato's voice slurred more deeply with resentment. "No!" He slammed his hand down on the table. "We'll leave my father out of this." He waved his arms wildly. "It's them. You can't make a fool out of me in front of them. They think I'm captain. Why can't I?" Suddenly his voice was petulant.

"They are wrong and you are wrong, my friend. You are no leader, and the sea demands leaders. Respect is the font of leadership, and true respect is underlain by fear. They may like you, Renato, but they fear me. To captain your father's boat would be to place it and your crew at peril. It's not like it was here tonight, all bombast and noise. You're better as a mate, and, like it or not, I am the superior leader."

Renato frowned, trying to straighten out his thoughts. When he spoke the words came tumbling out. "You're no leader. Leaders are men. You don't even . . ." He stopped, and his eyes became cunning. He leaned forward heavily. "You give me no choice, then. I call upon the Pact of Equals to decide. The captainship of the *Half Moon* will be the prize."

Bernard's eyes were wary. "What will be the challenge?"

"Elena Armetti, the vineyard owner's daughter. Remember how she spurned Antonio at the masquerade ball last year? And he's not the only one. She cares about nothing except her horses, I hear. But neither one of us has ever tried to woo her."

Bernard did not answer. Renato went on. "The wager is, we both pay court to her. We have two months before we sail. The first to bed her captains the *Half Moon*. One of us will find out how our fair Elena rides something besides a horse." Even drunk, he knew the task would be difficult. But because he was drunk he didn't care. Nothing mattered but the chance to best Bernard.

Bernard's was cornered. Renato had called on the Pact of Equals – their boyhood term to give proper solemnity to contests – which had over the years become an almost sacred accord. One could not invoke the Pact lightly, and once issued, the Pact could not be denied, though its terms might be mutually amended.

Bernard had issued most of the challenges over the years, and had usually won – though several times only because he had succeeded in altering the rules of the original test to his advantage. Renato never seemed to realize this, and had been loath to call on the Pact ever since that embarrassment two years ago when he had had to be pulled out of the water with success in sight. He had been convinced that he was the faster swimmer, and had almost made good on his challenge. He hadn't counted on exhaustion, and had to watch from under a blanket on the beach as the slower but stronger Bernard splashed to victory. In the celebration and backslapping that followed, it didn't occur to him that he had invoked the Pact on a two-hundred-yard swim, and that Bernard had swayed him into changing the terms by eulogizing about the glory of swimming across the Bay.

But now Renato had called on the Pact. Bernard weighed his words carefully. "I accept the challenge. But Elena's father is not the kind to take anyone meddling in his daughter's pantaloons lightly. It could be bad for our families. Then, there's the matter of arbitration. How will we know who is the victor?"

Without giving Renato time to think of a reply, Bernad continued. "Some evidence? Too crass for gentlemen. Which is another reason why Elena won't do; why no one girl will do. The choice of lady must be our own. Each of us must go out and conquer the virtue of a fair damsel. Also, the time devoted to this quest is far too long – and if you'll forgive me, Renato, too trivial – to warrant extended energies."

He looked squarely at Renato, and mustered up all the bravado he could. "A week. One week today, we meet at the Café Loretti with our conquests."

He forced a lascivious smile. "We'll ask Umberto to wait on us. He likes us both, and is a fair man. If only one of us brings a wench, then he is the winner. If neither of us does, then we extend the time of the wager. In the probable case of us both bringing a lady, we shall ask Umberto to decide who has made the fairer conquest."

As he noted Renato's nodding approval, Bernard smiled to himself, and thought of Angela, his family's new servant. He'd done it: changed the rules in his favour. There was no possibility of Renato procuring a girl within the week to rival Angela's beauty. It might cost him a bit of money and charm to secure Angela's cooperation. But servant girls were so predictable, and so pathetically willing.

Bernard extended his hand. "The Pact of Equals."

Swaying precariously, Renato rose to his feet, to shake Bernard's extended hand. The wine splashed in his goblet. "To the Pact of Equals."

He thrust his glass at Bernard's so violently that both glasses shattered. The wine gushed like blood to the table and onto the rug beneath.

Renato swayed as he chortled, "Wine and women – I love them both. More than you, Bernard. More than you."

There was no one else in the room, and nothing more to say. They left the broken glass where it lay and went out into the night. It was raining softly and the streets were deserted. Renato stumbled off to find a carriage, but Bernard walked back up the hills through the dark. He was drunk enough to ignore the rain, but not enough to banish the conflicting thoughts in his brain. He would win the bet, but could he face the test? The soft voice at his shoulder was quiet, and from behind the hiss of the rain on the road the noises of turmoil began to echo through his head. Shrill voices, growing louder, confusing him with their tormented babble. He hurried now, fleeing from the vibrations pounding in his ears.

The lowlands of the Ligurian hills swept down to craggy cliffs in a green-brown haze, barren but for patches of hardy cactus, and pine copses in sheltered areas. The land was little cultivated, virtually unchanged since the Roman legionnaires had stamped it with the seal of Empire almost fifteen hundred years earlier.

Usually Bernard was conscious of the moods of the sea whenever he walked near the cliffs. This morning, however, he hurried, head bent into the breeze that blew uncharacteristically cool from the Mediterranean as he walked the well-trodden path from the villa towards the ocean. He turned off the path and headed into a pine grove, which in turn opened to a ravine that pointed to a break in the cliffs. For five minutes, Bernard picked his way along the ravine floor until he came to an inconspicuous cleft in the earth, almost concealed by a jumble of rocks and thorn bushes. After moving several rocks, Bernard crawled into a space just wide enough to accommodate his shoulders. For twenty yards or so, he inched his way down through the dark until the passageway opened up into a cavern about the size of two rooms. Shafts of light from overhead crevices gave a bare illumination to the dry cave.

In the dead silence, Bernard unhurriedly began his ritual. He lit two lanterns on the floor, throwing one wall into irregular relief. Next, Bernard spread a blanket and sat cross-legged facing the illuminated wall, his eyes fixed in concentration.

The images on the wall came and went. He had talked to them all at one time or another. He saw the horse, the dove, the sceptre, and finally the familiar face of his inner self which guided his hand whenever he visited this chamber in the earth. The face looked at him knowingly and smiled. His feelings about women tumbled through his mind: disinterest, boredom, anger, and more recently, a crawling revulsion. Suddenly he flinched. The face was gone, disappearing into a mosaic of protrusions, ledges, and shadowy recesses.

Then he saw her. Soft grey with a gently sloped nose. Her eyes were dark, and her mouth was open in a sneer. Was it Angela? He willed her away. He blinked once, twice, but she was still there. He turned his head away, and abruptly brought it back. Her face mocked him from the wall. He forced himself to look, while silently pleading her to go. Then miraculously, through his confusion, he saw her transformed. She was smiling now, not sneering. It was Angela. As he sensed her eyes beckoning to him, he felt himself nodding, and a strange electricity coursed through his veins. Then one lamp went out, and she was gone.

The noises in his head had faded away. Bernard folded the blanket and returned it to its niche, and after extinguishing the remaining lantern, crawled back through the passageway to the world above. He scarcely felt the freshening wind behind him as he retraced the muddy mile to his father's villa. He knew now what he had to do. But first was the matter of Captain Pasqual Cordoba.

~ ~ ~

On the docks of Genoa, a gang of sweating sailors worked in the afternoon sun unloading the Birous cargo from the *Star of Lisbon*. One stack of cloth bolts was already under canvas in case of rain, and a second was taking shape on the dock. Beyond the *Star of Lisbon*, a second ship lay at berth, listing heavily to port. She was bound from Athens to Marseilles, and had limped into Genoa three days earlier. Her cargo had been removed and lay stacked on the pier. On board, preparations were underway to remove her to the repair dock across the bay. "Christ. It will take us till midnight to get this unloaded." muttered Pedro Diaz, first mate on the *Star of Lisbon*. Another hour to change piers, and another ten hours to load the Greek cargo. He cursed his skipper's greed.

Cordoba was wrong to have dumped the Birous cargo in favour of a better offer by the Greek, even if a transcriber's error in the contract gave him the right. Not good business. Not at all. *And he's not even here to see the job done*, thought Diaz bitterly. Came down sick rather suddenly. How convenient.

If he had been able to see his captain at that moment, Diaz would have dismissed his suspicions about Cordoba's neglect of duty. Cordoba lay on his bunk, his face ashen from vomiting and his face bathed in sweat. His penis burnt like fire. His bladder was full, but the pain of urinating made relief unbearable. He moaned with pain, his mind tormented by thoughts that he might be afflicted with the disease he dreaded most. "Stinking bitch," he growled to himself. He shut his eyes but no sleep came.

Through senses dulled by pain, Cordoba heard a tap at the door, and then a voice. "Captain Cordoba. It's Bernard Birous. May I come in?"

Cordoba had been expecting an angry Vincent Birous. Not his brat. He had not been looking forward to dealing with an enraged bull like Vincent Birous. His pale son was another matter entirely.

He had barely opened his mouth to groan something cutting when Bernard was in the room, standing by his bunk. Cordoba forced himself to one elbow. "What do you want?" he muttered thickly.

Bernard, dressed expensively in a silk business suit, looked about the cabin, tapping his hand with his cane, noting the jumbled disarray of clothes and bottles. On a table was a decanter of murky water with a dirty cloth beside it.

"Let me understand you properly, Captain. Our contract with you stipulates that you sail for Marseilles tonight. The shipment is direly needed by our customers, who already await your arrival with anticipation. Yet, if I am not mistaken, I see your men unloading our cloth onto the pier. I am told that you sail tomorrow with the cargo from yonder Greek vessel." He waved his arm towards the porthole.

"Read your contract, pup," Cordoba croaked. "The date of arrival was unspecified. An unfortunate omission from your point of view, but quite lucky for me." He wiped his brow with a filthy handkerchief. "Besides, the Greek has a greater need. And, damn your rich hides to hell, so have I."

Cordoba wanted to say more about his indebtedness; about how the Birous family could easily suffer this minor setback, but Bernard's voice cut in. "You don't look well Captain. Not at all. Indeed, methinks you would be wise to enjoy your ill-gotten profits as soon as possible. From what I am told, you have likely been plagued with what we in Genoa refer to as the Patrone Pox. Only last month I saw an employee of a friend succumb to its horror. He was quite blind and raving mad at the end, poor fellow."

Cordoba suddenly felt nauseated. "The what? I . . ."

Bernard smiled, turning the one chair backwards and straddled it to face the sweating figure on the bunk. "Gina Patrone, the whore who lives not a mile from here. Dark-haired, well past her youth. She has a nude painting on one wall. Shall I go on?"

Cordoba just looked at him, dreading what was coming next.

"She's rotten with disease, you know. Ah, there are many stories to be told about our Gina. Some men have been known to send their enemies to her while posing as friends. Reckless youths have devised a gambling game whereby the loser has to bed her."

Bernard leaned forward, and touched his cane to Cordoba's groin. "The pain will only intensify, you know."

Cordoba recoiled as if from a snake. His eyes were filled with tears. Like most seamen, he accepted venereal disease as a cruel lottery. Now he had lost. Already he wanted a priest and the cleansing darkness of the confessional. He closed his eyes and whispered, "Jesus, Mary and Joseph."

When he opened them, Bernard was standing by his side holding a small vial of white cream. "No, Captain. I imagine those three don't care enough to help you, but I might be persuaded."

Though Cordoba said nothing, his eyes betrayed their interest.

"Listen carefully, for what I say to you I will say once only. You are right in your assessment. We will endure this travail. The Birous family may lose money, and even some goodwill, but we will survive, no matter what you may do. On the other hand, you, my careless friend, will not. God knows how many foolish ones have perished because of the Patrone slut's foulness."

He held the jar close to Cordoba, turning it over slowly in his hands. "You see this, Captain? Such a common-looking thing. But it might well be your salvation." He smiled encouragingly. The lies tumbled easily from his lips. "My chemistry tutor at the university developed this substance a year ago in order to save the life of his most brilliant student. Like you, the young man had been careless in his dalliances. I myself saw him when his condition was worse than yours is now. He applied this ointment to his member for two weeks. The cure, though gradual, was complete."

Cordoba's eyes flickered with excitement. "How much . . . ?"

Bernard raised his hand again. "We both have needs, Captain. If you sail with the tide this evening with our cargo, the ointment is yours. If not . . ." He shrugged his shoulders.

With a visible effort, Cordoba struggled to his feet. He lurched towards Bernard, who easily moved out of his way.

"How do I know you're telling the truth? What I have is probably nothing, and will disappear in a few days. I'll tell you what I think. I think you're a damned liar."

Bernard smiled. He dropped the jar into his pocket and moved towards the door. "As you wish, Captain. You are a disgusting fellow and a rogue, and what happens to you will be no loss to anyone."

His hand was on the doorknob when he turned. "One more thing. Please have your men secure the Birous cargo well. I expect to consign another ship within the week. In your condition we may even beat you to Marseilles." Laughing loudly, he had closed the door and was walking away when he heard Cordoba's strangled tones. "Wait!"

He was standing at the door to the cabin, bent double and leaning against the jamb for support. "All right, curse you. All right. We have a bargain." He reached for the jar, then winced at the strength of Bernard's grip on his arm.

"Not so fast, Captain. All in good time. First we tell your first mate the change in plans. Then the ointment."

Ten minutes later, a frenzied Cordoba lay on his bunk, still sweating profusely, his penis coated with the thick gel. Bernard was walking briskly away from the dock. As his cane tapped the stone gateways and wrought-iron fences, he chuckled to himself. The Sardinian barman and Gina Patrone had done their work well. The combination of arsenic in his wine and the liniment with which Gina had lubricated herself had given Cordoba the desired symptoms. Still, Bernard stayed near the waterfront until he saw the *Star of Lisbon* weigh anchor and move silently out of the harbour to the open sea. Without the salve, Cordoba's symptoms would have disappeared within a day. The mild irritant in the ointment would keep him worried until he got to Marseilles. After that, it didn't matter. His only question now was whether he would pay Gina Patrone the additional seven coins he had promised. He thought not.

~ ~ ~

In her small room in the servants' quarters behind the villa, Angela Pietro was deep in thought. Two gowns lay on her bed. One had been a gift from a former lover. The other she had stolen from the selfish daughter of the last household she had attended in Spezio. She chose the shimmering green taffeta dress because it stretched tighter over her bosom than the more elegant red organdy gown she had stolen. Besides, having bustle, the red one was inappropriate for what she had in mind. She dabbed some of Lucinda Birous's cologne between her breasts, and fell to brushing her long, dark hair. To be invited by the master of the house to hear his poetry was one thing. To be asked on an evening when his parents were away was quite another.

Bernard was already in the library, standing with his hands behind his back, looking out at the sea. The balcony doors were open and the sound and

15

smell of the ocean freshened the room with a briskness he did not feel. His "Gerusalemme" translation was marked up with three untidy versions of a verb he normally would have translated with ease. He had turned to his beloved Bach on the harpsichord, but the notes were lumbering and lifeless.

He was going to face the one test he had always avoided. The cave had ordained it, and though it had always guided his course unerringly, he still felt ill at ease. The quiet voice at his shoulder was whispering good things about the delights of love, but he knew he was supposed to feel some desire, some relish at the thought of fondling female flesh. He had even tried to tell himself that it shouldn't be of concern, and that he might be best served to withdraw from the contest. Did it matter who captained the *Half Moon*? Was an encounter with a tawdry female of any import at all? But nothing worked, and for the first time in his life, Bernard Birous was frightened.

That women were inferior creatures did not worry him. Some of them made passable conversation, and he knew a few who had some modest talents. His concern was over his own certainty. He was a chosen one awaiting his destiny. He would be told when the time came. In the meantime, he should listen to the inner ones and keep himself in a state of readiness. Yet, though his guiding spirits had told him to conquer the woman and to humiliate Renato, for the first time he was not at one with them. But he must not deviate tonight. The soft one, and the cave-Angela had to be right. He just wished it were over with.

Bernard barely heard the tap on the door. He opened it to see Angela standing there shyly. The girl was taller than he had thought; her dark eyes met his at a level distance. He mustered the words, forcing a bravado he didn't feel.

"Angela, my dear. How breathtaking you look. Come in before you disappear into the night like a beautiful sunset."

He ushered her into the room, and motioned her to sit down. He had already decided on his strategy. First, flattery to relax and enrapture her. A glass of port while he read his poetry with proper feeling and intimacy. He would kiss her softly at first, then intensely. By the time he had undressed her, he would be ready. He knew he would. And afterward, he would have proven himself the master. She would be only too glad to go with him to meet his friend at the Café Loretti. Taking no risks, he would ensure her loyalty by giving her some money from his father's pouch. After next Tuesday she would be just a servant girl again. He would probably have to get his father to dismiss her.

"Thank you, master Birous," Angela replied looking about the softly lit room. She too, had done some mental rehearsing. She would be worldly, and would make it easy for him without being brazen.

She didn't sit, but went straight to the shelves. "I spend more time clean-ing this room than any other. I shouldn't be telling you why. But I will. Can you think why?" Her voice was coquettish, teasing.

"Because books are difficult to dust?" Bernard replied.

Angela laughed merrily. "No, no, silly." She dropped her voice confiden-tially. "But it is because of the books. I read them. I even took one to my room one night. But you won't tell, will you?"

"You *read* them?" Bernard was truly incredulous.

"Not all of them. Just some." She touched a volume of Vico. "This one's my favourite. I weep when I read the poem about the maiden who drowned trying to save her lover."

Bernard took her arm, ignoring the sudden pain behind his eyes. "Angela, you seem to be a most remarkable young woman. Now, you sit right on this couch while I pour us each a glass of port. I want you to be relaxed when you compare my verse to the romance of Vico."

Angela sat down. Her instincts were jangling, but she didn't know why. She forced an encouraging smile. "I will love your poetry. Do you write much?"

"No. Actually I spend most of my spare time translating books, or reading. The subject doesn't matter much. I just enjoy accumulating knowledge."

Behind her back he frowned, annoyed at himself for his candour. Then he carried the two glasses of port to the couch and sat down beside Angela.

"To lovers of poetry." He touched her glass, and they both drank. "Who taught you to read? I must admit, it has me intrigued."

"My uncle lived with us when I was a little girl." She smiled and took another ample draught of port. "He taught me and my brother. My mother said it was a waste of time for me. Do you think so, Master Birous?"

"Of course not," Bernard replied, opening his eyes in mock astonishment. "Except, if you couldn't read, then you wouldn't have read Vico, and then you wouldn't have known how really bad my poetry really is."

They both laughed nervously, and Bernard found himself thinking how much he wanted to be anywhere but here with this slattern. Gathering himself, he leaned forward and touched her on the knee. "Call me Bernard, please Angela. Tonight we are just two people talking about poetry."

Angela lowered her eyes, not moving her knee from his lingering hand. It felt cold through her gown. "All right. Bernard. May I hear your poetry?"

Bernard went to the desk and picked up a piece of paper. He had written the poem hurriedly a few hours earlier. It was abominably bad verse and he well knew it.

"I wrote this a year ago during a journey to Spezio – your birthplace, I believe. I was lonely at the time, and a solitary rock on an abutment overlooking the sea seemed to share my loneliness." He sat down beside Angela, then moved closer to her until he could feel the warmth of her thigh against his leg.

He smiled at her. "The light is better here, don't you think?"

Angela returned his smile and pressed her leg to his. "Yes, much better," she breathed.

Then Bernard began to read. He hoped the emotion in his voice was convincing.

> You stand alone through time,
> Watching without seeing.
> Listening without hearing,
> Living without breathing.
>
> You count the days by your own dying,
> Torn by the wind,
> Ravaged by the rain,
> Rotting into the earth.
>
> Should we be one,
> I would embrace your defilement
> Your solitude, my loneliness,
> Each unloved, one and together.

Time hung suspended as Bernard lowered the paper and looked at Angela. Her eyes were moist and her hand was on his arm. Conscious of his own laboured breathing, the ticking of the clock, and even the sound of the distant waves, Bernard paused on the brink of resolve. Then he plunged over.

Angela came willingly into his arms. Her mouth was soft and yielding under his. He kissed her for what seemed like a long time, and felt her probing tongue. His arms tightened about her as he levered her back on the cushions. She reached up for him and pulled him down on top of her. But even as he crushed his mouth harder onto hers, his mind was already receding from its resolve. He gasped, feeling suffocated, then almost blindly thrust his hand between her thighs, forcing it upwards. He left it there, probing desperately, while waiting for something to happen. It didn't. But he had to go on. He pulled the strap of her gown down until her breasts were exposed. The ugly mounds repelled him. Then her arms were around his neck, drawing his head down towards the flat nipples.

Even as she pulled Bernard's head to her breast, Angela could feel her body's resistance. The arousal that usually came easily in response to the touch of lips or feverish hands was lost in a welter of other emotions. Bernard was behaving in much the same way as those who had made her moan and writhe, yet she felt detached, almost like an object. She normally exulted in the pleasure her nakedness gave to men. Now she felt embarrassed. The press of his open mouth and his probing fingers brought no desire. Through the veil of confusion, she remembered her promise to herself. Her fingers fumbled with the buckle of his belt.

Bernard was close to tears. He recoiled from the saltiness of her nipple but left his mouth there, trying to stifle the gorge rising in his throat. He was scarcely conscious of the girl's hand fumbling at his breeches, and barely felt it close around his flaccid penis. He could feel the bile now, bitter and unrelenting, oozing between his teeth to soil Angela's white breast. He opened his eyes to find hers, unexpectedly open, large and frightened. With a cry he lurched to his feet, stumbled through the open door to the balcony, and vomited.

As the ghastly scene unfolded before her eyes, Angela almost instinctively retrieved her gown and draped it about her bare shoulders. Her thoughts raced in turmoil as Bernard straightened up and wiped his lips with a linen handkerchief, which he dropped into the night.

After a moment at the railing, Bernard turned to her. "My apologies, Miss Pietro. Doubtless something I ate. Still, it's a vision not foreign to your worldly eyes, I imagine." He forced a benign smile. "Please get dressed. As you can see I have no stomach tonight for such matters."

He turned his back on the girl, and began scratching with a pen at the "Gerusalemme" translation. His hand was shaking.

Angela said nothing as she dressed. Her confusion was rearranging itself into connected images. The dark head convulsing on her breast and the cold, tiny penis lying lifeless in her hand. *I have no stomach tonight for such matters.*

Even as she tried to straighten her hair, she saw Bernard pick up a purse from the desk. She knew what he was going to do. Tears welled in her eyes as Bernard walked across the room, the pouch jangling in his hands. Through her fury, Angela was barely conscious of Bernard's voice saying something about the Café Loretti, and lively conversation with people of gentle breeding.

"All you must do, Miss Pietro, is to be attentive to me before my friends, so it will appear as though we are lovers."

With a cry, Angela lunged forward, dashing the coins from his hand and scattering them across the carpet. The words tumbled from her lips: "No! I won't take your money. You think you can pay me like a whore? I'll tell you one thing, sir. Every chambermaid and livery boy in Genoa will soon know that the son of Vincent Birous is a eunuch who could never satisfy any woman. The only thing that comes up around him is his food."

With a shriek of hysterical laughter, Angela fled. Bernard remained standing, staring at the door for fully ten minutes after Angela had slammed it behind her. His face was almost trancelike as he fought to bring logic out of confusion. Only the clenching of his fingers gave any indication of his agitation.

He heard a noise at the front entrance. His parents. They had returned early. Quickly, he retreated to his room. Once inside and lying on his bed, his pent-up emotions broke their barriers. "Vessels of the Devil," he whispered to himself as his eyes filled. Then, for the first time in his adult life, Bernard Birous cried, his long sobs muffled against his pillow.

~ ~ ~

The next day, Bernard awoke late and had picked morosely at his poached eggs until they congealed into an inedible mass on his plate. He left the villa in disgust, pursued by a whirlwind of voices. For the next six hours he had walked narrow dirt roads and little-used paths that took him into olive groves, beyond to the higher grazing slopes and back to the rocky coastal headlands, trying to escape the strident voices and flashing lights that bedevilled him, until he had finally collapsed, exhausted.

The sun had almost dropped to the rim of the ocean when Bernard awoke. Now the voices and lights were less insistent and his head did not ache as much.

Retrieving his jacket he rose and began walking, with no particular destination. He had failed. Sullied by a woman. Misled by his guiding spirits. He stopped and looked out to sea. Then, a voice came to him, clear in its insistence, soft in its sympathy. *You have not failed, Bernard. Your experience with the vile woman was the gateway to your destiny. The cave will define your path.*

He turned and headed toward his sanctuary, less than half a mile distant.

An hour later in the gathering dusk, Bernard was hurrying back to the villa. His steps were purposeful and confident, as though a great weight had been lifted off his shoulders. He had seen the woman again, and this time she was sneering evilly. She didn't look like the servant girl anymore, but she was woman and she was foul.

It all made sense. His experience with the chambermaid slut had been a warning. Because he had wavered in his resolve, evil had tried to seduce him. He had touched her sickening lips, and had run his hands over her putrid, writhing body. And he had been rightly repelled. It would not happen again, ever.

But if the first image had vindicated him, the second had excited him beyond imagination. Awesomely imposing, it had extended the whole height of the cave. The cowled shape, face hidden in recess was unmistakeable. So was the embossed strip of the scapular covering the chest, and the beckoning outstretched hands. And he had counted them, the seven shadows that had danced behind the robed figure. His senses were overcome by the crescendo that welled from the throats of a cheering throng. He was being called to his destiny. To Rome, and the priesthood! A domain where women were neither needed nor wanted. A realm where power was both mystic and real. Men had always used the Church, but none had ever used it the way he would. It was so obvious. Rome! Ideal for one like himself chosen for greatness. The way was clear. He would speak to his father immediately.

~ ~ ~

For all his bluff heartiness, Vincent Birous was an astute man. Three decades in the volatile world of shipping had taught him to read people like his son would read a book. Yet standing outside his son's room the previous evening with a bottle of port and two glasses, and hearing the muffled sobs from within, he had found himself at a total loss. The coins strewn across the library floor, too, had puzzled him. So had the lingering fragrance of his own wife's scent and the small lace handkerchief he had found on the leather couch. Yet, for all his imaginings, Vincent Birous was not prepared for the shock his son's appearance had given him at the breakfast table that morning. The boy looked ghastly. His dress was uncharacteristically careless, his face taut and white, and his eyes held a look that Vincent had seen often before, but never in his son. He had seen it in enemies he had bested, captains he had bullied, and opponents he had thrashed in smoky taverns from Marseilles to Naples.

The bolt of realization had come at the end of the meal. As the new maid, Angela, approached the table carrying coffee, Bernard had mumbled something, lurched to his feet, and fled from the room. Now it all made sense. His son had at last behaved like a foolish boy. He had gotten himself involved with a pretty servant girl, and probably a wild one at that. That was enough to worry Vincent. Maybe she had given him something. That type often carried all sorts of nasty things in their pleasure boxes. Most were easily cured, and he couldn't have been dallying long enough with her to have contracted anything serious. Blackmail? An old trick, but easily foiled by a worldly and understanding father.

Vincent was going over some unpaid accounts when his son entered the library and took his place opposite the great oak desk. When he spoke, his words came in excited gusts instead of his usual measured tone.

"Father, I must speak to you on a matter of utmost importance." He produced a bottle from behind his back, and placed it on the desk. "So important to me that it shall be toasted, with or without you."

Good God! thought Vincent, watching his son pour red wine. *What's the young fool done? If he thinks he's going to marry that cheap tart . . .*

Aloud he said, smiling, "By all means, Bernard. You know, my father once said that there were only two kinds of surprises. Good and bad. And they involved either money or women. Now, which is yours? Although I'll vouch I've got more than an inkling. Nothing that can't be resolved sensibly, I trust."

He leaned back in his chair as Bernard placed the two goblets on the desk.

"Well, Bernard, to what or whom shall we be toasting?"

There was a long silence. Neither man raised his glass. Something was already jangling in the back of Vincent's mind. His son's voice was measured and deliberate, just as it was when he faced an adversary. "Father, I am going to enter the priesthood. I think you should know. The business, I mean."

Vincent felt like he had been hit in the stomach by one of his burly seamen. His thoughts about the girl disappeared as he struggled to reply. "The priesthood! I thought you were less a man of God than I am. You, a priest! With all you've got here." Vincent was recalling the many jibes he had heard his son make about the mendacity of men of God who valued the things of this world more than they did the spiritual glory of the next.

Bernard's reply was unemotional and curiously flat. "The call, father. I received it today." He did not elaborate further.

Vincent was about to respond with more vehement protestations about his son's misplaced values when he saw the look in Bernard's eyes. The blazing determination, underlain by something else more frightening, stopped the words in his throat. When he did speak he was surprised at the resignation in his voice. "What Order are you going to join? The place of study? Your immediacy? I mean, if you are serious, these things need due consideration."

Bernard's reply came quickly. "The Dominicans. I shall be a Dominican. I shall seek entrance to Santa Sabina in Rome."

Vincent nodded. It made sense. Lucinda's uncle was a Dominican, and like all well-read young men, Bernard was familiar with the high reputation of the Order for its intellectual rigour. In these times of Papal rejuvenation, Rome was a good place to study. The suddenness, however, presented some problems.

"Santa Sabina, eh? I would have thought that you might have chosen the fine monastery at St. Thomas'. It's the chief Dominican House in Italy, I understand, and not far from Rome. Still, knowing you, I imagine you have your own reasons."

Bernard nodded, saying nothing.

His father continued, "It's unfortunate that you go so soon. I need to arrange an introduction to the Prior at Santa Sabina. This should be done before you prove your fitness to him. The truth of the vocation, I mean."

"It will be easy, Father. I shall take the letter of introduction with me." He reached for the untouched wine goblet. "Now, shall we drink?" He raised the pewter towards his father.

Though Vincent's thoughts were in turmoil, he felt strangely removed. Bernard, a priest! The absence of passion. The missing ingredient. Could the priesthood be the answer? He had no doubt that Bernard would not only take Holy Orders, but advance himself grandly in the cloth. The Dominicans would not receive the humble man of God they might expect. "The ways of God are wondrous," his mother had often said. Here was living proof.

"To your new life." Without acknowledgement from Bernard, they drank. Vincent broke the ensuing silence. "Ah, Bernard. I know someone who will be delighted that her countless rosaries and novenas have not been in vain. We must tell your mother immediately."

~ ~ ~

Lucinda Birous did not disappoint her husband. God, the Blessed Virgin, and Catherine of Genoa received immediate, tearful tribute. A private conversation with all three would come later. Lucinda embraced her son and her husband joyously, and to Vincent's surprise and Bernard's veiled amusement, Lucinda suggested that they all take tea even though it was not the proper hour. It was that kind of news.

The next week was spent in frenzied preparation. Lucinda insisted on supervising her son's luggage. He packed books, she, clothes. Bernard had difficulty persuading her that the Dominican ideal of poverty precluded the notion of turning his cell in Santa Sabina into a gentleman's suite. She at last settled for one large trunk which was duly loaded on board a Birous vessel bound for Naples.

It was unfortunate, Bernard thought, that his mother had such a love of the Church. With her love of walking and affinity with things intuitive, she was in some ways like himself. He found it mildly amusing to think that she now believed that he shared her steadfast faith. Not that he wouldn't exhibit the proper piety as necessary. He hoped his mother wouldn't be too sentimental on this, his eve of departure. He'd just have to endure it, and excuse himself as soon as he could.

He found her door ajar, and after knocking once, entered the room. Lucinda was completing her ritual of evening devotion: selected readings from the New Testament, or lives of the Saints, followed by the usual rosary, litany to the Blessed Virgin, and individual supplication. She was sitting on the couch reading St. Paul. She smiled when she saw her son, and then rose to greet him with a light kiss. "Bernard, I can scarcely believe what has come to pass. All my prayers answered at last. And now you go so far away, and I'm not even sad. Well, just a little bit."

She took his hand and they both sat. Bernard began awkwardly as he fought off his unease. "I'm glad you're happy for me, Mother. It's something that I have to do."

Lucinda nodded, and then leaned forward eagerly. "Was the call strong?"

Before he could reply, Lucinda went on, her voice earnest. "When I was a little girl I waited for the call. I wanted to be a nun so much, but God didn't call me. I used to feel I was unworthy until I read about Catherine of Genoa. She wasn't a nun, and look what she did. All those visions and saintly work among the poor. She had a husband, but not a son like my Bernard who is going to be a priest, a great priest."

Bernard sighed, "Mother, you make it sound like I'm already canonized. I am just starting out. The studies are hard, I hear, and the time is long."

"It will not be hard for you," answered Lucinda, shaking her head. "You have had the call. How did He call you, Bernard? A voice? A light? A revelation rolling in from the sea like thunder?"

"No, Mother. None of those things. I just suddenly knew what I wanted to do."

Lucinda remained skeptical. A vocation was a clear individual request from God, often dramatic. It couldn't be just a feeling. Otherwise she would have become a nun.

"They'll ask, you know. The Dominicans will ask you about the call. Catherine of Genoa was in the confessional when a dazzling light gathered itself about her, almost blinding her confessor. And suddenly, Catherine saw her future life lying out before her like a road to heaven. It was miraculous." She nodded sagely. "Yes, the Dominicans will want to know about the call."

"I'm afraid the good Dominicans will have to be satisfied with but a feeling. Candidates for the priesthood must if nothing else be honest, my good Mother."

He rose to his feet. "It's getting late, and I leave early. The ship sails with the tide in the forenoon." He bent down and patted Lucinda's cheek." Good night, Mother."

As she watched his retreating back she answered, "Good night, dear Bernard. I shall miss you." The last words were almost murmured. She returned to prayer. The glow in her body had to be repaid with much prayer this most special of special evenings. Even as she knelt, her thoughts turned to the gold coins she had placed between his clothes. She had been hoarding her own money for years. Now it was Bernard's.

Outside in the hallway, Bernard thought to himself, *Thank you, Mother dear. If it was good enough for Catherine of Genoa, then it's surely good enough for the Dominicans.* He knew now what he would say about the call: he will have been alone in prayer, the light of revelation soft and ethereal. It was ironic that his entrance to the inner sanctum of the priesthood should be partly enabled by reference to what was obviously a wildly demented female. *Just like all of them.*

~ ~ ~

Lucinda did not go to the ship to fare Bernard well. She stood alone on the wide steps as her son and husband boarded the carriage. Vincent drove. No servants gathered around as was customary when a household member departed. Bernard had insisted that they instead be given a day of rest as his farewell gift. Lucinda watched until the carriage was out of sight, then, half-crying, began twisting the rosary beads in her hands.

At the dock, Vincent made sure everything was loaded and that the cabin had been prepared according to his instructions. He took two envelopes from his pocket.

"Your letters of introduction, and a little money. Your mother doesn't think you'll need the latter." Vincent forced a laugh.

Bernard took the envelopes, annoyed that Vincent had chosen to obey Dominican regulations and give him only a pittance. There was a moment of awkward silence.

It was Vincent who proffered his hand. "Farewell, Bernard. I know you will do well in God's work, but it is also good to remember that time clears and cleanses the mind. Should all not go favourably, you can always return. The Birous business will welcome you."

Bernard took his father's hand, but did not return the affectionate clasp on the shoulder. His words were level. "I think not, Father. Farewell. I will write should there be a need. Now I must go and unpack."

He was at the below-deck hatchway when Vincent's voice stopped him. "You're sure there's nothing you want me to do . . . Things I can attend to in your stead?"

The ghost of a sneer appeared on Bernard's face, and his words were edged with something Vincent felt but did not understand. "Yes. Tell Renato Santini that I give him the *Half Moon*. He'll understand. And one other matter, Father. Not that it concerns me greatly, but you'll do well to dismiss the thieving chambermaid immediately, and without references."

Then he was gone.

Lost in his thoughts, Vincent walked back to his carriage. With Bernard gone, the business would suffer, and he himself would have to work much harder. But he would be in control again. Definitely, Bernard meant more prosperity to the Birous enterprises. He also brought more disquiet. Deep down, Vincent both knew and hoped that Bernard would not return. His son had another destiny. He didn't believe for a moment that the chambermaid was a thief. His peasant mother had told him stories as a boy about instruments of good and evil. How God and the Devil sometimes sent special people to Earth to do their bidding. In some way, his son had been touched by this servant girl, and it would seem that she was an instrument of God, not the Devil. But he, Vincent Birous, a man who had always relied heavily on his instincts, was not certain, not at all. He would dismiss the maid tonight, but not without references. Practical God-fearing men took no chances in matters of heaven and hell. He felt suddenly better as he turned his horses' heads towards home.

~ ~ ~

In his cabin, Bernard lay on his bunk, a damp cloth pressed to his forehead. They were back. The voices and the lights, shrieking and flashing against his ears and eyes, and filling his head with an unbearable pain. For a long time his sweating body convulsed as he fought their relentless assault, until he fell into a fitful sleep. He was still asleep when the ship weighed anchor and slipped wraith-like into the sudden fog that had billowed in from the southwest like a grey ghost.

Rome, June, 1832

As Salvatore Tettrini read the letter, he paced the floor of the small; cold room, scarcely conscious of the young novice who waited nervously by the door. *Strange, thought Thomas Rivarola, that the good Prior should be so disquieted by this application.*

It was the talk of the monastery: a rich man's son from Genoa wanted to join the Order. Old Mario had seen him the day he first came to visit the Prior, and that night at refectory had described the handsome black coat, embroidered waistband and silver-buckled shoes worn by the dark-eyed young stranger. The Dominicans did not receive many such novices these days. The arrogant Jesuits were back in favour and had ingratiated themselves with the pious Pope Gregory, filling his head with visions of a modern theocracy in the Papal States – with themselves in charge, of course. It was no wonder that ambitious young men were joining the Society of Jesus rather than the Dominicans.

We are fast becoming true friar-preachers again. Rivarola smiled happily at the thought before bringing his attention back to the room. Why was his superior so visibly upset? At that moment he would have gladly forfeited a plenary indulgence to find out.

"That will be all, Brother. You may go. I shall summon you if necessary," Tettrini said with his mind clearly elsewhere. He closed the door behind the startled young man.

Tettrini returned to his desk, and after carefully arranging his white robe, sat down in the plain, straight-backed chair. He set the letter down beside the one he had received three weeks earlier, folded his arms meticulously as he always did, so that no skin showed, and gazed unseeingly at the simple crucifix on the wall opposite.

He had been the Prior of the monastery at Santa Sabina for over two years now. Though it had of late fallen on hard times, its halls had been witness to centuries of learning and tradition. At the time of his appointment as Prior, he had been informed that the Master General had chosen the venerable monastery to lead the Dominican Order on its path to regeneration. Discipline and mental proficiency would be rewarded at Santa Sabina, and Holy Orders achievable in less than the nine long years that awaited novices in other Dominican houses. In time only the very best candidates would enter Santa Sabina. Tiredly Tettrini rubbed his eyes. But not yet.

Santa Sabina's location in Rome, close to the power hierarchy of the Catholic Church, was an offsetting factor to the primacy wielded by the Order's parent house at St. Thomas'. Devoted to the ideal of community activity and the spreading of the Gospel, the Dominicans had marched to supremacy within the Church in the sixteenth and seventeenth centuries, only to be superseded within the Vatican by the more evangelical and politically ambitious Society of Jesus.

The trivia of administration was bad enough, Tettrini thought, and the turmoil that beset Rome was most disquieting. But could he long withstand what he continued to see inside his own walls? Sadly, in spite of the advantages offered by Santa Sabina's special place on the Order's road to reform, almost all those who answered God's call possessed hands better suited to the ploughshare than to the pen. Tettrini recoiled from the ignorance of the novices, and cried inwardly every time he had to teach a rustic Catalan or ill-disciplined Neapolitan the rudiments of language and logic. Was this the legacy of the noble Aquinas and Bonaventure? A pedestrian mass of white-robed illiterates?

In his time at Santa Sabina, Tettrini had yet to see Holy Orders bestowed on a candidate who approached his concept of the Dominican ideal. Why, the best he had now was the repulsive Alphonse Battiste. Tettrini cringed at the thought. Where were the Thomas Campanellas, the Ignatius Dantes, the Alphonse Chacons? Nowhere! And where were the coveted invitations that summoned priests from Santa Sabina to the seat of power? Sadly there were none to join the manipulative black-frocked Jesuits at the Vatican. Yes, the Dominicans had come on hard times. And Santa Sabina was supposed to make things better. Perish the thought, if these last two years were any indication. He picked up the letter dated four weeks earlier and turned it over in his hands.

He recalled his pleasure when he had first read it. It was not the prospect of a vocation from a prosperous, well-educated family that excited him; he had seen too many dilettantes to be impressed. No, it was the testimony to the young man's brilliant academic record that stirred him. More than that: the boy was a linguist. In Bologna, a close colleague of Tettrini's, Giuseppe Mezzofanti, the greatest linguist of the day, had told Tettrini that one brilliant purified mind trained in many languages was worth a thousand missionaries. With the dogs of secularism baying outside every church in Europe, a Catholic renaissance was needed more than ever before. Was Santa Sabina about to discover a defender of the faith worth a thousand men? It was a refreshing hope.

~ ~ ~

The day after receiving the letter of introduction, Tettrini had welcomed Bernard Birous into his study. It had proven to be an audience like none he had ever experienced.

Mario had ushered the important-looking visitor in with an air of defer-
ence not at all typical of the irascible old priest. Worse still, Birous's bearing
made it all seem somehow natural. His shoulders were thrown back like a man
used to giving orders. His dark eyes flashed about the room, taking everything
in, before coolly settling on Tettrini's. His handshake was firm but perfunctory,
and Tettrini was surprised to see his visitor sit, uninvited, facing him across the
plain, oaken desk like an equal instead of a potential novice. There was a hint
of a smile about the tight lips, but the unblinking eyes betrayed nothing.

Following his usual custom, Tettrini had begun with polite conversation.
He had inquired about family, the Birous business, and Genoa in general. The
answers were polite but short and largely uninformative. Feeling slighted,
Tettrini had decided to test the youth before referring to the vocation. The
young upstart clearly needed a lesson.

He set his favourite trap and asked Birous what he thought about the
widely accepted reconciliation of Aristotelian thought with that of St. Thomas
Aquinas. He was astonished at the ease with which the issue of comparison
was avoided. Instead, Birous gave a cogent delineation between rationality and
faith, and how the two coalesced to define Catholic theology. By the time the
discussion was exhausted, Tettrini found himself being forced to reply in the
negative as to whether or not he had read the original text of Aquinas' "Summa
Contra Gentiles." Later translations, his guest had explained airily, tended to
blur the angelic doctor's acuity.

Tettrini had then tested the youth in French, ending the discussion
abruptly upon realizing that he was being patronised.

Remembering his annoyance both at Birous and at his own inability to
control the situation, Tettrini grimaced as he recalled his final attempt to match
wits with the man. Tettrini's own English was quite good, and he was fascinated
by English poet John Milton's attempts to give definition in verse to the endless
struggle for Mankind between the forces of Good and Evil. Convinced that even
this supremely confident young man sitting opposite him would be ignorant
of the writings of a seventeenth-century English Puritan, Tettrini had asked
Birous if he had read *Paradise Lost*, a most important work containing elements
crucial to Catholic thought. Birous had simply smiled benignly before dis-
missing the epic as an overstated exercise in religious tedium. If one had to
read Milton, Birous preferred *Samson Agonistes*.

Tettrini was taken completely by surprise when he glanced up to see
Bernard Birous standing, the young man's hands gripping the edge of the desk
as he leaned forward, his eyes boring into Tettrini's. "I much prefer another

English poet. He is not like Milton, enslaved to the mirages seen by illiterate desert wanderers."

Birous's face was flushed and his full lips were twisting with intensity as his hands clenched and unclenched. "He rests now in his grave, gone a few short years – unnoticed, unloved, and for the moment, unremembered."

The voice rose higher. "But William Blake will remain a giant long after Milton's servile morality has been consumed by spiritual fire."

Tettrini listened, open-mouthed, as Bernard's words came from deep within him. The voice was nothing like Tettrini had ever heard before.

> "The Shadowy Female shudders thro' heaven in torment inex-
> pressible!
> And all the Daughters of Los prophetic wail: yet in deceit,
> They weave a new Religion from new Jealousy of Theotormon!
> Milton's Religion is the cause: there is no end to destruction!"

Then Bernard had smiled and his voice returned to normal. "That was Blake, Prior. An interesting message, don't you think?"

Parrying for time, Tettrini muttered that he needed to know more about this strange English poet. He gained a couple more minutes by pretending to take notes before returning to the discussion.

They had spoken next about Bernard's vocation, and his reasons for choosing the priestly life. Tettrini was less than impressed with Birous's account of blinding white lights and prayerful rhapsody. He didn't seem the type. Besides, nineteenth-century vocations were generally less spectacular. The Middle Ages were over. Still, it all went to show how serious this young man was about entering the priesthood. Tettrini was interested in his visitor's reasons for selecting the Dominicans above other orders.

"Because they were given to me." The voice Tettrini heard was flat, emotionless.

Tettrini could think of nothing to say. He felt drained. Bernard looked at the older man inquiringly. "The time of preparation? Is it true that at this monastery it is possible to receive Holy Orders as a Dominican in less than the customary nine years?"

Tettrini did not try to hide his knowing smile. "Ah, now I understand why you chose us instead of St. Thomas'. You are right. Usually the time period is at least nine years. One year of postulancy, another as a novice before Simple Vows are taken. Then three more years of Philosophy and Solemn Vows before the final four years in Thomistic Theology. However, our Master General has seen fit to adopt a new course in the interests of rewarding diligence and ability while paving the way for a more powerful and enlightened Order."

Bernard's response was swift and direct. "How long? What is the least time I must spend here before I leave as a priest?"

Tettrini pursed his lips thoughtfully before he answered. "That depends on one's capacity for rigour and study. The postulancy may be less than a year. The novitiate, another, no less. A brilliant mind might attain the requisite philosophical knowledge in a single year. But the Theology. That is another matter entirely"

He met Bernard's gaze levelly. "We are not prepared to ordain anyone who has not been in this monastery for less than five years. No one, you understand! Should you be Bonaventure himself, you would not be sent into the world before twenty full seasons within these walls. We also consider that six years comprise the taxing limit of intellectual, physical and moral rigour. There will be regular, exacting examinations, of course. Dilettantism has no—"

Bernard's voice was impatient. "Am I to understand that the righteous minds who direct the affairs of this place are as interested in equitability as they are in imposing rigour?"

Tettrini seemed surprised. "But of course. Adversity and challenge are the true masters. We only recognize what is."

"Good," said Bernard, satisfied. "Then it is settled. I leave here in five years."

"You presuppose much."

Once again Tettrini felt the intensity of those burning eyes. "No, Prior. You shall convey Holy Orders upon me in the summer of 1837." Then to himself he murmured, "It is foreordained."

Tettrini did not catch Bernard's last utterance, and was too tired and polite to ask for elaboration. He ushered his visitor out, explaining that accepting a vocation demanded time. Time for him to pray and discuss with his superiors, and time for Bernard to visit the holy places of Rome, and to think, and to pray for guidance. They would meet again in three weeks. Mario would travel with him back to his quarters.

When Birous had gone, Tettrini slumped in his chair. His eyes closed as he strove to arrange his thoughts about this remarkable young aspirant. A brilliant mind counterbalanced by something that beset him from within. A man who proclaimed a desire to do God's work, but who evinced pride and arrogance.

The merits of the vocation didn't bother Tettrini. Such instances usually resolved themselves anyway. But to turn loose within the dispirited, ravaged ranks of his once proud Order a brilliant but potentially uncontrollable icono-clast was another matter entirely. He thought the risk was manageable, but what if he was wrong? Even as he pushed the palms of his hands into his eyes in the childish gesture that his novices so gleefully imitated, Tettrini knew what he had to do.

Tettrini had met Luigi Lambruschini ten years ago when the great Cardinal, then a bishop, had given an inspirational sermon to the novices about "Lambs of God," and "Lions of God." If anyone could guide him, Lambruschini could.

~ ~ ~

Bernard was making his way down the Corso past the Borghese Palace. The sun was hot on his back, its warmth blending sluggishly with the dank odour from the tawny waters of the Tiber. Near the Church of St. Peter in Chains just off the Via de fiori Imperiale, he stopped and entered a small shop. Above the door, a faded sign, "Books Sold and Repaired," hung listlessly in the still air. Inside the cool, dim shop he was greeted enthusiastically by a short and portly man who pointed mirthfully at a box of books lying beside the counter. "Your books are ready for your examination, good sir. A cardinal himself would be proud to place them in his library."

He laughed noisily at his own humour, then watched expectantly as Bernard picked up a volume entitled *Acts of the Apostles*. The inside leaf showed the inscription of the Benedictine Order, and the printing date was 1750. After noting the thumb-worn cover and the fading title print, Bernard opened the book randomly. He nodded approvingly as the incoherent but powerful visions of Joachim of Fiore leapt up at him. Quickly he examined the others. His favourite works, all hidden respectably between proper ecclesiastical covers. Not St. Thomas' *Summa*, but the heretical writings of a contemporary Venetian mystic. The mockery of Rabelais disguised as psalms and cantos. The complete works of William Blake posing as articles on canon law.

Santa Sabina allowed certain proper books in a novice's cell. It was all part of the monastery's special status, the old monk, Mario, had told him. Self-imposed enlightenment did not always have to be rigorous, so the Prior had informed them. As long as it was pious enlightenment. Bernard had no doubt he could convince Tettrini of his insatiable appetite for works of the soul. Yes, the interests of literature would be well served in the long months that lay ahead.

He straightened up. "It is satisfactory. Have them delivered at once. You know the address." He produced a bag of coins. "Payment as we agreed. For your work – and your discretion."

"But of course, Excellency," gushed the proprietor, snatching the pouch and stuffing its contents into the back of a drawer below the counter.

Half an hour later, Bernard turned off the Via Aventino just behind Santa Sabina and entered the terraced courtyard of a small hotel. Vines clung to the white walls, and pots of blooming flowers were suspended from oaken pegs protruding from the balconies. He had stayed at this hotel since his arrival in Rome. It was perfect: close to the monastery, well kept, and moderately priced. He entered his room from the balcony and closed the door. Everything was ready: the wardrobe of costumes, together with makeup; a place to write; a made-up bed; storage facilities for books, and a cupboard which the obliging landlord had agreed to stock weekly with seasonal fruits, pastries and breads. The poor fellow had never had a yearly renter before, and he was delighted to accommodate this generous, prosperous young man who apparently would be using the room only on his infrequent and sudden visits to Rome.

He looked at his pocket watch. It was time for his final task. He needed to know the ideal route between here and Santa Sabina, and the time it took to travel it. He glanced around the room one last time, and let himself out the same way as he had come in.

It was dark before Bernard returned with the information he needed. Two trips had told him that by hurrying he could reach the gate of the monastery in just under eleven minutes. Three more, he had calculated, to gain entrance through the gate, or over the lowest section of wall on the south side. He was assuming that in true monastic tradition, all inner doors in the monastery would be unlocked. Walking unhurriedly, the same journey took him eight minutes longer. As he climbed the stairs to his room he had found himself wondering how often he would be able to escape the cloistered confinement of the monastery, and for how long. Much would depend on the rigour of daily practices inside the walls, and his own ingenuity in overcoming them. One's spirit was of course always free, but sometimes the body had to be liberated as well.

Before he closed the door of his room, Bernard looked out at the darkening city. He could barely make out the stark outline of the Circus Maximus, its crumbling walls an enduring reminder of rule by the mighty; when lesser men were allowed to spend their petty blood on the sands. By God, how he hated the streets! The dirty squalid figures passing him aimlessly; the lurching carriages with their faceless inmates, and the strutting human baggage that used the trappings of prosperity to advertise a shallow arrogance. Oxen without yokes, horses without halters, falcons without hoods. But one day he would be recognized and he would lead.

Now, in the silence of his own place, Bernard could afford to recognize the pain. He threw himself down on the bed and closed his eyes. He had tried to quiet the voices with concoctions from the apothecary, but they only laughed and hurt more. Even in sleep they haunted him, bringing wild, fitful dreams.

He pushed himself into a sitting position, his head in his hands. If he hadn't had that experience yesterday, he probably would abandon the priesthood, and leave Rome forever. He would return to his cave, and if the voices did not go away, he would seek peace in his own way, by his own hand if it necessary. But yesterday, at the Quirinal he had seen him – Pope Gregory XVI. The sight of the white-robed figure, hands held high in benediction over thousands of hushed, bowed heads, had elated Bernard. It didn't matter that Gregory knew none of the throng that paid him homage. Even as he turned his back on them, they cheered. This was power. In that ecstatic moment of realization, the voices had stopped momentarily. His head was clear. He stood there transfixed until the papal carriage had disappeared. Then Rome again became foul and alien, and the crescendo in his mind threatened to lift his head from his shoulders.

~ ~ ~

Cardinal Luigi Lambruschini walked to the window and looked out at St. Peter's Square, now almost deserted in the early dusk. He remained there unmoving for a couple of minutes before turning to the man who sat on the comfortable velvet-covered divan. "Very interesting, Salvatore. The only question is, can he be controlled? Potential only becomes power when it is harnessed. Two things need to be applied to your young novice, Salvatore. First, testing; then, moulding."

Lambruschini sat down beside Tettrini, who noticed for the first time how the set look of the aristocratic face and the depth in the eyes reminded him of Bernard Birous.

"If this Birous is serious about the priesthood, then he will have to be groomed – not obviously, of course – but sufficiently so as to be ready for service in the Lord's name after his Holy Orders are taken."

Tettrini nodded. "How do you propose I proceed?"

"Salvatore, do not give him the habit immediately. Let him endure a postulancy that will test his resolve. Make him perform the most menial of tasks. Put him on his knees often. Invoke the rule of silence rigorously. In short,

Salvatore, your new postulant should embody all the penitential sufferings of monasticism. At least six months of a privation that St. Dominic himself would welcome."

"And then?" Tettrini was doubtful.

"If his resolve remains undiluted after this period, then you begin the moulding process. Allow him to enter his Novitiate, and afterwards, his philo-sophical studies. Use Santa Sabina's special status to advance him as necessary. You tell me he desires to complete his requirements in five years. So be it, if he proves able."

Lambruschini squinted in concentration, and seemed to weigh his next words. "You may want to send him beyond your walls for language studies. As I understand it, the boundaries of your dispensary powers allow such licence under extreme circumstances. I trust you understand, Salvatore. Either this young man warrants bold measures or nothing at all. Remember, my friend, caution can be an encumbrance as well as a palliative. Rules only guide Man; they do not define his purpose. As for myself, I would like to be kept informed, and, should all go well, be allowed to observe our remarkable aspirant at least once before his ordination."

"I shall give your words careful consideration, Eminence. I confess, I am both stimulated and vexed by this vocation as I have been by no other. I shall pray that I am on the true path in my actions."

Long after Tettrini had left, Lambruschini remained in deep thought. The Church desperately needed renewal. Young men with fire in their bellies would be the wind that sailed Mother Church into the coming secular century. Old men such as himself and Tettrini were merely rudders to keep Her from cap-sizing. But such young men were difficult to find.

At his next appointment an hour later, Lambruschini had difficulty keep-ing Tettrini's young Genoan out of his thoughts.

~ ~ ~

The following day dawned wet and drab. Bernard had risen early and break-fasted in his room. He was dizzy from the noises hammering behind his eyes. He must gather himself and focus his thoughts. He walked to the balcony and gazed toward the grey sky. A speck became a form, and a small bird landed in the courtyard just below him and began pecking at the ground. By God, how he hated birds. Feathered carrion. One had flown at him when he was a child, sending him fleeing into the arms of his mother.

Then he saw the cat, its mottled fur blending perfectly with the drab shrubbery against the courtyard wall. On soundless feet it approached the unsuspecting bird, the tip of its tail twitching in silent anticipation. It came closer, then paused; then forward again. Bernard was breathing hard. The cat was now less than a metre from its victim. "Now," breathed Bernard, easing his body forward to the edge of the balcony. The cat was gathering itself. Its cold yellow eyes were narrowed and its ears flattened in a silent killer mask. Bernard's muscles tensed, his breath frozen in his mouth.

He must have moved enough to break the cat's trancelike fixation, for it turned its head to look at him. He matched its unblinking stare, urging it to return to its quest. *You are so close, my silent friend. Take your prize.*

Neither really noticed when, but when their gaze broke, the bird had taken flight. The cat left haughtily to seek satisfaction elsewhere. Bernard walked back into the room feeling drained. He looked at his pocket watch for something to do, and realized that it was time for his appointment. As he walked to Santa Sabina, he found himself thinking about the cat and its failed mission.

~ ~ ~

Salvatore Tettrini had felt the familiar pain in his joints as he knelt at mass praying for reassurance. Not guidance, for he had made up his mind about Bernard Birous. As he savoured the special prayer time following Holy Communion, Tettrini was already welcoming Bernard Birous into the Order.

When Mario ushered Bernard into Tettrini's meeting room, they found the Prior at his desk, reading. Tettrini did not rise to meet Bernard, but motioned him to take the chair opposite his desk. For fully five minutes he ignored the younger man, who contented himself with a detached gaze, first about the room, and then beyond Tettrini's shoulder to a painting of the Madonna visiting St. Dominic. Finally Tettrini spoke.

"I shall be frank, Mr. Birous. There are many things about this vocation which disturb me. Your previous lack of religious involvement are not of primary concern. Loyola, even the great Augustine, lived dissolute lives before hearing the call of the Lord. No! What concerns me is something far more disquieting. What I detect in you is an irreligious quality. You show more pride than humility, more arrogance than meekness, more wilfulness than acceptance, and, saddest of all, more rage than love."

Bernard was on his feet, his face a flushed mask of anger. He was surprised by the sharp bite in Tettrini's voice.

"Sit down, Mr. Birous. I have not finished."

Tettrini waited until Bernard was re-seated, seemingly unperturbed by

Bernard's hostility. "As I was saying. In normal times I would be most confident in advising that the cloth is not for you."

Tettrini shifted in his chair, paused as if weighing what he was about to say, then went on. "But these, Mr. Birous, are not normal times. The future of the Holy Mother Church has never been as precarious as in these dark days. The early persecutions, the heresies, incursions by infidels, the scourge of Protestantism are as nothing to the insidious malaise that is sapping our strength. There is movement everywhere away from us. The nations of the world are becoming more Godless by the day, more defiant in their rejection of the Church in temporal matters. Increasingly, they open their doors to rule by the unfit. This new threat, Mr. Birous, has its own deity. It worships on the altar of secularism.

"It is for these reasons that I look at your vocation, or what we shall prefer to call a vocation, as a possible sign sent by the Almighty in His infinite wisdom for those to see who would. To survive and flourish as She must, the Church will not only need champions of faith and piety. She will need leaders strong of intellect, unrelenting in resolve, and if need be, ruthless in execution. Qualities I detect in you. So convince me, Mr. Birous. Tell me how you would have our Church rise above the Godlessness that threatens to subsume Her."

Bernard said nothing for a long minute. Instead, he rose, went to the single shelf of books that broke one brown drab wall, and searched the titles. Then he resumed his place in front of Tettrini and crossed his legs. "May I, too, be frank, Prior? I assume you wish honesty."

"Of course Bernard. In God's trust, I listen to you."

If he had noticed the change in Tettrini's tone, Bernard gave no indication. His voice was as measured as if he had been giving an exposition before his tutor at university. "You are both right and wrong, Prior. Correct in asserting that our Church is weakening in strength; correct in averring that our mission is one of restoration. Wrong, however, in lamenting the erosion of our direct influence in the affairs of governments so clearly obsessed with secularization.

"The days of the overtly temporal Church are gone. We are going to have to spread a new spirituality that will envelop men with its ardour. We infuse this spiritualism into the peoples of the world, and we will have harnessed the forces of coercion to our end: A force that transcends national boundaries, class, and culture. Our power will be greater than ever before."

Bernard paused, obviously exhilarated. Tettrini's voice was measured as he raised an eyebrow. "I have two questions for you, my idealistic young crusader. This new spiritualism. Have you given thought to its definition, and how its power will be promulgated?"

"There is no need for definition, for like all true spiritualism, it must live through itself. To spread the word, we need legions of believers who will not rest until the world is remade in God's image. But to inspire these zealots we need a Pope, Prior. A Pope who looks inward, not upward, for his mission. A Pope imbued with a light that draws men to him. Such a man recognizes those like himself, and these are the new apostles."

Bernad's eyes blazed as he gripped the arms of his chair. He looked to Tettrini for a response.

Tettrini weighed his words carefully. "If I understand you correctly, you are suggesting that we go out and find a man-made image of Christ, who will then inspire a new spiritual awakening throughout Europe, and ultimately the world. I myself know of no such person."

Bernad leaned forward. "Believe me, Prior. I have seen such people. They do not know their own power. The one the Church needs is there waiting. It is for us to find him."

Tettrini felt the unease again, sensed the powerful aura of this remarkable young man. Both knew what his words had meant.

Tettrini shifted in his chair, and looked at his fingers. "Let us assume that such a leader could be found, and that he occupies the Papal Chair. How would he go about bringing this awakening to fruition?

Bernard's reply was confident. "It cannot begin in Spain and Portugal. They will never again be great. Britain is too much like us, and hates us dearly for it. The Holy Roman Empire's days are numbered. The New World countries are too young, too volatile to sustain their fervour. They also have no tradition which lends legitimacy to purpose. France meddles enough already. She sees the Vatican as her personal domain. Her spies are everywhere. It is the greatest irony that the nation the Church considers her closest ally is in effect her worst enemy."

" Where, then?"

"The northern Protestant states. The German principalities are divided now, but this will not last. The mood of Europe is towards unification. A spiritual renaissance in a united Germany would thrust the Church into a position of dominance not seen since the Reformation. All it needs is a symbol, and when the people are ready, the symbol can be easily contrived. The seeds can be planted when, how and where necessary. But a sower. We must have a sower."

Bernard waited expectantly.

Tettrini's mind was racing. The whole notion was absurd. The young fool was blissfully ignorant of the role of petty politics in the election of Popes, and the idea that some kind of Joachimist Third Age of the Spirit could be brought about through the actions of a single figure, no matter how charismatic, was far-fetched. It was the daring of the vision which impressed him. That, and the intensity with which it was conveyed. He rubbed his hands together as he thought, *Yes, we have a leader*.

He rose, and walked to the chair where Bernard sat. The young man looked up at him, surprised. Tettrini extended his hand.

"Welcome, Bernard Birous, to the noble Order of Friar Preachers. May the dignity it imposes on you be commensurate with the faith and loyalty you carry with you as you do God's work."

As he walked Bernard to the door, he explained that, following the necessary preparations, Santa Sabina would receive him within the week. After Bernard had left, Tettrini felt suddenly tired. He wanted to rest. Instead he dropped to his knees and began to pray for himself, his sins and the Order he loved.

Outside in the darkened hallway Bernard smiled inwardly to himself. The first step had been taken on the road to his destiny. Then as the pain engulfed him like a wave, he winced and leaned against the wall, his throbbing head just a few inches away from a painting of an unsmiling Reginald in a beggar's garb. If only the demons in his head would go away.

CHAPTER II

The door of the small house opened, and Martin Goyette stepped out into the bright sunshine. Though he held the black crepe-draped cross reverently, his lips moved wordlessly with the sounds of sorrow and anger. His uncle Antoine had told him once that these were the two very worst emotions because they fed on their own impotence. And now he was dead.

Behind Martin came the hearse, borne by four pallbearers paid by the curé to come from another parish. A lone woman dressed in black and sobbing into a black, lace-trimmed handkerchief came next, and behind her a group of elderly ladies. Every now and then one reached out to console the one who walked alone. There were no men but a few onlookers who watched silently as the small procession made its way to the high-spired church and the neat well-kept cemetery which surrounded it. Inside, the church was dark and sparsely decorated. Martin placed the cross on top of the casket and knelt behind the woman who was hunched forward, alone in the first pew. A single priest celebrated the requiem Mass. The two side altars were empty, and no choir sang.

Afterwards, the knot of mourners gathered at the graveside. The curé concluded the service with a brief importunity to God about the frailties of Man, and with proper funereal intonation committed the body of Antoine Cousineau to the earth. Martin removed the cross from the casket, which was then lowered into the ground. As the first clods of earth clattered over it, he gestured towards the undertaker. Embarrassed, the man looked to the curé for guidance. Then even as the spades continued their work, Martin leapt into the hole and pried away a crucifix from the casket. He thrust it at the undertaker, who accepted it wordlessly. Still looking very uncomfortable, but gathering himself, the undertaker approached Jeanne Cousineau, whose muffled sobs were quieter now beneath the heavy mourning veil. She took the crucifix numbly nodding her thanks. She remained for a few more minutes until her friends took her by the arm and led her to one of their homes for further comfort.

~ ~ ~

Half an hour later, only Martin Goyette remained beside the neat mound that marked Antoine Cousineau's last resting place. Later, a modest headstone might be added. Martin hoped that after he went away, some charitable soul might tend to his uncle's grave. His mother would, for as long as she lived in St.

Timothee. And that of course depended on other things. Idly he picked up one of the wilted white flowers that rested sparsely on the mound and began plucking at the petals. Already a sudden wind was dispersing the rest in white and green fragments. A half smile crossed his face as he dropped the petals to the ground.

"Good bye dear Uncle Antoine, and thank you."

Then he laughed at the sky, a hysterical laugh that had overflowed his anguish. He had lost his friend and teacher, and much worse. Yes, much worse.

For three hours Martin sat at his uncle's graveside. With Uncle Antoine gone he had nothing to keep him here. Maybe he should leave as soon as possible to take up his life as a painter. His father would neither stand in his way nor aid him financially. Yes, things would be difficult, but he couldn't be more aimless and dispirited than he was at present. He would ask his mother what she thought when he paid his respects to her household that evening.

Martin stood up, brushed the grass from his homespun trousers and looked at the church looming over the graves like a giant shadow. He was suddenly struck by one of his uncle's favourite ungodly fulminations. *Where were you, God, when I needed you? Sitting locked up in a veiled box with only a red light for company. You can help no one there.*

He thought of it like many things his uncle said. Sacrilegious, but made inoffensive somehow by his booming jocularity. Now his beloved Uncle Antoine was gone, struck down quickly, painlessly. His only wish answered by a God he had never worshipped.

Antoine Cousineau's death was not mourned in St. Timothee for he was neither of God, nor of them. Not to partake in the ritual of the village and attend Mass on Sunday was to turn one's back on both God and Man, a gesture the villagers would neither accept nor forgive. The three bells did not toll their intervals of three to announce the death of a male parishioner. No one would carry the casket even though they held Jeanne Cousineau in high regard. Curé Lalleland had refused Martin's request and offer of payment for a second-class funeral service, and allowed only the respects embodied in the simple third-class funeral. No one attended the requiem Mass and burial except for a few of Jeanne's friends – and Martin, but he was from another parish. Jeanne would live in the village as a respected parishioner, and when she died the bells would toll and everyone in the village would attend the funeral. For the villagers in St. Timothee, the circle was again closed. There were other things brewing on the air that late summer.

Now, mired sorrow as well as anger at the villagers for their callousness,

41

Martin's resentment flared anew about the Christian precepts that supposedly governed their lives. Still thinking about a God who made good people behave badly, Martin Goyette made his way to the village store owned and operated by his friend François-Xavier Prieur.

~ ~ ~

Even standing on a chair on tiptoes, François-Xavier could scarcely reach the top shelf. He teetered precariously and was about to get down and place a large book on the chair when he was interrupted by a laughing voice.

"Allow me, François. You'll kill yourself. How many times have I told you to buy a ladder?"

"Martin. Yes please. Right there beside the two lanterns. Good. You're right of course, Martin. I do need a ladder. A tall one."

Drawing himself up to his full height of five feet three inches, Prieur stepped back and looked at his visitor fondly. "Let us go out on the porch and talk. I have something exciting to tell you, Martin. Even on this sad day for you, my friend."

They sat together on the porch of the store, facing the street and the blacksmith's low open shed. Prieur rocked excitedly in his father's old chair that he had brought with him from the family farm.

"Just this week, Martin, I was invited by Rapin, the Patriote leader in this village, to join Les Frères Chasseurs. I was inducted immediately and given the rank of Castor." Prieur puffed out his chest proudly. "Les Chasseurs, Martin. They are everywhere in every village from St. Benoit to Odelltown. Thousands more over the border with money and guns will join us when the time comes."

He gripped the edge of the chair. "It will be different this time, Martin. This time we will drive the British from our land."

"Wait a minute, François. You were not active in 1837. Neither was I. We lost. Some say the British were too lenient. Amnesty to all and a holiday for some in Bermuda. It will be different this time; the British will be less tolerant to those they see as traitors. François, I would give this whole matter careful thought before I grabbed an old rifle or a pitchfork and took on the British army. Your friend Papineau. Where is he now? The revolution has failed, François. It never had a chance last year, and it is no different now."

The little man leaned forward eagerly. "You are wrong, Martin. We were foolish the first time. Isolated, and without sufficient heart. But we have witnessed the desecration of our farmlands. The British continue to raise our rents. We have to liberate our land. It is our sacred duty."

"Sacred duty! Be reasonable and think, François. You are a God-fearing man, far more than I. The Church will not condone violence."

"Wrong again, Martin. Mother Church is with us." He shook his head angrily, rebuffing his friend's interjection. "Not the bishops in Montreal. They are in league with the British. But our own curés are with us. Do you think I would have become a Patriote had I not Curé Lalleland's blessing?"

"Curé Lalleland has blessed the revolution?" Martin was incredulous.

"Not exactly. But he charged us all with doing God's will without mentioning loyalty to the British. It's the same thing." Prieur went on. "You must join the cause, Martin. Les Frères Chasseurs will welcome a man such as yourself."

"And what might that be, François?" Martin was smiling.

"A loyal Catholic and lover of our native land who does not wish to see her destiny denied by foreigners. Join us, Martin, and fight."

The door to the store opened, and a woman with a young child entered. Prieur got to his feet.

"I must go my friend. A man of means and property never rests." He laughed before continuing. "It's why I was given the rank of Castor, of course. The Patriotes must be led by men of respect and integrity."

Regardless of military ability or experience, Martin thought to himself.

It would come to nothing. He had heard of these Frères Chasseurs. His brother, Joseph-Narcisse, had been a member for months and was an active recruiter. For what? As far as Martin knew, there was too much fear of the British to fire a successful revolution. The French had no money, no guns, no leaders, no organization, and most of all no will. No, Martin Goyette's problems were more personal, but hopefully less insoluble. His revolution was with himself, not the British.

~ ~ ~

Jeanne Cousineau was praying and did not hear her son enter through the open front door. It was almost dusk. The sky was pink behind the high grey clouds dusted with a rosy glow. Though the room was not dark, two candles were lit on a small table covered with a wide linen cloth. A crucifix hung on the wall above the table and two framed pictures sat behind the candles. One was of the Sacred Heart. Christ's right hand pointed towards His exposed heart resting in flaming tongues of burning love. The other was of the Madonna. Her hands were crossed across her breast, her eyes raised heavenward. In the middle of the table was a small figurine of the Madonna, her hands spread beckoningly. Countless polishings over the years could not belie its great age. Martin's eyes were drawn past his mother's kneeling back to this ancient and time-honoured Mary. Without really understanding why, he fell to his knees and, with his eyes fixed on its simple splendour, prayed for Uncle Antoine.

Martin had just turned fifteen when he discovered that Jeanne Cousineau was his natural mother. When she had written to him from St. Timothee explaining the circumstances of his birth, things Martin could never understand suddenly made sense. The dark-haired woman with cold hands who lavished all her affection on Joseph-Narcisse, and later on the younger children. The indifferent father.

As she had explained to him in that long letter, and then again afterwards when they met, François Goyette had not told her that he was married, had not admitted the existence of a six-year-old son. But her vision of marriage was shattered when François admitted his deception. She had cried when he said that he would raise the child as his own, but in her heart she knew it was for the best. The child of a respected and prosperous notary faced much better prospects than that of an unmarried seamstress, so she had agreed to François' stipulations that she go to Montreal for her confinement. He himself came to the hospital and took the baby from her arms. The baby would appear in Chateauguay as an adopted child, and all was well in the public eye.

Privately, however, her son endured the pain of the loveless child. François Goyette could not abide the boy's physical imperfections. His deformed lip was unmistakably the mark of the mentally enfeebled — it made no difference that the boy did reasonably well in his studies.

Though Jeanne Cousineau knew none of this, she carried her sorrow and her secret for fifteen long years until the sudden death of Gabrielle Goyette. But though she loved Martin dearly as her son, they could never proclaim their relationship. She had never married and lived simply but respectably in St. Timothee. It would be too much. She would be disgraced and maybe excommunicated from the Church she loved. Any meeting would have to be under some guise or in the secrecy of night.

Then Antoine Cousineau returned from who knows where. Jeanne had not seen her brother in over thirty years, ever since he went down the St. Lawrence during the war with the Americans to seek his fortune. Crippled, half blind and irascible, but not without means, he just turned up one day with a trunk and stayed.

The night Martin met him he had arrived wet and miserable from St. Clement, where he had just commenced work as a store clerk. Martin had poured out his story to his mother and the new uncle, who sat silently smoking a foul stubby Irish pipe. François Goyette had for all purposes banished Martin from the family home and notary business in Chateauguay. Living with virtual strangers in a parish he didn't know, beside one of the most hated seigneuries in Lower Canada, and with a job he despised and which paid a pittance. A father who ignored him. A mother he couldn't have. What was he to do?

"Stop feeling sorry for yourself. Learn English and leave." Antoine Cousineau spoke the words without emotion. The blue eyes looked steadily at Martin.

Blindly, irrevocably, he was drawn to Antoine Cousineau that night. They talked for a long time afterwards. Friend, mentor, surrogate son, teacher, confidant, questioner. An interchange of needs that through time was bonded in the only love either had ever known.

Through Antoine, Martin learned of places beyond the few parishes he had visited. Most villagers in Chateauguay had never been beyond the parish. A few had been to Montreal, or even to the United States, but Martin had never met anyone who had crossed the endless sea. Antoine told him of places where the sun shone hot all year round, and where men and women exposed parts of their bodies in natural dress. He listened with fascination about the mighty storms at sea that tossed ships around like corks in a bathtub. He heard about great cities like Paris, London and New York where ideas flowed freely as wine. Antoine's face lit up with nostalgia as he poured out his stories to his enraptured nephew over the next months and years.

First he taught the boy to speak English.

"The superstitious peasants in this place may despise them. They hate them because they see themselves in bondage. We all hate our masters."

Antoine wagged his finger in Martin's face. "But they also speak the language of the future. And since they will not go away, we must learn to survive like they do."

"So we can become better than they?" Martin had interjected excitedly.

"No, so we can understand them and ourselves better. Who knows? We may produce a new breed of man in this place, this valley, the land itself. Not English nor French but both, each to itself and with the other."

"But there is talk of revolution now," said Martin. "Some say it will not be long before we will rise and drive the British from our land. Louis Joseph Papineau has many followers among the Patriotes."

His uncle had spat on the ground. "Papineau is a dreamer, and the English will win. Make no mistake, Nephew. Now onto other things. Your English lessons begin today."

Martin's lessons continued through the foment of 1835–37, and when the troubles erupted in St. Charles and St. Eustache in the fall of 1837, Martin quietly practised his English and played checkers with his uncle.

Martin's English was proceeding quite well when Antoine bestowed his second gift on his nephew. Unlike his new language, which was a secret he could never divulge until he left the cloistered hostility of Chateauguay or St. Clement, this one need not be hidden. They had been sitting on the riverbank watching the boats and the green farm-dotted hills beyond when Antoine produced pencil and paper for both of them.

"Draw," he said abruptly.

Martin's shock showed in his reply. "I have not been allowed, Uncle. Papa says it's for lazy ones and wastrels."

"Your father's a fool. I thought we were agreed on that. Now draw. Anything you see."

Martin drew for over half an hour, oblivious to the fact that Antoine had been watching him intently for half that time, his own unfinished sketch sitting idly in his lap.

He took the sketch from Martin's hands. The figures were crude, stylized but evocative. The trees were bowing and the boats were bending as if they were trying to kiss the river which fomented through heavy pencilled lines in a succession of whirlpools. When Antoine handed the sketch back, he said, "Now we know what it is you have to do."

Two months later paints, palette and easel arrived from Montreal together with some books. "An investment," his uncle had chuckled happily. Martin was delighted. He now had an ambition. When he had sufficient money, he would leave St. Clement and the other villages and go away to study painting. To Montreal, New York, Paris. And when he became famous he would come back and take his mother and uncle to where they could live as a real family away from eyes and minds who, to use his uncle's favourite phrase, "substituted pre-judgement for truth and called it God's will."

~ ~ ~

Jeanne Cousineau looked at her son lovingly. Yes, he was a fine-looking boy. Tall like his father, but with a kindness and an understanding of eye that François Goyette lacked. Blue eyed and fair, he had a smile that made people happy. His speech was slower than that of most young men but his voice was rich and soothing once you got used to it. She wondered about girls. She would find him most handsome, were she young again, but she was his mother. He had never talked about girls except on one occasion when he had mentioned his admiration for the betrothed of his brother, Joseph-Narcisse. What had he said? That he liked Domitile but that she could never love someone like him.

"You know I will not be able to come and see you as often, now that Uncle Antoine has gone. Will you miss him, Maman?"

"Not as much as you, my son. We were so unalike. His scorn for the Church. The words I didn't understand." She shrugged resignedly. "But yes, I will miss him. He laughed so loudly."

Martin wiped a tear from his eye. "I, too, Maman."

He took her hands and led her to the dining table. "But Uncle Antoine's going from us has made it more necessary for me to decide. I don't want to stay here, and I don't want to leave you. But I can't see you."

He shook his head despairingly.

Jeannne Cousineau patted her son's hand. "You must pray, Martin. Pray, and then put yourself in God's hands."

"That has always confused me, Maman. How will God let me know what He wants?"

"Things will unfold and you will be part of them, and in your heart you will feel God's guidance. But." Her voice suddenly became softer, more intimate, "The Holy Mother. She is the best one to ask. Jesus will do things for her like any good son will do for his mother. Pray to the Lord through the Madonna."

She got to her feet abruptly. "Now let me make you some of the bean coffee you like, and then you must be gone. You will travel more slowly in the dark, and you must be at your work tomorrow."

Chateauguay, Lower Canada, August 15, 1838

The Goyette family home was among the most imposing in the village. Built on two levels with large stone chimneys at each end, and set on sturdy stone foundations, it exuded an air of homey respectability. Visitors climbing the railed stairway to the front door entrance had good reason to believe that Notary François Goyette was indeed a fortunate man. Though it was the middle of the week, no one worked on this special feast day honouring the Assumption of the Blessed Virgin Mary to Heaven, and the whole Goyette family had gathered to attend Holy Mass together to honour the Virgin Mother, and then afterwards to dine on the bounty of the land around the big table with the curved arm chair at one end.

After dinner, the three men stood together in the small drawing room.

François Goyette was talking, but looking only at the younger man on his right. The other man, younger still, was listening politely although every now and then his eyes would steal a glance at the pretty, dark-haired young woman who was helping clear away the dishes from the long table.

"Be Careful, Joseph. This time you're a marked man. The British will not forget 1837, and if something happens in 1838, men may die for events in 1837 for which they have been pardoned. British justice." François Goyette laughed mirthlessly.

Joseph-Narcisse Goyette merely shrugged. "You forget, Papa. This is not a game. This is not something we have to win as much as something we have to do. We tried last year and failed. But we learned."

His handsome features were flushed with emotion, and his usually quiet cultured voice was ablaze with fervour. "It's simple, Papa. The British have to be banished from our land. Whether it be now or later. Me or someone else. Martin here. Or his son. Our sons. It doesn't matter who, how, or if, but when?"

"And you really believe that the 'when?' is now?" The elder Goyette looked uncertain.

"I do, Papa. We have the whole country covered to the border and to the east and north of Montreal. The Frères Chasseurs are as numerous as sheaves in a fine field. Nelson and Coté in the United States have the military means to move at a moment's notice. At the signal we'll isolate Montreal, take Sorel, and move in numbers on Quebec herself. The British will have no more choice than they had in the American States seventy years ago. Think of it, Papa. Masters of our own house. The new republic."

Martin spoke for the first time. "Do you really think you have the support, Joseph? Organizing secret groups, and talking about great support from the south does not ensure success. I am not as sure as you about our collective will. And has anyone ever seen this American army? Will the American government stand by while their own citizens cross a border to invade a country held by a formidable potential adversary? The Americans might be reckless, but they are not stupid."

It was François Goyette's turn to interrupt. Though Martin had echoed his own fears about the incipient Patriote movement, he could not allow his bastard son to tarnish any ideals held by his favourite first-born.

"If every great leader held your qualms, Martin, we would all still be under feudal vassalage. Joseph-Narcisse talks about duty, honour, a call above self. Sometimes freedom must be bought with blood and courage. Could you pay the price Joseph-Narcisse is willing to pay, Martin? Maybe we shall soon see."

Martin fought the anger rising within him. "I am not questioning Joseph's nobility, merely his practicality."

Joseph-Narcisse was looking at him intently. "I see your point, Martin. But I think we can win. I know we can."

"Are you a member of the Frères?" It was François who spoke. His voice was heavy with sarcasm.

"No, Papa. Unlike Joseph, I don't think we can win."

Joseph-Narcisse's eyes held a strange gleam. "Does it matter, dear brother?"

It was a female voice that broke the silence. François Goyette wheeled on his future daughter-in-law, angry at her effrontery.

"If you love something enough, the consequences of pursuing it do not matter. Martin is not like you, Joseph dear. He hasn't yet decided the depth of his love. When he does, he will seek to claim and then defend it. Isn't that true, Martin?"

There was a nervous silence. Joseph-Narcisse beamed inside. Few men in Lower Canada could boast a wife as beautiful or as courageous as Domitile. François was speechless with rage. He'd speak to Joseph tomorrow. This head-strong young woman who was about to become his son's wife needed a good talking-to. Martin reddened. Domitile was looking at him, her dark eyes wide and openly appraising. For a fleeting instant he met them and read their message. He mumbled something about his love for the land and excused himself to join his younger stepbrothers on the back veranda playing checkers.

The Seigneury of Beauharnois, Lower Canada, September 1, 1838

The road to the small farmhouse was a quagmire. The heavy rain that had saturated the grain-filled fields for a week had slackened to a steady drizzle that hissed in the night.

The shapeless forms, hidden behind heavy hats and coats, arrived singly, some on horseback, others on foot, squelching ankle-deep in the muck. Some slipped on the embankments that guarded the foundations of the stone house, muttering at the clumsiness that might have betrayed their approach. Each knocked four deliberate well-spaced raps before the door was opened. By ten o'clock, all were assembled inside.

There were twelve young men, mostly in their twenties or early thirties. Three wore clothes that showed they did not work with their hands. The greetings were friendly but subdued. There was little conversation. Some helped themselves to the soup simmering on the iron stove. Others smoked or took a swig from the bottle that was being handed around. Above them, the occasional cough of a sleeping child could be heard. The oldest of the group, a man approaching fifty, kept looking at the clock on the wall, parting the curtain and staring out into the wet night.

"I wish they would hurry," muttered Joseph Dumouchelle.

Five more long minutes passed, then a sound on the porch followed by the four heavy raps on the door. Dumouchelle quickly ushered the two newcomers in.

"I'm sorry we are late, but we couldn't get away. Brown stayed late drinking with a couple of traitors from Beauharnois." François-Xavier Provost was apologetic. The little innkeeper in St. Clement was known for his punctuality and had realized the concern his delay would have caused.

"Of no consequence, François," growled Dumouchelle as he assisted the other man with his wet greatcoat. "Just as long as you weren't followed."

"We weren't," said the second man tightly.

Chairs were pushed forward, but neither of the two men sat. It was Provost who spoke after gaining the attention of the others, now whispering among themselves and eyeing the other man interestedly.

"Thank you for coming my friends on such short notice. But these are exceptional times, and there was good reason." He motioned towards the other man who was cleaning his spectacles with a white linen handkerchief.

"Six of you are members of our brotherhood. As requested, you each brought a trusted friend. Welcome, one and all. We hope that you too will become one of us this evening once you have heard our guest expound our cause. We are honoured this evening by the presence among us of a great Patriote. Chevalier Thomas de Lorimier is well known by Patriotes throughout the land. A man hated by the British as much as he is loved by those who wish to be free from their yoke. Tonight he has asked to speak with men of Beauharnois. Accord his words careful ear, for as he will tell you, our time is at hand. Brothers, Chevalier de Lorimier."

~ ~ ~

From his chair Martin Goyette watched the stranger closely. He had heard much from Prieur about de Lorimier: his brilliance as a debater, his courage, and most of all his fervent belief in the cause. He had gotten to know the village wheelwright, Toussaint Rochon, fairly well, and at the inn that evening, Rochon had asked him to accompany him to a secret meeting that he might find interesting. Though vaguely aware of Rochon's involvement in Les Frères Chasseurs, Martin had agreed mostly because he had nothing better to do.

Now, witnessing all this secrecy, and with the sight of de Lorimier not two meters from him, he was beginning to realize his own unwitting involvement.

Martin could not see de Lorimier's eyes hidden behind the heavy green spectacles, but he could feel their piercing gaze nonetheless. de Lorimier's voice was husky, as if he had strained it. He moved his hands constantly as he spoke. They were white with long tapered fingers. The nails were rather long for a man, Martin noted.

"Thank you, Patriote Rochon. That this foul night has not marred your enthusiasm gives me both heart and confidence.

"I see before me faces I have never met before. Yet I see all of you every time I address a gathering such as this. The faces of men heavy with despair instead of with the hope that should mark the countenances of the young. We are all thus afflicted in these sad and sorry times. But none I am sad to say, more so than the hapless residents of Beauharnois."

Murmurs of assent rippled around the room. Martin found himself wondering. His eyes narrowed as he waited on de Lorimier's next words.

"*Beauharnois* means 'consistently loyal and reliable'" De Lorimier sniffed scornfully. "Are these qualities but fine-sounding names for apathy and meekness? How many of you are farmers?"

Nine pairs of hands showed themselves.

"And how many of you have succession?"

"None of us. We're all the first born." growled a stocky young man with arms like tree trunks. "Why do you think we're here?"

Another voice interjected. "My father has saved. My younger brother by two has succession, but my father says we could borrow for my own farm if the Englishman, Brown, would sell some of the land he has been holding."

The mutterings became louder at the mention of the most hated name in the parish. Theodore Brown was the land agent and permanent resident of the manor house at Beauharnois. He oversaw the operation of the entire seigneury for his master, Edward Ellice, the man they called "Bear," the fur trade and merchant baron long retired to England to enjoy the fruits of his commercial empire.

de Lorimier was quick to seize the opportunity. "It is said in Montreal that Brown is keeping 120,000 arpents of land off the market. Away from you and your birthright. Stories are rife that when it is sold it will be to wealthy Englishmen. In time it is expected that you will be all gone. Think of it, friends. One hundred and twenty thousand arpents of the best land along the St. Lawrence kept away deliberately from the trusted hands of families resident for almost two centuries, by foreign slime who seek also to evict all. How many of your brothers and cousins have already joined the landless masses in Montreal?"

Dumouchelle was on his feet. His face was livid with rage. "My brother-in-law has subdivided his land into parcels so small he is now impoverished. Grain prices have reached levels so low that those who have borrowed cannot repay and many have already been evicted. And still the English raise the taxes."

"One eighth of all my maple syrup. Half the hay in my father's best field." The voice was young, the speech thick and uneducated.

de Lorimier pressed on relentlessly. "Are any of you aware that Ellice's brat and his aristocratic bitch of a wife are in our country now?"

Only Martin nodded. The rest just looked at each other.

"He's one of the English blueblood, Durham's lackeys. Secretary, they call it. He wants to visit his inheritance." de Lorimier laughed derisively. "His inheritance. What a sacrilege! And do you know what he's been saying in Montreal? That his family owns the finest seigneury in the land. One that has been made more modern and profitable by improvements."

He waved his pointing finger around the room. "He says that his French peasants are not sufficiently grateful. 'No better than animals,' the good lady has been reputed to have uttered in polite English circles."

"We have had enough," Dumouchelle roared turning to the others. "We take back the land. No, we do more. We reclaim our country."

"You are right of course, Joseph. And we have tried the peaceful way, and were ignored."

"We also tried revolution. Last year remember, Chevalier. We failed. Dismally, I might add." It was the first time Martin had spoken.
At first de Lorimier seemed taken aback by the peculiar speech, but he understood well enough to respond angrily. "I do not need you to remind me, Sir. I was there. We lost not because of lack of will or ability. We were poorly organized and isolated. This time it will be different."

A hum of excitement filled the room.

"Let me explain how it will be different this time. We have new leaders. We were divided last time. Papineau is no revolutionary, but Robert Nelson and Cyrille Coté are. For months they have been raising money and support in the United States where there are many who hate the English as much as we do. They have raised over seven million dollars. They have already proclaimed the republic. Our own notes are soon to be printed, and distributed to the sons of freedom for their work in ousting the tyranny of the British."

He raised his hand to stem the gasps of delight at the news of this secret and wonderful revelation. This was the stuff of revolution.

"There are stores of arms hidden throughout the country, in every parish, in places known only by your own leaders, and an abundance of more rifles and cannon secreted in warehouses close to the border. Eight thousand rifles to take Chambly alone."

de Lorimier went on expansively, "Thousands of well-armed Americans only wait the command from Nelson to pour across the border to assist us. The English here have been divided by the actions of the so-called reformer, Durham. There is talk that he will be leaving soon, and when he goes the English will be leaderless."

"What about Colborne? It was him in 1837 and he is still here. Rise, and you rise against Colborne." Though Martin tried to temper his words, the rebuke was general and loud.

"You still do not understand, my skeptical young friend. Where is your patriotism? Colborne will be powerless in the face of the total popular sentiment we will bring to bear. You understand. This time we have organized ourselves so that our revolution will be complete, down to the last man."

de Lorimier dropped his voice to a confidential whisper. The group craned forward in conspiratorial unison to catch his words.

"The British are divided among themselves. Durham has lost all spirit and leaves in a short time for England. As for Colborne, he is more dispirited. He thought he was going home in 1837, and he is still here. Talk is that he is sick and tired of Canada and the Canadiens."

"But our real strength this time, my friends, are Les Chasseurs. The British are already frightened. Two thousand Frères in Montreal alone, and another ten thousand to the north and south. Thousands more in Trois Rivières and Quebec, and all the way down to the border. The lodges of the brotherhood are organized, as some of you know, to move quickly and efficiently into readiness for battle."

"How?" All eyes turned towards Martin, then back to de Lorimier.

"A hundred men to each lodge. Ten platoons of ten, each led by its own raquette who in turn is answerable to the lodge castor. Above the castor is L'Aigle who is responsible for co-ordinating the lodges of an entire district. Overseeing all military operations and receiving his direct orders from our president, Robert Nelson is the Grand Eagle. He is a man of much military experience and vision."

"And his name?"

It was Dumouchelle who spoke. "Only members of the brotherhood are permitted to know such things, Martin. Our bond is total secrecy and commitment. That is why we will win."

"Joson is right. But we have said enough, and it is time to go on to our purpose here tonight. Les Frères Chasseurs will be the agents of the revolution. We have the organization, the men, the arms, and most valuable, the will. Who here is ready to take the oath and undergo the rites of initiation?" de Lorimier's eyes were blazing as he drew his audience to him.

Five pairs of hands shot eagerly into the air. Toussaint Rochon looked imploringly at Martin who sat stone-faced staring at the stove.

"And you, my young friend?" de Lorimier's words held the edge of impatience.

Martin shook his head. "There is too much I do not understand. Too much I do not feel. Too much I do not believe. The British will win. Rhetoric we have aplenty. But that will not be enough, and I do not want to be a martyr. No, Chevalier. Les Frères are not for me."

de Lorimier nodded. His voice was terse. "You have my sympathy for your bloodlessness. Now leave us. We have things to do."

He turned to Toussaint Rochon who looked embarrassed. "Can we depend on his silence, Toussaint?"

"Martin is no traitor. He should be allowed to go in peace."

"Martin who? is no traitor. What name are you known by?" de Lorimier raised his voice questioningly.

"Goyette," replied Martin dully. He just wanted to leave.

"Hopefully, we will see you again. As a man of conviction. As a Patriote. But now, you are a stranger who has no place in this house of freedom. Go from us this time, Martin Goyette."

He heard no words of farewell as he embraced the cold rain. It had been a big mistake to have come. de Lorimier was a fanatic, like Joseph. He was not about to become one of their sheep.

"Why then, O God, do I feel so empty, so full of nothing?"

No one heard him. The wind plucked the words from his mouth and hurled them into the wet empty night.

Quebec, Lower Canada, September 9, 1838

The Castle of St. Louis in Quebec was a plain baronial edifice with a wide verandah that commanded a panoramic view of the St. Lawrence River. Yet, even with this magnificent setting amid four acres of wooded land including two fine gardens, it resembled more the home of a respected English gentleman than it did the official residence of the Governor of Lower Canada. The outer walls, once fortified against attack, now stood decayed and crumbling, while visitors passing through the courtyard to the plain wooden front door found their nostrils assailed by an odoriferous invasion from the nearby stables as well as from a fetid empty structure that loomed obscenely against the unspoiled greenery of the woods beyond. Some whispered it was an ancient French gaol where prisoners had languished at the Governor's pleasure, and where the lost souls of the departed sometimes wailed in the night wind. By comparison, the interior of the Castle of St. Louis was more opulent, containing several spacious apartments, the most impressive of which were the official quarters. Since it devolved on each Governor to furnish his own suites, they were particularly fine this year, for the resident Governor was well known for his elegance of taste and love of things fine and genteel. John George Lambton, Earl of Durham was a man of utmost discernment when it came to matters of refinement.

He was evincing it now, flicking disdainfully at an offending speck on the lapel of his black immaculately tailored jacket. and motioning imperiously to the man sitting respectfully silent across from him on a stiffly-new divan. Edward Ellice rose and delivered the papers to Lambton who then waved him away with a flaccid gesture of the finely manicured fingers. A slight breeze from the open windows barely rippled the heavy bronze-coloured velvet drapes. Yet the dank smell of the river faintly tainted with the nose-crinkling odour of burning pitch overcame both the fragrance of flowers set in ornate porcelain bowls, and the incense taper smouldering inconspicuously in a brass stand beside a cameo portrait of four children. Ellice looked at the thin spiral of smoke and then at Lambton who unconsciously was smoothing his grey streaked hair as he read. He had tried to dissuade his superior from displaying this painful reminder of his lost family, struck down suddenly, cruelly with the scourge that continued to ravage the Lambton household. But it was to no avail. John George Lambton, First Earl of Durham, and now Governor-in-Chief and High Commissioner of British North America was not known for his tractability. So the portrait stayed, an occasional item of intimacy among the regal trappings and the retinue of imported courtesan finery which had accompanied the aristocratic soldier and diplomat to the shores of New France to face a maelstrom of discontent. A bloody ferment that had seen French speaking peasants, English farmers, displaced American anarchists, and other petty souls take up arms in 1837 against the might and right of Great Britain. He had arrived in May, setting up court in Quebec with a lavish formality not seen since the days of Compte Louis de Baude Frontenac and the Ancien Regime. The Chateau St. Louis had become his hallowed hall of justice from where he bestowed the reforming enlightenment of British Whiggery on the colonial masses. After all he was not known as Radical Jack for nothing. Clemency without capitulation served better ends than high handed repression. So he had not executed the ringleaders of the rebellion, but had exiled them to Bermuda. Those who had escaped to the United States he had forbidden to return to Canada under pain of death. It was as simple as that. He had placated the people, and afterwards they had come as welcome visitors to his court at the Castle: clerics, notaries, merchants, and ignorant farmers with the smell of the earth clinging to their boots and fingernails. All wanting the justice that an enlightened Britain could give them. He had also gone among them, visiting the towns and the parishes where he had been painful witness to the yoke of feudal oppression. Yes, he had listened well, dwelling long and hard on the ultimate solution to this most vexatious problem. He thought he knew the answer. The fault in Lower Canada was clearly racial, resting as it did on the ideals of absolutist and feudal France. It was a peasant society with no middle class and therefore bereft of hope for future progress. Any solution would have to take this into account, along of course with the parliamentary reforms that would surpass those in Britain, which, if so far bravely promulgated by Whigs, had been only tenuously grasped by the Tories and other lesser denizens of Whitehall.

Across the room, General John Colborne, his sword resting lightly on the tip of one gleaming black boot saw things differently. When the rebellion had come in the fall of 1837, he had been ready. The battles were short. The victories, complete. Sadly though, the aftermath was less impressive. Colborne's communications with his two main field commanders broke down. The result was unsanctioned pillagings, burnings, desecrations, and a smouldering enduring hatred among the French speaking populace towards the British and their coldly efficient leader. They spat his name venomously in parishes along the St. Lawrence from Quebec to Montreal and beyond, and down the Richelieu to the American border. le Vieux Brulot, the symbol of brutality. All of which bothered Colborne not a bit. The realization came gradually and alarmingly to him that Durham was not interested in returning the Canadas to the benign enlightenment of true British military rule. He and his rabid cohorts were talking increasingly about political union of the two English and French speaking colonies, and worse still, of concentrating more political power in the hands of elected assemblies. Colborne's sensibilities recoiled at the thought of mob rule run rampant. Power was a sacred trust, honoured and tempered by those fitted to exercise it. Certainly it could not be delegated to farmers and petty shopkeepers. Tin was still tin no matter how much it was shone to look like silver. And so he had listened to them snapping at the servants, and afterwards debating at length about liberty and the rights of Man, over haunches of roasted venison, and silver plates piled high with the fruits of peasant labour. Ellice's wife tittering behind her fan and making comments fit only for men, and the rest of them, loud, brightly festooned, and full of ambition. He loathed the banquets, and by the end of the summer had also come to despise the gaunt figure who sat at the head of the table. The dark eyes set back in the humourless face, the authoritative gestures of the long thin fingers, and most of all the air of dominance that reached out towards him like a slap in the face. An irate certainty encircled the pampered visage of John George Lambton, Earl of Durham like a thin wispy halo, and the rest of the world be dammed. And now he was leaving.

~ ~ ~

"I didn't see you enter, General." He motioned to Colborne to approach.

Irritated, Colborne kept his silence, but took his time in approaching Durham's desk. Still, his training took over involuntarily and he found himself standing stiffly at attention before the man whose military experience and ability mocked his elevated position.

"Your messenger said you wanted to see me, Your Excellency."

"I shall be departing on the first available ship. You, General, are now in charge of all affairs in this place. My work is done here, but not done altogether. I will have my say. Later, and in London," he added to himself.

"Thank you Excellency for your trust in my abilities." Colborne smiled slightly at Durham. "But I hope such confidence will not see me here in this place for too long."

Durham looked slightly surprised. "But of course. How could it be otherwise? There is quiet throughout the land. You will have little to do until a permanent governor is appointed. He, on the other hand, will have much to do if he proves to be the right man."

"My duty is clearly understood, Your Excellency as is my direction. May I take my leave by your grace. Preparations are necessary. There is much to be done."

Durham appeared confused, as if he hadn't been listening. "Preparations? Much to be done? About what? The new governor is the man who ..."

It was the first time Colborne had ever interrupted the man who was no longer his superior. He took enjoyment in the fact, noting the look of astonishment that creased Durham's usually set features.

"Revolution, Lord Durham. I speak of revolution. It is imminent you know."

A brisk salute to Durham, the barest of nods to Ellice who looked dazed, and Colborne was gone. His sense of satisfaction did not last, however. The rare smile which he had allowed himself vanished in the afternoon sun as he made his way towards his austere office in the cheerless grey edifice they called the Citadel.

~ ~ ~

The Upper town of Quebec was dominated by the Citadel, a massive fortress which enclosed a circuit of almost three miles. Built from the same grey granite, quartz and dark slate as the rock upon which it sat, the Citadel consisted of high stone walls, batteries and works that carried to the very edge of the precipice and the river 350' below. Sir John Colborne hated the place. It was cold in winter, was poorly heated, and gave him an overwhelming feeling of confinement. On a curved battlement just below his window, the British flag fluttered idly from a serrated flag pole. Intermingling with the two sentries who were patrolling the battlements was the usual knot of sight seers leaning over the walls and pointing to the bustling town below. Over thirty craft under sail and one steam packet lay at anchor in the still grey waters while in the distance the blurred shapes of dull green hills disappeared into a mist that had risen suddenly from the Atlantic. Yes, it was a peaceful enough scene, Colborne thought. The Citadel was an impressive reminder to any foreign naval power that British might in Canada stood firm and resolute. The trouble was that the danger lay not in the waters below him. It was elsewhere, beyond those hills in the neat white villages that nursed dark resentments.

~ ~ ~

After some time, Colborne turned away from the window, and settling himself in the old but comfortable writing chair, dispatched his orderly with instructions to fetch Major General Clitherow immediately. It was time to act, and Clitherow was about to get his chance. Rumours of a second insurrection had been rife all through the summer. Discontented farmers along the Richelieu and the border areas were said to be arming for revolt, supported in their cause by American citizens prepared to cross the border as an invading force. Though he had no illusions over the depth of smouldering resentment along the valley, Colborne nevertheless had remained sceptical over its capacity to spark another revolt. His subordinate however was less sanguine, and had pressed him to bolster the military presence along the Richelieu downstream from Sorel. He had given Clitherow short thrift. After all the man had not been in the country long enough to make strategically valid military judgements. Now, in the light of intensifying reports of musterings and arms movements, the ever cautious Colborne was beginning to feel the familiar janglings of alarm. If Clitherow was right, then they were dangerously isolated particularly if the American reports were anywhere near accurate. The United States government appeared indifferent despite importunities by Durham himself. Their armies were eyeing the new republic of Texas, and the border with Lower Canada was guarded by scattered patrols not much bigger than a corporal's guard. Damn Durham and his pride. While he took to his heels like a petulant schoolboy, he left the soldier to fight in his place. But at least he was in charge. Much better to fight a battle unencumbered by advice or direction from a superior who had barely earned a cornet's ranking. Still he wished he was in Iona. Tiredly he rubbed his eyes and waited for Clitherow.

~ ~ ~

Clitherow knocked once, and half a minute later stood at attention before his superior. Behind Colborne, the tired eyes of the late King William IV looking absurdly quizzical in a sailor's hat gazed back at him. The formalities were brief. Hatless and at ease in each other's presence the two officers talked for a long time until the sun was low in the sky. Durham's leaving, they both agreed, left the colony in the hands of men who should never had had to relinquish it in the first place. Rebellion was probable and possibly imminent. They railed at their helplessness in the face of the covert nature of their threat: the secret brotherhood which turned peasants into soldiers and frustration into fanaticism. Their real fear however was the disposition of the Americans. One may not like or respect such ill-disciplined rabble but when their numbers were reputed to be over forty thousand prepared to bear arms and another quarter of a million in total sympathy, even the most professional of military men may be excused for feeling a measure of trepidation. Yes, they would have to watch the border, closely.

Beauharnois, Lower Canada, September 10, 1838

Theodore Brown was a big man with a weather-beaten face, reddened latterly more by excesses of rich food and the bottle than by the elements he had endured along the fur-trading streams west of Hudson's Bay and beyond to the great limitless North-West. Though age and the privileges of authority had curbed the natural aggressiveness he had employed to serve his own ends, he remained intolerant towards anything that did not concur absolutely with his concept of the correct order of things. He only admired one man in the entire world, and that was his employer, Edward "Bear" Ellice, the man who had single-handedly saved the fur trade by bringing the warring Hudson's Bay and North-West Companies to a merger. The son of an old Nor'wester himself, Brown had heard his father talk with great respect about the Ellices, and when his aching bones made it too difficult to make the long fur trading trips west, he had approached the great man himself when the Bear had made one of his infrequent visits to Canada in 1836. Impressed by the big man's initiative and with his knowledge of French, the Bear had offered Brown the job of manorial resident and manager of the seigneury of Beauharnois.

Brown readily appreciated what he had to do to earn the Bear's favour. Though he had been resident manager for less than two years, he viewed his accomplishments with some satisfaction. A new mill, better roads, plans for a canal. Thousands of acres of land held in speculation, and more all the time with evictions brought about by loan defaults. Just two days earlier he had met a delegation of some of the more prosperous farmers wanting land for their sons who did not have succession. He had refused them all. He thought for a moment that Charles Roy was going to attack him. He wished he had tried; it would have made an excellent example to have responded to provocation by breaking a French head. Still, when they had threatened armed retaliation, he had followed prudence and had called his loyal volunteers together. Farmers who owed him money or favours. Men who feared him more than they hated him; cautious men; men bound by religion more than anger; men ruled by their wives more than by their supposed invisible leaders. They had all come, bringing their weapons as requested. He had exhorted their fealty to Beauharnois before confiscating their guns and storing them in the cellars.

That was two days ago. Today he had a more pressing duty. One that he didn't particularly like. Edward Ellice, his only son, and his wife were visiting the seigneury. Brown didn't especially like Ellice. The man fancied himself too much the aristocrat, and worse still had begun to interfere, even hinting that he mightn't return to England with Durham. Both he and his stuck-up bitch of a wife liked Beauharnois and were visiting with increasing frequency. At least Brown had one thing in common with Ellice. They disliked the French peasants as much as he did. In any case, he doubted whether the pallid younger Ellice would have the nerve to countermand any of the Bear's directives.

Brown heard the carriage approaching the manor house and, after peering through the draperies at the tree-lined driveway, gave one final glance around the drawing room and then joined the servants at the front door to greet the honoured guests. Another couple accompanied Edward and Jane Ellice. All four were hot, tired, and dusty from the trip. They did not want Theodore Brown around while they discussed the journey and their plans for the next three days, which suited Brown. He was only too glad to escape the cool, refined surroundings of the most detested manor house south and west of the St. Lawrence.

He laughed. The Ellices believed they were welcomed by the peasants as benevolent squires. The silly simpering fools. He swallowed dryly, feeling the need for a drink. Half an hour later he was on his fine grey, smelling the river air as he made his way down the narrow rutted road that led to St. Clement.

~ ~ ~

The Angelus bells were ringing as Martin crossed the last "t" and closed the account book. Usually he took his lunch either on the back porch or in the small room behind the office. Today he decided to go to church. The last week had been anything but tranquil, and his restlessness and uncertainty were bearing more heavily on him each day. He had never felt this way before. He'd laughed when Uncle Antoine had called him a "tomorrow" person, but now he had to admit to himself that Uncle Antoine had been right as usual. As he walked, he thought of Father Morin. The elderly parish priest at Chateauguay had had a favorite sermon. To him, hope was the greatest of virtues, and at the commencement of every season and also on Pentecost Sunday, he gave an impassioned plea for his parishioners to assuage their toil and sweat beneath the ever cool and invigorating panoply of hope. Martin had always enjoyed these sermons and remembered himself nodding in agreement as the gentle, grey-haired Father Morin applied spiritual salve to minds that were throbbing increasingly with an ungodly disquiet. But being young, Martin had not known what the good cure was trying to effect in his more truculent parishioners, and instead had assumed optimistically that God's will had good things in store for him as well. For instance, he had anticipated that things would get better in time with his father. Now as he passed the small stone houses with their flowering gardens and neatly kept vegetable plots, he found himself dwelling on realities. If anything, he was becoming more estranged from Francois Goyette. His banishment to this place was a clear signal that he was not wanted. He recalled the relief in his father's eyes when they had parted. A formal handshake, a letter of introduction and a firmly closed front door were his final reminders that he no longer had a home in Chateauguay.

The sun had come out again and its warmth was pleasant on his back as Martin made his way towards the waterfront and the cluster of buildings that comprised the business heart of St. Clement. He saw the approaching rider in the distance and noted that he was galloping the horse faster than necessary, especially near the cottages that dotted the approaches to the village. Then he noticed the dog lying under a tree on the other side of the street. It was an animal of dubious breed that seemed to belong to no one in particular. Martin had often patted it, and at times had shared his lunch in its slobbering happy company on warm days when he sat on the porch. It spied him now, and wagging its tail began a headlong rush across the street towards him.

The rider could have reined in. If he hadn't re-directed his mount's head, he may have missed the dog altogether. The image was frozen in Martin's mind. The rider crouched lower in the saddle, spurred the grey, and with a jerk of the reins descended on the dog who realized the danger too late.

A single piercing yelp split the air followed by swirling dust, and a muffled curse. The rider shouted at Martin before continuing down the main street. As Martin bent to tend to the limp form he could already see Theodore Brown turning the grey's head back towards him. He was still standing in the centre of the street when the horse loomed above him, snorting, turning sideways and exposing the large beefy form holding the riding whip menacingly in his left hand.

"You senseless idiot. I should have you arrested. You're a public danger. My horse lost a shoe because of that mongrel." Brown gestured angrily towards the dog lying lifeless in the dust. A trickle of blood stained the dust. Its eyes were glazed open and already a fly was buzzing at its open mouth.

Martin took the scene in, first incredulously and then with mounting anger. But the heated words froze on his lips before he could utter them. The menacing figure on the horse was Theodore Brown, a powerful man who used his fists as readily as he did his tongue or his influence. He kept his voice calm and reasonable. "The dog is not mine, Sir. It belongs to no one apparently." He fought the words but went ahead, "It is unfortunate that you were not able to avoid him. He was an agreeable animal."

Without thinking, he bent to pick up the dog. It lay in his arms, strangely heavy and feeling like a broken doll.

Brown reacted angrily. This was insolence pure and simple. This misshapen French whelp ignoring him to flaunt a dead cur in his face. "Not so fast, halfwit. It's your carcass. Your responsibility. You'll pay for the shoe or I'll take it out of your hide." He raised the whip threateningly.

Martin looked about him. A knot of people were standing off to the side, watching. He knew most of them. A couple were friends. He swallowed hard. His legs felt weak and fear pulled at the pit of his stomach. Then as if closing his eyes to the existence of his adversary, he turned his back on Brown and, still carrying the dog, began walking away towards the onlookers. Deep inside him a voice called silently out to them. *Help me, Pierre. Jocelyn, you're big and strong. You will not stand by and see me beaten. Please.*

Nothing happened. They stood stone-faced, silent, unmoving. Martin kept walking. His arms were heavy and blood pooled in his palms beneath the dog's warm fur. He was conscious of the cursing behind him. He quickened his steps, fighting the urge to run. Then he heard the galloping hooves. They were on him now, and instinctively he turned to face his pursuer. He dropped the dog to shield his face from the whip that swished towards him. It bit into his cheek, and as he screamed in pain the horse caught him with a lurch of its rump. He stumbled and as he reached out blindly to support himself, his fingers clawed at the grey's tossing head. Terrified, it reared high, its front hooves slashing the air. Martin tried to jump clear. It was too late. A hoof smashed into his hands as he tried to protect his head. Then another struck his chest. A blur swept across his eyes and pain sent him to his knees. He pitched forward into the dusty street. By the time the first rescuers had reached his prone body, Theodore Brown had spurred his limping mount out of the village back towards the manor house at Beauharnois.

~ ~ ~

The room came into focus gradually, spinning wildly before beginning to coalesce into indistinct shapes. Martin first tried to sit up, but fell back wincing at the tug of pain in his ribs. His head throbbed and his right hand, which was heavily bandaged, ached.

He was lying on a hard cot. The white sheets were pulled tightly about him. A long table with assorted bottles and silver instruments sat in front of the window. It was then that Martin realized he was in a hospital. No, an office. A doctor's office. Above a desk cluttered with papers hung two framed certificates, and between them a large crucifix. Martin fixed his eyes on it, blinking and waiting for the Christ to come into clearer focus.

"The older patients like it," said a voice. Martin looked up, startled. The man was young, about his own age, with tousled curls of brownish hair. He wore a long white coat and in his hand was a flat chart with a pencil attached by a thread to one corner. The man was writing on it as he spoke. "It gives them a sense of security to know that God abounds in a place where death lurks close. You'd be surprised how many times I have come in here to see a patient on his knees praying before it."

"Where am I? Who are you?" Martin was surprised to hear his voice sounding so weak.

"Doctor Jean Baptiste Henri Brien. You are in my office. Now lie still. You've had quite an experience. You're lucky to be alive really." He held Martin's wrist and counted softly to himself. "I think I'll keep you here overnight. There's a danger of concussion after taking a blow like you did. I think you'll be all right though. You should be able to go home tomorrow, but there will be no work for you for a while, I'm afraid."

"Am I going to be all right?" Martin's voice showed his concern.

Brien laughed, "Oh, yes. You'll be fine . . . in time. You have at least one broken rib. Very painful, but since no lung was punctured, not serious. Your head should heal without complications. The blow was glancing. You'd proba-bly be dead otherwise. It's your hand I am most worried about."

Martin looked doubtfully at his heavily swathed arm. "My hand?"

Brien looked serious, and examined his chart, avoiding Martin's question-ing gaze. "Several bones were crushed, I am afraid. The healing process will take time and recovery will be slow. It's why you cannot work. You will have to be careful about exercising it the right way. If you do, in time maybe you will restore full usage."

"Full usage? What do you mean?" An empty painting easel jumped before Martin's eyes. "I want to be a painter. I still can, can't I?"

Brien looked confused. He patted Martin's left arm consolingly. "Give it time, Martin. It's possible. It's so difficult to tell at this early stage."

"But it mightn't?" Martin persisted.

"No," replied Brien simply. He fumbled for something further to say. "You can always pray."

"Why?" The tone was sharp and angry.

Brien looked up, startled. Martin was sitting up in bed, His face was flushed and his words babbled forth. "It's all God's will, isn't it?" He went on letting the frustration show in words that held the edge of tears. "I suppose it was God's will that allowed that hulking barbarian to come to amongst us, drunk half the time and riding roughshod over anything that gets in his way. Dog. Man. It doesn't matter. I hope the bastard rots in hell. If it's God's will of course." He tried to laugh and lay back on the sheets, drained and dizzy.

Brien sat on the bed beside him and wiped the perspiration from Martin's face with a white cloth. Through eyes that were already closing in exhaustion, Martin was conscious of Brien, heard the words that he uttered.

"Yes, Martin. God's will will be done. That much every good Catholic knows. However, for Man to act in anticipation of this will is a matter only for zealots. A Catholic land ruled by Catholics. Could God want otherwise?"

Chateauguay, Lower Canada, September 20, 1838

It was still light, with the afternoon sun hanging low in the sky. The two men lay flat, concealed from view by the charrette's high boarded sides and mounds of loosely piled hay that covered the floor in uneven depths. Up at the front of the unwieldy-looking vehicle, the driver made little attempt to hasten the two horses' lazy gait, but turned his head often to converse with the man who sat beside him. Both were dressed in homespun farmer's clothes. Though occasionally they waved to workers in the grain-filled fields, the obvious placidity of their journey was uninterrupted by neither oncoming vehicle nor stoppage.

The sun had just dipped behind the pastured hills when the horses approached a large farmhouse guarded by three tall trees and an assortment of crude rail fences. About fifty metres from the house, the man beside the driver removed a white handkerchief from his pocket and wiped his brow with deliberate slowness. From the centre dormer window, ahead and upwards in the gloom, a faint returning flutter of white broke the dusk. The driver, grunting approvingly, guided the charrette into a barn at the side of the house. The two men in the back clambered stiffly to the ground, brushing the hay from their hair and clothes. The right hand of one was heavily bandaged, and he moved as though he were in pain. The driver peered into the dusk and then signalled to the others. Huddled against the darkening sky the four made their way in single file to the open back door of the house. The first three men entered into the warmth of the kitchen. The short man who had driven the charrette stayed outside, watching. Soon it was pitch dark and only the glow and smell of a pipe betrayed his presence.

There was one man only in the kitchen, sitting at the table eating a piece of bread. He rose and greeted the first man.

"It is good that you are here early, Joseph. My wife and children will be returning earlier. They're at my brother's."

"Good, Louis," said Joseph-Narcisse plucking a bit of hay from his coat. "Is everything ready?"

Louis Guerin nodded, and then motioned towards the two other men standing awkwardly by the door. "Only two? And one a cripple. He won't be worth much."

Joseph-Narcisse laughed and patted the farmer's shoulder good-naturedly. "The cripple is my brother Martin. The other fellow is Joseph Duquette. He works in my father's office but has a strong thirst for battle, a burning hatred of the British and a love of our motherland."

Joseph Duquette beamed at the praise. The wild dangerous look that Martin had seen in him on the journey out was replaced by the appearance of a rapturous puppy. Martin inwardly thanked Joseph for sparing him an equal treatment of patriotic rhetoric.

Guerin grunted a welcome and shook Duquettte's hand. He looked at Martin, then at his bandaged right hand. Martin stood until the farmer turned his back without saying anything. Joseph-Narcisse took him by the arm. "You wait upstairs, Martin. We'll do Joseph first. Louis will come for you when it is time." He inclined his head towards Guerin.

As Martin followed the stocky farmer up the well-worn staircase to the sleeping areas, he fought the urge to turn and run. Had he known where to go, he would have.

Sitting on one of the homemade beds, Martin rested his chin in his good left hand. He looked at his throbbing right hand and gingerly tried moving a finger beneath the bandage. Nothing happened. Only more pain. The hand would not get better, he was sure. His career as an artist ruined before it got started. Was it anger or despair that had led him to seek Joseph-Narcisse out to join Les Frères Chasseurs? He wanted to strike back at Brown, but to risk his life in a cause in which he had little confidence and less faith? Then he had tried to tell himself that if Joseph and the others were right, and the British banished, he would stand an excellent chance of being rewarded, possibly with an important post in the new government. Joseph-Narcisse would be very prominent, and would help him. He was sure of that.

But as soon as he realized he was falling prey to blind hope, his optimism vanished and he was miserable again. It was only this afternoon as he prepared to board the charrette that the truth came to him: for the first time in his life he was doing something uncertain, even risky, for his own sake. The decision was his alone. He only wished he felt more positive about the outcome.

Martin looked up as the door opened. Louis Guerin motioned him to come, and together the two of them descended the stairs to the kitchen. Neither Duquette nor Joseph-Narcisse was there.

"Close your eyes tightly, and leave them closed," Guerin said. Martin obeyed. The door opened and he was pushed, stumbling, into the next room. Before he knew it, a blindfold was drawn about his eyes and a heavy hand pushed him to his knees. He knelt for several seconds, conscious of movement but no sound. Then a voice broke the silence. It was familiar but Martin could not place it.

"You, Martin Goyette, have come to take the sacred oath of Les Frères Chasseurs. These things you will now swear.

"You will observe the signs and mysteries of our brotherhood, never reveal-ing nor speaking of them except to another member. You will live henceforth by the crossed rifle and dagger, honouring its rules to the death if need be."

The voice droned on, exhorting Martin to repeat the solemn oath after him. As he uttered the words, Martin found himself concentrating more on the speaker's identity than on the heavy words of the oath.

"All this I swear without restriction, consenting that, failing in any part, I shall see my property destroyed and my throat cut to the bone."

As he intoned the last word, the blindfold was ripped away. Martin blinked in the sudden light. A dozen weapons were pointed directly at his heart and the eyes behind them were unsmiling and grim. The man closest to him had a pistol. Martin noticed that the hand that held it was shaking. He looked into the eyes of Henri Brien.

Bologna, August 6, 1221.

Heat waves danced off the cobbled streets as the young monk lowered his burden to the ground and wiped his sodden brow impatiently. He was weary but he must not tarry. He had brought this water many miles for his beloved master. Cold water from the spring high in the hills above this fever-ridden place. He flexed his shoulder muscles painfully before stooping to retrieve the two goatskins, relishing their coldness against his hot skin. Ahead of him, through the haze, he could make out the low white walls of St. Nicholas of the Vineyard. He broke into a trot, his flat sandals slapping across the burning stones as he ran. He entered the priory through the iron gate and open kitchen door. Once inside, he hurriedly poured cold water from one of the goatskins into a shallow earthenware cup which he carefully carried along a narrow, lightless corridor to a room on the north side of the house. An older monk emerged and wordlessly took the cup from the out-stretched hands, acknowledging the entreaty in the younger man's eyes with a tearful shake of the head. Just before the door closed before him, the young monk caught a glimpse of the frail white figure on the floor. With a faint cry, he dropped to his knees, and through muffled sobs, began to pray.

Inside the room, Brother Rodolph held Dominic's head in his arms. He was crying softly as he wiped the sweat from the fever-racked face. The others in the room shuffled uneasily, their white robes rustling against the hard, stone floor. The room was stiflingly hot and windowless. Outside, the blowflies festered the heat with their obscene droning.

"He's asleep," said Brother Ventura. "He took but a little water."

Then he knelt, the others following him to the ash-covered floor, fingers twisted in the heavy rosaries that hung from their waists. Across the line of bowed heads, Ventura looked at Rodolph. Both were crying now. They had seen too much death to pretend otherwise. The end was near.

~ ~ ~

Dominic Guzman was where he felt closest to God. On the floor among the ashes, lowly and penitent. His beloved Master would soon take his wretched body which offered nothing noble, save chastity. He smiled as the visions of his life rippled before him.

He saw the Albigensians mocking and spitting at him. He blessed them even as the spittle rolled down his cheeks. His eyes were bright as he knelt before Pope Honorius receiving the mantle of the Order he had founded. He saw himself in the snow, praying outside a priory he had founded on a mountainside in his Spanish homeland. He reached out to touch Brother Jordan as the two of them walked the marshlands of Saxony, rejoicing in their empty bellies and threadbare garments.

The visions rolled away for a moment.

Then he looked into a blurred image which became Cardinal Ugolino, his friend and patron. They were sitting together on a stone bench in the terraced gardens in Lombardy talking about the future of the Order. He could even smell the damp, brown earth that clung to their sandals.

The slight body shuddered as the visions became more real and painfully sweet.

It was Reginald. Dominic saw him clearly. He was sitting up in his sick bed in Rome. He had seen her in the night and she had cured him.

He cried out in his sleep. Rodolph bent and gently bathed his fevered face.

~ ~ ~

A midafternoon shaft of sunlight lanced through the dim cell to rest on the empty bed, when Dominic regained consciousness. He saw Rodolph and smiled with his eyes. There were more in the room now, brothers like Blessed John who had come from Salerno to be near him. No one knew what to say. Moved by their mute anguish, Dominic spoke to them, the effort visibly sapping his waning strength. "Do not weep, beloved ones. Do not sorrow that this frail body goes. I am going where I can serve you better."

Then he lay back breathing shallowly, but his eyes remained alive and aware. Heeding Brother Ventura's sign, the friars began preparing for the solemn recommendations for a departing soul.

Dominic watched them, and when they were ready he moved his hand and whispered, barely audibly, "Begin."

The intonations filled the cell. Dominic moved his lips with them.

Subventi Sancti Dei. Come to his help O holy ones of God.

Dominic saw her. She came through the mist beyond the tear-filled faces and prayers of his brethren

Occurrite Angeli Domini. Come out to meet him ye angels of God.

She was smiling, and her hands were outstretched. He raised his arms towards her.

"Mater Dei," he cried silently.

Suspiciente animum ejas, offerentes eum in conspectu Altissimi. Taking his soul and offering it in the sight of the Most High.

There was a moment's silence as the last words of the office died away. For an instant, the figure in death's repose was Dominic Guzman, founder of the Order of Dominican Friars. With the release of an anguished weeping, he became their saint.

~ ~ ~

Brother Ventura could not afford to grieve brokenly like the others, who milled about Dominic's body like lost children. He motioned Rodolph to his side. "We have but little time, Brother Rodolph. Many will be coming soon to be with our beloved master one more time. Prepare his earthly remains well. Not that it would concern him if it were otherwise," he added to himself.

Half an hour later, Rodolph was alone with his master. Gently he washed the pale face, and combed the thinning, grey-streaked hair and matted auburn beard. When he removed the ill-fitting robe from Dominic, his eyes filled with tears as he beheld the monstrous, heavy chain entwined around the emaciated body. It had performed its task well. Recent bruises and old scars told of ongoing, relentless agony. It took Rodolph several minutes to remove the testimony of penance from Dominic's body, so embedded were the twisted links in the flesh of the wearer. After he freed the body, he put the chain aside, already resolving its future as a holy relic. He might not have noticed the leather link, except for the way he had held the chain while laying it out on the floor beside the body. Upon closer examination, he found that the leather was really attached to the link by two strands of light gut. Curiosity got the better of him, and his fingers worked for a few minutes freeing the leather. A piece of yellowed parchment fell to the floor. Rodolph picked it up and stared at the heavy bold script. The words were unfamiliar to him, but seemed to be names of some sort.

He pondered for a moment, uncertain. He had seen Dominic's script, and was sure that the words in front of him had not been written by his master. Yet they were clearly significant; worn through time on a penitent's belt. He had heard from Brother Ventura that the great Cardinal Ugolino was coming from Venice to be with Dominic. His Eminence knew Christendom and Dominic like no other. His mind made up, Rodolph placed the piece of vellum in the small pouch he wore around his neck, and fell to his precious task of preparing his saintly leader for burial.

~ ~ ~

Cardinal Ugolino, once Ugo of Segni, now Bishop of Ostia, knelt alone in the small chapel dedicated to the Holy Mother in the hills above Bologna. It was cooler here than in the city, and he needed to both pray and think. His Office finished, he walked outside to the cool pines and gazed at the city below him. His thoughts were on Dominic.

It had been a fitting funeral. He had presided over the burial after sealing the plain wooden coffin himself. Patriarchs, bishops and abbots from near and far had swelled the train behind the bier until the interment in the Church of St. Nicholas of the Vineyard. Dominic had been buried as he wished, beneath the feet of his brethren. Ugolino's gaze shifted to the unfinished walls of the new priory rising from the brown hillside, and admired Dominic for his constancy in ceasing construction because its grandeur mocked the Order's ideal of poverty.

"Oh, Dominic," he murmured. "You left nothing of yourself but everything of your soul."

Ugolino frowned as if remembering something vexatious, and extracted the piece of parchment from his canon book. Embarrassing. Puzzling. Perhaps both. He, Ugolino, was a man of letters who had seen most of the Catholic world, yet the names meant nothing, belonging not to antiquity, nor to Biblical reference, nor even to the shadowy world of heresy. Of one thing he was certain. The words had been written by Reginald. He had seen too much of the brilliant professor's work on canon law at the University of Paris to be wrong. Never a man of prevarication, Ugolino returned the parchment to his book, and started down the hill to the convent, and the solitude of his cell.

Cardinal Ugolino spent most of the evening on his knees. A virtuous man, he prayed this night not for others, nor for Dominic's soul, but for personal guidance. Rodolph arrived after the other monks had retired. He was breathless from hurrying. "The business of the priory, Your Eminence."

"Ah, those figures, good Rodolph. The way they appear from your quill in rows of perfect balance.

"I have spoken to Brother Ventura. He is at one with me. The Paris priory and Matthew will welcome the worldly skills of Rodolph. They are too spiritual, I fear. A little business sense is not ungodly." Ugolino chuckled at his own good humour.

"Paris, your Eminence?" Rodolph was already imagining when it would be, and wondering if anybody he knew was there.

The two men talked for the next few minutes, mainly about Dominic. Rodolph did not pursue Ugolino's reference to Paris. The concept of personal preference was as alien to him as the meaning of the script on the parchment he saw lying on Ugolino's table.

The two knelt together and prayed, each as one, and with the other. Rodolph felt Dominic's presence guiding him as he had promised. Ugolino saw blessed Reginald in the bosom of the Lord. Were they both nodding approvingly, or was it the cursed sleep seducing his body? He rose first, and went to a small bench where he had laid out his writing materials. By the flickering candlelight he copied out the names written on the parchment, and when he was finished, he showed it to Rodolph, who nodded. Then, slowly and clearly, he spelled out his instructions. The original list was to rest with Reginald; the other he would keep. Both agreed it was a suitable solution. Rodolph had felt Dominic's approval. He was certain spiritually, and that was all that mattered. Ugolino was less than convinced. The blend of intellectual clarity and emotive transport that constituted true prayer had given him a direction. He was, however, too much of a man of God to even hope he was right. "The Lord's will be done."

CHAPTER III

Santa Sabina, December, 1832

Bernard Birous shivered in his thin robe and put his hands under his armpits, ignoring the rosary beads which fell unneeded to the floor. He could see his breath in the chill of the empty chapel, and wondered what mental activity in the ensuing two hours could banish the numbing cold that pinched at his ears and stiffened his joints. He grimaced as he shifted his kneeling position, and longed for sleep. Every Friday evening for the past six months he had prayed before the Stations of the Cross, a rosary and sustained prayer in front of each of the fourteen frozen images depicting Christ's passion and death. He found that by reciting the Aves out loud he could enjoy the companionship of the reverberations of his own voice. There was little comfort in the silent thoughts that filled his mind during the other periods of the week when he was rarely alone. The wretched creature who occupied the second pallet in his tiny, damp, stone-walled cell, and who stared at him in the night through sleepless, red-rimmed eyes, violated his privacy. Only on Friday evenings in this hellishly cold edifice to icons could he be at one with his thoughts.

He had not expected life in the monastery to be so rigorous. He had hardly heard his first Mass when Tettrini informed him of his special spiritual needs. The uncertain nature of his vocation necessitated a sustained purgative period, akin to Christ's ordeal in the desert. The road to true purification.

The restrictions were many. Unlike his fellows, he could not converse during refectory. The other novices avoided him as if he were a leper. He thought he saw compassion in one pair of eyes, but was too caught up in what was happening to him to care. He had the tools of manual work in his hands far more often than the books he loved. His hands were bloodied, then callused to insensitivity. He looked at his hands, clasped now, cold white in the candlelit gloom, and repelling. The stench of excrement clung to them and invaded his fingernails no matter how hard he tried to bite them to the quick. No one ever helped him in his daily ritual with the night soil pails, emptying the foul muck into the pit behind the cow barn, or mixing it with a branch to a brown soup to be worked into the tired earth in the garden.

He rubbed his eyes, fighting fatigue. He must not waver. They would be watching, waiting for the weakness that would banish him to the misery of the "Disciplinii." He had been to that dreadful hole only once, very early in his novitiate, when he had overslept. Forced to kneel and pray for hours on boards with upraised crosses that embedded their imprint into his knees. Never again.

He hated then all. Loathed them for their mute servility. Despised them for their hypocrisy. Preaching the Dominican ideal of chastity while committing lustful acts before the glassy eyes of the very icons they worshipped. But he would stay, though he had to live the life of a beast amid stupidity and blind ignorance He had no choice. His destiny demanded it.

Bernard could barely genuflect, his knees were so stiff. For an instant he was tempted to spit on the floor, but decided against it. Eyes were everywhere in this stone hell. Painfully, he made his way from the chapel through the vaulted passageway that led to the dormitories. He passed his own cell, and felt the eyes searching him from the mass of straw in one corner. He fumbled for the alcove and found the small recess in the wall just beyond his cell. Barely large enough to accommodate a small table and bench, the alcove was his public work place, an open cage, facing others, beside others.

By the flickering light of a single candle he worked, the quill moving across the paper slowly, mechanically as if the hand guiding it was detached from thought. He had been told to make six copies of William of Thierry's *Meditations* for distribution to the Philippine priories. This was his last copy, and by now he detested every maudlin, rambling word.

Why they couldn't send over printed copies to grace the libraries of the witless neophyte Christian Asians was beyond him. But it was like everything else he had to do in this place. In six months he had accomplished nothing that a cage of trained parrots couldn't have done. He had memorized the Offices of the Dead and the Virgin Mary, not to mention over a hundred psalms – some of them lengthy, and all of them banal. If he had been allowed to speak, he could have told them that he was very familiar with the writings of Augustine, Anselm, and Bernard. But no! These too were thrust at him to be regurgitated as undisputed truth. Augustine with his ascetic gibberings, Anselm and his unorganized meanderings about rational faith, and worst of all, Bernard. That witless buffoon who seduced the minds of fools with hysterical bedtime stories from the Sinai Desert. All an unthinkable waste of time, and an unpardonable insult.

An hour later, Bernard wrote the final word, and without bothering to read his work over, gingerly shuffled to his cell. Once there, he dropped to his knees, aware of the eyes behind him in the dark. He thought about food, his library, the sound of the sea as he entered his cave, and the sight of Pope Gregory receiving adulation. After the appropriate time, he lay down on his straw bed. Across the cell the other figure turned to face the wall.

As he lay curled up in defence against the chill in the room, Bernard turned his thoughts to his cellmate. *Yes, you miserable, cunning piece of offal. Close your worthless eyes and be at one with the vermin in your sack. You think you torment me, but you don't know what victories you have already given me.*

Bernard smiled to himself in the dark. The tribulations within this cheerless place were nothing to the hellish forces that had lifted their imprint from him, leaving blessed relief and peace. He had had no headache for six months. The voices were gone, all except the soft, familiar one who whispered things to him that no one else knew. Not these baleful walls that imprisoned his body, nor the slime opposite him whose heaving carcass even now filled the room with noisy sounds.

February, 1833

From his study window, Salvatore Tettrini could see the young novice working in Santa Sabina's fields. He was standing on top of a laden mule cart pitching hay to the cattle that were milling about, lowing impatiently. Tettrini noted the rhythmic swing of the wide shoulders, and nodded approvingly. Bernard Birous had withstood his ordeal admirably. Privation had melted away the softness of body and replaced it with a sinewy resilience. His thinner face gave greater prominence to the strong jaw and burning eyes. The eyes of a zealot, or a fanatic? Yes, thought Tettrini, *we have banished the haughtiness, but not the arrogance. We have locked the man-boy away forever. But what have we released?* He wished he knew. Answering the knock, he went to the door to receive his visitor, the other novice who was tormenting his thoughts.

Tettrini had found Alphonse Battiste's vocation difficult to accept, but had yielded to the enormous pressure applied by the Bishop of Lombardy. The elder Battiste had promised the Church a goodly portion of his extensive landholdings upon his death, since with his only son a priest, he would have no one to manage them. Interestingly, the family wanted the boy in Rome, in a monastery where rigour and self-denial were practised as true virtues. The bishop had been evasive when Tettrini tried to probe further.

The young man was most unbecoming in appearance and demeanour but was, as he soon found out, not unendowed with other abilities. Reprehensible abilities that would probably mean a promising future given the inclination of the Church toward political and temporal matters. Ingratiating, clever, shrewd and ambitious, Battiste exhibited proper outward piety, did extremely well in his studies, and had given indication of outstanding oratorical skills. He was also a manipulator, a liar, and a tyrant. The other novices were afraid of him. Tettrini had knowledge, but no real proof, of his abject bullying and frequent violation of monastic rules. There was no spiritual beauty behind Battiste's physical ugliness, just more ugliness.

Battiste now faced him across the room looking like a distended white slug. Fat hung on the smooth round face in pink, meaty jowls. The tiny eyes were red-rimmed, and darted furtively, avoiding direct contact. His whole head was totally hairless, His shiny, oily pate, and the lack of eyebrows gave his face a flaccid, bulbous appearance. He sat now with his chubby, sausage fingers splayed obscenely across his stomach, waiting expectantly for the praise he was sure Tettrini was going to shower on him. He was certain he had what the Prior wanted.

Tettrini broke the silence. "Brother Battiste. It has been more than six months since we last talked at length. I believe it is now time we did again."

Alphonse Battiste smiled slyly. He knew full well why Tettrini had placed him in the same cell as Bernard Birous. Had seen through Tettrini's suggestion that he, Alphonse Battiste, the most gifted of all the novices, could assist the new penitent by example and silent companionship. The Prior had needed a spy, and today he wanted his spy's report. Well, he would get it, and if he was right, Tettrini would be pleased.

Battiste's voice was a sibilant wheeze oozing out through cracked, yellow teeth. "I have done as you requested, Father. For six months I have watched, and tried to lead by example. When you spoke to me after Mass this morning, and said you wanted to speak with me in private, I prayed and pondered long and carefully these words I now say to you."

Liar, thought Tettrini. Aloud he said, "Go on."

"He kneels, but he does not pray, Father. He works, but his mind is not on God. He writes the beautiful words of the great ones in the night, but his quill is filled with contempt. His composure masks a mind that roils in venom. His brooding silence is but an unsettling protest against the things of God."

Tettrini mused as he listened. It was just as he thought. The jealous and malevolent Battiste could tolerate no rival to threaten his self-imposed dominance among the novices, many of whom suffered his tyranny in Christ's name. Although Tettrini believed that Birous was not among those who would "inherit the earth," who else was better able to sniff out his potential than a cunning rat?

"Thank you Brother Battiste. You've been very helpful. I shall give your words today careful thought. Stay with Brother Birous a while longer. Santa Sabina may be a better place for it."

Battiste was disappointed. He had expected more. Yet he was not displeased.

The conspiracy was not to end, and he would take advantage. He licked his lips, and for an instant there was a glittering behind the pink slits of his eyes.

"But of course, Prior," he wheezed. "We all do but God's will." He wanted to stay and ask Tettrini what he had heard about the Austrians marching on Lombardy, but the Prior seemed preoccupied, and ushered him out without even a simple benediction.

Tettrini closed the door and returned to his desk. He took out his handkerchief and wiped his nose. By all in heaven, that foul man had a stench about him that assailed his nostrils. Yet he was serving his purpose. If they were left together, Battiste might discover something which would justify Birous's expulsion from Santa Sabina. On the other hand, Birous might just slay Santa Sabina's fat pink dragon.

~ ~ ~

It was late in the week when Tettrini joined Bernard Birous at prayer. Afterwards they talked. Tettrini told the young postulant that he was very pleased with his dedication, and that his purgative period was now over. He could converse with the others, and would commence his novitiate immediately. When Bernard asked about bringing his own books to his cell, Tettrini had replied that such was within the sanctions of Santa Sabina's discretionary powers, but sadly not just yet. Brother Battiste would be remaining with him for a short time yet. Reasons of space. In the light of the new times, Tettrini had grand plans for the six empty cells in the west dormitory. A study room where less rigorous works of literature might be enjoyed. Tettrini knew that Bernard would both understand and approve.

~ ~ ~

Alphonse Battiste always occupied the same place in the chapel during the compulsory one-hour private prayer vigil in the Holy Presence. The monastery allocated four such periods daily to be observed according to choice. Battiste usually chose the pre-dawn hour only partly because of his restless sleeping habits. It was the least popular hour, and often he could be alone. From his place in the back pew on the Epistle side of the altar, he had a side view of anyone approaching the entrance to the chapel and could easily move unnoticed from his sitting position to a proper kneeling pose. His recent lack of privacy had added a more urgent reason for unobserved solitude. Even as his mind wrapped around his Ignatius, he closed his eyes blissfully, slid his ungainly bulk lower in the pew, and reached under the folds of his robe.

He had loved the gardener's son as soon as he had laid eyes on him. Though only ten years old, Ignatius had hot sensual eyes, and a brown lissom body that inflamed his senses He had easily befriended the boy, enticing him to the barn with a promise of sweets, and a ride on his snow-white pony. Ignatius had cried a little when Battiste had pulled his breeches about his knees. But he had bent willingly. Afterwards, he had paid him well, threatening him with a sound beating, and his father with dismissal should he ever betray their secret.

They met often after that. Pretences were easily contrived. After all, even then he had been sixteen years old, and as the heir to the estate, a figure of some authority.

Then came that bittersweet day. It was Ignatius' fifteenth birthday, and they were in their favourite space on the bed in the room off the stables where the stable boy slept during foaling season. It was the day Ignatius made proper love to him for the first time. He felt the wild pleasure, remembered biting his lip between frenzied gasps, hoping it would go on forever. Then the slamming door, and the chill of sudden discovery. His father stood framed against the nodding heads of the oxen in their stalls, his face taut and thin-lipped, the riding crop resting against his thigh.

Ignatius was flogged savagely and at length by his father, then sent away with his family without references to beg in the streets. But Alphonse, too, was banished to this place to pray for forgiveness, and to let the rigour of the monastic life purge the lusts from his flesh. His father's uncompromising hardness, and his friendship with the Bishop of Lombardy had sent him here. To a new life, a life he found less reprehensible than he had imagined. Except for one thing. He longed for Ignatius.

~ ~ ~

Battiste stirred in sudden alarm, feeling the hardness in his hand evaporate. Someone was entering the chapel. He hoped it was Bernard Birous. It wasn't. It was Thomas Rivarola. Battiste watched the broad-shouldered friar take his place in the front pew, the rosary twisted in his thick hands, beneath the bowed head and silent, moving lips.

"Peasant imbecile," Battiste muttered to himself. He reached for himself again, but this time he thought of Bernard.

There was something about the dark-haired young novice that frightened Battiste. He was stronger, and much more imposing in body than most of the pale-faced young men who followed God's bidding in this cheerless place. But it was not just his physical appearance that filled Battiste with unease, for he was also beautiful, with long eyelashes and full lips that he would love to kiss. No, what frightened Battiste was something else entirely. Something from within, something wild and dangerous. He had told Tettrini the truth of his thoughts about Birous despite the fire he brought to his loins. He feared this man, but he could also love him. He let his thoughts drift off to the pleasure in his hand.

The previous day, Battiste had watched Bernard take communion and as he knelt beside him at the rails he felt the emotions that tore at his thoughts. Battiste was delivering the High Mass sermon on Sunday from the very pulpit that loomed to his left, the first novice to be so asked. Even before the peasant storyteller, Rivarola. The Prior himself had told him that men's blood boiled when he spoke. Battiste took the host on his tongue, all the time eyeing the dark-haired young man whose elbow he allowed himself to touch. Afterwards, he was pacing up and down the courtyard as he always did when thinking about the magic of his words, when he again saw Birous. Furtively, he retreated into the gloom of the sacristy door, and, breathing heavily, let his eyes build the love, hate, and then hope in his fevered mind.

~ ~ ~

Bernard was back at his father's villa. He was in the garden reading a book on the Hauran Druses, those treacherous Arabs who protected their women through veils and red slippers, while observing their status as equals. His hands burnt like fire as he held the vile testament, but he could not let go. Suddenly, magically, the book closed, and he was able to stand. Then he saw the servant girl coming towards him, naked, out of a blurred mist that was both light and darkness. He lay down, trying to hide, but she prostrated herself beside him. He could smell her foul breath, and felt her hands encircle his waist. He wanted to force them away, but his arms felt fixed in place. He sensed her putrid lips on his neck and face, and, though he tried to twist away, he tasted them, gaping open and drooling into his mouth. Bile rose in his throat, choking the scream that would not come. Then her head crept between his legs. For an instant he felt her roiling tongue, sicky and hot. He felt as if he would die. With a last effort he forced the scream to his lips. It echoed in his mind. He woke, sweating and panting.

Battiste wanted to pair his silent gestures with the words of love he felt. He opened his mouth to speak, extending one hand to caress a cheek he couldn't reach. Instead, a knee smashed into his face. He heard the crunch of bone and tissue and his own yelp of agony. Choking on his own blood, he scarcely felt the strong arms drag him out of the pallet and throw him against the stone wall. He slumped to the floor and crawled to a corner where he cowered, protecting his bloodied head with his arms. He stayed there for over an hour, whimpering through the red mist of pain from his shattered nose. When the grey of morning told him that he might leave in safety, he lurched to his feet and stumbled through the pre-dawn light to the sanctuary of the chapel. He knelt, still trembling with fear and shock. This time he did not occupy the back pew.

February, 1834

Bernard Birous barely heard the chanting as he knelt, scarcely noted the aroma of the incense as it wafted in a blue spiral from the thiruble into the heavy still air of the chapel. As he mouthed the responses, his eyes moved beyond the bishop's bowed head to rest on the mosaic behind the altar. It depicted beggars in white robes kneeling before a cloud out of which shone a radiant light that bathed the worshippers in a soft glow. Bernard blinked once twice, then watched the mosaic come to life with his own image. He saw it smiling through the cloud, acknowledging the supplications of those who knelt below it. Bernard basked in its approval as he intoned the Simple Vows that pledged him to the Dominicans. He heard himself renounce all worldly possessions, and then, as Brother Bernard Blake, rose to receive the blessing in his new name.

"Birous" was gone forever — so would have "Bernard," had the Order's stipulations allowed. But no! A new name must co-exist with an old. Tettrini had at first resisted his choice of Blake, preferring instead a more proper Christian name. But Bernard had insisted, and had prevailed in spite of the Prior's reluctance.

Later, outside in the crisp winter air, he began to feel a sense of freedom. His novitiate was over.

June, 1834

Thomas Rivarola did not enjoy Philosophy, or the lecture rooms, or the Master of Studies. He hated the writing boards, the rows of hard wooden desks, the narrow windows, the cold, grey formless reading rooms, and worst of all the terrifying figures at the lectern. Today, he was staring numbly at a page of Descartes when he heard his name. He stumbled to his feet, and waited nakedly for the embarrassment to follow. He didn't care what the question was. No matter how hard he tried, the twists and convolutions of philosophical thought were beyond him.

Suddenly, he saw the white-robed figure in the front row, the new novice from Genoa. The one they had tried to break during his Postulancy, and who had just begun to take Philosophy classes. He was standing, not looking at the one at the lectern, but at the class, waving his copy of Descartes in front of him. Without waiting to be recognized, he began to speak.

"I come to this class for the first time today to read René Descartes, and find that – limited, contradictory thinker though he was – he is being misused in a place devoted to the furtherance of knowledge."

The Master of Studies' eyes bulged with disbelief and rage. This from a mere student was effrontery beyond all gall. "Sit down, you impertinent boor, and cease your gibberish. I find your appalling ignorance more insufferable than your social graces. You are even more ignorant than you look. I will surely assign you a plenitude of reading from Descartes to edify your plebeian mind."

Bernard's answer was sharp and challenging. Rivarola felt the spell as he hung on every masterful word. "Not from this book, I trust. Three errors on the very page of study. Whoever translated this must have learned his letters in a barnyard."

The class laughed nervously. Rivarola just sat, motionless. He liked barnyards.

"Line number ten. According to the text here, Descartes asserts that the mind and brain are one. This is wrong. His concept of clear and innate ideas forced him to see the two as independent of each other. And on line twenty-six, one should add "motion" to the list of innate ideas.

"And on line fifty-one, the most absurd error of all. The merely imaginary object which the mind puts together from adventitious and innate ideas are not fictitious but factitious ideas. If the rest of this wretched discourse is as rife with falsehoods as this single page, there is little use in pursuing the subject seriously."

He sat down amid a stunned silence.

Father Paulo Venturi had left the lectern and was standing in front of Bernard. There was an hysterical edge to his voice. "You are presumptuous and impudent, Sir. You wish to debate Descartes with me?"

Bernard didn't even rise. His voice was mocking, indulgent. "But of course. I suggest we begin with his earliest work, the *Essay on Algebra*, followed by *The Discourse on Method*, and *Dioptric*. I also believe we should leave *Meditations on First Philosophy* and *Principles of Philosophy* until after we have dealt with his last work, *Treatise on the Passions of the Soul*. The latter is most interesting and in my opinion shows Descartes for what he really is. Don't you agree?

The silence was deafening.

"When shall we begin? Following this class? I would further suggest we work in Descartes' own French. The native language is crucial to true philosophical understanding."

There was a hum of excited murmurings in the room as Venturi fought not only for control of the class, but of his own emotions.

If the truth be known, the Master had allowed his acuity to wane over the years. His notion of valid philosophical thought ended with Aquinas. Venturi's knowledge of the Jesuit-trained rational philosopher was enough to enlighten ignorant students, and little more. Certainly not enough to debate Descartes in French with this upstart. Impossible! He'd wait. Aristotle in Greek. Now that was another matter entirely. Yes, he'd have his day.

"I shall satisfy myself later on the validity of this account on Descartes. In its place we shall now take up Abelard."

Venturi asked no questions of the class during the remainder of the lesson, and was mercifully glad when his tormentor remained silent. He did, however, find the level appraising stare, disquieting, and was most glad to escape the room.

~ ~ ~

Afterwards, an awestruck Rivarola approached Bernard thanking him profusely for his timely intercession. Bernard replied that he hadn't noticed, but agreed to walk with Rivarola to the reading room. He made a show of conversing amiably with Rivarola, who he soon discovered was a farmer's son from Catalina. He had noticed how the monks at the monastery gathered about Rivarola, enjoying his wit, and glad to be in his company. Although Bernard saw little merit in the man's evident compassion, piety and unselfishness, who better to work in his noble cause than an unwitting peasant who could captivate men? His joust with the Master of Studies had had at least one desired effect. The Rivarolas were not men of destiny. They could, however, be useful to his.

Bernard smiled to himself as they walked. He wondered about the other effect he had hoped to achieve with Venturi. A few more like encounters, and the good Master might be only too willing to allow him to write the philosophy examinations before the year was out. Three years of Philosophy in six months: it was a delicious thought. Yes, he would be out of Santa Sabina in less than four years.

December, 1834

The examination papers lay in a neat pile on Salvatore Tettrini's desk. Six months earlier, the Master of Studies had burst into his study, more agitated than Tettrini had ever seen him. It was Brother Bernard Blake who had upset Venturi so; after only a handful of classes, he was refusing to teach the friar-student any more. After calming the hysterical Venturi, Tettrini had once again appealed to Luigi Lambruschini. The cardinal had gently suggested that an especially rigorous round of examinations would bring the young Genoan to humility.

"Or perhaps, Salvatore," Lambruschini had said, leaning across his desk, "the examinations will prove him to be as exceptional as we thought he might be."

Skimming a few pages from the top of the pile, Salvatore Tettrini brandished them at Paulo Venturi, who was sitting sullenly, biting his lip. "Brilliant, Paulo. The most cogent and well-reasoned responses I have ever read from a student. More than that, this is the work of a master."

Venturi shifted in his chair. "Yes. He works through the minds of the Great Ones with much facility," he said sullenly.

"Our decision then, Paulo?"

"We have no choice, Prior." Venturi shrugged his shoulders. "We can teach him nothing more here. Or at St. Thomas'. Turn him over to Giuseppe. You have the dispensary power. Our saintly, patient one is welcome to him."

Tettrini was already wondering how Giuseppe Palermo, Santa Sabina's Master of Theology, would fare. Better, he assumed. Palermo was far less tempestuous, and more wise in the ways of mortals than Venturi. And there was always the Thomistic Oath. No, Bernard Blake would not have the same freedom of expression in Theology. Tettrini brought his mind back to the present. "The Solemn Vows? He should take these as well?"

Venturi met his gaze levelly. "We have no choice there as well. As you have already and so pragmatically put it, he has the right. I pray that you are correct with this candidate, Salvatore. He frightens me."

Mustering a confidence he did not feel, Tettrini put his arm on Venturi's shoulder. "God's will be done, Paulo. We are but His instruments."

He watched Venturi's retreating back until it disappeared around the cornice that legend said, wept tears at the death of Fra Angelico. "Yes, Paulo. I do pray. More than you know."

~ ~ ~

Sometime in the spring of 1835, Bernard found that he had a friend in Thomas Rivarola. The realization came suddenly and not without surprise for he had never intended to take the gregarious, simple Rivarola seriously.

There were many in his village, Rivarola had told him sadly, that found no solace in the Lord. That's why he was becoming a priest. Why he had allowed his younger brother to claim his title to the small family farm. Not for him were the missions, nor the seats of power in Madrid or Lisbon. He was going back to his birthplace to return a straying flock to the Lord's sweet embrace.

Yes you can, Bernard had thought. *You can do all these things. You could make stones* cry out with your words. You shall work your wonders with your fellows. But not for the Lord alone, nor in wretched Catalina. But for me also, and in faraway Saxony, Bavaria or Denmark where ears are more sensitive, minds more receptive, and hands more willing.

Gradually but unmistakeably, the diffidence Bernard bore towards Thomas Rivarola was withering in his mind. They were walking back from classes soon after Bernard had begun attending courses in the great Hall of Theology. Rivarola, still struggling with Philosophy, was talking animatedly about how Hegel was essentially anti-Christian. Bernard who had been listening intently as he had been doing of late with Rivarola, suddenly grabbed the big man affectionately by the arm.

"Excellent, Thomas. We will make a philosopher of you yet."

Rivarola beamed happily, delighted by flattering words from the person he most wanted to impress. For Bernard, it was a moment of epiphany. He'd actually felt proud and happy for another person. He smiled inwardly, and absorbed the implications of this new sign. He'd always known that his destiny would lead him to rule over the minds and hearts of men. He had told Tettrini that apostles were needed for the new Renaissance. But now he knew who his Apostles would be. He laid his arm across Rivarola's shoulders, and laughing together, they entered the afternoon gloom of Santa Sabina's main hall.

May, 1835

"Put them down there, Thomas. That's good." Bernard stood back to allow the burly Rivarola lay down the box of books in the corner of the cell.

Rivarola picked up a copy of *Histoire de Saint Leger*. "I am impressed, Bernard, by your love of mediaeval Church literature. Would that I were so interested."

The big man didn't read French anyway, so even if he opened the book he wouldn't notice that it was actually a copy of Rousseau's *Emile*. Just one of his precautions: every sequestered book was in a foreign language. Most prying eyes wouldn't find fault with his library, even if they had taken the time to look. Except Battiste that is. But he doubted whether Battiste would ever enter this cell as long as he was the occupant.

As if reading his thoughts, Rivarola spoke teasingly, "Books in place of Battiste. You must have been persuasive, Bernard, to convince our Prior to allow you books in your cell as well as the banishment of Alphonse. I do pity that poor wretch for his ugliness of mind and body. I shall have to try harder to treat him as one of God's children, even though he dislikes me intensely."

Bernard was busy arranging his books. "Oh, I don't know, Thomas. There is nobody who cannot like and trust you in time. Not even Battiste. Has he not been a different man since that terrible fall he had in chapel? "

Bernard went on, "As for the books. Dispensatory licence, no?"

They laughed at the reference to Santa Sabina's special niche in the Order. Everyone in the monastery had learned to use the argument to secure some small measure of privilege.

Rivarola looked about the cell and began bouncing on his feet. "This is the time I miss my farm the most. Spring, when the smell of life is everywhere. Don't you feel it, Bernard?"

"Yes, I do admit a change in a last couple of weeks. Mario with his flower-pots. Rising in light instead of darkness. Yes, Thomas, I too am feeling freer, but not because of the season."

He lowered his voice. "When I spoke to the Prior just yesterday he granted me another special dispensation, one which I must confess surprised me greatly." The latter was not true and he even regretted just a little, lying to his friend. He had not been granted the dispensation. He had requested it.

Rivarola raised his eyebrows, a sure sign, Bernard had discovered, of his high interest.

Bernard went on, "I have been given permission to study languages at the University of Rome. Certain Theology classes have been deemed expendable, providing I can evince advance mastery. Since I am familiar with Aquinas, Master Palermo has seen it fit to become my advocate with Prior Tettrini."

Rivarola laughed warmly. "Bravo, Bernard." It was so good to see his friend smile. Bernard's privacy pained him so. Though Man was meant to do God's bidding, it didn't mean he had to be always serious. Rivarola was sure his Maker enjoyed a good laugh, probably often.

"I'm hungry," said Bernard. "I wonder what swill our inept novices have concocted up for us this evening. I do declare the food was better when I took my turn last month."

"Oh, I wouldn't go that far," replied Rivarola. "And besides, for unskilled town lads, they are quite acceptable."

"But you would eat anything. Raven yet."

"True, true. You're right. Raven is very good. You have to boil it first."

"With the feathers on or off?"

"Depends on how hungry you are."

Rivarola's laughter earned him a disapproving look from one of the priests in residence. Reprimands in God's house, however mild, usually upset him greatly. This time he exulted in the quiet but unmistakable humour in his friend's eyes.

CHAPTER IV

Montreal, Lower Canada, September 27, 1838

Martin Goyette heard the Angelus bell and knew the time. He was standing behind Bonsecours market watching the milling crowd. In front of him two urchins sat on the ground, one guarding a small cage containing a bird. A vegetable vendor wheeled his barrow towards the market building, and beyond him two men were leaning against the rail that overlooked the river. Martin wondered whether or not one of them might be the man he was looking for. He pulled the piece of paper from his pocket, and read the message again, even though by now he had memorized every word.

His castor, Henri Brien, had given it to him the previous evening saying no more than it was from de Lorimier directing him to come to Montreal on a matter of some importance. He had just arrived and had taken his place among the crowd of market goers just outside the sellers' entrance. He was still eyeing the two at the rail when suddenly he noticed the man with the cap who had been one of a group sitting on some sawhorses listening to an old fiddler. He straightened up, touched his cap and began picking his nose with deliberate slowness. Martin watched fascinated as if he were in an audience. After a minute or two, the man wiped his hands on his trousers, flicked at some dirt on his knee, and began walking slowly past the tall stone market building. Martin followed at a safe distance. About ten minutes later the man stopped outside a neat but inconspicuous-looking house. He paused before knocking and went inside. A minute later he re-opened it to receive Martin and without saying a word led him to the back of the house and a courtyard garden where two men sat sipping coffee.

de Lorimier saw Martin first and rose enthusiastically to greet him. "Brother Goyette, welcome. I am pleased that you were able to come on such short notice. You found my instructions easy to follow."

Martin extended his left hand, "Greetings. As you can see, Chevalier, I have time on my hands. And yes, your instructions were quite explicit."

"Come join us," de Lorimier motioned to a vacant chair, and gestured to the other man. "This is John Picote de Belestre-MacDonnell, a great Patriote whose house we have the honour of utilizing for our noble cause."

de Belestre-MacDonnell beamed happily and shook Martin's hand profusely. "Welcome, Brother. The Chevalier has told me grand things about your enthusiasm. We have need of men such as yourself."

"I am honoured that the Chevalier thinks so highly of me." Martin's eyes rested coolly on de Lorimier as he spoke but the other man didn't seem to notice. Instead, de Lorimier was fussing with a pipe. He lit it and watched the blue smoke lose itself in the afternoon air before speaking. "Your hand is getting better, I trust."

"Not really. The pain is less, but the movement has not returned."

"You can fight, yes?" de Belestre-MacDonnell's voice was full of hopeful indignation.

"I'm not sure. I could use a pistol, I think."

"Ah, there are things a soldier can do without pulling a trigger. In fact, that is the reason I asked our young friend here today, John."

de Lorimier continued without giving the older man a chance to reply. "Martin, do you remember what you said to me that night at Joson's farm?"

"That I didn't think you could defeat the British. That you – I mean we – needed more than rhetoric and promises to be successful. But here I am myself. I have joined you. So you can see I have changed my mind."

de Lorimier picked up on the obvious sarcasm. "I can see, my young friend, that you have your own reasons for joining Les Frères." He looked at the bandaged hand. "Revenge, perhaps. It's always a good motive."

Martin thought of Theodore Brown and envisaged his body lying in a pool of blood with himself standing above it, gun in hand. It gave him no joy, just a sickening feeling of uselessness.

"No. Not revenge. But it doesn't matter. And I still believe it will be very difficult to oust the British."

"But we must try?"

Martin was surprised to hear the uncertainty in de Lorimier's voice.

"Of course we can win. The British have no real stomach to face an uprising the magnitude of what we are about to perpetrate," de Belestre-MacDonnell was defiant.

"That is what we have to find out, John. The magnitude of our strength. We know that of the British. But it is our own will that will turn the tide."

de Belestre-MacDonnell seemed surprised. "You have heard the Grand Eagle. He is confident."

de Lorimier's reply was sharp. "I am afraid I do not share the same level of faith in Edouard-Elisee Malhier as you do, John. I'm not sure Coté and Nelson do either. But we have no one else. Of course, his courage is unquestioned. It's his leadership and practicality that concern me. He's the eternal optimist, and that worries me somewhat. Which brings me to our young friend here."

He turned to Martin. "I have a task for you, Martin. A task in the name of Les Frères and the cause. We hear only positive reports from everyone who visits this house. But they all want the cause to succeed so much that they could be blind to reality."

"What about you, Chevalier?" Martin's voice was level.

"Me also, I do admit. But I am also beginning to feel the need for some measure of assurance. It is for this reason that I want you to journey to the parishes and villages along the Richelieu, and beyond the border. Talk to the Eagles, Castors, Raquettes, any of our number. Then seek out Robert Nelson, Cyrille Coté and the Grand Eagle himself. Assess the reality of our position both in the United States as well along the Richelieu, for that is where the battle will be won or lost. Number of men, guns, cannon, and most important, discern between revolutionary foment and mere discontent . As you yourself have stated, one is wise not to mistake the one for the other. The British will not suspect you, even though they will be wary of travellers. You will be perceived as harmless." de Lorimier stammered the last words in embarrassment. Both knew what he meant. Martin had been the butt of too many jokes about his appearance and speech to be misled.

"But you are also very shrewd, and given your natural skepticism, will not be led to believe what is not so. Besides, you speak English and that will be a decided advantage."

"How do you know I speak English?" Martin was surprised.

"Dr. Brien. He told me about your encounter with Theodore Brown. In your delirium, you were talking to someone . . . in English. One can learn much by listening, especially when it is thought that you do not understand."

Martin thought to himself before replying. "So I go on this journey. And what if I am led to more surety about my present doubts? Will it make a difference?"

de Lorimier examined his long fingers. "It might. We will just have to see, won't we?"

The man whom Martin had followed suddenly materialized at the table. de Lorimier gestured towards him. "Georges will give you money and acquaint you with our various signs of identification and recognition. They change with each parish."

Martin felt the other man's hand on his arm. It gripped tightly. "You gave an opinion once, my friend. Now find out the truth." He sighed and patted de Belestre-MacDonnell on the arm. "You see Martin, as I have said, even if John or I could go in your stead I might wonder about our objectivity. We are zealots. You are not. At least, not yet."

"You have a month. In one month you will tell me of the real readiness of

Les Frères Chasseurs between here and the border, and the strength and disposition of our American allies. We will meet at the house of Henri Brien on November first. It should give us enough time to reassess if we have to. It has been a late harvest. Nothing will happen before the middle of November. God speed, my young friend."

He raised his glass. "To Les Frères Chasseurs and the cause."

"And to the good news our young friend will surely bring," said de Belestre-MacDonnell as he touched his mouth to the goblet.

Martin watched both men drink. His face was impassive. When they had lowered their glasses, he raised his own.

"To the truth."

New York State, just inside the Vermont border west of Aulberg, October 31, 1838

Martin saw the bridge faintly at first through the rain. The stone arch crouched there like a medieval gateway. Beneath it was a dark void and the sound of rushing water. Martin urged his mount forward and down until he was directly underneath the roadway. He dismounted, and throwing the reins over a jumble of rocks clambered upwards away from the binding wet clay to the cold dry earth beneath the bridge supports. He sat there, shoulders hunched forward against the chill listening to the sound of the rain just above his head. He looked at his watch. He could spare half an hour no more. Feeling the lump against his hip, he suddenly remembered the bread. He fished it from his pocket, and began munching it through the water that dripped from his sodden hat, relishing its warm flavour against the roof of his mouth.

He wished he could cry. The futility rose in him sickeningly like he was watching something terrible and couldn't look away. The truth was just as clear. It was useless. The revolution was nothing more than a grotesque exercise in self-delusion. No, it was worse than that. Good men were going to die, slaughtered like pigs in the very fields they had vowed to make free. He looked at his hand whitened like a dead fish in the gloom. Would their blood be on him? Could he avert the inevitable? He closed his eyes against the dark and waited for the drumming above him and in his chest to recede.

~ ~ ~

Long before he got to St Albans and the tall well kept house from where Nelson and his lieutenants plotted their grand return to Canada, Martin Goyette was disillusioned. Using a different set of identification signs he had met the

American Brotherhood, and heard talk of revolution for the first time in English. Yet, unlike in Lower Canada, the sentiments sounded hollow as if a game was being played with no one certain of the rules. It was as if they saw themselves as noisy supporters whose commitment to armed involvement was at best, possible, and even then predicated on the assurance of success. As for a ready supply of arms, there seemed, if anything to be less certainty as to its procurement or existence. Beyond the indigenous supply of assorted farm and private weaponry, the American Brothers were as ill-equipped as their Canadian comrades, and should they decide to cross the border, and Martin entertained serious doubts over that eventuality, they were little more than cannon fodder.

~ ~ ~

Martin was daunted when he met Robert Nelson in St. Albans. The man had a powerful confident presence. He spoke loudly and intensely, and Martin was quick to note how such an impressive presence could easily sway others to his will. Money was readily available, Nelson had explained airily after reading the letter from de Lorimier that Martin had carried. A mighty arsenal was now being assembled for rapid shipment to Aulburg. Afterwards, he had met the others. Dr. Cyrille Coté who spoke eloquently and graciously but who looked at him like he was some specimen on the laboratory table; the strutting Grand Eagle, Edouard-Elisee Malhier and his vainglorious utterances. It was difficult to take the comical little fellow seriously, and even to Martin's untrained eye, he posed as little more than a military sham. Lucien Gagnon watched him all the time. He alone of them all had the sinewy body and the hard eyes of the true fighter. Martin could not look at him and instead tried to swallow his fear.

The next day he was in Albany at an address given to him by de Lorimier, at the home of Pierre Hamelin, a banker who had once practised law in Montreal. A revolutionary like themselves, de Lorimier had explained, but a realist, and therefore in these days of high emotion, a man who could be believed. He would have definite opinions about the nature of the proposed American support for the revolution. The fat little banker proved to be astute, with bright round eyes that blinked wisely behind clear spectacles. As he had watched Hamelin's stubby bejewelled fingers tapping impatiently on the desk, Martin had realized that de Lorimier was wrong about his friend's revolutionary fervour. Chevalier de Lorimier had made the mistake of equating Hamelin's clear hatred of the British with the seething resentment of the rebel. Hamelin told Martin in no uncertain terms that the seven million dollars supposedly raised to cover the costs of battle was a myth. His bank had recorded no sizeable unexplained shifts of funds, no run of small withdrawals. It was the same with other banks, even those in New York and to the north. Unless Robert Nelson and his mysterious unknown American supporters had incredibly substantial financial reserves, which Hamelin doubted, or had already acquired a massive arsenal of weaponry, the revolution would be fought with Canadian guns. Martin recalled how the little man sighed as if realizing something important. He had pointed a finger in Martin's face and begged leave to qualify his last remark. Men might indeed pour across the border in numbers to support a revolution, he acknowledged, but only if it was already won.

Though he was impatient to leave at once, good graces had prevailed and Martin had dined with Pierre Hamelin. He had scarcely tasted the food, and had later declined Hamelin's offer to accommodate him in his own home. He had to get back to Montreal, to de Lorimier, at once. The madness must be stopped. He had to get to de Lorimier and to Joseph-Narcisse, to François-Xavier, Toussaint. All of them. His friends, and friends of their friends who were even now preparing for a battle, blindly confident that their certain victory would be enabled by allies that Martin now knew were as ephemeral as the dreams they held of a new nation along the St. Lawrence. He had to stop them.

~ ~ ~

The rain had eased to a cold drizzle. Sliding and slushing in the mud, Martin led his mount from under the bridge to the roadway. He mounted painfully and with difficulty, trying to coax some feeling into his right hand by placing it against the warmth of his chest. He had barely crossed the bridge when the upward movement of his horse's head caused him to draw on the reins. He saw and heard the figure at the same time. It emerged from the dark woods beside the road like a black spectre, and in a moment was confronting him. A horseman in a wide hat and dripping cape. The thrill of fear coursed through him.

"Who goes there?" Martin's voice sounded weak and hollow.

"You are Martin Goyette?" It was a woman's voice, its tone authoritative, unafraid.

"Yes, who wants to know?" As soon as he uttered the words Martin cursed himself for his stupidity. How could he have been so careless?
The woman urged her mount close, trying to get a better look at him in the dark. Martin could not make out any of her features. Yet, she seemed satisfied about him, and drew back nodding her head. A moment later he knew why.

"You have the voice they spoke about, and you sit a horse well with the reins in your left hand. Follow me. They are waiting for you at the border."

"Who? Who waits for me and why?"

"The British, you fool. Who else?"

Then she was away heading for the trees beside the road. She didn't look back. After a moment of hesitation, Martin followed her into the sloppy dark, already conscious of the familiar frailty that had so easily overcome him. Here he was following a perfect stranger through the night to God knows where, and he didn't know why. Fear had clouded his judgement. He tried to keep her in sight as they galloped through the trees, along well worn paths, and across several swollen streams. The woman rode recklessly and expertly, stopping several times to allow him to catch up. Even had he known the area as she obviously did, Martin would not have been able to stay with her. She allowed no respite, and spoke no words – just a toss of the head to indicate direction, and she was gone again into the night like an impatient, shapeless wraith.

They rode for what seemed like a long time. Martin found himself falling farther behind as both he and his mount flagged under the pace. He would lose sight of her, then she would be there, featureless and forbidding, her horse prancing beneath her. Once he asked for a rest. His voice must have lost itself in the night, for she was gone again before he reached where she had waited. He thought he heard a laugh but attributed it to the freshening breeze, cold and biting from the north-east.

The farmhouse just emerged out of the night, a yellow light shining in the distance which gradually became a shape. Soon Martin could make out fences and a house. The woman reined in at a gateway and gestured for Martin to dismount. She took the reins of his horse and pointed to the house.

"Employ the knock of the Parish of St. Valentin. You are expected and will be admitted."

She left Martin standing there as she led the horses around the back of the house. To a barn, Martin supposed. He tried the iron gate and was surprised when it fell off its hinges, clunking to the ground with a noise that seemed horrifyingly loud in the night. The steps to the house were loose and creaked loudly, and as he knocked his pattern on the door, Martin noticed that the window to his right had been boarded up where a segment of pane had broken.

The door opened a fraction and a frightened face peered at him. "Martin," it breathed joyfully.

A moment later a thin hand grasped his wrist and ushered him inside. Martin gazed about the room, adjusting his eyes to the unaccustomed light. He was in a kitchen. Frugal, about the same size as his mother's in St. Timothee, and like a hundred others he had known, but lacking somehow their simple refinement. A fire blazed in an iron stove on top of which a large pot simmered pleasantly. The rich aroma of vegetable soup made Martin realize how hungry he was and his mouth watered.

His host must have read his mind, "Help yourself, Martin. Madeleine will be some time yet. I will get some bread. It is good to see you again."

For the first time, Martin turned to face the other man. He didn't recognize him at first, then his eyes widened. "Jacques. I didn't recognize you. It is you isn't it?"

"Yes, it's me, Martin. With spectacles and without the cap."

"The same voice, though. We spoke together for a long time that night, Jacques."

The little man beamed happily. "I thought you mightn't remember me."

Martin remembered him all right. Jacques Verdon, the most timid and fearful of the Brotherhood he had met with in Odelltown a few weeks earlier. He had selected him as the most likely source of information. Sadly, as eager as Jacques was to talk of the revolution, he had proven useless. The poor fellow knew nothing of value about the Brotherhood's real preparedness for battle. It had been a wasted, futile two hours.

The steaming bowl of soup broached no discussion. Neither did the chunks of thick brown bread that soaked it up. Jacques sat with him, talking all the time.

"Another mile and the British would have had you. They've been waiting for days. We were lucky to have found out. Clitherow has his spies everywhere. One was doubtless in the inn when we met, listening, watching."

As he ate, Martin recalled the strangers whose eyes he had felt on him from time to time. He had dismissed these misgivings at the time, attributing them to fear.

"About a week ago, Clitherow began moving men towards the border in increasing numbers. A platoon stationed itself at the border road and has stopped every traveller coming from New York, sometimes keeping them for several hours. They were clearly looking for someone."

Jacques threw out his thin chest and went on proudly. "But I discovered who that person was. You, Martin. The British were looking for you."

He lowered his voice confidentially. Martin had to strain his ears to catch the words. "I go to the inn in Odelltown as often as I can. The owner is a friend and he leaves me be, and gives me a room when fatigue from reading too much overtakes me. I heard Clitherow himself and his officers talking in the next room. The walls are thin and I have the ears of a fox. They were seeking a traitor. Then I froze with horror. Clitherow mentioned the man with the deformed lip and the useless right arm. You, Martin, you are their traitor. Our Patriote, their traitor. I rushed to inform my Castor. He talked to other brothers and after much debate it was decided that the Verdon family should intercept you and take you to a safe place, our farm. The British are everywhere in Odelltown. You are safer here. And since my sister rides far better than I, it was she who went. She would have gone all the way to Aulburg if need be. She is a brave one."

Jacques was standing now, pacing the room. Martin, who had finished the last of his soup, watched him, the realization that he was in mortal danger hitting him like a jolt in the stomach. Him, a traitor? He had to get away from this place. Back to Montreal at once. But he was so tired and the thought of the long cold night ahead was too much. Instead he heard himself saying, "You are kind, Jacques, and I thank you and your sister for saving me. I should be able to make my way safely if I exercise proper caution. The British have no reason to believe that I am not still in New York. A rest in a warm bed for the night, some bread and cheese for the journey, and I will leave with the dawn's light."

Jacques' eyes were moist with emotion, "Yes, my brave friend. A warm bed and food you shall have. But," He looked nervously at the door, and seemed to be gathering his courage, "might I speak briefly with you on a matter of great importance? At the cost of an hour's sleep, you will pay any debt you feel you might have to the Verdon family."

Martin's aching body longed for the warmth of a bed and the oblivion of sleep. He would need all his energy tomorrow. Then he saw the pleading in the blue eyes behind the thick spectacles, the tremor in the thin white hands. He owed this man.

"Of course, Jacques. Sit and talk."

"Like a friend?"

"Yes, To a friend who is in your debt."

"I will be as brief as possible. If Madeleine comes I will have to stop. You will understand."

Martin bit his lip, stifling a yawn. Jacques' voice was low and urgent. "It's my sister, Madeleine. She . . . she . . ." It was as though he was searching for a word, for when it came out it was like it was just plucked from the air. ". . . jeopardizes the revolution. Would you talk to her, Martin? Tell her that she places our lives in danger through her wilfulness. She won't listen to me. Sometimes I think she hates me, hates everyone like she says she hates the British. You are young, brave, and a person of privilege in the Brotherhood. She might listen to you. Stop her, Martin. Stop her from doing the evil things she does against those whom we owe fealty. The manor, the Brotherhood, me. Everyone. I only joined Les Frères to honour my friends. I am no fighter."

The little man's lip was twitching and he began to cry. *He's terrified,* thought Martin. Without thinking he pulled his still-wet handkerchief from his pocket and handed it to Jacques. "Easy, friend. Take your time. I'm listening."

Jacques wiped his eyes and clenched the handkerchief in his hand. "She used to be so good when our parents were alive. They both succumbed to the fever of 1834. Even after that she was dedicated to the farm, helping as much as possible, assuming much of the work, and abandoning her dream of entering the convent."

Jacques shrugged his shoulders. "There were only the two of us, and I am no farmer, as well you can see. I was going to study law in Quebec before Maman and Papa died. Then everything changed and though I was nominally the head of the house, it was really Madeleine. I didn't mind. I understand the necessity of these things."

"Go on, Jacques."

"When she met Claude I was very happy. He was a farmer from St. Jean. A good strong man and steadfast in the faith. He did not have inheritance, and thus would have farmed this place and I would have been able to study law. Madeleine was very attached to him . . ."

"What happened, Jacques?"

"Claude was killed at St. Eustache in 1837. He was shot coming out of the church where he had prayed for the courage to lay down his arms and humiliate himself before the British dogs. He died a Patriote. It was never the same after that. Madeleine did not cry at the funeral, and after that she was different."

"How?" Martin was intrigued by this sad, strange tale.

"In many ways. She neglected her work at the farm. The other women grew afraid of her silences and the anger always blazing in her eyes. She wanted to join the Brotherhood and fight the British, but as you well know, this is not women's work. She then fell to accosting strangers and extolling on the abominable depths of Colborne's soul. Her outspokenness and disregard for person or property has made me fearful. I once saw her with a knife hacking at a picture of the British flag."

Jacques shuddered and slumped forward in the chair. His thin fingers bit into Martin's arm. "Talk to her, Martin. Try to make her understand. I do not know what to do anymore."

~ ~ ~

As Madeleine entered the kitchen her wild grace sent a tingling through Martin's body. She did not speak, but flashed her dark eyes about the room. She was tall, and her dark hair glistened in wet strands about her shoulders. Martin's mouth was dry as he met her gaze and read the scorn, intensity and anger in her eyes. He swallowed and rose to his feet as if anticipating an introduction. The silence was deafening. Even the scraping sound of Jacques stirring the soup ceased. Slowly she advanced towards him. She had changed her clothes and now wore a white lace-trimmed gown. The lace trimmings of her bodice rose and fell as if they were alive, and he found his eyes hovering at her breasts. They evoked a desire in him he had never before known. He knew he should look away but couldn't. Martin's forced himself to speak, and his voice sounded faint and trembling.

"You're Madeleine. Jacques has told me of your bravery." He gestured his head towards the silent figure, who was stirring again. "I'm Martin Goyette and I am in your debt." He attempted a bow and hoped it looked impressive.

"You were easy to find. I expected you sooner." Madeleine said, turning her back to him. She took a bowl of soup from Jacques and sat at the other place at the table. Martin wanted to say something but couldn't. Instead he folded his arms and watched her eat. The silence was awful. Martin's cheeks were hot. He couldn't face her eyes and found himself looking again at her breasts.

"I shall retire now with your permission, my young friend." Jacques' voice startled Martin so much that he jumped. Jacques blew one of the lamps out and lit a candle to carry to bed. He looked anxious. "Sleep well, Martin. I will awaken you at dawn. You should be able to get away before the sun is up, although I fear only more rain and snow."

"He need not be wakened. He is not a child," Madeleine said.

"You are right of course, dear sister." Jacques dropped his eyes apologetically.

Embarrassed, Martin tried to interject, and even as he spoke he felt her angry eyes on him. "No, no, Jacques. Do not concern yourself. You've been kind enough already." He shook the other man's hand. It was limp and cold. His eyes, though, were bright and pleading.

Jacques bowed towards his sister. "Sleep well, Madeleine. You were brave tonight." Then he was gone. Martin could hear his footsteps shuffling, then diminishing upwards. A door creaked in the distance and Martin found himself alone with her.

Though he was sure she would not speak, Martin tried waiting, casting his eyes about the room as if seeing its details for the first time. He knew he had to speak, and not just because of his promise to Jacques. His hands felt cold as he realized how desperately he didn't want her to leave. Yet she frightened him.

His words were supposed to sound casual but he knew they didn't. "Jacques tells me you would fight the British if you could. Do you think we will fight? Do you think anyone will fight?"

"Cowards won't. Will you?"

Martin was surprised by her directness. "Yes, I suppose I shall, but I'm not sure we can win."

"Then you are a fool." Madeleine laughed strangely. Her wild eyes immediately became crafty. "But you first must become a believer."

"Yes, we will need spirit, Madeleine. But will it be enough? Guns! We must have guns and lots of them. And men to use them properly, and other wiser men to tell the others how and when to use them. It will not be easy."

As he looked up to gauge her response, Martin watched fascinated as Madeleine put her hand on the hot iron stovetop. When she spoke her voice was toneless, as if she were talking to no one. "It burns but it harms me not, for I am blessed. As you shall be."

Martin wanted to tell her to stop but his tongue was locked in his mouth. The white hand on the hot stove mesmerized him. After what seemed an eternity, she removed her hand and came towards him. Martin shivered with excitement. He heard her voice again, quieter but with the same flat tone.

"We will crush the British. You are the instrument. You will stack their bodies on pyres in a flaming testimony to She who guides us."

"I, Madeleine? She who guides us? I do not understand."

She was standing close to him now and her hair smelled wet and sweet. Suddenly he wanted to touch her, to lose himself in this strange wild creature who seemed to belong to another realm. He reached out his hand, feeling her soft arm beneath the white sleeve. "You can tell me, Madeleine. I am your friend. Tell me more about your thoughts."

Madeleine seemed not to notice his hand, but as if a barrier had suddenly broken between them, she seemed to see him for the first time. Martin's mouth was dry and there was a strange ringing in his ears. Unable to help himself, he stepped closer to her, greedy with passion. She placed her hand in his, but her eyes held him back, even though their ferocity had softened into a strange intimacy.

"Come."

He followed her, conscious of the warmth of her hand and his own urgency. She led him outside. The rain had stopped but the sky was still starless.

Martin shivered in the cold and stumbled twice in the dark. Her hand held him steady and suddenly the barn appeared before them. The door opened easily and they were inside. He could feel the straw under his feet and heard the rustling movement of animals disturbed in the night. His teeth chattered uncontrollably as Madeleine allowed a horse in a dark stall to nuzzle her hand. Her words were coaxing, intimate and full of love. Twice more she stopped to talk to other animals girlishly, with soft words and kissing sounds. At last they came to the far end of the barn. To the right Martin caught the pale glimmer of light under a door. Madeleine pushed it open and led him inside.

They were in a small bare room, heavy with the smell of leather. Mismatched rugs were strewn on the earthen floor. In one corner a stove glowed red, and above it the flue leaked wisps of smoke that lost themselves to the night sky through cracks in the roof. A made-up cot rested against the length of one wall, and above it clothes hung from nails driven into the rough boards.

But it was the Madonna that dominated the room. Nearly two feet high, the old plaster statue sat on a long table draped with a heavy white cloth, surrounded by lit candles in brass candlesticks. The figure was chipped and grimy, but the Virgin's features were still sharply defined, and in the flickering candlelight her downcast eyes appeared open, her face warmly radiant.

Then Madeleine's hand forced Martin down and he found himself kneeling beside her on the bare floor, facing the flickering tabletop and the figurine of the Madonna. Madeleine was murmuring urgent prayers. Martin kept his eyes closed and waited.

The sputtering of a candle made him suddenly aware that Madeleine was no longer beside him. He opened his eyes to see her standing, looking intently beyond the altar. Her eyes were wild, moving as if focussing on something that wasn't there. Then she spoke in a light and breathless voice that made her sound like a little girl. Her hands were outstretched in greeting. "O Holy Mother. I am here. I have done as you asked. I have brought a male, one who will lead us in the fight against the British."

The sputtering candle died.

"Yes, Mother. We shall have to purify him. Rid him of the folly that binds him to man-priests. Make him worthy to crush our enemies in Your name."

Her hands were at her waist, and as if in a dream Martin watched her raise the gown above her head and drop it in a crumpled heap. He gasped. She was naked beneath it. He could hear his own shallow breathing, could feel his whole head dizzy with desire.

Madeleine turned and came towards him. Closer, closer until he could see every outline of her magnificent body, and smell the musky warmth of her flesh. Blindly he reached for her.

He was holding onto her, kissing at her neck and ears while she tore his clothes from him. Awkwardly he tried to help and guide them towards the cot, but Madeleine forced him down so that he was on his back on the floor in front of the altar. The lighted candles swam before his eyes and he could see the figurine's eyes on him.

The Verdon Farmhouse outside Odelltown, November 2, 1838

The grey misty drizzle made it seem later in the afternoon than it was. The kitchen was already in need of light when Martin backed in through the door with an armful of wood. After feeding the fire, he pulled up a stool and warmed his hands. For a long time he sat in the gloom half-listening to the footsteps in the room above, and wishing with all his heart that Jacques had been wrong. The hour of the Revolution had come at last.

He and Madeleine had been tending to one of the horses. She was in a cheery mood, laughing, tugging at his arm and bending her head close to his. Then Jacques had ridden up flushed with excitement and blurted the news out breathlessly. The rebellion had begun! The call to arms had been received this forenoon. He was to report to Hercule's blacksmith's barn at seven the following morning. Then with a joyous invocation of freedom and the motherland of Patriotes, he had disappeared into the house.

In the kitchen, Martin raised his eyes to the thumping noises above him. Jacques was still there. Packing what? Preparing for the nightmare? The debacle was about to begin for all of them: he, Jacques, de Lorimier, Narcisse, François-Xavier, Toussaint. He sighed bitterly. He had been going to warn them; now he was going to join them. *Oh, Madeleine, why couldn't it have been otherwise?*

After Jacques had left them, he had tried to talk to Madeleine, to tell her they would be safe. That the fighting would not touch them. That a new life awaited them somewhere else – south, across the sea, anywhere. But she had become rigid and had thrust herself from him, and the wild look he already dreaded came back into her eyes. She had spat the words at him: she would shed British blood in the name of the holy Mother, and he would, too. The holy Mother had chosen him as her agent of death and would not be denied. Then she had ridden away, shrieking prayers to Mary, her hair flying in the wind and her countenance blighted with the mask of madness.

Martin got up and went to the window. Madeleine had been gone for over three hours. Who knows where? Already he was lost without her. She was wilful, unfathomable, changing her moods like a capricious woman would change gowns. She was a passionate lover arousing him to heights of pleasure. A rabid high priestess of doom talking to empty air and calling it the Virgin Mary. A playful little girl talking to the animals. A haughty autocrat demeaning Jacques and treating him like a simple child. And most fearsome of all, an avenger driven by a frenzy that glittered in her eyes like crystals of ice.

Though she frightened him, she also drew him in helpless fascination, like a beautiful serpent. Martin knew it and he didn't care. As though hypnotized, he found it easy to let her make the decisions and hope that time would take care of any initiative he might have. Softness, calm would come to her in time. Her dementia would disappear, in time. Everything would be all right. Even the rebellion.

~ ~ ~

When Martin heard her coming he rushed to the barn to meet her. He found her quiet, preoccupied. She had been talking all this time to the Holy Mother about the rebellion.

"She wants to speak with you. She will appear when we light the candles."

Afterwards they knelt in the room before the flickering lights and the figurine. Martin was wondering what he should be doing, when Madeleine nudged his arm. "Look! She's coming." Then she hissed, "Don't talk. Listen."

Martin focussed his eyes where Madeleine was looking. Madeleine's lips moved wordlessly, her face shining with the same look he had seen the previous evening. Several minutes passed before he heard Madeleine whisper, "We will do as you ask, Mother."

Madeleine kissed him for a long time. Martin felt her tongue and he reached at the folds of her clothing, but she drew away. Her eyes widened and a sly smile betrayed her excitement. She suddenly darted from him and stood in front of the candles. "Now you too have seen and heard her. Now, you, like I, have a cause. We will bring the holy Mother her chalice filled with British blood. Will we not?"

Martin nodded numbly and put his arms around her. He felt her racing heart and kissed her brow as she rocked gently in his arms, humming tunelessly like a child. Over her shoulder he could see the candles and the statue of the impassive Madonna.

CHAPTER V

Rome, July 1836

The little man in the turban sat cross-legged on the floor. His high-pitched voice was chanting tunelessly to the accompaniment of a strange reedy instrument somewhere behind the dingy orange curtain. In the small dark theatre, half a dozen people listened intently. All were young and shabbily dressed. Some were smoking pipes that emitted a sweet, bluish smoke that hung in the stale air. The thin voice quickened to an excited babble, and the scrawny brown arms began gesticulating wildly, offering a benediction in the name of his new Trinity to the eager faces in front of him. The mind, the elbows, and the penis. Father, Son, and Holy Ghost inverted. The penis to father the seed of truth. The elbows to smite the enemies of the Father, and the mind to resurrect its own sanctified spirituality. He repeated his bizarre blessing half a dozen times before throwing himself to the floor to rest motionless in the fetal position. When the discordant sounds of the reed died away to loud and enthusiastic applause, he sat up expectantly to receive his audience, who gathered about him like excited children.

After about ten minutes, the noisiest and most vociferous admirer kissed the little man on both cheeks, and waving gaily, moved slowly towards the curtained entrance. His movements were jerky, and the hollow cheeks and dark circles about the eyes suggested a deep and lingering malaise. His dirty brown hair hung about his shoulders in untidy strands. He wore only one sandal, and his shirt and trousers betrayed age, neglect and the smell of the sewer. Outside in the afternoon sun of the Piazza Colonna, he leaned against the wall for support and coughed into his shaking hands. He staggered down the Via Del Corso, past the street vendors peddling religious curios. He cringed in fear as a French captain touched his sword and ordered him to move to the other side of the street. It took the bent, shuffling figure an hour to traverse the kilometre between the bath-house theatre and his destination. He hunched beneath an oak until the evening dusk made him a shadow.

Half an hour later, Bernard Blake removed the last of the greasepaint from his face. On the bed lay the ragged garments and wig. He dressed unhurriedly. First, the white tunic, followed by the white scapular and black cappa which covered his shoulders and breast like a mantle. He wore his capuce off his head around the back of his shoulders. He would don the cowl when he was within sight of the monastery. He detested the tonsure, his latest capitulation, for he had taken great pride in his long dark hair. Renato had told him once that it gave him an imperious air, which he had taken as a compliment.

Now, as he surveyed himself in the looking glass, he felt a sense of satisfaction. If all went according to plan, he was less than a year away from Holy Orders, and the road to his destiny. Prior Tettrini had hinted of a possible position of importance, but hadn't elaborated. He wasn't surprised. After all had he not been ascribed by Master Palermo himself as one of the finest students ever to read Theology at Santa Sabina? At the University of Rome, his proficiency in languages was so highly regarded that he had already been offered a prestigious teaching position upon his ordination. But teaching was for fools, worthwhile only if the entire world was your classroom.

Eating a peach, he thought of his afternoon at the theatre. The man was clearly a fake, and probably quite mad. In that sense it had been a distressing afternoon. His disguise had been excellent, though. He had attended operas as a pompous overdressed businessman, and one paganistic play as an Austrian military officer. Usually, however his disguises consisted of wig and beard, supplemented by inconspicuous clothing. He had dined in Rome's best restaurants, once at the next table to Albert Kuehler, and had visited numerous art galleries and museums unnoticed.

This afternoon, however, had forced an experiment in something he had never tried before. He needed to be someone else, and act out a part from beginning to end. And he had succeeded. More than that, he had enjoyed the experience. The notion of being with people, hearing their thoughts and observing their actions while giving nothing of yourself except through the role you had chosen to play, was intoxicating. At first, his use of deception had simply provided an opportunity to walk through Rome unobserved. Afterwards, he had assumed that his increasing interest in disguises represented his rebellion against the loss of individuality demanded by the monastic life. Now he knew better. Bernard had learned to assume other bodies. It was another sign. He dropped the peach pit into a wicker basket, and after checking that his goodly pile of coins was still safely concealed beneath a loose tile under the bed, he retrieved an assortment of books from the walnut desk and let himself out through the balcony into the black heat of a Rome summer evening.

Bernard Blake entered Santa Sabina through the front door, and went directly to the Community Room, and the big black book. He wrote his name, and beside it, the time of departure and arrival back at the monastery. Under the heading, "Destination and Purpose of Forsaking Monastery Walls," he wrote, "Tutorials in Norwegian, University of Rome, Riva Room." He closed the book and glanced at the clock in the corner. Good! He had gotten back late enough to have missed Holy Hour, but sadly not enough to risk omitting his nightly vigil in the chapel. Thankfully, the chapel was deserted. Not that it mattered. His outward piety was undeniable, and, if the fools realized it, genuine in its own unique way. He knelt in the front pew and fixed his eyes on the vaulted wall behind the altar to the mosaic of small tiles and the kneeling figures, heads bent in prayer. In the evening darkness, the candles on the altar threw the patterned figures into irregular relief, just like in his cave by the sea in faraway Genoa. He wanted to talk with his Blake about his wonderful experience in the disguise of a wasted vagabond. But Blake wouldn't come. The figure that emerged and which would not leave was unmistakably his mother. She looked bothered. Shrugging, he blinked her away, and after a fitting low genuflection, left the chapel.

St. Thomas' Monastery, near Rome, October, 1836

The girl was young, about fifteen years of age, and clearly overawed. Her heavy homespun clothing, sturdy boots and ruddy complexion left little doubt about her peasant background. Maria Balboni held her rosary beads tightly in her hands, and kept her eyes down as she followed the portly figure in white, and the other tall man who wore the crimson of the cardinal. Another priest came up quickly, and gently guided the young girl to a chair in the middle of the room. She sat there, naked in her vulnerability, not daring to look at the dozen white-robed figures who looked from her, to their Vicar General, to the cardinal, and at each other in mild curiosity.

The Vicar General of the Dominican Order for Italy, Thomas Tippoletti introduced himself to the novices particularly those from Santa Sabina whom he did not see as often as those from St. Thomas'. He explained that this special convening of selected novices from the two monasteries had been occasioned by an unusual request he had received from the newly appointed Secretary of State for the Vatican. Gesturing towards the tall grey-haired man sitting directly behind him, Tippoletti assured the novices that the great cardinal would soon allay the curiosity he was sure they all were feeling.

Luigi Lambruschini introduced himself as one interested in hagiography, and a long-time champion of the Dominican Order who had sought their Vicar General's indulgence on a matter of personal interest. The group was clearly intrigued as Lambruschini held their close attention. All except the dark-eyed figure in the front row who kept his eyes, not on the cardinal, but at the young woman sitting nervously a few feet from him. Lambruschini who had identified Bernard Blake earlier, fell to studying him even as he addressed the group.

The cardinal spoke easily but directly. After thanking Tippoletti for his charity, he came quickly to the point. "The young woman you see in front of you, Maria Balboni, may have been blessed like none of us in this room. On three occasions. she has claimed a visitation from our Blessed Virgin. She and her two sisters and a friend were spoken to by the Holy Mother on a hill just outside her village in southern Calabria. It has fallen to me to speak with this young woman and attempt to verify the truth of her experience so that the Church can rightly identify the incidence of a miracle.

He left the lectern and moved to the girl's side. "Who better to assist me in my task than a group immersed in hagiography? For, my young seekers of knowledge and truth, in God's name I remain somewhat confused in reaching a conclusion in this particular incidence. Did this woman see the Holy Mother, or is her story but a fabrication. You are about to test your powers of interrogation, while aiding me immeasurably. Each of you will be allotted five minutes to question this woman in the presence of the others. We shall then meet together to discuss our conclusions. We shall commence immediately and in the following sequence."

He read the names from a piece of paper. Bernard Blake's was the last name called. Lambruschini had his arm on the girl's shoulder as he reminded the group. "You will keep this child's age in mind as you question her. As you can see, she is frightened and not used to such august surroundings."

For the next hour the girl responded unceasingly to an ongoing torrent of questions in a voice so soft and subdued that several students had to move closer in order to hear her. The questions focussed mainly on what the Virgin had said, and details of her appearance. The more insistent questioners tried to involve her in contradictions. Others referred to specifics of location, time, and the precise position of the witnesses. One even tried to suggest that she had been drunk. Despite Lambruschini's earlier warning, the questioners invariably were caught up in their own emotions. Strident, sharp tones, at times reduced the proceedings to the level of petty courtroom histrionics. To the experienced Lambruschini, it was obvious that the girl was withdrawing into herself. Her answers became shorter and more uninformative. By the time the novice before Bernard rose to his feet, the girl was thoroughly cowed and virtually useless as a reliable source of information. Just as Lambruschini had both expected and wanted.

As he called Bernard Blake's name, Lambruschini thought to himself. *Now, my brilliant but ambitious friend, we shall see what magic you can work on the minds of lesser folk.*

Bernard Blake did not stand like the others, but moved his chair closer to the girl. His voice was soft and encouraging. "Maria, my name is Bernard Blake and I am studying to be a Dominican priest. Have you heard of St. Dominic?"

The girl nodded dumbly.

"Our Holy Mother appeared to him too. She gave him the very first set of rosary beads quite like the ones you have."

He reached out and patted the girl's hand. She flinched at this touch. "Maria, I'm not going to ask you about the Mother Mary's visit to you. If you say she came to you, then it must be so." The girl's eyes widened, and her shoulders relaxed visibly.

"Do you like stories, Maria?"

Surprised, the girl nodded cautiously.

"I'll tell you my favourite if you tell me yours."

Another nod of agreement, this time more forcible.

Bernard spent a minute briefly sketching the Genoan legend about the doe that saved the life of the archer who had tried to kill her.

"Now tell me yours, Maria."

The girl began haltingly as she related the fable about the eagle that every year laid a golden egg which she then hid in a cave, building over the years a huge nest of gold. By the time she was finished her story, Maria's voice was animated and confident.

"Do you and your sisters ever go looking for that cave and that wonderful, gleaming golden nest that must surely reach to the roof?"

"Yes," breathed Maria excitedly

"And do you expect one day to find it?"

"Oh yes, I'm sure its in a cave on the other side of the hill near Agglio. We'll probably find it next year."

"I'm sure you will. Maria do you tell your sisters stories?"

"I do, but it's hard making up new ones so that they will listen. They used to like stories about our Lord Jesus' miracles. Now they want different ones and it's hard to make up good ones." She sighed in vexation.

Bernard nodded understandingly. "I will ask just one simple question about Mary's visit to you. Did you want her to come? Had you asked God to send her?"

"Yes. I prayed every night for a year. I even gave up sweets one Lent so that she would come."

"Who are you praying for, to come now?"

The girl looked startled. "How did you know I was praying for someone else? I'll tell you anyway. It's Mary Magdalene."

"Why, Maria? Why Mary Magdalene?"

"Because she is so beautiful."

"And do you think she'll come?"

"I know she will."

"Just like you knew Mary would come."

"Yes." she replied firmly.

Bernard again patted the girl's arm. This time she smiled back. "Thank you Maria .You've been very helpful."

He returned his chair to its place and sat down. Most of the class were looking at him as if he were insane. Lambruschini's hand was on his chin, his thoughtful eyes gazing steadily at Bernard. His face showed nothing, but the racing tick at his temple betrayed his excitement.

~ ~ ~

An hour later the group re-assembled in the magnificent Casanate Library. The library was said to rival that of the Vatican as the finest in all Christendom. Over 25,000 volumes, many of them priceless treasures of Christian antiquity, occupied the deep shelves of polished wood and marble. The floor was heavily carpeted to mute noise, and wide windows opened to light and the sweet earthy smell of the fine garden that surrounded the library on three sides. The Dominican students had been placed at the ornately carved oaken table in the centre of the reading section, and as they sat, all eyes were fixed intently on Lambruschini, who was sitting with his arms folded at one end of the long rectangular table.

The Cardinal wasted little time in getting the discussion underway. What did they think about the testimony of Maria Balboni? Did she see the Virgin, or didn't she?

The ensuing debate was lively and at times, heated. Most of the students felt that the girl's story was credible, but were divided as to its implications for Church action. A vociferous few were adamant that she was nothing but a self-seeking liar. Others voiced the opinion that she was in all likelihood, demented. Bernard Blake took no part in the discussion, but lounged back in his chair lightly drumming his fingers on his thigh.

His eyes met Lambruschini's as the cardinal directed his question. "Deacon Bernard Blake. You have said nothing. Please enlighten us on your thoughts on the matter of this visitation?"

Lambruschini was surprised to find that the intensity of the reply belied the speaker's apparent nonchalance. "There is nothing to say along the lines of this discussion. The point is not whether or not the peasant saw the Virgin, but rather lies in the surety that she believes she saw her. Reality comes with our own perceptions, and may be supplemented by the visions which we conjure up to guide us."

"Heresy," one student muttered.

Lambruschini's tones were measured. "Are you suggesting that not only Maria's, but all previous divine interventions, have been no more that individual perceptions, and not based in any external reality?"

Bernard felt the threat. *Easy, Blake,* he told himself. *Remember your destiny.* He knew how dangerous Lambruschini could be despite his courtly demeanour.

"No, Eminence, I would never suggest as much. But revelation is not only a very holy, but is also highly personal, and, like a thought, does not exist until shared. The real miracle, therefore, lies not in the revelation itself, but in the change it wreaks in the receiver. Which brings us back to this grimy child. While she truly believes she saw the Virgin, she possesses neither the spirit nor the missionary vision to take it beyond herself. She can be of no further interest to the Church in this regard. I would suggest, your Eminence, that you remark favourably on her faith, present her with gifts honouring the Madonna, and send her back to Calabria."

The class erupted in an angry uproar. Recriminations were directed against Bernard Blake who remained unperturbed. When Lambruschini finally restored order, he concluded the discussion. Ten minutes later he was in his carriage, and on his way back to the Vatican. He had had his answer. Bernard Blake had impressed him. But, yes. Tettrini was right. There was something else there. And like Tettrini, he wished he knew.

February, 1837

"He's ready, Salvatore. The examinations in Theology are quite superfluous, really. I sometimes think that he could examine me. Anthony Palermo spread his hands in mock surrender. A smile hovered around his lips.

Tettrini let the words hang in the air for a full half minute, then looked at his old friend. He respected Palermo for his piety and intellectual clarity and liked him for his understanding and honesty. Whenever possible, his Master of Theology was also his confidant. "Then what say you, Anthony?"

"Ordain him, Salvatore. At Easter with Alphonse Battiste and the two others who have laboured their nine years."

"But he has been with us less than five. Dispensation or no, do you think I dare? Battiste himself has almost seven full years, and he is our most promising."

"No, he isn't. Not by three years or more. Ordain him, Salvatore. Let him leave us."

The two men's eyes locked as understanding flashed between them.

Palermo went on, "A position awaits him at the Vatican. It is as tenuous as Lambruschini's. No?"

He's right, thought Tettrini. It was whispered that the gentle but stubborn Pontiff would soon tire of the threat posed by Lambruschini's ambition. Then where would he be? In spite of his doubts, Tettrini knew that he had gone too far to compromise the risk he had taken with Bernard Blake. The Cardinal had encouraged him. Let the Cardinal now assume the responsibility for that encouragement. In Rome, and at the Vatican.

"I see your point, Anthony." He wagged his finger. "But, let us prepare the most rigorous examinations. Have him abandon all outside studies, and intensify the demands of prayer and abstinence. Bernard Blake's Lent begins earlier this year."

Palermo rose to leave. Tettrini stopped him with a look. "Are we wrong, Anthony?"

The Theology Master looked at him understandingly, "In God's name I do not know, Salvatore. Of one thing only am I certain."

"And that?"

"He does not belong amid the faith and honesty of a House such as ours." He gripped Tettrini's arm, "Let him go, old friend. Let God's will be done."

Afterwards in the darkening light, Salvatore Tettrini gazed into the orange-tinged sky, past the spire of Santa Sabina, east and north towards the mighty enclave where many men and one God-man ruled the Church. "Take him, Lambruschini. Take him. And may God help us all."

CHAPTER VI

St. Clement, Lower Canada, November 3, 1838

Thomas Chevalier de Lorimier sat in the dim drawing room of the Hotel
Provost, an untouched mug of dark ale on the table in front of him. The other
three men were standing, warming their backsides by a crackling fireplace.
Two were drinking red wine, each from his own bottle. Outside, a grey forbidding day, heavy with the threat of rain, spread a cold mantle over the
deserted cobbled square and the frozen grass bordering the waters of the St.
Lawrence.

de Lorimier broke the silence. "News, gentlemen. News of the most serious consequence. We have a message from Vermont: the call to arms. The
rebellion has begun." The beginnings of a cheer split the air, quelled by
de Lorimier who held up his hand.

"God trust that we have much to cheer about. I wish I shared your enthusiasm, my fellow Patriotes."

"Why, Chevalier? You have been our inspiration," said François-Xavier
Provost.

de Lorimier shrugged. "I have been thinking much of late, François. I am
not so sure any more over whether or not we hate the British enough. Even
at this minute I await news from one of us who may be able to guide our decisions." He spread his hands lamely. "He is not here. He was to have been, but
he is late." Embarrassed, de Lorimier could hear his own voice rambling. It
sounded like someone else.

"It's too late for that now. The call has been made. We answer it." Henri
Brien reached again for the wine bottle.

"He's right, my Chevalier." Victor Rapin spoke quietly. "The summons.
Was it from our President? Is Robert Nelson ready?"

de Lorimier nodded, passing the message to Rapin.

"Then to delay is treason. Our course is clear"

"You're right of course, Victor. I simply would have liked . . ."

Brien's voice held the edge of challenge. "What would you have liked,
Chevalier?"

"It is of no consequence, Henri. The die is cast."

"Your orders, then?"

"We assemble here in the square tonight at eight. Each castor with his
own men, armed, and with provisions to stand a night and day's march.
Victor, you procure the cannon. Henri, you send a messenger to Chateauguay

and have Joseph-Narcisse Goyette join us with all the Patriotes he can muster. Doubtless we shall have received word from Dr. Nelson as to when we march and where."

~ ~ ~

During the afternoon, Edward Ellice and his wife and children, together with Jane Ellice's sister and family, arrived at Beauharnois cold, tired and dispirited. They had bid farewell to Lord Durham two days previously and Jane Ellice was not at all sure that they shouldn't have been going back to England with him. She had one of her headaches and the children were irritable. As they set about preparing for the evening meal, no one in the party thought it strange that few people had been noticed about the manor house, so customarily alive with activity in the month after harvest, or that they had seen so many men walking the roads in groups and clusters.

Theodore Brown did, though, and he was worried. Farmers had been drifting off in twos and threes for two days now, and he didn't like it. No one at the mill. Yesterday his annual livestock sale, the most popular event of the season and the grandest gesture of his magnanimity, had been attended solely by his loyalists. When he went to the village in the afternoon, it, too, was empty. With growing disquiet, he spent a couple of hours rounding up a dozen or so volunteers, telling them to meet him at the manor house at eight o'clock that evening. A few had grumbled, but they all had come in the rain. By nine o'clock he had dispatched them to strategic positions about the manor with strict instructions to notify him in the case of anything untoward. He had mentioned his misgivings to Ellice, and was rewarded with a shrug and a bland aristocratic smile. He had then retired to the fire with a bottle of sherry he had pilfered from the ample cellars in the basement, just off the big storage area where he had stored the weapons he had so wisely commandeered.

St. Clement, 8:00 PM

de Lorimier looked out at the group in front of him. There were about a hundred, and more were in the other three buildings. He didn't know how many there were altogether, but they had been coming all afternoon and into the night. Young and old. Some with old rifles. Most with pitchforks, or swords fashioned from scythes. The bundles of food suspended from their weapons gave them an absurdly festive appearance. Their faces showed a mixture of enthusiasm and uncertainty, and, as he took his place in front of them, de Lorimier could sense their expectancy.

"Brother Patriotes," de Lorimier was surprised to hear his voice sounding so calm. He should be hysterical with fervour, but he felt only weary. "The rebellion is at hand. We march on Beauharnois tonight. Now."

A loud cheer split the air and a hoarse voice was heard above the rest. "We burn her, like they did to us."

de Lorimier held up his hand and waited until the hubbub died down. "There will be no blood spilled unnecessarily. What we want are the guns that Theodore Brown has stored there. The manor will be ours until the orders come to march again. To Montreal, to Sorel, or wherever our President sends us."

"Three cheers for Robert Nelson."

Three resounding roars went up.

"Three cheers for the rebellion."

The noise was deafening.

~ ~ ~

Jane Ellice heard the commotion through a dream-filled sleep. She awoke slowly, driven to reality by the swelling volume and urgency of the noises outside, and then by the empty place beside her in the bed. She pulled a nightgown about her shoulders and went to the window. She could see nothing clearly, but it was apparent that there were many people outside. The waving torches and hoarse shouts were directly below her on the grassy lawn where they used to take afternoon tea in the summer. She stood watching for a few minutes before going to check on the children. She found her sister and her husband Alfred in the hallway, looking confused.

"What is wrong, Jane? What are those noises?"

"It's probably nothing, Lucy. Just a few men on some grievance or other. I'm sure Edward will be back soon to tell us about it."

Afterwards in her room, she tried to pry open a window so that she could hear better. It was no use. So she lay in the dark wide-eyed, listening, her heart pounding like a hammer against her chest.

~ ~ ~

Martin had met them along the road less than a mile from Beauharnois, a wet mass trudging in the slush and mud. He found Joseph-Narcisse even in the dark and after a joyous reunion was escorted to de Lorimier who was riding a fine black horse at the rear of the cavalcade. de Lorimier greeted him soberly.

"It's begun, as you can see, Martin Goyette. It doesn't matter now what you think, or anyone thinks. It's too late."

"We will lose, Chevalier," Martin whispered. "You know that, don't you?"

de Lorimier looked grim. Suddenly, ahead of them, yells and report of rifles split the night. An order was barked and the front ranks broke, wheeled to the left and right, and disappeared into the dark.

"They'll surround the house," said Joseph-Narcisse. "Brown probably has men posted."

Soon the leading formations were at the iron gate that opened up to a wide driveway that led to the front door of the manor. More shots were heard, followed by the sound of breaking glass. Riding beside de Lorimier, Martin could make out a swinging lantern in the distance to the front and left of the wide front stone steps. It was Theodore Brown and another man – smaller, paler and dressed as if he was out for a Sunday walk.

"Edward Ellice," said a familiar voice. Martin turned to see the frightened eyes of Henri Brien.

de Lorimier tried to muster an air of authority, but his words were hesitant. "Theodore Brown. Tell your men to lay down your arms. No harm will come to you. You have my word. You are now prisoners of war."

Brown's face was set with an indignant rage, but his eyes were crafty. Sensing de Lorimier's indecision, he resorted to the bluster that was his most effective weapon when dealing with his docile peasants. "Like hell. This is treason. Get out of my way or I'll . . ." He started forward, shoving his way between two horses. de Lorimier sat motionless. Fear gripped Martin, and to his right Henri Brien, looking startled, was actually moving his mount from Brown's path. Brown was suddenly blocked by the huge form of Joseph Roy. Roy planted one hand against Brown's chest and brought the flat side of an iron spade into the side of his jaw. Brown yelped with pain, then went down under another blow that sent blood spewing from his nose. Roy drew his boot back to kick him, when Joseph-Narcisse barked, "No, Joseph. Enough. The revolution will be peaceful as possible, even when we deal with scum." Men moved in and pulled the shaking Roy away.

"Tell them, Brown. Tell your men to lay down their arms, or should I ask Joseph to do it for you?"

Martin took a measure of satisfaction in seeing how quickly the chastened, bleeding manager hastened to obey the order. Hardly had brown's dispirited men emerged from the dark when Joseph-Narcisse turned his attention to Ellice, who was standing in the rain, his fine shirt glued to his skin and a look of fearful panic on his face.

"Your arms, Sir. They are in the house. Do you give permission for my men—"

It was too late. A few of the bolder men had already rushed into the house. Whoops of joy soon announced that they had found the weapons. The larders and wine cellars too, thought de Lorimier. The rebellion had scarcely begun and it was already going wrong.

Brien was as pale as a ghost and de Lorimier himself seemed to have slipped into the role of silent observer, his heavy coat bundled up around his ears and his blue eyes expressionless behind his heavy green spectacles. Acting cool and decisive, Joseph-Narcisse took over. Ellice, his brother-in-law, Brown and the rest of the shaken volunteers were trussed securely and loaded onto a cart for transportation to a detention centre in Chateauguay. Horses, tools and all vehicles were confiscated and lined up facing St. Clement. Then with Martin at his side, Joseph-Narcisse entered the manor house. The next hour was spent trying to restore some measure of order, although it was impossible to restrain the ransacking of the finest wine cellars west of Montreal. The stored weapons were checked together with all available ammunition, and wagons were loaded with enough food to sustain a three-day march.

Martin was just beginning a search of the house when he saw the big fellow, Joseph Roy, again. He had a bottle in his hand and was lurching drunkenly along the first landing. Martin watched him stop at a door and put his ear to it. His hand wavered as he aimed the pistol at the lock, splintering it with a single shot, devastatingly loud in close quarters. He stood grinning in the open doorway, and Martin heard a woman's voice. It was frightened but controlled. "What do you want? Leave us alone. We have children here."

Martin thought quickly. Already feeling weak in the knees, he joined the big man and put his arm affectionately about his shoulders. "Joseph. These are gentle English ladies, and not the spoils of war. We are not the Americans or Godless English. We are Catholics, and by all in heaven, the holy Mother would never forgive us if we behaved like animals. Now I know for a fact that there is an excellent bottle of fine brandy in a cabinet downstairs in the drawing room. Why don't we go and find it?"

He steered Roy towards the staircase, talking soothingly to him all the time. When he was certain that Roy's steps would take him to the bottom, Martin turned and dashed back to the room where Jane Ellice and the other women were. "Save yourselves if you can," he hissed in English. "Everyone is master tonight and I cannot guarantee your safety. Go to the strongest room. Lock it and bar it until the drunkenness subsides and reason returns." He bowed formally and hurried to join Joseph Roy.

~ ~ ~

Martin left Joseph Roy happily ensconced with the brandy bottle, and after joking with several groups now happily drunk and sleepy, had stepped outside to check on what was happening. He found several Patriotes mounted on Ellice's horses patrolling the grounds. The barn doors were wide open, and assorted goods were piled on carts ready for dispatch. The night had an air of random excitement, much like little boys who had done something daring but who now didn't know what to do with their newfound status. Now, as he joined his brother and de Lorimier, sitting together in the drawing room, he felt suddenly tired.

Joseph-Narcisse was showing no such lethargy. His voice was urgent and his handsome face was flushed with excitement. "Look, Chevalier. I'm right and you know it. What have we here? A hundred rifles at the most, and not as much ammunition as we expected. Outside we have three hundred men. Another hundred back at St. Clement. More assembling at Bakers Field down the road. And we have guns for less than half of them. A great chance we are going to have against British artillery, with pitchforks! Chevalier, we must have more guns. You and I both know where we can get them. Every man among the Mohawks has a fine well-oiled rifle. Our Indian friends won't mind giving them to us. After all, their chief—"

"Is my kin." de Lorimier sounded weary. His family relationship to the Chief of the Mohawks at Caughnawaga was something that he would sooner forget. He tried to sound convincing. "Joseph, I agree we need more guns. But I doubt whether our Mohawk friends feel much sympathy towards us. Georges, I'm afraid, bears a strong measure of loyalty towards Colborne. I think he is probably afraid of him more than he is of us."

"Then we'll just have to persuade him to part with his weapons. The easy way or the hard way." Joseph-Narcisse patted the pistol tucked into his belt. "We need the guns, Chevalier. Orders to march may come from Nelson at any time. We could be fighting the British tomorrow." Joseph-Narcisse rose to his feet. "I leave at once. I will take sixty or seventy men and some wagons. With luck we'll be back by mid-morning. Martin, you come with me. I may have need of you."

Martin looked startled. "I can't fight Joseph. You know that. I can barely hold a pistol."

Joseph-Narcisse laughed. "Who said anything about fighting? It's your counsel I may need, and your sharp eyes. Mine have read too many books."

Martin sighed. "As you wish, Brother. That is, if the Chevalier doesn't object." He gestured towards de Lorimier. "Shouldn't you tell him your other idea? I'm sure he'll be interested."

de Lorimier looked up questioningly.

"If we held the Mohawk Reserve at Caughnawaga, we could declare it an independent country. It might make our potential American allies more willing than ever to join us."

"And how might that be?"

Joseph-Narcisse spread his hands. "If captured they could claim status as regular prisoners of war instead of revolutionaries. It might help."

As they left, Martin turned to look at de Lorimier who hadn't even glanced up. His brow was furrowed and he was trying to enter something in a black book he had on his knee. It looked like figures.

He knows, Martin thought.

The Caughnawaga Mohawk Reserve, November 4, 7:00 AM

The cavalcade had moved slowly through the dark and it was after dawn before the first crude shelter and wooden sign told the riders that they were on the Caughnawaga Reserve. The road to the main village wound through groves of spruce interspersed by frozen partially cleared fields. A few cattle poked away at the wet earth, and somewhere over the knoll of a hill the bark of a dog told the Patriotes that they were nearing the village. Joseph-Narcisse sent orders back through the column to avoid unnecessary noise. It would be much better, he had whispered to Martin riding beside him, if they could have caught the warriors while they were still in their beds. Now, it was better that they stop and make final plans. Joseph-Narcisse raised his hand. The group came to a milling, uncertain stop and listened while Joseph-Narcisse went over the details once again. Keep all weapons concealed. Let him do all the talking and above all, act friendly unless they heard the order to attack. There would be no trouble, of course, but it was no use being unprepared.

No one saw the woman. Clad in fur, she blended with the dark ground like a shrub. Quickly she broke into a trot, sloshing through the woods and fields and across partially frozen brooks. Panting, she arrived at the Church where Georges de Lorimier was hearing Mass. He was in his usual place on the end in the back pew. She genuflected and whispered urgently into his ear. White men were coming. Lots of them. With guns.

~ ~ ~

The sight of the lone man walking towards them on the muddy road caught Joseph-Narcisse and Joseph Duquette by surprise.

"It's de Lorimier," whispered Duquette through clenched teeth. "He must have seen us coming. But why is he here alone without his braves? Why is he here at all?"

"He knows, Joseph. News of the revolution must have reached him. He wants to parley. Find out what we want. Well, he'll soon know," said Joseph-Narcisse.

Georges de Lorimier was prematurely stooped. Arthritis had twisted his body, and he looked more like a scarecrow than a venerated tribal chief. Catholicism had tamed him to the point where he spoke thickly accented French in a high feeble voice, and habitually carried rosary beads instead of a gun. He was twisting them in his hands now as he approached the mounted men and spoke.

"Greetings, my friends. What brings you to our home?"

"The revolution, my venerable chief. Surely you've heard of it by now. We are about to drive out the British and reclaim our land."

"Which you took from us." de Lorimier was smiling faintly.

"There's enough for all of us, Chief de Lorimier. We will see to it that your people live freer and more prosperously. You have the word of Joseph-Narcisse Goyette."

"But why are you here? How can we help you? We will not fight the British. In their way they have been generous."

Duquette spoke harshly. "It doesn't matter, old man. We don't want you. We want your guns. You have many rifles. We will borrow them and when we defeat the British we will give them back to you. We'll even wash the blood from the stocks."

Chief de Lorimier's eyes narrowed. "Another of your kind, Amury Girod, invaded our brothers at Oka in the revolution less than a year ago. Guns were taken then, violently. Will you be any different?"

Joseph-Narcisse's voice became hard. "I am not Girod. Still I warn you that I shall have to insist."

The chief twisted his beads and closed his eyes. His lips moved in silent prayer. When he spoke again his words were level. "Yet by all in heaven I do not see the hand of a friend here. By whose authority do you come to us and make such demands?"

Joseph-Narcisse's pistol appeared from nowhere, pointing straight at de Lorimier's heart. "By this, chief. This is our authority."

~ ~ ~

The scene unfolded before Martin like a blur, yet long afterwards he was to recall vivid details as though he were seeing it all again for the first time. A series of wild yells split the air and dozens of Indians broke from the woods on either side of the road, with guns in their hands. The terrified horses fought for their heads as the Patriotes tried to free their hidden weapons. Moving astonishingly fast for an infirm man, de Lorimier grabbed the reins of Joseph-Narcisse's horse and wrenched sideways. As Joseph-Narcisse wrestled for control, they were on him. Martin saw him dragged off his horse into the mud. He saw a clenched fist come down. Then volleys of gunfire turned the horses into mad things. War whoops, screams of pain, and the slosh of bodies falling to the ground intermingled in a hideous cacophony. It was all over in a few seconds. Riderless horses galloped past him, and Martin saw a few riders escape through the trees. Without thinking he whirled his mount around, and spurring its flanks mercilessly left the ghastly scene behind him. He forced his right hand to the reins and rode wildly until he and his horse were both exhausted. For a long time he leaned over the neck of his steaming mount, the gorge of fear still in his mouth and his heart pounding like it would never stop.

St. Clement, 8:00 AM

On the wharf at St. Clement, François-Xavier Prieur crouched behind a barrel, pistol in hand, and watched the steam packet the *Henry Brougham* manoeuvre herself alongside the long wooden dock. Behind him in a shed waited fifty Patriotes while a hundred more watched from the windows of the houses adjoining the wharf. As soon as the mooring lines were secured, Prieur gave the signal. Within two minutes a hundred and fifty men swarmed over the deck of the steamer. The boilers were shut down, and about fifty frightened passengers herded on deck. Prieur allowed them time to complete their toilet, and, leaving the captain and crew on board under heavy guard, then escorted the female passengers to the Hotel Provost and the village presbytery. The men, including two British officers bound for Montreal on official business, were bound and trundled off to the detention camp at Chateauguay. It was all over in less than half an hour and a proud, excited Prieur rode to report his bloodless victory to Chevalier de Lorimier: a boat that could carry many soldiers was now their prize.

A little over an hour later three wagons arrived from Beauharnois. On board were Jane Ellice, her sister, their children and the rest of the women interned overnight at the manor house as official prisoners of war. Prieur was with them, explaining in deferential fashion as the group huddled together in the wet square, that they would all be quartered in the presbytery under the care of the village curé, Father Quintal. He apologized for the inconvenience, and promised the ladies the utmost courtesy and consideration. He waited for some response but the women were cowed, frightened and did not say anything. Jane Ellice, however, looked steadily at him, and Prieur was relieved when he thought he saw gratitude in her cool blue eyes.

By noon, under a steady cold drizzle, the village of St. Clement resembled an armed camp. Men with guns were everywhere. They guarded the roads out of the village, screening the women bringing food supplies and extra clothing for their husbands and sons. They stood outside the homes of known loyalists, rifles at the ready. They lined the deck of the *Henry Brougham*, and six were posted around the presbytery to ensure security for its gentle inmates. Two hundred or more wandered about. Some drank and smoked. More went to the church to pray. Most just sat in groups and talked. Some of the older farmers visited their homes. A few just drifted away. James Perrigo tried to conduct some drilling exercises but soon yielded to the cold. As the afternoon wore on, the mood in St. Clement changed from restlessness to frustration. When would they march? Watching from a window in the Hotel Provost, Thomas de Lorimier wondered how long he would be able to hold them. Damn Nelson, he thought. What's the man doing?

Montreal, 10:00 AM

In the new cathedral, the pride of Montreal, the priest was just completing the communion and Mass was almost over. It had been a different sort of Mass, interrupted continuously by clamour on the street outside the church and by the sound of bugles competing with the peal of the bell and the softer resonance of the altar gongs. The congregation was visibly disquieted; only the older ladies prayed as though nothing was wrong. Several men in the congregation exchanged fearful glances, but no one left his place. When the priest, preceded by his four acolytes, disappeared into the sacristy, the congregation sat in silence instead of making the usual quick exodus. It was a suspension in time, a twenty-second sanctuary before whatever lay beyond. Then a young man in the front pew finally rose and genuflected. The rest followed, trailing along the aisles to one of the four private and five public entrances.

Outside in the cold gloom, the army was waiting. The Place d'Armes in front of the church was a sea of dull red, and in the forefront were the cannon, their ugly maws trained directly on the church and their gunners standing at attention with lighted matches in their hands. A woman screamed, another fainted, and the crowd began a panicky movement back into the church.

British soldiers appeared from all sides, grasping arms and hauling men from the steps. When it was finished more than thirty men were lined up in single file in the street. As their names were verified one officer wrote details in a small brown book. They were then marched off to Montreal jail. No charges were laid, and no reasons for detainment were given.

~ ~ ~

As the afternoon wore on, and more new arrivals came to overcrowd the cells, it became increasingly clear that the British had been more in tune with the activities of les Frères Chasseurs than even the most pessimistic of the jailed dissidents might have been willing to admit.

That night, as Colborne went over the lists of political malcontents, rebel sympathizers and Frères members now languishing in prison, he had two further reasons to feel more secure. The Irish and Jewish of the city were not part of the revolution. Still better news came from the surrounding countryside. The northern counties were quiet – there were a few mutterings but nothing more. As Clitherow had put it, the peasants in the northern villages were far more frightened of Colborne that they were of les Frères. It was the south he had to worry about. At least now he knew where to deploy his forces.

He sent for Clitherow, who told him that there were several volunteer companies of loyalists in the south ready to march on a moment's notice: one at Lacolle, one at Hemingford to the west, and another on the east bank of the Richelieu. In another two or three days he would have the regulars marshalled in Montreal. The Grenadier Guards, the First Dragoons Guards, and the 7th Hussars, as well as four regiments of infantry, two of artillery, some five hundred volunteers and about four hundred Indians. In all, a force of over eight thousand men would be ready to do the Queen's bidding. Colborne smiled, told Clitherow to keep him informed, and went to bed secure in Montreal, and secure in the belief that he had things well under control.

St. Clement 4:00 PM

Martin rode towards the village slowly, his head full of conflicting thoughts. It had been a long day, and he had spent it riding aimlessly, trying to fashion meaning out of the chaos in his mind. Joseph-Narcisse was gone, captured, possibly dead, for a cause that was doomed from the start. In a way Martin envied him. He was a true zealot who believed that his course was necessary and just. Most of the rest were mere participants, men who believed in the cause as one might cheer for one player in some game. Only this was no game, and, God only knew, the opponents weren't equal.

They didn't realize it, of course. Men like Joseph-Narcisse mightn't care, viewing death as a price to be willingly paid if need be. But the rest? Once they realized that their lives were in real jeopardy, most would melt away like an early autumn snow. Those who did stay, whether out of ignorance, blind allegiance or simple indecisiveness, might indeed die, but when they did it would not be as martyrs to a noble cause, but as victims of their own frustration.

Then there was himself. He did not live the cause. He was not like Toussaint, either, who wanted to vent his anger, or de Lorimier who deep down wanted another solution. Not like Joseph Roy who never thought beyond today, or Joseph Duquette who adored Joseph-Narcisse and would follow him to hell. And certainly not like François-Xavier Prieur who believed that simple men could wreak miracles if they had God's approval. Martin sighed. Then what was he? Ahead, he could see the distant village and the sentries on the road. He would be among them all again soon. What would he tell them about Joseph-Narcisse? What would he say about his own desertion? That he was afraid? That nothing burned inside him? Not dreams of destiny or the new republic. Not God's love. That was a laugh. God liked nonsense syllables; God was fear. Madeleine was love.

The two sentries on the road greeted Martin, happy to see another survivor of the Caughnawaga debacle. Six others had already returned with the sad news. Martin could see doubt in the sentries' eyes. They were young farmers as far distant from their homes as they had ever been in their lives, two days removed from their loved ones. Only one had a rifle, an antique relic of the 1812 war. Even before he left them standing in the mud, Martin had made up his mind: he would start with Henri Brien. The terror on his face the previous evening had given him away.

Martin found Henri Brien in his office. He looked pale and dispirited, and, as Martin expected, was very receptive to his overture. They talked for a while and compiled a list of names, which Martin pocketed. They left the office together to find the castors. Brien headed immediately towards the Hotel Provost, and Martin set off for the shed beside the blacksmith's shop, where long tables had been set up for serving food.

~ ~ ~

Soon they were all gathered in the drawing room of the Hotel Provost, some standing, some sitting, all waiting: de Lorimier, Prieur, Rapin, Perrigo, Provost, Guerin, Dumouchelle, and all the other castors. The two groups eyed each other nervously. The men with Martin shuffled uncertainly, waiting for him to speak.

It was de Lorimier who broke the silence. He addressed the group but his eyes were on Martin. "Henri tells us that you want to confer with us. Have you news, or is it something else?"

Martin cleared his throat. His words were slow, deliberate as if he was choosing them very carefully. "I, we will be brief, Chevalier." He gestured towards the others. "I speak for them, and we speak for many."

"Go on. We're listening."

"We request, Chevalier, that you send every man back to his home. Now. Tonight."

A ripple of excitement ran through the room.

"It is useless. This rebellion is a farce. We will lose. Many of you facing me now realize it as well as I do. I have just come from the food shed. They say there that thirty have gone this very day. More will leave on the morrow. There is no news from Nelson. Seventy of our best men are in the hands of the Mohawks. We have a paltry supply of weapons and no promise of more. The British will not be as merciful this time. Colborne has already promised that."

"He's right, my Chevalier. To stay is to die or perish on the gallows, or rot in jail." Michel Longtins' sombre tones contrasted sharply with Martin's emotion.

"But it doesn't matter, Martin. Whatever happens now, we are still dead men. We have taken prisoners. We have been recognized." James Perrigo looked at his feet, shaking his head.

"If we bring Edward Ellice back from Chateauguay and throw ourselves on his clemency we could still win the day," said Martin. "Some of you are friendly with him. His wife and family have been treated well. There has been no bloodshed. François-Xavier, you dined on board the *Henry Brougham* this very evening with the captain, did you not? They could be persuaded. We are not criminals."

A hubbub broke out. Martin could see them wavering. de Lorimier was scratching his chin, Rapin was nodding and so were several others. *It's going to work*, thought Martin. *It's going to work.*

It was the little man, Prieur, who finally held his hand up for silence. "You don't understand. Yes, I dined tonight with Captain Wipple. He will remain my friend until he opposes us. Then he is my enemy. We joined the cause to free our land, to drive the British from our shores. Some of us were prepared to die. To break up now would be to deny everything we believe in. We have right and God on our side. I say we stay until everything is truly lost. For now we are still Patriotes and proud of it."

He approached Martin, and drawing himself to his full height whispered the words. "I pray, Martin my friend, that you are guided by right more than fear."

Martin gripped Prieur's arm. "I swear I am right, François-Xavier. I know about Nelson and the Americans. The Americans won't fight."

"But we hear that thousands have crossed the line and are waiting now to march on Montreal."

"I assure you they haven't. The American resolve is soft. No one will cross the line. Nelson has little money and few guns."

de Lorimier spoke, "It is clear that if Martin is right," he paused for a moment before continuing, "and I believe he may be, then we have a decision to make. But we all must hold true. Either we all go or we all stay. Agreed?"

Some nodded in agreement, others muttered to each other. "We pray and then we vote. God will guide us." Henri Brien was fairly sure which way the vote would go, but wanted to make sure. The solitude of prayer usually brought men to practical decisions.

A loud knock came at the door A muddy courier was ushered in and de Lorimier read his message. A frown crossed his brow and then he sighed in resignation. "It's from Robert Nelson. He's in Napierville. We are to be ready to march on an hour's notice. We can expect our orders at any time."

"You were wrong, Martin," Prieur said softly. "Nelson is in Canada. He must have the men and the arms. The revolution proceeds."

Dumouchelle took up the chant, then Guerin. "The revolution proceeds." Then some started singing. The rest looked at each other in confusion. Martin stood there, stunned. It was all over.

CHAPTER VII

The Vatican, May, 1838

Within a week of receiving Holy Orders Bernard had been summoned to the Vatican for an interview with Cardinal Lambruschini. The great trial of his novitiate over, he was finally at the threshold of the portals of power.

The great Cardinal had greeted him warmly, as if they were old acquaintances. Over tea and disgustingly sweet biscuits, they had discussed politics. Metternich's grand design for Europe, the industrial superiority of Great Britain, and the awesome potential of the still-fledgling American States. Lambruschini had waited until the table was cleared of silver and China before coming to the subject of their meeting.

Bernard was not surprised to learn that Lambruschini knew of his thoughts on the need for spiritual revival within the Church. But then, inexplicably it seemed, Lambruschini changed the focus of the discussion by referring to Pope Gregory's interest in fostering a cultural renaissance within Rome, the Vatican, and ultimately the Church herself. Lambruschini had been expansive. His Holiness was interested in the establishment of a matchless archival repository in Rome. A place where the priceless treasures of Christian antiquity could be stored and made available when necessary to Catholic scholars. A linguist and translator like Bernard Blake could be of invaluable service in assembling the most relevant manuscripts from monasteries all over Europe. At first Bernard did not grasp the implications of Lambruschini's statements. He was already imagining himself lost in the morass of mindless treatises and arcane translations. He was even wondering how he might gracefully refuse when realization swept over him. Carefully rearranging his thoughts, he allowed his enthusiasm to match Lambruschini's before adding that he would also welcome the opportunity to speak with the most facile monks.

The Cardinal had not disappointed him. Bernard recalled how Lambruschini's eyes had bored into his own, full of understanding. Lambruschini wanted more than Christian antiquities – much more. Bernard Blake felt again the coursing excitement in his blood, saw again the huge ring on the hand that was opening the door to his destiny, and read the words etched in the pale grey eyes. *Seek out the leaders, Bernard Blake. Seek them out even as you plant the seeds of hope and ambition that will produce a legion of zealots.*

Now, sixteen months later, Bernard rubbed his eyes and longed for sleep. The work lay in front of him in dusty boxes, bags and assorted folders. Notes, records, compositions, letters, manuscripts, and books from a score of monasteries throughout Europe, the result of two separate trips over the past sixteen months. An original text of Thomas of Nietro's *Forty Hours' Devotion* was found in a priory in Breslau. The House of Studies in Antwerp had yielded an almost complete copy of *Bullarium Ordinis Praedicatorum*, the most comprehensive collection of papal bulls ever assembled. A priest fleeing from one of the disbanded German priories was accompanied by a heavy metal trunk containing a copy of Pius II's edict granting German priories the dispensation of eating meat three times a week to compensate for the cold weather and the absence of good wine. Thomas of Stella's constitution of the Blessed Sacrament Fraternity was found at St. Zita's in Palermo, while at Erfut, Saxony, hidden away in a damp cellar, was the text of John Tetzel's sermons on the merits of indulgences preached to hostile crowds amid the turbulence of the Reformation. In a sheltered priory beside a frozen river in Lithuania, Santes Pagnini's seventeenth-century translation of the Bible lay in a velvet-lined box on top of fully a dozen small dictionaries composed by French encyclopedists, and better yet, a rare sixteenth-century text on martyrology Bernard Blake shook his head despairingly. It was all too much. The task of classifying and organizing this vast array of archival material was his and his alone. Translations had to be made, as well as the proper cataloguing. It would take him months, but his special situation demanded it. As Cardinal Lambruschini had told him on the day of his appointment, "Legitimacy must always advertise itself." And so he had travelled deep into the German States collecting archival material of significance for transfer and preservation in the fine repository in the Vatican. The assignment proved far more arduous than he had feared. Not only had he difficulty in persuading some of the more possessive Priors to relinquish the testimonies to their heritage, but he had no idea that the task would involve such intense perusal of faded and often useless documents, not to mention enduring the often rambling interviews to secure oral supplementation and elaboration on local historical backgrounds. It had been a frustrating exercise, and now the worst was to come. He sighed, and felt the tender spot in his aching back. He wouldn't have really minded this onerous task if the real reason for his visits had been more fruitful. At least he had something to show for his archival search. Sadly, his real intention had produced mainly frustration. Lambruschini would be upset, and might be disillusioned enough to doubt the plan that he had so carefully and persuasively set in place over a year ago. To add insult to injury, Bernard had heard that the odious Alphonse Battiste had been posted to the Vatican. He doubted he could long delay a meeting with his old enemy.

~ ~ ~

Cardinal Luigi Lambruschini's highly polished black shoes made little sound as they paced the thick grey carpet of the spacious office. Behind him, the folds of the floor-length grey drapes moved slowly in a warm breeze which even in the forenoon was already heavy with the earth sweet odour of freshly cut grass. On the table in front of the other man were two empty teacups and a plate of whitish biscuits with red centres.

Lambruschini's pacing stopped and he stood directly in front of Bernard Blake who was looking at him soberly. *The flash in the eyes is not as bright*, thought Lambruschini.

"I see you have collected much material. Good. His Holiness will be pleased." He took a biscuit and munched on it thoughtfully. "The other matter. Have you satisfied yourself?"

Bernard Blake was silent for a moment. When he replied his voice was even. "The news is not good, I'm afraid, Eminence."

He wiped his lips with a napkin, rose to his feet, and began pacing the room. Lambruschini watched him patiently. "My journeys bore no fruit. I spoke with priests who were but servile self-doubters. I listened to plaintiveness when I wanted to hear words of passion. I saw feebleness when I was looking for resolve."

He stopped, and looked away, but his lips were twitching as though he had more to say. Then he continued. "I travelled to monasteries set on mountains hidden in cloud and fog, and where the veils of the seventeenth century are pulled low over the minds of bookmen. In Belgium and Holland, the priories are permeated by the babble of libertines. On the plains of Saxony, I was assailed by our brethren fleeing in fear from foment. In Lithuania I found our houses as wretched as the miserable land which sustains them. Hostility in Hungary, and confusion in our own Roman provinces. There are no leaders, only everywhere, the hollow emptiness of the dispirited."

"And all this came as a surprise, Father?" Lambruschini said, rifling though a newspaper lying on his desk. "I would have thought . . ."

The younger man's voice was higher. If Lambruschini noticed the interruption he gave no sign. "When I was in Santa Sabina, there was a monk there whom I befriended. He was big of body, simple of intent, but noble in spirit. When he spoke, the others were drawn to him like birds to corn. It was my thought that sufficient men like Thomas Rivarola would walk the halls of far-flung monasteries."

He hit his hand on the table, shaking the vase of red roses. "Not one, Eminence. Not a single soul with the fervour of a Rivarola. Let alone the inspiration or the magic words. Yes, Eminence, I was surprised. No, disillusioned." Bernard hung his head.

When Lambruschini spoke, his voice was at first so soft that Bernard had to strain to hear it. "There is a force afoot in Europe which demands change. Quick, sudden, even bloody. Our Church is seen as an enemy, and those who would hold her banner high now cringe with the fear of the uncertain. To be a champion of the Church these days is to be an enemy of progress."

"You have discovered what I already knew, Father. You have seen for yourself the hopelessness of our cause, and as a consequence the need of solutions that are both political and expedient. You will now begin to understand why my policies, deemed so cautious by some, are in reality rooted in necessity. I will admit your hopes of a spiritual uprising tantalized me, and certainly I felt that if anyone could discern the seeds of such, it would be a fluent linguist, politically untrammelled, perceptive, and possessed of his own mystique. In short, Father, you."

He spread his hands expansively. "Which is why I sent you, of course. Your failure simply confirms my fears. The rise of secular governments will continue to erode the power of the Church. They are stepping into the void created by our own apathy."

Bernard Blake's impatience showed. "Then we lose, Eminence."

"No," Lambruschini barked. Bernard was taken aback by the force behind the cardinal's voice. The older man's eyes bored in on Bernard, who uncharacteristically found his confidence shaken.

"The seeds of a revival will not flourish on their own. We must both sow and nurture them. Father, we must contrive a miracle."

"I don't follow you, Eminence."

"A miracle will restore our credibility if the conditions are right. God will be seen to have returned to earth to succour His Church. You must understand the passion of Man for miracles."

Bernard thought for a moment before answering. "I see what you mean. A sign. A manifestation of Divine intervention. Let the populace rally the clergy, and the clergy of course can then be . . ."

"Exactly, Father. We understand each other."

The excitement clearly showed on Lambruschini's face. He waved the newspaper he was holding in front of the surprised Blake. "Here we may have just found our miracle. You read Norwegian, I understand."

Bernard nodded.

"Read this and tell me if you find it interesting. It arrived today from a respected friend who is now our legate in Sweden. It appears he knows the author of the article and speaks quite highly of him."

Bernard took the newspaper, noting its Christiania origin and month-old date. The headline "Strange Sights in Bergen" was followed by three columns commenting on the strange experience of a seventeen-year-old girl who had seen a vision in the meadowlands above her home. The author reported that the girl's description of the vision closely paralleled that of St. Dominic even though she was not a Catholic – indeed, she had no religious affiliation. The writer concluded the account by stressing again the fact that though the young woman was neither mentally feeble nor illiterate, she was as unfamiliar with the Virgin Mary as he himself was with snake charming.

Bernard Blake looked up to see Lambruschini looking at him quizzically. "Well, Father. What think you?"

"Another one like the peasant girl from Calabria, it would appear. The same basic idea. Women appearing, dressed in blue." He shrugged. "It's happened before." Bernard Blake tossed the newspaper back on the desk, and turned to Lambruschini. "Eminence, if we are going to contrive a miracle, then let's go about it in a way that will yield the most fruit. Bear with me while I explain myself. When I was travelling through Bavaria, some peasants showed me a spring which they said had healing powers."

He noted Lambruschini's quizzical look. "Do not be in a hurry to be skeptical, Eminence. The phenomenon has some basis in reality. An article published recently in a French scientific journal attests to the powers of some mineral waters to relieve and even remedy certain muscular disorders."

He looked at his fingers carefully before continuing. "We seem therefore to have some scientific basis for an incidence of divinity. Our Bavarian spring might be used fruitfully to work miracles in the name of our new spiritualism. The area is favourable politically, and with the right subjects, we could produce, not only the miracle, and proof positive thereof, but the individual conviction that spreads like weeds in a garden."

He gestured towards the newspaper lying on the desk. "With the Scandinavian girl we have nothing but fanciful illusions. A demented woman-child, a peasant as vacuous as the cows she milks."

He sat down expectantly and watched Lambruschini's face. His argument was sound. He knew it. Of course he could not reveal to his Superior the crawling feeling that the account of the female had given him. It had taken every ounce of resolve he possessed to get through the encounter with the Balboni girl. No, a miracle with a female was out of the question.

He was scarcely conscious at first of Lambruschini speaking to him. "Perhaps you are right, Father. But there is another side. The healing power of waters is not spiritual in itself. We would have to embody its miraculousness through an individual. It could be done, mark you. But not easily. On the other hand, an unwitting living symbol of direct contact with divinity is already elevated beyond anything we could contrive. With the right interpreter to guide her, this girl could become a stand-in for the Blessed Mother herself."

Bernard Blake's reply betrayed misgivings more than the disquiet he actually felt. He forced the steadiness in his voice. "Only if she has the qualities, Eminence. Comely enough to match the popular vision; simple enough not to realize it, and above all, the presence to transcend her being."

He laughed before continuing. "A female, with one foot on earth and the other in heaven. But where will her mind be, Eminence? No, I like the mineral waters idea better. All the variables are ours to control."

Lambruschini studied Bernard's face carefully, trying to read meaning into the young priest's words. His voice was suddenly conciliatory. "Bear with me a little, Father. Your mineral waters are still there to be used as necessary."

He twisted the plain crucifix that hung about his neck. "I do have faith in the miraculous, Father Blake, even if you don't. I have strong feelings about this occurrence, and I have prayed much this day. You will go and investigate this girl. It may be nothing, but remember one thing, Father." Lambruschini wagged a finger towards Bernard Blake. "People, not ponds, move the Church. Now go out and find our sign from God."

"And if I do?"

"Then we will have begun, won't we?"

"And if I don't?"

"That will depend on you, won't it? I have a feeling that you will find what you need to find. The Virgin appears to a Protestant in the Northern states. Should this girl be genuine and possess the presence that the Balboni girl lacked, and if we are careful in our deployment, we may still turn the tide. It's worth the trouble. Two months, Father. We have a little over two months before our Congress with France and Austria."

He looked squarely at Bernard. "Either way, Father, it is a gamble." He smiled a cold smile. "For both of us."

Bernard did not reply, silenced more by the tightness in his chest and the hammering behind his eyes than by Lambruschini's tone of finality.

The Vatican, late June, 1838

He was young and well-dressed, but wore his expensive clothes awkwardly, as if they belonged to someone else. Both hands were stuffed into the pockets of his tailored cotton jacket as he slouched through the dusk down the via Crescenzio towards the Piazza del Risorgimento. He leaned against a doorway for a few minutes, scanning the darkening square before moving on. He circled behind the extension to the Vatican Museum, glancing over his shoulder to make sure he was not being observed. The grass felt soft against his feet as he crossed the green lawn in front of a large rectangular stone and brick building which he entered through an unlocked door at the rear. He climbed two flights of stairs, resting on the first landing to catch his breath, before making his way down an unlit hallway. He finally found the door he wanted. It was marked "For Private Use Only. See Secretary for Key." He spent a few seconds rearranging his clothing and patting his blonde hair to make sure it was in place. Then he knocked four times, two soft, and two loud. The door opened just wide enough for an arm to usher him into the room. Immediately he was enveloped in a tight embrace. He felt the hot urgent lips on his face, and the large bulk pulling him forwards towards the couch in the centre of the room. Then he closed his eyes and saw nothing. Even as he felt the clammy hand reaching blindly, tugging at his belt and pulling at his trousers, there were no words. Then as the head left his face to writhe on his groin, he sensed as much as heard the phrase, garbled in its passionate frenzy. "Ignatius, my love."

He clenched his eyes shut as tightly as he could. Desperately he forced his lovely Ahmet into his mind to induce the swelling in his groin. Though the tongue was not as tender as Ahmet's and the teeth bit more hurtfully, he smiled triumphantly at the delicious stirring, and with Ahmet smiling at him from the ceiling, he reached out.

~ ~ ~

Afterwards, Alphonse Battiste lay on the couch watching the younger man dress, his eyes never leaving his body. A fleck of saliva still clung to one corner of his mouth. "You were supposed to come last night, my love. It's been a week now."

"Alphonse, you are so unreasonable." The voice was petulant and the full-lipped mouth pouted its agreement. "You don't know how difficult it is for me." His eyes never left the mirror. A second later he knew he would pay the price.

Alphonse Battiste's face hardened and his voice lost all traces of endearment. "Of no matter now, Ignatius. If you don't come, you are not rewarded. You could find yourself back in the poorhouse where you lay in rags. A miracle you called it then. But everything has its price, my love. Even miracles."

Ignatius said nothing. The face in the mirror stared back at him, still handsome, but puffier than it used to be. And the narrow waist that brawny sailors once liked to encircle with their callused hands was thickening. Yes, he'd have to watch himself. Alphonse Battiste might be the most repulsive of his lovers, but he paid the bills. Without him, where would be the fine clothes, the wine, the pleasant room he called his own, and the coins that jangled so comfortingly in his pockets?

Ignatius walked to where Battiste was sitting. He knelt before him and stroked his cheek. "Alphonse, you know I love you the most. Please be nice to me. I will surely cry if you don't."

The gesture seemed to please the fat priest. Ignatius was going to mention his shortage of money when Battiste brought the matter up. Ignatius was not to worry. He would have all the money he would need for his trip: a journey, sadly, that would keep them apart for a month, possibly longer.

"I don't understand," said Ignatius, shaking his head.

"You do not need to, my beautiful friend. You simply go where another man goes, and tell me everything he does. But Ignatius," Battiste held up one pudgy hand, "he must not know of you. Follow him silently but see everything. When he reaches his destination, you will write to me weekly. And upon your return you will repeat everything you know. Everything. Then I will be generous, and you will be grateful, and we both shall be happy."

"This man. Who is he, and where does he go?" Ignatius was already envisaging a trip to Paris. Maybe the man was comely.

"He is a priest. A Dominican, and he goes to Scandinavia. In three days." Battiste withdrew a piece of paper from his pocket. "A copy of his travelling arrangements up to his arrival in Christiania. Where he goes from there is not certain. My office has not been informed of his travels within Scandinavia.

"During Mass tomorrow, I shall show him to you. I shall kneel directly behind him, and follow him from the church. He is dark with wild eyes. You cannot mistake him."

Breathing heavily, Battiste extracted a bag of coins from the drawer of a table which served as a book stand. "This will prove ample for all your needs. We will meet once more before you go."

He reached for Ignatius and kissed him wetly. "Be careful, my love. This is a bad man, and dangerous. I will want you back safely in our bed. Soon."

Ignatius stood, confused. Something was wrong and he didn't know what it was. Only that he had to be very careful. The coin brought no warmth, and neither did the litre of red wine that three hours later condemned him to a dreamless sleep on the very bed he was to have shared with his virgin-slim cabin boy from Abyssinia, his Ahmet.

Bergen, Norway, April, 1838

Signy Vigeland shivered in the cold, and pulled her dress more tightly about her shoulders. Her stiffening fingers were useless against the reeds of the flute, so she put the instrument down on the grass beside her, and blew warmth into her hands. The mist had rolled in suddenly from the sea. She hadn't noticed it rise above the cliffs, and float towards her place by the big rock. It was there before she knew it, a grey clamminess that blocked the sun and filled the air with a wetness she could taste.

She needed to move, to stretch a little. There was no way she could traverse the journey back to her parents' house. Not in this light. She wouldn't have, even if she could. She loved the eeriness of fog. It drew her in, magically, and she could hear the notes of the reed played by Balder himself as he watched with love in his eyes. Signy raised her arms dreamily and began to dance. She was not Signy any more. She was a frost maiden, born out of the very droplets in the mist, and now seeking Balder's pleasure. Her lissome body etched itself against the greyness as she twirled and swayed, oblivious to everything but the music in her mind. As she arched her back in supplication to her beloved Balder, her long blonde hair touched the ground in a golden shower. She danced on, twisting and turning across the sodden meadow towards the crevice that cut its way to the cliffs, the sea spray, and the churning turmoil on the rocks below.

Then she noticed it. Signy stopped dancing, and stood motionless, breathing heavily from exertion. There was something there, coming out of the shrouded mist. For a moment she thought it was one of her father's cattle. But they were all gone to the other pasture beyond the stone fence. She could make it out, now. A person walking – no, floating towards her. A formless shape that gradually became a woman. Signy gasped. Could it be Frigga? As a little girl she had played games where Frigga had taken her across the sky to Valhalla, to her son, Balder, and to the wheel which spun golden threads that were never used. But that was so long ago before she learned to play the flute well, and spend all her free hours practising the notes that Olaf had taught her.

The woman was closer now. Signy could see her face, beautiful and serene.

Her skin was as fair and pure as a silken sheet. Her eyes though, were dark, and she could not discern the look in them. The white veil over her head concealed her hair, but Signy knew it was fair like her own, and the slender hands held a string of what appeared to be beads. She stood before her, silent, and as Signy watched, one white hand reached towards her through the mist.

"Frigga," she breathed. "O Silent and Wise Mother of Balder. Have you come to me at last?"

The figure in blue smiled wanly, and Signy saw her lips move in speech.

"Signy, Signy. where are you?"

The sound came from behind her. Signy turned, distracted, to see her father looming out of the mist. Beside him was their sheep dog, wagging its tail in lively anticipation.

Her eyes returned. They were met by the shapeless wet ground and its grey shroud. The figure was gone.

Bergen, Norway, July, 1838

Down the hill in the handsome house beside the sole school in Bergen, Olaf Hanson had finished his evening meal. He had dined alone on smoked fish and baby carrots from his own garden. His housekeeper, Ingrid, had cleared the table, and after bringing him a cup of strong, black coffee in his study, had gone home to her own family. He had asked her to leave a brewed pot on the stove. He doubted whether he would be retiring before midnight this evening. He picked up two of the three books he had had Ingrid retrieve from his library shelves, and began rifling through them. A panegyric by a Franciscan scholar entitled *The Glories of Mary*, and Jordan of Saxony's *Life of St. Dominic*. In the former were detailed the occasion of several visitations by the Virgin considered significant by the Roman Church. They invariably followed the same pattern. First, only a visitation; then a pronouncement attesting to identity, and on the third occasion, a message, often oblique, even symbolic, but a message nonetheless. The parallels with Signy's vision were uncanny, yet the child had no knowledge of the Virgin, and had if anything, manifested her father's well-advertised suspicion of churches and churchmen.

He remembered the first time the girl had told him about the vision of her Frigga. The child had been full of excitement, telling him that she had seen Frigga, but not to tell anyone, especially her mother who was always accusing her of fanciful thinking, and not her father who would just put his hands on his hips and laugh. Frigga was to be her secret. Olaf had humoured the girl. She had played extremely well that day, and had earned the concession.

While she described the woman who had come to her, Olaf had sat bolt upright in his chair when he realized that it was not Frigga who was being described, but the Virgin Mary. Afterwards he had gone to Jordan's *Dominic*. The details were identical: veil, beads, expression, posture, garb. Though he was aware that Signy was no ordinary child, he hadn't thought much about the incident, attributing it to coincidence or to a half-remembered recollection of something in past experience. Until two weeks later when Signy had burst into his study for her lesson, breathless with excitement. Frigga had come again in the same place. She knew for certain that it was Frigga.

"She didn't tell me that her name was Frigga, but I know it is." The deep blue eyes were wide in their conviction.

"Did she speak to you? What did she say?" Olaf recalled how disturbed he was when he heard Signy's reply. It fitted the pattern, but imposed a further puzzling dimension.

"I asked her her name, and she smiled and said, I can't remember it exactly but it was like this. She said, 'I am she whom you invoke every evening. The mead has been brewed for him, the hope of God.'"

She went on, her words running together, "I talk to Frigga on nights when it is dark and quiet, and I am with my own thoughts. I ask her about her son, Balder, and if I will ever find an earthly man to remind me of him. I think Frigga is telling me that she is ready to send him to me. My Balder. Don't you agree, Olaf? I shall practise very hard today. When he comes, he will want me to play for him."

Afterwards, he had written the letter to his newspaper friend in Christiania. Why? He didn't know. He wasn't a Catholic and, God knows, it had been a long time since he had entered a church. Gods of love and mercy didn't rob men unnecessarily of their legs. But something had moved his pen that night. He didn't mention the words uttered by the vision. He couldn't; it was too incredible to be true. He shivered. And too frightening to be a coincidence. He had checked as soon as Signy had left his house. The vision's first sentence paralleled exactly the words attributed to the Virgin when she spoke to St. Dominic. The second sentence closely matched words spoken by a wise woman to Odin as originally recorded in the *Elder Edda*, that great fragmentary collection of ancient poems upon which much of Norse Mythology is based. There was no possible way the child could have knowledge of either. He had decided then that he would wait and see. He had plenty of time. After all, he wasn't going anywhere, and the pattern, if it was a pattern, had yet to be completed.

Olaf sipped the coffee and perused the third book carefully. His own priceless copy of the *Elder Edda*. It was more than two centuries old, and there was not a scholar in a hundred who could read it like he could. Half an hour later, he sighed and dragged himself to his bookshelves. He should have had Ingrid get more down. Using his cane he knocked half a dozen more to the floor, and pushed them over to his chair. All dealt with the same two subjects, Roman Catholicism and Norse mythology. Two hours later he threw the last one to the floor in frustration, and rubbed his eyes wearily. Nothing!

That very day a third visitation had brought Signy running wildly through the rain to a lesson she wasn't supposed to have, completing the pattern. Signy had been more confused than excited this time. Frigga had come again in the mist and rain. She only stayed a little while and seemed very sad.

Though Olaf had tried to be calm, he had been conscious of the urgency in his voice. What had Frigga said?

Signy had been puzzled. It had been very windy and Frigga's words were not as clear as before, but she thought she had uttered, *Blessed is the fruit of my womb.*

"Balder, O Mother?" Signy had asked.

Frigga had shaken her head, "No. Greater than Balder." Then she had been plucked away by the wind.

The child had been very upset. In her book, the one Olaf had given to her, and which she kept in her secret place so that her parents wouldn't find it, there had been no story about Frigga having another son. Olaf had consoled the girl saying that there was much in Norse mythology that he did not know himself but that he had books which did, and he would consult them.

Could Frigga be having another son, one that belonged to our time? Signy had sounded hopeful and Olaf was happy to encourage her. He then suggested that she play her new piece for him. The high praise he laid on her afterwards was genuine. She seemed much brighter, and chattered about how Nels Lingren had smiled at her in school that very day, and touched her arm later when they were preparing bread for the younger children. Olaf had listened patiently, laughing when she did, and noting the lateness of the hour, had sent her home.

Olaf left the books on the floor, and painfully made his way to his bed in the next room. Suddenly he was feeling light-headed and dizzy. He extracted two white pills from a vial on his bedstand and after swallowing them without water, laboriously levered himself between the covers. It was barely dark and he could still see the hands on the Ormolu clock on the wall. Twelve-thirty. He was very tired but he knew sleep was a long way off. He had much to think about. It was the one thing he could still do well.

Olaf shifted painfully onto his side. The soft patter of the rain had stopped and he could hear the steady dripping into the oaken rain barrels outside his window. Signy was unlike the usual female subjects of visions, who were typically poorly educated and of limited faculties. The girl was intelligent and perceptive. Even her flights of fancy were typical of girls her age. He knew nieces and daughters of friends who made Signy seem like a Stockholm banker by comparison. She had loved Norse mythology when he had introduced it to her during a break in her lessons. He had even given her a simple book of stories that had been his as a child. She often rhapsodized about Balder, Frigga and Freya, but, as he recalled, nothing to indicate an inordinate fixation. The influence her father had on her was shown in her half-serious, half-jesting remarks about how God received only praise when things went well, but that we had to blame ourselves when they didn't. He had to agree with her there.

Yet Signy was different. She was like no other person he had ever met. It was not the girl's beauty, or her inner purity and simplicity. Goodness knows, he had seen enough beautiful women in his time, a few of them just as fine under the skin, to be overwhelmed by this flaxen-haired slip of a girl. It was something else. Like she was born to a destiny. She possessed a rarefied presence that transcended her beauty, one which was grounded solely by her music. And now this. It was frightening.

Groaning, not all because of the pain in his legs, Olaf forced his mind away. Instead, he focussed on the message which completed the pattern and to which he could assign no meaning. It hovered in front of his eyes for only a short time before sleep claimed him.

Olaf woke with a start even though the room was still in gloom.
My God. The message. It had been there all the time. He had missed it because Signy had misheard. He had to be sure. It took twenty minutes for him to knock the book down from the library shelves. He opened it with shaking hands. *The Office of the Rosary and Litanies to the Holy Madonna.*

He found the prayer. "Blessed art thou among women and blessed is the fruit of thy womb . . ." Signy had said that the vision had said "my womb," but also that it had been windy, and that she couldn't hear clearly. If the vision had said "thy womb," then the message was clear. Olaf shuddered and for the first time in ten years, he wanted to pray.

CHAPTER VIII

St. Clement, Tuesday, November 6. 2:00 PM

Prieur received the news from a frightened-looking Patriote. An army of regulars and volunteers some eight hundred strong were marching on the Patriote forces at Baker's Field about five miles down the road from St. Clement.

de Lorimier and his officers retired to the Hotel Provost to consult. It might be wise to move from their present position; the mood in the village was tense. There had still been no orders from Nelson. Rumours abounded of defeats, bloodthirsty loyalists, and mustering armies. A diversionary force to fight at Baker's Field might stem the tide of desertions until Nelson gave them the word to march.. Within two hours, four hundred Patriotes led by de Lorimier, James Perrigo and François-Xavier Prieur moved out for Baker's Field. Martin was with them, miserably nursing his throbbing right hand. No one had sought his opinion. All of them, even de Lorimier, seemed to be avoiding him. Only the thought of Madeleine stopped him from running.

Montreal, Friday, November 9, 1838 8.00 AM

Under a grey sky, made all the more sombre by the uneasy silence on the streets beyond the wrought-iron barracks' gates, Colborne reviewed the troops in full salute and then joined them as they began their parade to defend the Queen's realm. Civilian bystanders stood for over an hour watching the troop ferries move back and forth across the slate water. Three hours later the re-assembled formations commenced their march to the Richelieu. The banners of the regiments fluttering idly in the slight breeze preceded the phalanxes of the cavalry and the rumbling gun carriages with their ugly burnished cargo, and behind both marched the endless red files of the infantry.

Above Odelltown, Noon

Madeleine Verdon felt the rifle cold against her cheek and lined its sights up on the heavy wooden door of the church. They were in there, probably a hundred of them. Above the church on the road she could see many more. Redcoats and volunteers. They came from all directions, converging on the church and the stone buildings surrounding it. As she nuzzled the rifle resting steadily on the low stone fence which shielded her and the rest of the Odelltown Patriotes, a slight thrill ran through her body. She couldn't miss from this range. She wished she had more ammunition. Only thirty rounds had been issued to her with the admonition to use it sparingly.

This morning the men had at last been given the chance to do what they had been boasting about for months. They had mustered just after dawn in the blacksmith's shop and Madeleine had wondered at seeing so few there: no more than a score, all clearly uneasy. The quartermaster, a kindly man with white hair, had looked at her understandingly when she had tucked her long hair under a woollen toque and given her name as 'Jacques.' Later, the castor had led then in prayer. A small fearful man with bulging eyes, he had trembled and stammered, and she had wanted to laugh. Then they had all marched out to this place to fight.

Here behind the wall, they had waited and watched while the British reinforced the church. A few were in the curé's house; others were in the two wooden buildings that stood within the quadrangle formed by the stone fence. There had been no shooting yet, only the movement of the British in front of them and muttered words of encouragement whenever another Patriote arrived to take up his position. Madeleine wished it would begin. She had a good feeling. Many British were going to die this day.

Thirty feet away, her Castor was not so sanguine. Where was the force from the north? It should have been here by now: thousands of Patriotes with cannon and horses, led by the president, Robert Nelson, himself. He looked at the sky nervously and got out his rosary. Beside him, others did the same. Madeleine kept her eyes fixed on the church. She hoped they would burn it when all inside were dead.

~ ~ ~

Madeleine heard a distant rumbling, and then the sharper sound of firing rifles, coming closer. Redcoats were retreating up the road towards the church. Some were turning and firing as they ran, kneeling down, rushing their shots before getting up and resuming their panic-stricken flight. Behind them she saw the Patriotes, led by a tall man with fair hair. They were taking more care with their shots. She counted at least three redcoats prone in the snow. The shooting stopped suddenly as the Patriotes took up their positions behind the stone walls. There was a loud swish as a thrown torch lodged itself in the roof of one of the wooden buildings within the quadrangle. Minutes later, a dozen or so men came fleeing out. Three were cut down by Patriote bullets before the rest reached the safety of the church.

~ ~ ~

From his position well away from the embattled church Robert Nelson watched the proceedings with interest. The redcoats and their volunteers were trapped in the church. It was going to be a great victory. Still, prudent men took no chances. Glancing around to ensure that no one was watching him, he moved backwards into the trees until he was hidden from view. He remained mounted and kept his horse's head turned towards the path that wound deeper into the woods.

Suddenly the doors to the church were flung open and volunteers poured out, fanning wide to the left and right and filling the air with maniacal yells. Behind them came the cannon. Lines of riflemen kept up a steady volley at the Patriote defences while the gunners trained the cannon on the walls.

Madeleine heard the boom and ducked instinctively to protect her head. The air was filled with dust and falling stones. When she looked up, she gasped, frozen momentarily by the scene which met her eyes. A section of the wall was ripped away and where it had been was a tangled jumble of bodies, some still twitching. The ping of a bullet off the wall just inches from her head galvanized Madeleine back into action. With the sweet hot smell of blood in her nostrils, she trained her rifle on the lines of standing riflemen, trying not to hear the dreadful screams that followed the intermittent boom of the cannons.

She saw them advancing towards the wall. All around her was a confusion of panic as the Patriotes broke away from their shelters and ran. Some had thrown their weapons away. Near her on one side a wounded Patriote had his beads out, while just to her right the grey-haired quartermaster was loading and firing methodically. Across the quadrangle, the fair-haired man was standing on top of the wall yelling for his men to follow him. Nothing happened and Madeleine saw him drop out of sight.

They were lined up nicely like ravens on a fence, a kneeling, standing, firing formation that kept coming closer towards her. "Thank you, Mother," she breathed. She squeezed the trigger. A redcoat clutched at his face and toppled forward. She fought to control her breathing as she reloaded. Twenty seconds seemed like hours, but neither the grey-haired one beside her nor the British dogs facing her in an evil wave could do it faster. Bite the cartridge cover. Pour the powder down the muzzle. Ram the cardboard and shell home. Raise the piece, aim, and fire. The one kneeling in the centre of the line took her next shot in the stomach even as he fumbled to reload. She was excited now and breathing hard. The Holy Mother was guiding her hand. Her movements with the ramrod became more fluid. She was an instrument of revenge. She smiled as another redcoat sunk to his knees. He was screaming, his face a blob of redness. They were closer now and she could make out their features. They were young, drooling at her and their eyes were filled with evil. They were going to hurt her, take her away from the holy mother. But the holy one wouldn't let them. Together they were invincible. She fired again. A lurching falling figure disappeared into the smoke and dust. She looked down at the cloth that held her ammunition. She had five cartridges left. No matter. They would all be dead by then. She could feel them close around her, pressing, smothering her. Their guns were levelled, but the only sound was a ringing in her ears. The glorious Mother herself floated in the cold blue sky. At peace, above all this noise and confusion. Rapture overtook Madeleine's body. Her rifle once again obeyed her and she fired into the advancing ring of her tormentors.

Baker's Field, 1.00 PM

The stove had been allowed to burn too low, and only a few embers glowed dully in the ash-filled grate. Chevalier Thomas de Lorimier shivered, and flexing his arms got out of the armchair. Outside the frosted window on the bare brown grass in front of the farmhouse, the Patriotes were assembling in loose military formation. Prieur was there, counting the rifles and assigning their owners to the lead ranks. James Perrigo was there too, a ramrod-straight figure despite his age, the only one of them with any military experience.

The Patriote squatting awkwardly in the bare branches of a maple tree looking intently to the east suddenly began waving towards Perrigo. It could mean but one thing. The volunteers were coming. Hundreds of them had been reported to be moving in their direction as early as this morning, and now they were here. It was time at last.

The cause was lost, de Lorimier knew. He also knew that he could do nothing about it. Not now. Not after all he had done . . . the speeches, the exhortations, his own grand designs and finally the decision he had sanctioned just two days ago in the Hotel Provost. They had to go through with it. He grabbed his pistol, cold in his clammy palm, and pulling on his greatcoat joined Perrigo on the steps of the farmhouse. His eyes caught a bird wheeling in the grey sky. Yes, it was a good way to die.

James Perrigo had few instructions for the troops. Surprise was the essence of any successful charge. Shoot to kill and don't be squeamish about wielding a scythe if close quarters were reached. Three whistles would be the signal to fall back. It was all attack otherwise. Prieur would be field leader and Claude Nevue would be second in command. Martin Goyette would act as courier, and it was best if the Chevalier did not take part, for all would be lost should he perish. Then, with he and Martin astride two of Baker's horses, Perrigo watched the excited Patriotes move out towards the field to their left. Once the first fence had been cleared, they broke into a yelling running frenzy, surmounting the hill and descending on the surprised volunteers on the road beyond. Martin's eyes widened and Perrigo smiled as the volunteers turned and fled, four of their number left prone on the road.

Some of the Patriotes had their swords out and Martin saw one volunteer straggler cut down from behind, screaming and clutching at his bloody neck. Martin felt sick. It was going to be a massacre. This was not the way. Blood on his hands, on everyone's hands. Whatever happened afterwards, they would all hang for today's events. He had to do something to stop it. He looked at James Perrigo pleadingly and hoped his voice sounded convincing. "It could be a trap, Mr. Perrigo. A ruse to entrap us. More could be waiting down the road. Call the men back, Mr. Perrigo. Please."

"No, Martin. There's not enough of them. There must be more some-where." He glanced behind him towards the farmhouse and the seemingly deserted fields beyond. "The danger may lay elsewhere. To our rear. It's a pin-cer movement I'm afraid of, not an ambush. Wait here." Perrigo spurred his mount back the way they had come.

~ ~ ~

Ten seconds seemed like an hour. As Perrigo's horse clattered into the distance, Martin urged his own mount into a gallop and soon he was beside Prieur who was standing waving a pistol and shouting encouragement to his men.

"Fall back, François-Xavier," Martin shouted. "Orders from Mr. Perrigo."

"Fall back?" Prieur was incredulous. "Why? We can rout the lot of them and get their guns. Victory is—"

"No, François-Xavier. Blow the whistle."

Prieur hesitated. He looked down towards the running figures now fifty yards ahead of him on the road. A volunteer took a bullet and stumbled to the ground. Prieur swallowed, shook his head slightly and then brought the whis-tle to his lips. He blew it three times, loud shrill sounds that Martin scarcely heard.

"Again François-Xavier. Again."

The Patriotes returned reluctantly, and with harsh questions. A great victory had been denied them. Why? Not a single Patriote had been scratched. The enemy was in disarray, yet it was the victors that did the retreating. Why? Prieur was furious and de Lorimier, still panting from his run from the farmhouse, was scowling. Everyone was glowering at Perrigo who sat his horse calmly, a piece of paper in his hands. Martin looked from Perrigo to his comrades and back to Perrigo again trying to control his fear. Perrigo finally held his hand up for silence. "Fellow Patriotes, listen to me. François-Xavier acted wisely like a good officer should. He believed the order came from me. It didn't. Many more Loyalists would be dead now were it not for Martin Goyette. He gave the order to fall back."

"Then he should be shot." Joseph Roy moved menacingly towards Martin amid angry mutterings.

"Leave him be, Joseph," Perrigo said sharply. "Coward though he well may be, he has probably saved us all from the gallows."

"What do you mean?" asked someone in the front.

"I received this from a courier even as we were fighting." He handed the paper to de Lorimier. "Bad news, comrades. Colborne is marching with thouands of redcoats. We were defeated heavily at Lacolle. Dr. Coté and Lucien Gagnon have fled for the frontier. The force at Boucherville which was to have taken Chambly has dispersed. Nelson is gone and the Grand Eagle has fled also. The same with the Patriotes attacking Laprairie. Men came together, then broke up in confusion before completing their missions. Everywhere men are returning to their homes. We are advised to do the same."

"Disperse?" said François-Xavier Prieur. "What about the revolution? We have come too far now."

"It's over. Can't you see?" Martin was on the edge of tears. "It always has been."

~ ~ ~

They talked through the night, each man being allowed to voice his opinion. By morning it was decided. de Lorimier, Perrigo and the other leaders would try to make their escape to the frontier. The rest would simply return to their homes. Prieur would go back to St. Clement and consult with the Patriotes still there. The coward Martin Goyette would go with him. Should the St. Clement Patriotes decide to fight on, the coward would have to die the second death of thousands.

Saturday, November 10, St. Clement 11.00 AM

François-Xavier Prieur and Martin did not speak on the journey from Baker's Field to St. Clement. Prieur kept his silence through praying and ignored Martin who rode morosely behind him. Martin knew he should flee, and cursed himself inwardly for continuing this journey into hopelessness. It wasn't cowardice at Baker's Field, or at least he told himself it wasn't, but if he ran now there would be no doubt. He couldn't face that . . . or Madeleine. So he rode with Prieur and hoped that even this most unlikely soldier would eventually see reason before it was too late.

Fewer than two hundred Patriotes greeted them at St. Clement. The rest had melted away. News had recently arrived: over a thousand men of the Glengarry Highlanders, dragging six pieces of heavy artillery, had crossed the stream at the foot of Lake St. Francis. They would be beyond St. Timothee by nightfall, and at St. Clement by morning. Prieur made his mind up quickly. An ambush. They would surprise the Glengarry's outside St. Timothee at the narrow place in the road where it passed between the river and an old stone wall.

The remaining St. Clement Patriotes exchanged nervous glances and mutterings. Basil Roy spoke up. "We are only a few ill-equipped men. They are thousands. Their vengeance on our families will be even worse, I am afraid, than their thirst for blood tomorrow."

A vote was taken and general agreement reached quickly. They would leave at once. The revolution had failed. Farewells were tearful, and one by one the Patriotes slipped into the night. They would return to their families and hope that the British would be merciful or better still, ignorant.

At last, only François-Xavier Prieur and Martin remained. The little man seemed drained and his voice held the edge of desperation. "It won't be as easy for us, Martin. We are marked men. de Lorimier has many enemies and both of us will be counted among his friends. We will have to flee south. They will be watching for us. Traitors everywhere."

Martin put his arms around the other man's shoulders. "You are a courageous man, François-Xavier. You believed much, only to lose. But not everything. You still have your freedom. It will have to be taken from you, and if we are cunning that will not be easy. And you still have me. I am your friend."

François-Xavier Prieur looked at Martin through tear-filled eyes. "I believed in our homeland, but it was not to be. God's will has been done and I will now pray for His guidance." He extended his hand towards Martin. "His love does not allow rancour or uncharitable thoughts. I forgive you, Martin, for everything, and will pray for your soul."

Martin took the outstretched hand. For François' sake, he forced a comradeship into his voice. "Thank you for your kindness, François. You are a true God-fearing man."

"We shall travel together? One can watch while the other sleeps."

"No, François. It's better that we go alone."

"All right." Prieur had his rifle and his bundle of effects tied to the muzzle. "May God be with you, Martin."

~ ~ ~

Martin thanked the clouds that blackened the night and kept him hidden. He heard at least two patrols, one passing less than fifty yards from him as he pressed himself against a thick spruce. He calculated that it must be almost dawn when he broke from the woods just to the south of St. Timothee. Though only the barking of a lone dog disturbed the stillness, he proceeded cautiously, and as he approached the cottage he found himself worrying over the fright he was going to cause his mother. Thankfully she was a light sleeper and heard his knock before it became too persistent or loud. He was inside within minutes warming his hands by the stove, which was soon heating a mouth-watering stew. He ate ravenously. Jeanne Cousineau said little, but just watched him eat, passing him more food and filling his cup with hot thick coffee. Only when he pushed the plate away, shaking his head at her gesture for more did she speak.

"It is good to see you, my son. The revolution does not go well, I hear. Will you be safe? Are they hunting you? There will be many burnings now." She blessed herself.

"Yes, Mother. It is all over. We should never have fought. I was foolish, and now I have to flee. They will be hunting for me. They think I'm one of the leaders." He patted his mother's knee. "But at least they won't harm you. It's the first time I have ever been happy that no one knows I am your son. They will have no cause to burn this house."

Jeanne Cousineau's face clouded with fear, then composed itself. "Where will you go? Will it be difficult to escape the British?"

"Many have already. I think I can succeed. If I travel by night and trust no one, I can be beyond the frontier in three days."

"You will need food and proper clothing."

"Yes, a pack with enough food for three days, and two sets of warm clothing. I know the country well, having just returned from New York. I also know a secure place to cross the border. I will be safe."

"And then?"

Martin shrugged, "Who knows? I will find work. I speak the language. And when it is safe I will come back for you . . . with Madeleine."

" I do not know of Madeleine. Why haven't you told me? Who is she?"

"I only met her a short time ago. She is brave and beautiful. Together, the three of us will live where we can be free. I am told that there are many artists in the United States and that some of them have fine homes with servants. When Madeleine and I marry you will live with us."

Jeanne Cousineau smiled, already envisioning a beautiful loving girl, and grandchildren. Then she frowned as if remembering something vexatious. "Your hand. Can you use it properly? Working will not be easy, particularly there."

Martin flexed his right hand. "It is not as bad as before. I feel some movement. I think I could even write some words if I had to. I may be able to paint within a few months. I speak acceptable English. I will seek employment as a salesman, a teacher. I know a man who works in a bank. He is important and will help me."

Jeanne Cousineau nodded. She went to the stove to get more coffee, but when she returned her son was already asleep.

~ ~ ~

She let him sleep all day, waking him only to guide him to her bed, and then much later when a pale cold dusk forced her to light the lamps. She had his food ready for him: good thick bread, cheese, nuts, some dried fruits, and biscuits soaked in honey. He dressed in Uncle Antoine's heaviest seafaring clothes. When he was ready to leave, he checked the night. It was pitch dark and a light snow was beginning to fall. He grunted. A good night to travel. Then he went inside to do what he hated most of all.

He faced her awkwardly in the warmth of the kitchen, dreading her anguish, and feeling his own bitter agony rising to his eyes in uncontrolled tears. She did not cry but held him close. He felt her breathing and smelled the warm cooking smells and a flower-like fragrance in her hair.

"Good bye, Mother. It won't be for long. I will be back. I promise you."

They were at the back door. "God will guard you, my son. I have sent the holy Mother with you. As long as you have her, no harm will come to you. I leave you in her hands."

He travelled easily that night, well rested and secure in his knowledge of the terrain. It would not be as easy the farther south he got. He saw the red glow in the sky around midnight and soon after caught the whiff of smoke. St. Clement. They were burning St. Clement. The dogs. What more could be expected? Retribution, grim and unforgiving had already begun and God only knew when it would stop.

Martin found what he was looking for soon after dawn: a bridge he could conceal himself under. He settled himself far back in the dark recess where stone met earth and turned to his food supply.

There among the cheeses, wrapped in a soft blood-red cloth, was the icon of the Madonna, the one his mother had told him had come from France

143

almost two centuries ago. No one knew its age but it had been passed on to the first-born female of the family. His mother had treasured it not only as a family heirloom but as a source of divine inspiration. As he turned the tarnished figure over in his hands there in the dirty gloom on frozen ground he could see little divinity in it. He sighed, re-wrapping it in the red cloth. He'd have to carry it. He couldn't throw it away.

~ ~ ~

Picking his way south, Martin avoided all habitation. The other fugitives would rely on Patriote sympathies to shield them on their dangerous journey to freedom, but he had no such faith. He ate sparingly and travelled only by night. Two more bridges and a haystack took care of the days.

He had seen several patrols and heard the cursing of the vigilantes as they plundered rebel property. All along the fields and villages the smell of smoke was heavy in the air. The desecration of the land was well underway, and not all boots that passed over the bridges that concealed him were British. He heard the clatter of wagons, women's voices and the sound of crying children as the dispossessed sought their own refuge.

It was just after dawn on the fifth day and he was surveying a bridge from the concealment of a spruce copse. His food was gone, and the steady numbing of his feet told him that he must risk a fire or face permanent incapacitation. Suddenly, his eyes narrowed. That bridge was the one he had sheltered under just before he had met Madeleine. He could even make out the stone road marker a few yards beyond the bridge. He was in New York. He was safe. Martin's hands trembled with excitement as much as from the cold as he counted his money. There was a village on the edge of the lake just a few miles to the east. The thought of a hot meal and a warm bed drove his feet forward. He still felt uneasy as he stepped into open view and crossed the bridge. His ordeal was over but he couldn't quite believe it.

~ ~ ~

He had eaten well, purchased some clean warm clothes, enjoyed the luxury of a hot tub, and was anticipating the bliss of an uninterrupted sleep in a warm bed with sheets when it came to him. Though it was barely night, he was readying himself for bed, adjusting the curtains on the window of his room in the small but comfortable inn he had found in Aulburg. Outside the window the frozen expanse of Lake Champlain reached into the gathering darkness. The night shroud that had hidden him from his pursuers was out there again. Hiding who? François-Xavier, de Lorimier. Were they safe like him or languishing in some filthy place, a prisoner or worse still, dead? Then she came into his thoughts, just appearing there as if she had been hiding all the time. My God! Madeleine. What if the British were seeking revenge on her as a Patriote sympathiser? He'd assumed she was safe, that he alone was the threatened one, but now after seeing all the burnings, and knowing of Jacques' involvement with Les Frères, he could not be sure of Madeleine's safety. How could he have been so blind, so wretchedly foolish? For ten minutes he paced the room, the thoughts racing around in his head in a confused turmoil. The bed that had looked so inviting was now more of a seductress. What was he thinking of? Sleeping like a coddled child while his loved one was facing turbulence and unimaginable dangers. He would go back for her. It wouldn't take him long, no more than a few hours. He could still get a horse at this hour. The place might be difficult but certainly not impossible to find. Cursing himself for his stupidity, but excited by the vision of holding his beloved Madeleine in his arms, Martin hurriedly dressed discarding his fine new clothes for the dirty but eminently more suitable garb of the former night traveller, and scarcely noticing the hardness of the little icon resting in one of the deep pockets. As he closed the door, he smiled at the bed. They would be sharing it in love in a few short hours.

He wished it weren't snowing. His mount, a sturdy beast more suited to the plough than to the road, seemed to move with agonizing slowness. They were three hours from midnight when they crossed the bridge, and now came the tricky part. To cross the border and find Jacques' place in darkness was no easy matter. To do so while remaining invisible was a task he had avoided thinking about. He did the only thing possible. He tried to retrace their route of – was it less than twenty days ago? It took him two hours, much of which was devoted to scouting ahead while his horse stood tethered in concealment, but suddenly there it was in the snowy darkness. Though no light glowed in the windows, Martin could tell that the house had not been burnt. Feeling much relieved, Martin dismounted and led his mount cautiously to the barn. Disturbed animals nickered nervously in the dark. Another good sign. By the light of a match he approached the tannery room and peered in. The shape of the table with the candles and large statue was barely visible in the cold gloom. The bed he could see was empty. Made up haphazardly, but looking strangely disused nonetheless. He felt the stove. It was ready for lighting and the metal was very cold to the touch. Then the match went out and for some reason Martin felt a foreboding chill. By the time he had reached the door of the barn he was running. She was in the house. She had to be. He was pounding on the door before he knew it. Loud insistent noises reverberating into the night, desperate heedless sounds that sought ears without caution.

The voice behind the door was frightened. "Who is it?"

Martin recognized the voice and almost sobbed with relief. "Open up, Jacques. It's me. Martin."

"Martin. It's truly you." The door rustled and opened. The scent of neglect hit Martin's nostrils.

The little man's appearance was a shock to Martin. He looked as if he hadn't tended to himself in days. He seemed thinner, smaller if that was possible, but there was a puffiness and unnaturally red colour to his countenance, and Martin could smell the liquor on his breath. His red-rimmed eyes held a wariness that belied the effusive welcome he had just received.

"Madeleine. Where is she? I have come for her."

Jacques was shaking his head. "You don't know? Madeleine is dead. Buried with the others who died for the cause at Odelltown. She died bravely, I am told. She was using my rifle. She was a fine shot. She could load and fire three times in a single minute. No other Patriote could do that." He broke off, sobbing.

Martin shook his head in disbelief. Jacques was obviously mad. The shock of the battles and the defeats. He might even be thinking that Martin was a traitor and was making the whole thing up to protect Madeleine. He approached the other man gently. "Listen to me, Jacques. It was you at Odelltown, not Madeleine. Women did not bear rifles in the Patriote cause." He patted Jacques reassuringly on the shoulder. "You know me. I'm your friend. I would never betray you or Madeleine. I love her as much as you do. Now take me to her."

Jacques seemed to have retreated within himself. He spoke in a monotone as if he hadn't heard what Martin had said. The words were flat and emotionless, slurred with drunkenness, and addressed to the air. Before they stopped however they had turned Martin's blood to ice. "She lies in the cemetery of St. Vincente. With Maman and Papa. I didn't say anything about her sickness. The Curé buried her on Tuesday last as a good Christian. May her soul rest in God's mercy."

Jacques went on. Martin stood there breathing heavily. It was true. Madeleine was gone. He could feel the tears deep down filling his guts with a heaviness that would later rise to his eyes and then in time flood his mind with the despair of bitter-sweet memories. "I let her go in my place. I didn't want to, but I was afraid. She would have been angry with me. I had no choice, don't you see?"

Martin balled his left hand into a fist. He wanted to smash the pathetic little coward who had killed his Madeleine. He moved forward. Then he saw Joseph-Narcisse on the road at Caughnawaga, the dead dog and Theodore Brown, and the sight of the blood and the sound of the screams at Baker's Field. Then tears came, and drawn-out sobs that wouldn't stop. He put his head down on the table and wept, for how long he didn't know, but when he looked up the room was empty and in total darkness. Feeling more alone that he had ever felt in his life, he walked listlessly from the room out into the cold. It was snowing heavily now and a wind was whipping the whiteness around in a blinding veil. He couldn't leave safely in such a blizzard, but even had it not been so, he would have stayed. To say farewell to Madeleine.

~ ~ ~

Martin had the fire going in the stove in a few minutes. The lamps were lit and Madeleine's – their – room was soon yellow with light. He then lit the candles, and when they were all ablaze, he knelt before them. The bulk in his heavy coat seemed to disturb him and he extracted the Madonna from the pocket. He placed it on the table in front of the large statue. The candlelight caught her features and he found his eyes drawn to it instead of the space above the altar where Madeleine had seen what had inspired her. He knelt for a long time looking for Madeleine, or even for what she had seen. But Madeleine did not come out of the darkness to share herself with him in a last farewell, or better yet in a promise of their love. And neither did the other vision rise from above the altar to replace Madeleine with himself, to bond him with her while offering the consolation of revealed certainty. Nothing but the emptiness and the hissing sound of dying candles extinguished by the drafts that whistled cold between the cracks.

The fire had burnt itself out, and Martin lay in her bed shivering with the cold. He would stay here for a couple of hours until the blizzard stopped. He thought it was a long time that he talked to her in the darkness through muffled sobs until at last he fell into sleep.

~ ~ ~

There was a crash and Martin sat bolt upright in the bed. Six men in uniform and carrying rifles had entered the room. One kicked the altar aside as he approached and swung his rifle. Martin felt the searing pain of a rifle butt across his head. Rough hands then dragged him to his feet and shoved him towards an older man wearing the insignia of an officer.

"You are Martin Goyette?" The tone was arrogant.

Martin felt himself nodding numbly.

"I hereby arrest you on the charge of treason towards her Majesty and her subjects." The officer nodded towards a burly sergeant. "Let him dress and clap him in irons." He looked at Martin. "Traitors have no rights, bastard. Don't you ever forget that. Hanging is too good for scum like you."

It was then that Martin saw Jacques. He was standing behind the soldiers. The eyes held fear this time, and something else Martin later was to realize was shame.

CHAPTER IX

Bergen, August 4, 1838

Bernard mingled easily with the crowd of disembarking passengers, most of them summer visitors to the fjords. He followed an affluent-looking Swedish couple past the fish market and assorted buildings with gloomy dark court-yards that had little of the bright airiness of Copenhagen, and none of the sun-drenched colour of Genoa. Halfway down the narrow neck of stores and houses which comprised the town proper, the couple turned in at an inn. White and green with a gable roof on one side and a lower square tower on the other, it looked like a toy house. Even the brightly clad doormen standing on both sides of the low covered veranda that served as an entrance seemed unreal, as if snatched from a child's picture book.

Inside, Bernard was greeted effusively by a tall blonde man who looked as if he spent a lot of time in the sun. After a brief conversation, he selected a room with a view of the big hill he had seen from the boat. The small thin youth who carried his bag explained the hill was called the Fløyen, and it was over three hundred metres high. From the top, rivers, lakes and distant moun-tains spread below like the realm of a mighty king. In ancient times it was said that the Gods made days so clear that their chosen ones could see the icy spires of Valhalla coming out of the blueness in the place where mountains became sky. The boy was excited and wanted to talk more, but Bernard changed the subject, and asked if he had the acquaintance of a young woman whom he believed resided in Bergen. Her name, if he had it correctly, was Signy Vigeland. How could he find her?

The boy's eyes became guarded. He used to know her well when they were children playing in the schoolyard or in the fields below the Fløyen. But since she became beautiful, only the boldest of men would look at her.

"Why is that?" Bernard was mildly curious.

"Her father is a large and violent man who protects her fiercely."

"The girl is of age, is she not?"

"That is of no consequence, sir. Peter Vigeland vows he will kill the man who touches his daughter."

"Do you believe this?"

"Yes," replied the boy simply. He grabbed Bernard's arm urgently. "Stay away from her, sir. Talk to Olaf Hanson, the old cripple who lives in the big house next to the school. He will tell you I am right." He grabbed the silver coin that Bernard had placed on the table and scurried from the room.

After the boy had gone Bernard Blake stood thoughtfully looking out the window. The rain was easing slightly. Here was a turn of events he hadn't counted on. His satchel, containing a vellum-bound book, wig, greasepaint, and two changes of clothes, lay on the bed. Maybe he should revert back to the white robe. Even a brutish father would consider his daughter safe in the company of a priest. Annoyed with his own temerity, he dismissed the thought. There were always ways. A single conversation with the female would be sufficient to strip away whatever façade she had constructed to hide the dementia she passed off as reality.

He missed Thomas Rivarola more than he could have imagined. It was an alien feeling, and he fought it by remembering that Thomas' Holy Orders were to be bestowed before the summer was out. When he had laid Lambruschini's obsession with the Bergen simpleton to rest, he'd speak to the cardinal. With Thomas to follow him, things would proceed more equitably.

Everything had seemed so simple when he was in his cave. The soft one at his shoulder had whispered words to him about his destiny, the greatness that he knew would be his. He would control men, and move them towards a domain of his choosing. But what of this domain? It would not revere the female and it would be intolerant of ignorance. But beyond that, if the truth be known, it had no definition. Nothing to direct him beyond the fact that he would be Pope. The revival he spoke so passionately about to Tettrini and Lambruschini was more real to them than to himself.

His head was hurting and the pain screamed out more as his thoughts focussed on the creature who had brought him here, back in time to a place where the gloom of the Middle Ages lay like a pall. He lay on the bed and rested his head against the headstand. Unconsciously, he began to rock back and forwards. "Slime. Vile whore. Worthless temple of darkness."

He heard the noise before he felt the pain as the headboard broke free under the force of his skull. Bernard lurched to his feet to where it lay on the floor beside the bed. Snarling, he seized it with both hands, and brought it forcefully towards his face. Again and again his forehead struck it.

"Bitch."

~ ~ ~

Signy Vigeland watched the boat from Christiania slip below her father's house, wiped the rain from her face and continued with her daily round of household tasks. She was almost done, and after she had taken her father his lunch, it was practice for an hour before she went out to visit her aunt who lived above the bakery. It was the first time the house had been her full responsibility. He mother had had to leave suddenly the day before to visit an ailing sister in Eidfjord. She looked at the basket over her arm, counting its contents out loud. Gathering the eggs was a task she enjoyed. She smiled with delight at the small oval brown egg laid by her bantam, Riva. She would boil it to serve with the thin breadsticks that Uncle Sven baked every Saturday.

Half an hour later, Signy backed into her parents' bedroom, balancing a tray of food. Peter was on his side dozing, but on hearing his daughter enter, raised himself on one elbow and smiled.

"Papa. I have your lunch. Cold meat, fresh brown bread, and some of Hela's milk. Mama would want you to eat it all. I'll sit with you to make sure you do."

She set the tray down, and perched on the bed, grinning impishly. "I prepared only what you like. No pickled beets. We won't tell Mama."

Peter reached out and patted her thigh. "Ah, Signy. You tend to your Papa. What will I do when you go away? I wonder if having the most beautiful and the best flute player in all of Europe will be worth it."

Signy smiled and cupped his giant hand in hers. She kissed its gnarled roughness. She hated it when her father spoke about her leaving. She felt guilty about wanting to leave them, this house, Bergen, but her heart jumped at the thought that out there, beyond the mountains and the green waters, were exciting places, fine people, wonderful music, and her Balder. As she absently stroked her father's hand, her blue eyes became dreamy, and she began to hum the haunting lament that Olaf said she would only play well after she had truly loved.

She suddenly became aware that her father was not eating. He had pushed the tray down about his knees, and was looking at her strangely with moist eyes. It must be the sickness: a sore throat and dizziness, which the doctor said would go away with rest. She had never seen her father ill before.

"My appetite has left me. But before I rest, stand up and let your papa look at you."

The girl obeyed.

"Twirl around. Now pile your hair up like a lady of breeding."

He nodded approvingly. "Yes. A real princess who plays like a goddess. Now give your papa a hug, and leave him to finish his sleep."

As Signy left she heard him muttering to himself, "Sleeping in the afternoon. What next?" She didn't see him reach for the bottle under the bed.

~ ~ ~

Olaf Hanson looked up from his book in surprise. The knock on his door had startled him. So late in the afternoon. The knock was repeated twice more before he could answer, quiet yet insistent, as if his caller was not used to being kept waiting.

"Coming," he growled. He fumbled with the latch and opened the door.

He had never seen the man before, and thought it must have been a mistake, until he saw the flat, brown leather case. Another would-be genius wanting lessons he couldn't afford. He was young, bareheaded, and wet. Olaf noticed that he was protecting something under his light jacket.

"Herr Hanson. Olaf Hanson?" The accent was not native Norwegian, more southern Danish, with a pleasant lilting quality.

"Yes, that is my name. How may I be of help?"

"My name is Bernard Birous. I am from Marseilles, but no stranger in your land. I would like to talk with you on a matter of mutual interest, if I may?" The man's dark eyes were wide and solicitous.

The man was well mannered. Looked cultured and refined. Normally this would have pleased Olaf. Instead, he felt dizzily uneasy. He forced a smile, even as he gripped the door for support.

"Please come in, if only to get out of the rain. Now you know why they say that all babies are born in Bergen with umbrellas." He nodded at his legs before adding, "I travel neither far nor fast. But I talk well and listen better." He shuffled on his slippered feet through the long hallway, puzzled by his own strange reaction.

Bernard followed the old man into the house, scarcely noticing the quiet refinement which greeted his eyes. He was anxious to get the meeting over. He hoped the old fool wasn't garrulous. But as he entered the large study, he had to admit the impressiveness of the library. Unconsciously he fell to examining the books. Behind his back, Olaf Hanson watched him, his senses still churning.

"You know something about mediaeval saints, Herr Birous? An interest of mine for some time now. There was a time when the cloth had appeal for me. But that was before I discovered the flute."

Bernard turned towards his host who had eased himself laboriously into a hard-backed chair. "You are to be complimented, Herr Hanson, on a magnificent library, the equal of which I have rarely seen even in Catholic countries where the tradition of mediaeval sainthood is more venerated. I have some knowledge of the subject, but clearly nothing like your own."

He rubbed the book he held in his hand as if banishing some imaginary moisture. "Still, I must confess my gratification that I do not see a copy of this volume on your shelves. My pleasure of giving it to you would be thus denied."

He proffered the book to Olaf, who took it wonderingly.

"A copy of Brother Leo's *Life of Francis of Assisi*. My father's library had two." He smiled conspiratorially. "And since I had planned this visit on my next business excursion into Scandinavia, I thought to myself, Who better to enjoy a copy of this matchless contribution to the hagiographic tradition than a true connoisseur?"

Even as he took the book, Olaf was aware that unanswered questions were troubling him far more than the joy he would normally have experienced over such a gift. This dark-eyed young visitor whose presence filled him with unease. Who was he? How did he know of him? His interests? Why had he come? Something told him to be careful. He kept his gaze level as he forced the normalcy into his voice. "My special thanks, Herr Birous. I should refuse such a gift. But I won't." He laughed. "I am too fallible to reject such pleasure."

He kept the book in his hands, rubbing its cover absently, then leaned forward in his chair. "Now tell me. Who are you, my fine young man who speaks like a gentleman and a scholar and who bears fine gifts to broken-down musicians?"

Not taking his eyes off the older man, Bernard answered, "As I have indicated, my good Herr Hanson, I hail from Marseilles. My father owns a shipping business which has allowed me the advantage of extensive travel on his behalf, and the luxury of pursuits of abiding interest. Both came together in Stockholm a short time ago. It was my private passion which led me here to Bergen to you . . ."

He paused and surveyed the bookshelves as if weighing whether or not to continue.

Olaf shifted painfully in his chair. It was as though he were part of a play, yet in the audience watching it. He knew that it was ungracious of him to bypass the normal social niceties which dictated that the guest initiate the subject of discussion, but he had to confront those burning eyes.

"Since I presume you know who I am, I also presume that music is also, how did you put it, your 'private passion'. I teach very little these days."

Olaf saw the lazy, indifferent smile and shake of the head. He watched from outside himself as the young man opposite reached into his pocket, and extracted a cutting from a newspaper. Then a long white hand carried it to his face, a blackened assemblage of words on a scrap of ageing paper that belonged to another time. His shoulders hunched and he recoiled from it, averting his eyes to the book he was twisting in his lap. Olaf thought of the little church where he had prayed with his parents as a boy.

"This is what brought me to Bergen, Herr Hanson. I first read this in Stockholm, and promised myself that I would satisfy myself on my next visit."

Bernard went on enthusiastically. "Such accounts have long been my fascination. My last exposure was to a peasant girl from Calabria some years ago. But alas the child had an overly active imagination and I was left unconvinced. I must admit that I am also skeptical about this girl."

He lowered his voice, and shifted his feet nervously. "May I be frank with you, Herr Hanson?"

"If you wish," Hanson's reply was dull, but his eyes were darting like a trapped bird.

"I had a sister younger than I, who spoke to me of such visitations by the Blessed Virgin. The Holy Mother came to her at night while she lay quiet in the darkness, and promised her greatness."

He blessed himself, and took a deep breath before continuing. "She loved me dearly and became very distraught when I wouldn't believe her or lend her credence with our parents. Later she became very ill and passed on to her Maker. I have been disquieted ever since her loss, over my own lack of faith in her. I want to satisfy myself as to the veracity of these occurrences. I have read everything I can, and now try to involve myself whenever I am able. So far, Herr Hanson, my penance has been that of the non-believer. I yearn for release, and the comfort of truth about my sister."

Bernard spread his hands. "You understand, Herr Hanson. This need for assurance. Will you help me?"

Liar, thought Olaf. The persuasive words could not hide a malicious edge. Aloud, he said cautiously. "No! I'm not sure I do understand, Herr Birous. But that is another matter. What is it you want from me that is not already written there?"

"It is very simple, Herr Hanson. I would very much like to know your thoughts about this woman's apparent miraculous experiences. Are they genuine?"

Olaf Hanson felt trapped. His armpits were cold as he fought to arrange his thoughts. *Be careful, Olaf.*

The knock was deafening. Ingrid's voice, piercing. "Herr Hanson. Will you let me in? I have left my key at home."

The two men looked at each other. Olaf hauled himself to his feet and shuffled towards the door. "My housekeeper. Come to prepare my supper. She's always forgetting her key. But she's an excellent cook. If you'll excuse me for a minute.

"Coming, Ingrid." If she were younger and he less proper, he would have hugged her. He needed the time.

Inside the library Bernard sat in the chair, the piece of paper still in his hand. God, his head hurt. It was all so unnecessary. The female lunatic, this hellish place. For a moment he wished he had listened to his thoughts when they had suggested that he spend some time in Copenhagen and fabricate a story about the Bergen slut to Lambruschini. But the wily old pirate had written a letter to prelates in Stockholm explaining his mission. Besides, he had spies everywhere. He thought he had noticed a suspicious loiterer in Christiania. No, he had to go through with this, and this was the best way. A talk with Hanson – who seemed shrewd enough, for a wreck who lived in the past – and possibly a conversation with the woman – in Hanson's company, of course. Remembering his feelings when he spoke to the wretched idiot from Calabria, he was sure he didn't want to be alone in her presence. There was also her brute of a father. He wished Hanson would hurry. He wanted darkness and rest.

When Hanson returned to the study, he said nothing. He simply re-seated himself and stared at his guest, inviting him to begin.

He's made up his mind about something, Bernard thought. *So let it be.*

He stared back.

Olaf finally broke the silence, "So you want to know about the girl. Things that are not written there." He gestured towards the clipping.

He went on. "She is a simple person with some talent for the flute. Her imagination is vivid, and in many ways she is a child. No, that is not quite right, a woman-child. She is amiable, and will probably marry a fisherman's son of her father's approval, and live the rest of her days like her mother and her mother before her. The apparition has spoken to her on three occasions." He paused, and moved his lips wordlessly. Then he continued, "But she will not confide in me the words, if indeed she has memory of them." He nodded towards the paper in Bernard's hand. "As I have written, it is all there. The facts as I know them."

Olaf could feel his heart pounding. He did not know what was happening, only that he must protect his Signy. Mustering all his willpower, he looked through the space which separated them. His voice was firm and, he hoped, convincing.

"Hear me well, Herr Birous. The child plays well, but has no soul. I teach her because of a family obligation to her mother. A musician with ability but without soul is accursed. Doomed to reach for the cup of greatness but never to drink from it." He felt weariness coursing through him in a flood.

155

As he listened to the old man's impassioned words, Bernard felt himself relaxing. Just as he thought. She was a charlatan, just like the rest of them. He thought of the British ship that was leaving for Portsmouth in three days, and blessed his luck in having secured a berth that very morning. Two more full days in this hellhole were two days too much.

But something in the old fool's attitude towards her struck a discordant note. He chose his words carefully. "Although I am confused by your meaning, I do hear your words, Herr Hanson, and appreciate your honesty. It would seem that we are agreed on the subject of visitations." He gestured towards the vellum book on the table and rubbed his cheek. "The demands of the hagiographic tradition.

"But if I may be so bold as to suggest, you do have one advantage over me with this girl."

"And that?" Deep down inside, Olaf knew what was coming.

"You have personal acquaintance with the subject, and I do not. I know I may sound like St. Thomas, but might it be possible for me to meet with this girl? In your presence, of course. I could satisfy myself, and it may help my dear sister's memory."

"No, Herr Birous. That is neither possible, nor wise for that matter."

"I don't understand. She comes to this house for flute lessons, does she not?"

Olaf held up his hand. "Yes, you do not understand. Signy will talk to no one about these visitations. She fears laughter, her father's disapproval, and above all the betrayal of what she believes is her secret, shared by no one save me. No, Herr Birous, she will not talk to you about her secret."

Bernard's eyes glinted. A battle. Now this was more like it. This old idiot was no match for him. "No! No! No! Herr Hanson," he said, laughing. "I do not want to talk with this woman. I merely want to meet and observe her. I would seek her out myself, but I am told she has a protective, violent father. If her next lesson is soon, I could come here posing as a former music student. I could observe her while she takes her lessons. I must confess I know nothing of soul in music. But I am certain I would find her demeanour enlightening. Will you introduce me, Herr Hanson?"

Olaf felt trapped. There was no way he could politely refuse. Reluctantly he nodded. "She comes tomorrow in the early afternoon at two. You may meet her, then. But there will be no discussion about the things we have spoken of this day, and that will be the end of it. Are we agreed?"

"But of course, Herr Hanson. I am most grateful. Until tomorrow then."

They shook hands and Bernard left. For a long time afterwards, Olaf sat in his chair. He closed his eyes, wishing the vestige of nagging doubt at the back of his mind away.

August, 5, 1838

Signy Vigeland was exasperated. She had spent hours on the concerto that Olaf had set for her. She loved it. When she played it well on the hill near her rock, she envisaged the lover that Olaf had told her she must have before true mastery. But today when she was bursting to play it for him, all he wanted her to do was practise scales and go over some simple tunes she had discarded years ago. When she asked him why, he became annoyed and scolded her, which made her angry. Though she hated it when Olaf scolded her, she usually understood his reasons. Today was different. Olaf was not his usual self, not laughing and making funny faces when she made a mistake. It wasn't like him at all. Pounding the table and calling for discipline like Fru Helved and her dreadful exercise classes in school.

She came out of her reverie to see Olaf glaring at her. "You're not listening, Signy. I swear I've heard better high Gs from my kettle. Your embouchure is terrible. And your fingers. Are they mallets? What's got into you today?

He thrust the sheet of music at her. A child's bedtime story he had set to music. "Play it, Signy, slowly, and clearly. I want to hear every note as if it was the only note in the piece."

"But why, Olaf? It's so easy. It's been years."

"Last lesson I noticed a slurring of tone. A day on this will help." He patted her cheek. "Trust me Signy. The price of greatness—"

"Is humility. Yes, I know, Olaf. I suppose you're right."

As she began to play, Olaf watched her, half listening for the knock on the door, and thinking. He wished she had not worn the blue dress. She liked it because it made her look more womanly. Her hair, as usual, had been brushed until it shone. It spread itself over her bare shoulders. Only a blind idiot would not be completely taken with her beauty. The way her eyes sparkled when she smiled and the full lips that hinted of deep passion. If he kept her subdued, and if Birous was as pedestrian as he espoused to be, then things might be all right. Then Birous's pale face floated before his mind. A good-looking boy. The eyes! There was something captivating about the eyes. He closed his eyes and forced himself to listen to the deliberate notes of the simple tune.

Olaf sensed Ingrid even before she tapped on the door.

"Yes Ingrid. What is it?"

"A visitor, Herr Hanson. He says he has an appointment."

A moment later, Bernard Birous stood framed in the doorway. He did not look at Signy, who played on, seemingly oblivious to the interruption, but approached Olaf, who was still trying to rise from his chair. He shook his hand silently, nodding as he placed his left finger to his lips. He stood beside Hanson's chair, and watched the girl. Olaf wished he could see his face.

Signy raised her eyes casually for a cursory inspection of the visitor. She was used to interruptions; Olaf had many visitors.

Their eyes met and held. Signy felt her cheeks redden. Something leapt from inside her to her fingers. She moved her body slightly. Her lips caressed the lip plate. The notes changed, a child's bedtime story throbbing with an emotion she couldn't control.

Bernard's mouth was dry as he listened. Something terrible was wrong. His feet wanted to move closer, pulled by the blue eyes that held him helpless. His chest tightened, and there was a hotness at his crotch. He pressed his knees together, bit his lip for the control given by sudden endurable pain, and waited.

The music ended. Signy put her flute down, and sat silently. Olaf could feel her questioning gaze.

"Good, Signy. I think we'll work on the major scales for the next half hour." He swallowed before continuing. "Before you begin, I would like you to meet the son of a former student who has paid me the honour of an all too fleeting visit. May I present Herr Bernard Birous from Marseilles. Herr Birous, this is my student, Signy Vigeland."

Bernard could not believe it was happening. It was as though he were possessed. He reached out and took the girl's hand, never taking his eyes off her face. As he raised it to his lips to kiss it, he heard himself saying, "My pleasure, Frøken Vigeland. You play very well."

Her skin was like satin to the touch of his lips. His hand did not want to let go. He trembled inside and wished that Olaf weren't there.

As Signy saw the dark head bend to her hand and felt the warm moistness on her wrist, her breath quickened. Her Balder. Here in Olaf's house. The way it was supposed to be. She suddenly felt like the gulls that soared with the wind. "Thank you, kind sir. Do you play the flute?"

"A little. I enjoy listening more."

"Olaf, may I play my new piece for Herr Birous? I have worked very hard this past week. You haven't even heard it yet."

"No, not today, Signy. I am sure our visitor will not mind if we continue the lesson as planned. The scales, Signy. Every note equally clear through the register, in all twelve keys."

The next half an hour passed in a blur for Bernard. He stood transfixed behind Olaf's chair wondering what was happening to him, but not caring. Magically, wonderfully, the pain in his head was gone, replaced by a sweet emptiness.

Signy talked to Balder through the scales which she ran like a love sonnet. The notes whispered on a low cadence, softly entreatingly, and then spiralled up and across to Bernard, wrapping him in a passionate embrace that promised her love, her very life.

Only once did their eyes meet. A long look that made time stand still. The girl's head moved sideways slightly and her lips parted. Bernard desperately wanted to touch her again. He caught the animal sound in his throat and felt the moistness of tears.

Signy was still playing when Ingrid again came into the room. She talked urgently to him for a minute and then left hurriedly. Olaf got to his feet, fumbled for his canes and turned to Bernard. "It seems we have a problem A dispute over spending for our summer festival. I keep the books, and I am needed. If you'll excuse me."

He turned to the girl who had stopped playing. "Keep playing, Signy. I will be only a short time."

With a last look at Bernard, he left the room without closing the door.

Only the ticking of the wall clock broke the silence until the sound of voices was heard in the distance. A slamming door. Then silence again.

Signy's eyes were bright, her speech hurried. "I'll play it for you if you like."

"What will you play for me, Signy?" Bernard found the familiarity easy and natural.

"The special piece Olaf had me practice and then wouldn't let me play today. A beautiful Vivaldi concerto. I want to play it for you, Herr Birous.

"Antonio Vivaldi, a composer dear to my own heart. I would love to hear you play it, Signy. And please call me Bernard."

Signy put a finger to her lips. "Not here, not today. Olaf would be displeased. She blushed and looked confused. "Tomorrow on the hill above my father's house. It's where I practise every day. The flute gives my mother headache."

Bernard could feel his excitement. "Yes," he breathed. "I would like that. The time? And the place. Is it easy to find?"

"Everyone in Bergen knows the hill above Peter Vigeland's house. But you mustn't come that way. Papa is ill, and is at home instead of on the water with the fishing nets. He . . . He does not take kindly to young men. He would not be pleased if he saw you."

"How, then?"

Signy was animated. She pressed forward. "Go to the docks and ask for a rowboat. Tell them you want to go to Velda's Cove. There is a small beach there, and a path that winds its way up the hill to my father's field. No one must see you. I go there in the early afternoon. Meet me there. I shall play for you . . . Balder."

They both heard the sound of shuffling feet, and suddenly Olaf was there. He nodded to Bernard, and motioned to Signy to continue her scales. She picked up the flute and began to play. Her fingering was firm. The sound was clear. Her mood, indifferent. Olaf looked from one to the other, and after seating himself closed his eyes. Bernard smiled. He had caught her look. The promise of tomorrow.

Olaf sat in his chair, his crippled legs drawn below his knees like a child's. His eyes were closed, and he moved his head rhythmically with the scales that rose and fell with the metronome that had repeated its message over and over again through the years to this child who was now a woman. Consistency to self. A consistency he had violated through his own weakness. Had he been wrong? He remembered once in Paris when he was very young. He had gone against his instincts then, and played a difficult score before he was ready. He had been wrong. He could still feel the deadness in his heart. *Oh, God, Signy. What have I done?*

August 6, 1838

The day dawned bright and sunny, and Bernard rose early and took a walk along the docks to the sea wall that jutted into the depths of the fjord like a gnarled finger. He squinted against the sun as he caught the spiral of smoke rising from the chimney of the house that perched on a hill with its top lost in a wispy whiteness. For a moment he thought of the barren hills above Genoa. He could see his mother beside him as their feet disturbed the brown earth sending a warm cloud of dust into their hair and nostrils. He inhaled the salty air, and laughed at the sea, conscious of the freedom inside his head. No pain. Just the joy of being. As he began walking back towards the town, he noticed a small crab, disoriented somehow and dying on the edge of the wall, its tiny legs waving feebly in a slow death dance. He stopped, and without knowing why, picked up the creature. He was going to throw it far into the water. Instead, he clambered down over the glistening stones and laid it gently in a tidal pool. After rubbing his hands clean on a dry rock, he resumed his walk back to the inn. He hadn't felt this good for a long time. He relished what the day may bring, oblivious to the pair of eyes that peered at him through a spyglass in the darkened doorway of the warehouse that fronted the harbour.

~ ~ ~

Ignatius waited until Bernard was a hundred meters ahead of him, and then followed at a cautious distance, darting into a doorway whenever his quarry so much as inclined his head, or paused to examine a building. After he was satisfied that Bernard had returned to his room, he positioned himself opposite the inn in a small courtyard that allowed a clear view of the front door. He found the sunniest spot and squatting on his haunches began munching on an apple. He had been lucky so far, but even with the tourists, this place wasn't very big. And he wasn't following a white beacon any more. He had been surprised when the workers at the dock hadn't remembered a priest. But because he had no other choice, he had visited the inns, starting with the best. Imagine his shock when he almost ran into him near the front desk of the first establishment he had tried, just an hour ago. It was him, all right. He could never forget that face. He seemed friendly enough, smiling and apologising for his clumsiness. Without the robe he looked much less severe. Priests! When they donned the cloth they became insufferable. He wondered whether Battiste would be more pleasing if he weren't a priest. He thought not.

Ignatius was dozing in the warmth, and but for the lumbering passage of a loaded dray and the noisy screeching of gulls attacking its contents, he might not have noticed Bernard Blake leave the inn. The sun was high in the sky and Ignatius could feel his back, wet and itching from the stone wall. He got to his feet awkwardly, fighting a momentary flash of dizziness, and watched the priest who now was not a priest. He was heading back towards the quays. He was obviously not leaving the town; no ships were sailing that day. Only the clipper bound for Portsmouth, and she was not leaving until past midnight. Besides, he carried no luggage. Ignatius's curiosity gave way to concern when he saw Bernard Blake slap some coins into the hands of a short fat man who had just climbed from a small rowboat. His concern became panic when the priest took the fat man's place in the boat, and after a farewell wave, began pulling away from the dock. Ignatius waited until the boat had rounded the closest point before dashing to the wharf where the fat man was busy gutting his morning catch. Gathering himself, he tried to be casual, using his broken German to inquire about renting a boat. The fat man was apologetic. There were no boats to be rented this late in the day. Tourists and fishermen, he shrugged. Like the one who just took his boat. Going to Velda's Cove. There was nothing there.

His insides churning with frustrated anger, Ignatius returned to his cheap inn beside the fish market, and glowering over a bottle of frothy Norwegian ale, watched the tranquil waters.

~ ~ ~

Through a fitful, sweat-drenched sleep, Peter Vigeland could hear his daughter humming the tune again. He groaned and turned over trying to find a comfortable spot in the bed. Earlier he had tried to get up, but the ground spun too much and he had to lie down again. And he had been certain he would be able to fish today. "Signy," he mumbled drowsily, "What's that tune? I like it."

"It's the new one Olaf is making me learn. It's beautiful, isn't it?"

She came into the room and danced before his bed. "It makes me feel like I want to fly. Away to a castle in the sky. To a Prince on a golden throne."

"Castles in the sky? Princes?" He would never understand his daughter's wild fantasies. "Well by the looks of you, you seem more ready for a concert than flying. Aren't you practising this afternoon up on the hill? Or have you a lesson?"

"No, Papa. I am leaving for the hill soon. I have much work this afternoon."

"Dressed like that?"

"Oh Papa, don't be old-fashioned. Girls like to look nice even when they're not going anywhere special."

Peter looked at his daughter sharply. His eyes narrowed and for a moment he forgot the dizziness and pain in his head. This wasn't like her at all. "All right Signy. Go on. We both know how important your music is, don't we?"

Signy nodded eagerly. If she had noticed the edge in her father's words, she didn't show it.

Infuriated by his daughter's seeming disdain for his feelings, Peter turned to the wall. He would stay awake this afternoon if it was the last thing on earth he did. And watch the hill.

Ten minutes later Signy re-entered the room carrying her flute and some music scores in the wire cover her father had fashioned for her. She kissed his cheek lightly and with a cheery wave ran outside to her brother. Peter watched from his bed as she left the garden and began to climb, her long legs moving easily up the steep incline. Halfway up, she turned and waved. She knew he'd be watching. He waved back. There was a hard glitter in his eyes.

~ ~ ~

Bernard raised his oars and gently drifted in to the rocky beach. He hauled the boat in, wincing as the cold water splashed about his bare feet and legs, and spent five minutes securing it, first to a protruding branch, and then more wisely to a large rock at the end of the beach. Retrieving his shoes and stockings, he climbed the well-marked track that meandered circuitously around rocks and fissures before opening onto a wide undulating meadow, where there was neither shrub nor tree. Just isolated chunks of stone in an expanse of spongy green turf that rested on the sandy earth like a well-worn carpet. Above him and to the left, a huge grey boulder broke the line of his vision, and just beyond it a rough low stone wall stretched unevenly before disappearing over the crest of the hill. He saw the patch of blue at the base of the big rock before he heard the music wafting on the still air. Sounds, beautiful, poignant, that drew him forward until he could see her clearly.

Bernard approached her from the side. Signy was oblivious to everything but the music in her mind, and did not see him standing there in the shadow of the rock. For five minutes, they were each lost in the rich melodic baroque of Vivaldi. Bernard was enraptured. The girl was brilliant. He had never heard anyone play like that – the old fool had lied to him; Signy's playing was all soul. It was like a personal message, sounds for him alone, hanging on the air from the lips of this woman who had touched him in a way he could not yet understand. As the last note died away, Signy turned to look at him. She smiled, her eyes wide, expectant. "Bernard. I didn't hear you. Did you like my Vivaldi?" She giggled nervously.

Bernard squatted on the ground beside her. He laid the flat box and the small package at the base of the rock, and after removing his jacket spread it out on the turf beside her.

"It was beautiful, Signy. I had no idea you could play so well. You will be great one day. Few women play the flute, you know. It's a man's instrument, they say." He laughed. "You are about to prove them all wrong."

"Do you really think so? Olaf says that the way will be long and hard, and that I will have to work for a long time before I am good enough to play in the big concert halls." She rubbed the flute idly. "Sometimes I wonder whether the flute is for me. Other girls I know are marrying. Some this very summer." She laughed. "And all I do is practise the flute." She looked coquettishly at Bernard. "Do you think I am wasting my time, Bernard?"

Bernard was frightened but excited in a wild way. His head was clear. The pain was gone, replaced by feelings he had never before experienced. He was moving down an unfamiliar road. His hands were sweating and he could feel a hardness at his crotch. It was happening. Another page in the book of his destiny. Lines he could not have predicted. Even as he smiled and reached out to touch her hand he would feel himself closing his ears to the soft one, and to anything else that would try to prevent this headlong rush. "Play your concerto again, Signy. You, me and Vivaldi. I will close my eyes and listen."

As she played, Bernard found that his body would not stay still. He moved closer until he could feel her warmth, and rested a hand on her knee drumming lightly with his fingers as she played. As the final bars wrapped him in their sensual sweetness, his other hand reached under her thick hair and rested on her neck. A cow lowed in the distance breaking a silence that wanted no words. Signy put her flute down and turned her face to his. One hand reached out to touch his cheek. Bernard gently pulled her closer and kissed her softly. For a long time he drank in feelings strange, wondrous, but frenzied in their desire for more. He pressed harder and felt her respond. Her arms wrapped themselves around him and they swayed, locked waywardly in a hunger that could not separate them.

He didn't know what to do. He tried to undress her but was confused by the buttons and ties. Finally he pulled the dress roughly around her waist, and fell to kissing her white breasts, feeling the hardness of her nipples under his tongue. The surge in his loins was overpowering and he thought he was going to erupt. He fought against it and lifted his head to hold her close, whimpering into her neck.

As she held him to her, feeling the coarse cloth of his shirt against her breasts, Signy was crying. Not sobs of anguish, but the sweet tears of love. Her Balder had come to her. Instinctively she pulled at his shirt until he was barechested. She rubbed against him, and as they fell to their knees, she was conscious of the chain about his neck, and the small medallion that brushed by her lips as she moved her mouth across his chest.

Afterward, they lay together in the sun for a long time. Signy rested her head on his shoulder, one hand absently twisting itself in the thin silver chain about his neck. She had never felt this happy. She was a woman who had known love. There was no thought of the future. Only now, here, with her Balder. Bernard stroked her breast gently, at times kissing at her cheek and ear. He kept the turmoil on the edge of his mind, and like Signy, savoured the moment.

Her drowsy voice broke his reverie. "What is that about your neck, Bernard?" she said fingering the small medal. "It looks like Frigga."

"Like who?" Bernard was suddenly alert.

"Frigga. The mother of Balder." She lifted her head and looked at him earnestly. "Don't laugh at me, Bernard. But Frigga has come to me. Here on this very meadow. On misty days. Dressed just like that." She pointed to the medallion.

"How do you know it is Frigga?"

Her answer surprised him. "Who else could it be? I have often asked Frigga to come to me, and send me Balder. Now she has done both." she added happily, and rested her head again on Bernard's chest.

~ ~ ~

Peter Vigeland stirred as Signy entered the room and tiptoed by his bed to the clothing cupboard she shared with her mother. He opened one eye, looking vacantly at her back as he tried to clear his head. He cursed himself for his folly. The wakefulness he had promised had vanished with the half-bottle of fiery spirits that was only supposed to ease his aching head. If she had met someone up there it was too late for him to do anything about it today. He closed his eyes quickly as Signy turned around, and feigned a snore until he heard her singing and then laughing, playing with Refus the dog in the garden. He reached under the bed for his bottle, his mind seething with frustrated rage.

~ ~ ~

Bernard sat on his bed and stared blankly at the window and the Fløyen beyond it. His head was whirling, not with the familiar relentless pain, but with a jumble of emotions that could not be unravelled. He sighed. He must decide about these events. Assign meaning and priority to things strange, wonderful, and disturbing. This afternoon he had followed his emotions blindly, untrammelled by the soft voices and darkened images that usually defined his actions. He had known pleasure he had never dreamed possible, and a yearning for another person that lay strangely heavy on his heart even as it intoxicated his senses. He lay back on the bed, and closing his eyes allowed Signy to swim in and out of focus. When her face was clear and smiling, he was back with her on the meadow looking at the sky, content. When she receded into formlessness, her face became tiny, a chip in the mosaic that spelt out his destiny. He lay there while dusk crept in the room, until darkness blotted out the shapes, his eyes wide open, rigid and without sight. Only the slight tick at the temple betrayed life. For a long time the soft one whispered to him there in the gloom.

When Bernard rose, the hands on the pendulum clock on the wall pointed close to midnight. Though he watched the time, his movements were slow, unhurried, as if he were already elsewhere. He removed his wig, and took the white robe from his satchel. Within a minute, he was a Dominican priest again. His bag re-packed, he let himself quietly out the back door, and made his way through the deserted streets to the docks. He boarded the clipper, and after a brief conversation with the watch, was shown to a small cabin. Not grand, the mate shrugged, his English slurred with a brogue Bernard could not identify, but it was the best that could be done on such short notice. Within the hour, he could feel the swaying movement as the ship entered the deep channel of the fjord. Bernard lay on the bunk, and kept Signy on the edge of his thoughts. Yes, it was easier when he was not with her. For a while she had captured him. She had even whispered that he belonged to her. Tomorrow she was expecting him up there on the hill where he had not been Bernard. Just another man, saying things he did not mean, reaching for lips he neither wanted nor needed. He shook his head in the dark. She had served a purpose, one that would be understood in time. A pawn in his destiny. The hollow feeling of emptiness that gnawed inside him was only an emotional reaction. It would be gone tomorrow.

August 7, 1838

Ignatius woke gradually as if coming out of a stupor. Through the fuzziness in his brain, he tried to collect his thoughts. An empty bottle lay beside the bed. Suddenly he sat bolt upright, wincing from the pain that stabbed behind his eyes. He looked outside at the sun. It was high in the sky, and already clouding over with the promise of rain. How could he have been so foolish? He had drunk too much. He had not seen the priest return the previous evening, and now had no idea where he might be. He dressed quickly, stumbled out into the light, and took up his position outside the priest's inn. He waited an hour. Nothing! He spent several more minutes in indecision before starting to walk, as briskly as his aching head would allow, back the way he had come. Half an hour later he was in a rowboat scanning the rocky shore. There was only one small beach, and he could make out the line of a trail that climbed the cliffs. Velda's Cove. The priest went there yesterday. Why not today? Ignatius landed the boat awkwardly, tied it hurriedly to a protruding branch in the sand, and laboriously began the walk to the top, wondering what he would find when he got there.

Luckily her back was to him when he crested the rise. Otherwise she most certainly would have seen him. Ignatius dropped to his knees, and crouching behind a large rock watched the girl in the blue dress. She walked back and forth along the cliffs, passing a few meters from him as she searched the direction of the trail. She was clearly waiting for someone. After a while she retreated to a big rock in the distance. Seconds later Ignatius could hear the sound of a flute, melodic, sweet and, even to his untrained ear, full of sadness. She played for a long time before recommencing her restless pacing, looking towards the sea and the path that led to the beach.

A glint of metal attracted his eye, but he dared not move until the girl was gone. It seemed a long time before she left, walking slowly the other way towards a rough stone fence and a lower meadow. Ignatius felt cramped and wanted to stand, but had to wait until the girl was completely out of sight because she kept looking back over her shoulder. When she had disappeared, Ignatius rose and scuttled across the rocky path, where he found a miraculous medal like the one Alphonse wore. Blake must have dropped it yesterday. Ignatius put it in his pocket and stretched his aching muscles. Another wasted day. Where was the priest? Ignatius had no choice but to go back to his place by the inn, and wait. Absently he descended the hill to the beach. A piece of broken branch lay on the smooth grey stones. The boat was gone, drifting slowly with the out-going tide two hundred meters away in the cold deep waters.

~ ~ ~

Peter Vigeland drained the last drop from the bottle, and resumed his never-ending stare, focussing on a solitary bush near the crest of the hill. He was feeling much better. The dizziness had gone, and at one point he had even considered going down to his boat. But he hadn't. Instead he had spent most of the day in the big chair on the veranda. It was past mid-afternoon, and she was still not back. Another half an hour and he would go and find her, Them. He removed the cork from another bottle with his teeth, and drank noisily. The liquor flamed in his stomach and he licked his lips. In God's name he wished he were wrong. But he knew he wasn't.

This morning Signy had been unusually bright, laughing and singing about the house like a little girl. But her thoughts were elsewhere. Usually she chattered interminably to anyone who would listen. Himself, Ingrid, Refus the dog. Anyone. This morning she was oblivious to his presence. For a long time, she had sat in front of the mirror, brushing her hair and humming a tune he had never heard before. Then he saw her wearing her favourite dress, and his nose caught a whiff of his wife's perfume, a gift from her brother, Sven, when he had visited Stockholm two years ago. She had her flute case out early too. It was on the table by mid-morning and she kept looking towards the hill, impatience written all over her face.

"Signy, Why don't you stay here today and practise so I can listen?" Peter put as much sincerity in his voice as he was able, knowing full well the reply he was going to receive.

"Not today, Papa. I do my best up there. You know that." Her voice was airy, innocent. It infuriated him.

She pecked his cheek. "Good bye, Papa. I may be late. The concerto is difficult and I want it to be ready for Olaf by my next lesson."

She was halfway out the door, when Peter decided to test his instincts one last time. "Would you like me to go with you? I think I have the strength if we walk slowly. I promise not to disturb you."

Something died inside him when he saw her eyes. Wild, desperate. "No, Papa. You're too ill yet." She gathered up her flute and fussed about with some sheets of music. "Bye, Papa."

Before he could reply, she was gone, half running towards the path. No wave this time. Just the purposeful strides of someone who had a destination. Peter had started drinking before she was out of sight.

Through his half-drunken haze, Peter Vigeland could see Signy at the top of the hill. She was standing, looking back the way she had come. Then she began walking slowly down the path. It seemed to Peter that she took a very long time to reach the house. He feigned sleep and watched her as she passed his chair. She looked upset. Something had happened up there. That was clear. For a moment he thought of confronting her. No, she could wait. The bastard who had despoiled her couldn't. He could hear Signy rustling around inside the house, and the sound of dishes as she began supper preparations. Quietly he eased himself from his chair, and as steadily as he could, made his way up the hill.

~ ~ ~

Ignatius was more annoyed than worried. Someone would retrieve the boat. The path that the girl had taken had to lead somewhere. Cursing his carelessness, he left the beach and picked his way back up the incline and across the meadow to where he had seen the girl disappear. The well-marked path wound down to the outer edges of the town. Ignatius squinted and craned his head forwards. Something was moving, coming up the path. He could make it out, now. It was a man. Probably a farmer coming to check on his livestock. He had seen some sheep in the distance. Ignatius waved and quickened his steps.

They were about twenty meters apart when Ignatius realized that something was not right. The farmer had broken into a trot, his lumbering bulk weaving from side to side as he ran. He was yelling words that Ignatius could not decipher. Ignatius stood for a moment transfixed as the distance between them shortened. He could see the man's eyes now, and the huge hands that were already reaching towards him.

Panic-stricken, he began to run upwards towards the cliffs. His side was burning, and his breath rasped dry in his throat. At the crest, his aching legs refused to move, and, as he slowed to a walk, he turned to face his pursuer. He almost sobbed with relief when he saw the man far behind lurching unsteadily, and then falling heavily to his hands and knees. One hand pressed against his side, Ignatius began to run again, a stumbling half gallop that took him down the incline towards the shore. Twice he fell on the loose gravel before he stood cornered by the sea on the little beach. He splashed into the water, only to be driven back out by the numbing cold that took his breath away. Frantically, his eyes sought a hiding place. Beyond one end of the beach, the rocks piled unevenly. He climbed desperately, scratching his hands on the sharp rocks. He could hear the whining animal noises in his throat as he forced his body into a fissure created by a slanted rock meeting the cliff wall. A solitary bush afforded a small measure of protection. Ignatius lay wedged tightly, doubled over so that his dry mouth was pressed against the salty coarseness of the rock. He closed his eyes, and tried to control his breathing.

It seemed like ages. Ignatius could feel the pounding in his chest easing as his breathing became more regular. The tight thrill of terror remained, though, and he craned his ears, listening. All he could hear was the screaming of the gulls overhead and the slapping of water against the rocks. He was wondering how long he must stay there when he heard the sound, at first scraping softly in the distance and then coming closer. He buried his head in his hands and held his breath. The noise stopped and there was a moment of awful silence. He could sense the dark presence looming over him, but could not bring himself to look. Then he felt the grip of powerful hands on his shirt and he was hauled to his feet and thrown against the rock. He screamed as sharp pain bit into his back. Before he could recover, the hands were on him again, tightening about his throat. He struggled and kicked against his attacker's shins. A knee drove into his stomach and his legs gave way. The man's face was close to his and he could smell the liquor on his breath. He tried to speak, but no words came, just the sound of his own skull thudding against stone. He convulsed violently, drawing on air that wasn't there. Then everything seemed to stop. The lights dancing in front of his eyes became dim, and suddenly he couldn't hear the cursing anymore. Even his head was not being pummelled, but was only moving back and forwards slowly, rhythmically, as if in a dream. Then a wave of blackness enveloped him, and he couldn't see the man anymore.

Peter Vigeland dropped the limp form to the ground and stared at it dully. He was breathing heavily and suddenly he felt faint. He steadied himself against a rock, and after a minute began dragging the body, feet first, to the beach. He rifled through the pockets. The only thing of interest was a Catholic medal. Peter pocketed it.

He looked at the face more closely, and was relieved to see that it belonged to a complete stranger. Probably one of those vagrants who descended on the town during the summer months to prey on tourists . . . and young girls. He had credited Signy with better taste. The face was soft, weak. And not a Scandinavian either. He dragged the body behind some rocks above the water-line, and made his way slowly back up the hill.

~ ~ ~

Signy was reading in her room, and didn't notice her father coming down the hill. Signy looked up, surprised when he burst into her room. He was swaying slightly, and fury shone from his eyes.

"You didn't even notice I was gone, did you? Your mind on better things?"

"I did, Papa. I thought you had gone to your boat, now that you're feeling better. Is anything wrong?" Her eyes were wide with puzzlement.

"Is there anything wrong? I have a slut for a daughter, and you ask me if there's anything wrong. You take me for a complete fool?"

"What do you mean, Papa? I'm not a slut. It's not what you think." Her voice was trembling.

Peter put his face close to hers. "Are you telling me that you have not been meeting someone up there on that hill when you were supposed to be prac-tising?" He grimaced. "Oh yes, practising indeed. Practising what?" He slumped to the floor, but kept his head up, and the derisive anger in his eyes.

Signy came to him and knelt before him so that her eyes were level with his. "I won't lie to you, Papa. I never have. I would have told you yesterday. I wanted to tell you, but I was afraid. You become so angry. Yes I have met some-one. He is wonderful and I love him. He is kind, Papa. And gentle." She grabbed his arm urgently. "He is Olaf's friend. Papa. I know he will be yours too." She forced a small smile. "I think he is very handsome, Papa. Just like you."

170

"Stop!" Peter pounded his hand against the wall. "You are only a child. With a fine life ahead of her. I don't care who he is." His voice dropped to a whisper. "But he won't be touching you again."

Signy was suddenly afraid. ". . . What do you mean?"

Peter pulled the chain from his pocket and flung it at her feet. "I warrant you've seen this before."

She looked disbelievingly. The medal with Frigga on it glinted up at her from the wooden floor. Signy picked it up. "Where did you get this?"

"I took it from him. Up there." He gestured towards the hill.

For an instant Signy's heart leapt joyously. He had come after all. A flash of happiness that died with her as quickly as it had come.

"The rest of him lies at the bottom of the fjord. May the filth burn in Hell."

Peter picked himself off the floor and faced Signy who was still kneeling, white-faced and mute. "It is done. Finished. You understand." He rubbed his hands together. "We will go on as before." Nodding as if in agreement with himself, he went on, "Yes, you have a flute lesson tomorrow. The important piece you must know for Olaf. Now go to bed, daughter. I have some things to do. We will talk of this no more." He bent down and kissed her forehead and left the room.

~ ~ ~

Peter waited until it was dark before he lowered his rowboat into the water. Unseen, He rowed through the misty darkness to the cove. Retrieving the body, he weighted it down with rocks from the beach and piled it into the bow. When he was over the deepest channel, a gentle splash disturbed the night's silence as the body broke the surface of the still waters. Peter looked at the invisible ripples for a long time. He was suddenly very weary. The tears welled from nowhere. They just came. He rested his head on the oars and wept.

August 8, 1838

Peter Vigeland looked up sleepily as his daughter touched him on the shoulder. "Your breakfast, Papa."

"Is it morning already, daughter? I must hurry. The fish won't wait." He laughed.

As he ate, he watched Signy do her mother's usual duties about the house. She wasn't singing, but neither did she appear particularly upset. He had been right. His daughter was a Vigeland. This whole thing was probably harder on him than her. Dutiful daughters like Signy were quick to realize the error of their ways. He hoped she had learned a good lesson.

"Here is your lunch, Papa. I hope you are not too late for the tide. The other boats are out already."

"Ah, you're a good girl, Signy. Your Papa loves you." He hugged her and kissed her cheek, not noticing in his relief that she hadn't answered.

~ ~ ~

Constable Piet Halvorson looked up in pleased surprise when Signy entered the small room that served as his office. He sucked his ample girth in, and wished that he had taken more attention with his hair. There was no doubt about it: Peter Vigeland's daughter was a real beauty. "Good morning, Signy. What brings you to this cheerless place? You want to invite me to the summer ball. I'll have to ask my wife first." He laughed at his own humour.

But Signy was not smiling. She looked serious, and spoke as though she hadn't heard him. "I am here to tell you something, Constable Halvorson. Something you should know."

"What is it, Signy?" he asked wonderingly. An accident. A drunken sailor who had put his hand in the wrong place. Well, if it was, it was better for the poor bastard that she had come to him instead of her father.

"A man has been killed. His body lies at the bottom of the fjord. He is a stranger. . . ." She stopped, and Halvorson could see her fighting for control.

He pointed to a chair, and reached for pen and paper. "Sit down, Signy and rest for a minute. Now start again and tell me slowly how you come to know about this. Who has been killed?"

"It was my father. My father killed him."

Then she was gone, running out the door. Halvorson lurched to his feet awkwardly. "Wait, Signy. Come back."

~ ~ ~

It was raining again, and the fog was rising from the fjord. Signy Vigeland put the bundle down at the base of the big rock. Slowly she undressed, discarding her coarse outer garments like a butterfly shedding its cocoon. Her lips were painted and her hair hung loose on each side of her breasts in golden tassels. In the cold mist, her lace-trimmed white petticoat clung to her body like satin. Her slippers were pointed delicately with a single red rose sewn on each instep. She dabbed some perfume under her arms and on her wrists, and, humming one half of a Devienne duet, began brushing her hair, tying it back when she had finished with a dark blue velvet bow. Then she stooped and drew a thin silver thread from the bundle on the ground. It was cold as ice, and droplets of moisture gathered on the medallion attached to one end. She fastened the chain about her neck, and held the silvery oval to her lips before placing Frigga's face against the warmth of her skin. Still humming, she carefully slipped the blue dress over her head and walked through the mist to the cliffs. At the edge she stopped. Far below her the grey waters lay silent, cold, waiting. They had imprisoned her Balder, hiding his beauty from her in their green murkiness. She looked down searching for his face. He was out there somewhere in the greyness calling her. Signy watched a kestrel in the distance rise, its graceful wings dipping and cresting as it flew.

"Go, my beautiful one. Carry my soul with you to Valhalla. My body goes to Balder."

She spread her arms wide and plunged into the abyss. Falling, falling. Cold grey air bringing her home. She saw the face rising from the depths smiling at her, arms outstretched. She cried out.

"Frigga."

Paris, Spring, 1222

Rodolph had not been to Paris before, even in his many wanderings with Dominic. He looked forward to the university which some said was equal to that in Bologna. He found the convent of St. James well placed among the several churches which had sprung up around the university. Brother Matthew, the Prior, greeted him warmly, and insisted that he rest before Vespers. The Friar Preachers, Rodolph had discovered, were well established in Paris, following their humble beginnings three years earlier. Residents of the city flocked to hear them preach. Miracles were already attributed to them, and it was said that Reginald's sermon in the Church of Notre Dame a short time before his untimely death had inspired many to join the Order. Even that very day, Rodolph had seen one of their number, a rich man who had joined the friars after he had heard them singing in the cold streets one night as he lay in his warm bed. Ugolino was right, however. From the look of things in the priory, the friars could benefit from his organizational skills.

Brother Recaldo was one of the last of the friars to meet Rodolph. He had been preaching at Limoges when Rodolph arrived. They fell to talking after lauds one morning as they strolled along the riverbank across from the busy, muddy market. He listened as Recaldo told him how one could tell in spring if the vineyards would be healthy that summer. When it was Rodolph's turn to speak, he related to Recaldo the story of the names he had found on blessed Dominic's body. Recaldo listened intently, as Ugolino had said he would. He also agreed with Ugolino about Reginald, his one-time colleague at the University of Paris.

That night in his cell, Recaldo showed Rodolph the only worldly possession Reginald had ever carried with him, or even thought about for that matter. The small icon of the Holy Mother, standing hands outstretched in frozen humility was modestly cast in soft pewter. Reginald had told Recaldo that she had come to him exactly in that pose when he had been ill in Rome, and that she had cured his sickness. Recaldo took the icon reverently in his hands as he thought about Ugolino's solution. It seemed right and fitting for Reginald. The next evening the two friars worked secretly, long into the morning hours sealing Dominic's list inside the icon. After Matins, they brought the icon to the chapel, and returned it to its place on the Gospel side of the altar. Reginald had always turned his eyes there when he prayed. He felt he was not worthy to look at the tabernacle.

Rome, Fall, 1228

Ugolino had been Pope Gregory IX a year when he heard the news. He received it with sorrow and finality. One door was now closed to all except whom God would have. The plague had struck Paris that summer, and had taken Brothers Rodolph and Recaldo. They had both died, rejoicing in their pain, and the promise of paradise. Ugolino doubted whether either one of them had given a thought on his deathbed to the secret, shared by nobody else but himself.

CHAPTER X

John Colborne had called the meeting immediately he had completed reviewing the reports that that accumulated during his highly successful military campaign to the south. There were just three of them. Major General John Clitherow and Colonel Sir Charles Grey were both military men and therefore junior which meant that the meeting would be short and full of agreement.

"Two things are clear," said Colborne after tea had been taken, the informalities dispensed with, and the real order of business, underway. "The common courts of this country cannot be relied upon to dispense impartial justice between the Crown and her subjects. It is also equally clear that proper justice be done this time. This eruption, gentlemen, had its origns in our own maudlin, misplaced benevolence a year ago."

"I agree," said Clitherow. The newspapers are demanding retribution. We need to act promptly."

The third man was a tall, spare figure whose demeanour resembled more a professor than that of a military man. Charles Grey had been in Canada since 1835 when he had joined his friend, George Gipps, on a British appointed Royal Commission of Inquiry into the political troubles of the Canadas. Knowing Colborne, Grey realized the difficult position he had been put in. The man belonged to the eighteenth century. He would have to be cautious, choose his words carefully. He decided on the easy, confident approach. "Yes, I too agree. We have no choice. We can't let them go this time. We have to try them."

"I'm glad you agree, Sir Charles. But not the courts."

"What then?" Grey could still not see Colborne's line of reasoning which annoyed him because he saw Clitherow already nodding.

"A court martial, Sir Charles. We try them in a court martial. Major General Clitherow will preside. It will be a proper trial. Witnesses will be called and all proceedings conducted openly. The tribunal will be composed entirely of the military and its decision will be final and subject to no appeal."

"Except your personal pleasure," Clitherow interrupted.

"Of course," Colborne replied.

Grey sounded worried. "A court martial. Isn't that a dangerous precedent Excellency? The courts of the land are still sitting. There is no state of wartime emergency. British common law clearly states..."

"I don't care what British common law states." Colborne was annoyed now. "I do know we have had two rebellions in this place in less than a year.

There were no recriminations the first time. But by God there will be this time. I will continue to act under the provision of my ordinance."

"Even when there is no need?"

Colborne seemed to calm down somewhat. "But there is, Sir Charles. There is avery need. Let me finish." He then turned to Clitherow. "Major General, how many prisoners have we in custody?"

"Over eight hundred, Excellency."

"All guilty, but not all equally, Sir Charles. Therefore our justice will be equitable. Unrelenting, fair, but ultimately merciful. We will acquit most. A few we will exile." He went on, looking steadily at Grey, not Clitherow. "A certain number we will condemn to death. A few of these we will hang. The whole process will be protracted while the public interest runs its course."

Grey smiled to himself. Colborne had not forgotten his early teachings, passed down when times were more suited to the rights of the privileged than to the growing notion favouring universality of law: Mercy and terror, with the uncertainty of delay thrown in to accentuate both. The old firebrand if nothing else was predictable.

"The prisoners. They will be defended properly?"

"Of course," Colborne sounded benign. "The dictates of law will be followed. I have already decided on the names of the defence. Messrs Drummond and Hart. A good choice, don't you think, Sir Charles?"

Grey had to admire Colborne's instincts. The reputation of both attorneys was impeccable. "Yes, a most appropriate choice, Excellency. And I trust they will have the usual access to the prisoners, the normal time and latitude to prepare adequate defences."

Colborne looked at Clitherow and for a moment his eyes became guarded. He recovered quickly and went on expansively. "There will be some limitations. There are simply too many opportunities for collusion. False witnesses could be called at will, and most will willingly perjure themselves since they do not accept British law anyway. Also, most of the prisoners are illiterate. No, we have to be more arbitrary, I am afraid, than we would be in a British court of law.

"How much more?" Grey's question was direct.

"Proceedings will be entirely in English."

Grey sighed, "Of course."

Colborne countered the sarcasm with his own. "I am pleased that you understand. I have also decided that Drummond and Hart will not argue on their clients' behalf. They may advise, even read prepared statements, but no more. Each defendant will have to argue for himself."

Grey gasped, not believing his ears. "Excellency. You cannot do this. It's not right. The Crown will not accept it. The Privy Council will not uphold your actions."

Colborne was sneering now, "And who is going to tell them. The Privy Council has more to worry about than my use of precedent. I will give the Crown back its rightful domain, a peaceful domain where the carpings of blood hungry radicals will not disturb the lives of decent men and women regardless of what language they speak."

Grey rose to his feet. "I beg to inform you, Excellency that I will have to make your intentions known to the highest French speaking legalists in this place. I acquiesce to your actions no matter how much I find them opprobrious because I am your servant before our Queen. I am, however, also a gentleman born to revere the right of any man to a fair trial. You are impinging on these rights, and as such I feel bound by my duty."

Colborne too had risen. His face was flushed and there was a resolute edge to his voice. "As I am also, Colonel. Peace in the realm is of first concern. Equitability of justice will be the result of all this, and a few will hang. The right few. And now if you'll excuse us, Major General Clitherow and I have some further matters to discuss. Good day to you, Colonel."

"Will he make trouble?" asked Clitherow.

"Perish the thought. He's not that much of a reformer. Now let's get down to business." He handed Clitherow a list. "The names of the two prosecuting barristers and the twelve other officers you will need for the tribunal."

Clitherow took the list and skimmed the names. "All good men," he agreed. "One thing bothers me Excellency. Whom do we hang? We can't really go by the leaders. Most of them got away. I mean, how can we decide who dies and who doesn't."

Colborne laughed. "You don't, Major General. I do." Clitherow raised his eyes as Colborne continued. "First, we decide whom to try. That's your task. Let's say we settle on about a hundred. The rest were simply followers anyway, and we can release them over a period of days, even weeks. Those we try, we do so in groups of about a dozen spread a week apart. Special cases, we could try singly. Each trial should take you about a week so we should be finished in about three months. Enough time for the thirst for revenge to be slaked, and general interest to abate. Spread the measure of guilt in each trial. Acquit or exile some, and condemn the rest to death. You and I can then decide on which ones, and how many of those we hang. It all depends."

"On what?"

"The mood of the populace. It will be easy to read."

"I still need some guidance on the death sentence."

"That too is easy," replied Colborne. "Involvement in the last rebellion should be a major determinant. Also, known association with any death during either revolt should be given due consideration. The final reasons I leave to your own determination."

"And those?"

"Expediency and personal conviction," replied Colborne. "Laudable sentiments, don't you agree."

"The first trial. When do you wish it to begin?"

Colborne shrugged. "Now. As soon as possible. The infernal *Herald* says we are already too slow. They want their blood. Then we shall let them have it. Start with the group captured at Caughnawaga. We have a prime candidate for hanging among that lot."

"Who?"

"Joseph-Narcisse Goyette, the loudmouth notary from Chateauguay and a rabid enemy of the Crown. Except for the damned reformer Durham, he would have hung in 1837. He's done much to hurt us publicly."

"Any one else. I mean to hang?"

"In the first group. Oh, probably one more. We can decide that later." Colborne began walking to the door indicating that their meeting was over. "It's all settled then, Major General. We start the trials a week from today. The wheels of justice are about to turn.

Le Pied du Courant Prison, Montreal, December 21, 1838

The Pied du Courant Prison in Montreal was a solid three-storey edifice surrounded by a stone wall and patrolled by sentries whose stiff grey serge uniforms were as modern as the prison itself. The upper two storeys were reserved for lesser criminals, those whose minor infractions allowed communal living, and who did not warrant the scrutinous security of a barred cell. That was reserved for the ground block, which was divided into two-man cells fronted by a long corridor that in turn looked out through barred windows onto a large courtyard. Usually in the morning this space was deserted, given over to the gulls and other birds that wandered about as aimlessly as exercising inmates.

It was different this morning. The activity began on the large gallows which had been completed just a week earlier and whose platform rose above the stone walls like a macabre stage. A short hunched figure tended to the noose that hung menacingly from a thick horizontal beam. Other officials, two clad in the scarlet of the military, another civilian in a black suit and hat, and a young intense priest fingering his pectoral cross milled about on the gallows. At 8:30 the thick wooden gate to the right of the gallows swung open and the company of troops marched into the courtyard, the sound of their boots muffled by the murmurings and jostling of the crowds that had begun to congregate outside the walls. The soldiers halted outside the main prison door, and on an order from their mounted officer formed two lines about twenty feet apart, and extending to the steps of the gallows. The ceremonial aisle thus created, they ordered arms and faced each other stolidly in the cold grey light, and waited.

They came ten minutes later. Four guards and the man in the black suit. The two prisoners' hands were manacled and a long halter placed about their necks. Duquette was sobbing and didn't look at his parents who just stood mutely in the doorway to the cell. Just before they shuffled forward, Joseph-Narcisse smiled wanly towards his wife and father, and raised one manacled hand in a farewell gesture. Then with the priest leading the way, they passed into the cold morning light, between the scarlet unsmiling line of rigid troopers, and past the young priest now kneeling in the snow, pectoral cross raised high in a hopeless gesture of hope. At the foot of the wooden steps to the gallows they paused. There, Humphrey the hangman awaited them. Bent over double and hideously disfigured, he was a grotesque caricature of his macabre trade. He led them in a slow procession up the steps. Twice Duquette's legs gave way and he had to be supported, then pushed forward until they all stood on the platform. The man in the black suit gestured towards Joseph-Narcisse who walked evenly towards Humphrey and the trapdoor below the noose which was swaying slightly in the stiffening breeze. With a shake of his head he indicated his readiness. He had nothing he wished to say. Behind him the priest was on his knees and he could hear Duquette crying. As the noose was fixed about his neck he gazed out over the crowd spread before him and pressing against the restraining cavalry. Their faces were upturned, silent. The crowd, the city behind them, the cold grey river beyond. None of it was part of him anymore. Who could live in greyness where freedom was denied? He closed his eyes and waited. The trap was sprung. The crowd gasped and Joseph-Narcisse Goyette dropped cleanly into eternity. Minutes later a screaming Joseph Duquette took his place at the noose.

Le Pied du Courant Prison, Montreal, Monday, January 7, 1839

Twelve men filed silently into the bare room escorted by two guards. Once inside, the iron door was closed behind them and they were left to themselves. Still flexing his hand — it was a habit by now — Martin tried to survey his surroundings while the rest either talked or slumped to the stone floor in, what was by now to them, a familiar resignation. They were in the new prison and though no one had spoken of it during their short journey here, every man was aware that the next stage in their ordeal was about to begin. They were to undergo their trial, if one could call such a mockery of justice, a trial. Just passing the monstrous gallows still stained red with the blood of Joseph Duquette had done much to rekindle the terror that they had tried to bury during the endless weeks at La Pointe à Calliere.

As a guard had casually put it, the noose snapped some necks like a twig; others it just strangled slowly. Either way, it awaited them all.

The first to be taken away was Chevalier de Lorimier. Escorted by two guards, he disappeared down the gloomy passageway to return half an hour later white-faced and silent. Then Martin heard his own name being called. Whatever it was, it was his turn, and the fact that he was second on the list did not escape him as he proceeded past some more unoccupied cells to a room at the end of the corridor. He was ushered inside by the two guards who motioned him to a chair in the middle of the room, and then withdrew locking the door behind them. There were two others in the room. They were not prisoners and both were dressed in dark suits. The shorter one of the two, a stout man with a cherubic face, greeted Martin with a smile. "Don't be alarmed Martin. My name is Lewis Drummond, and this here is my associate, Mr. Aaron Hart. We have been appointed by the Crown to conduct your defence."

Hart nodded his concurrence. He was taller, pale and austere looking. His voice, however, was warm and encouraging, his French unaccented. "You and your comrades, the ones we will see today, are being arraigned for trial. It begins— "

"On the eleventh," Drummond interjected, producing papers from his briefcase. "Twelve of you."

"You are my defenders?" said Martin trying to gather his thoughts. "All this is very new to me. What am I supposed to do?"

"I have the charges here," replied Drummond. "A strong case, it appears."

"And our ability to plead adequately is jeopardized," added Hart. We can only advise you. Read a prepared statement. Delay proceedings while you consult with us. The real business of defence, I am afraid, will have to be in your hands."

"Witnesses for the defence have been very hard to procure. The time is so short." Drummond sounded apologetic. "The proceedings are conducted entirely in English," he added.

Martin gave the briefest of smiles. "I know the language. Could you please elaborate on the case they are making against me?"

Drummond and Hart exchanged glances. They had not had an easy time with this most difficult of assignments. Justice was not being served, and they were part of the whole legal mockery that was seeing men denied the rudiments of British law. But if Goyette could speak English and could muster some sort of counter to the arguments that were going to be thrown at him, either through persuasion or the procurement of plausible witnesses, he might stand a chance.

Drummond spoke slowly. "You will have to counter three main charges. Witnesses brought on your behalf on any, or all three will be most useful, but if previous cases in these court martials are any indication, that may not be an easy thing to do. First, they say you are a man of prominence in Les Frères Chasseurs. That a warrant was out for your arrest on treasonable charges even before the revolution began. That you were engaged in subversive activities in the United States. Can you counter these allegations, Martin?"

"Of course. I was simply acting on de Lorimier's orders. It was a mission of observation. I did no recruiting."

"But can you prove it?" Seeing Martin's look, Hart said, "I thought not. You were in the United States before the revolt?"

Martin nodded.

"On Les Frères business?"

"Yes, but . . ."

Drummond sounded worried. "And you have no witnesses, prominent persons who could speak on your behalf about the innocence of this journey?"

Seeing the negative look in Martin's eyes, Hart went on, "The second charge is that you proposed to burn down the manor at Beauharnois, and that you tried to instigate violence against Lady Jane Ellice and her family."

Martin was stunned. This could not be happening. "That's preposterous. I tried to help them. Lady Jane Ellice will tell you. I spoke to her."

"You'll have a fine time trying to call her as a witness," said Hart. We'd be laughed out of the court."

Drummond pressed on, "But the crown does have a witness who will swear to it that you were bent on violence or worse towards the gentle ladies."

"Who? What dog will swear to such a lie?"

"Someone the tribunal is most likely to believe. The manager of the Ellice estate, Mr. Theodore Brown. He has scars as testimony of his personal assault."

"It's all lies. Brown is a liar." Martin was almost shouting now. "Don't you believe me?"

Harts voice was gentle but firm. "It doesn't matter what we believe. Can you call any credible witnesses from that night to support you?"

"I don't know. I had just arrived. It was dark. There was the Chevalier, the innkeeper, my brother. I can't think."

Hart looked at Drummond resignedly before continuing, "It is the third charge which is the most serious, Martin."

Drummond was reading, trying to scan the piece of paper in his hand. "A Scottish farmer named Simon Macintosh. Are you aware of him?"

Martin shook his head. "The name means nothing to me."

"Well, he is prepared to swear that on the afternoon of Saturday, November 3, you were involved in the fighting which led to the death of his neighbour, John McBride. That you and your brother ordered the burning of his home and that in the shooting which followed you both fired weapons into the burning house as the victim rushed forth."

Martin's heart leapt. "I haven't seen Joseph-Narcisse since he tried to take the Indians' guns at Caughnawaga. He still lives!"

The two men looked uncomfortably at one another. Drummond finally cleared his throat and said, "Martin, your brother was hanged two weeks ago with Joseph Duquette. I thought you knew."

"No," Martin whispered, looking at his lap. He wondered whether Joseph-Narcisse had died quickly or had suffered at the end of the rope.

"But McBride was indeed killed by rebels from Chateauguay."

"I wasn't there. How can this man say it was me?"

"According to what is written here, he is familiar with your family. He said he recognized you by your, your, blemish."

Hart leaned forward insistently. "This is most serious, Martin. If this man's story cannot be refuted, then you almost certainly face a guilty verdict. Your brother can't be called as a witness now. If you weren't there, where were you, and who can you produce to substantiate it?"

Martin groaned inwardly. "I was on the road from Odelltown. I was travelling alone. I reached my comrades just as they were moving on Beauharnois. I spoke to no one that day. My haste was great."

The lawyers looked at each other. Drummond thought for a moment. "Is there anything else that happened in the revolt which might lead the court martial to give your other assertions credence? Anything verifiable which would diminish your level of culpability?"

Martin thought hard, then jumped at the ray of hope. "Yes. There is one thing. When we were routing the Volunteers at Baker's Field, I called the charge off. It was not my responsibility to do so, but I acted in good conscience because people were going to die. All of my comrades will gladly verify this."

Hart sighed. "I am afraid you cannot aver to that, Martin."

"Why? It happened as I said."

"James Perrigo, who was tried recently and who held command that day, has testified that it was he who gave the order to fall back."

"But he didn't. I did."

"Like with Theodore Brown and Simon Macintosh, it's not a matter of truth but rather who believes whom." Drummond rose and patted Martin on the shoulder. "All you can do, my young friend, is tell your story and pray that mercy is on your side. I and my colleague will do what we can, but without reliable witnesses . . ."

"I understand," said Martin dully, as he walked to the door. "There's nothing anybody can do now." He paused before allowing the escort to usher him away. "One question, if I may. What happened to James Perrigo?"

"He was acquitted. He left a free man." Hart looked satisfied. "It was one of our rare victories."

Friday, January 18, 1839

Lewis Drummond and Aaron Hart were in their places near the dock, both engrossed in a pile of papers on their desk. Beside them at a much longer table sat the three judges advocate, Dominique Mondelat, Claude Day and Captain Peter Miller. It was Miller who called Martin forward to the separate dock set aside for individual prisoners to plead their case. He read the charges loudly and spent ten minutes detailing their nature and severity. He then called the first witness. A door to the side of the courtroom opened to admit Theodore Brown. Though he was dressed ludicrously in a brown suit that was far too small for him, his florid face bore all its customary truculence. He stared openly, contemptuously at Martin before taking his place on the witness stand. The Oath sworn, he then proceeded with his damning testimony. Half an hour later Simon McIntosh gave a repeat performance, but he did not look at Martin, and kept his eyes down during the entire testimony. Then it was Martin's turn.

"The man you brought in here, Simon McIntosh. I have never seen him before in my life. I was nowhere near Chateauguay that day. Look at my hand." Martin held up his right hand. "It's been broken, very badly, and if you want to know, it was the other witness Theodore Brown who broke it. No, that's not quite correct. His horse broke it, but Brown was attacking me." Martin knew he sounded stupid but he had to go on. He paused and tried to gather his thoughts. But even as he fought for composure, he could feel the hostile eyes of the presiding judge, could sense the doom facing him across the long scarlet row of powdered wigs. Two of them were actually sleeping. Another held his hand in front of his mouth, whispering to his companion.

Martin swallowed before resuming. "I could not fire any weapon with this hand. Even if I were there at the farmhouse you spoke about, I could not have done the things testified to by the witness. Any one with my brother that day will—"

Martin froze. One of the tribunal, a fat red-faced Captain, was holding up a crude drawing before him. It was a gibbet, and swinging from it was a stick figure with a carrot-shaped head and grossly deformed face. It was speaking words, circled and written in crude French, "There must be something wrong with this necktie. I can't breathe." The officer next to the fat one took his turn with the drawing. His chuckle was audible to the whole court. Only the presiding judge seemed oblivious, gazing into the air vacantly. Down the table, the drawing was passed from one hand to another. More chuckles and smirks intermingled with gasps of outrage from the eleven prisoners who stood aghast behind their restraining rail. Alone in the dock, Martin lowered his head.

~ ~ ~

The trial came to an end on January 21, and three days later the prisoners were brought back to the Palais de Justice to receive the verdict and hear sentence passed upon them. Still manacled, they were led singly into a small room to face the three judges advocate, who sat together at a small table flanked by two armed soldiers. Though he was under no illusions as to what was coming, Martin nonetheless felt anew the familiar chill of fear as one rose and intoned the words that sealed his fate: "That Martin Goyette be hanged by the neck till he be dead at such time and place as His Excellency the Lieutenant General, Governor of the Forces in the Provinces of Upper and Lower Canada and Administrator of the said Provinces, may approve."

Wednesday, February 13, 1839

Neither of the two men had spoken for an hour. They both lay on their pallets, the silence broken occasionally by de Lorimier coughing or the rustling of Martin's bedding as he turned restlessly in the dark. It had been a long painful day, and Martin had been relieved when the cells were closed for the night.

Martin held the icon on his chest. It glinted dully in the gloom. "Chevalier.

You are not afraid to die? The rope, the drop, the snapping of your neck. It does not frighten you?"

de Lorimier's voice sounded slow in the dark. "No. It will be over quickly. My eyes will open, and since I have made my peace, I will see God."

"What will He look like? Who else will you know?"

"His face? I don't know. It will be bright and fill me with everything I ever wanted. Others will be there. Whether I will know some is not important, but we will all laugh together because we are seeing God."

Martin got up and took the Madonna to de Lorimier's pallet.

de Lorimier didn't see it at first. When his eyes caught it, he uttered, "Mon Dieu. The Holy Mother. Where have you been hiding her, Martin?"

"She belonged to someone I love."

"Come, Martin. Set her up there." He pointed to a low shelf where they kept food for cooking. "We can pray to her together."

"I can't pray any more, Chevalier. Ever since my Uncle Antoine talked to me about doubt, I have wondered about the empty words that I have uttered in the name of prayer, and even before that, I think. There are so many things I do not understand." He turned the icon over in his hands. "She is made of pewter, Chevalier. If we know who God is, why then do we pray to metal?"

de Lorimier blessed himself as if to banish this heresy, but spoke consolingly as though he understood. He took the icon from Martin. "She is made of metal but she represents the Virgin, so when we pray we pray to Mary through this man-made likeness. For me she is the soul of the Madonna." de Lorimier was thinking aloud more than debating.

Martin pressed on. "All the time?"

"No. Only when I pray to her."

It was Martin's turn to take the icon again. "A pewter Madonna makes the true Madonna real? Lends substance to belief on whim? I find that very difficult to accept, Chevalier."

"But you have to, Martin. It's the faith that ordains what the Protestants, and you apparently, see as icon worship." He held the Madonna reverently, "Icons such as this have been sanctified through revelation. Like faith which too is revealed, your Madonna simply lends physical being to spiritual certainty."

"Are you saying that revelation precedes faith?"

"No I am saying that faith is strengthened and made more real by revelation and that our representations of divinity are equally averred. Where the faith originates from for every man is not for me to say. In my case, it was taught at my mother's knee. Only the chosen ones are different."

"The chosen ones?" Martin was startled. Madeleine had used the same words. "What do you mean, Chevalier?"

"They form the bridge between earth and heaven. God sends them among us to do His will."

"And what will is that?" Martin was thinking of Madeleine. "Could a hopeless bloody fiasco be God's will?"

de Lorimier sounded weary. "That is not for us to divine. That He or His Blessed Mother have deigned to make themselves known to a chosen one is sufficient to incite in the hearts and souls of all mortal sinners a rejoicing and renewed faith in the true God. Only the chosen ones know on earth the rapture that awaits me two days hence."

"I still don't understand, Chevalier. Forgive me for my lack of faith or discernment, but what of those who are mad?" He swallowed before continuing. "I have heard of false chosen ones. Indeed, I have spoken to someone who claimed a celestial vision."

de Lorimier was quiet for a long time. Finally he answered, a childlike reply that told Martin nothing about God or the chosen ones but everything about the God-fearing Chevalier.

"I have read about the chosen ones: Paul, Augustine Dominic, Reginald, Francis. The truth of their experiences have been attested to by our holy mother Church. That is enough for me, for it could not be otherwise were it not so."

"I understand that, Chevalier. But would you yourself know a chosen one?"

"It would depend, I think."

"On what?"

"The piety of the subject. The consistency of the vision with the teachings of holy mother Church."

Martin could see Madeleine. He leaned forward earnestly. "What about intensity of feeling? An inner knowledge."

de Lorimier wagged his finger knowingly, smiling and nodding his head at the same time. "Now you are talking about faith. It all comes back to that, my friend. And now you begin to understand why I am not afraid to die."

It was Martin's turn to be silent. Certainly de Lorimier would not have counted Madeleine among the chosen ones. Not by that definition. But by his own? Martin remembered again the intensity he had experienced when he saw her transfixed by something above the altar she had created with her own hands. His lack of surety was because he hadn't shared it. But he had believed then, was sure now that she was seeing something in the air, something real that was guiding her actions far more profoundly than Uncle Antoine had ever guided his. Whose faith was more real, his or de Lorimier's? Madeleine had referred to him as being chosen. He hadn't understood what she meant. But if she had meant that she, a true chosen one, was also selecting him, then it made sense. If Madeleine had been a chosen one, in time she would have wrought conviction out of his doubt, purpose out of his uncertainty. And now he had lost her. Oh God! The realization suddenly hit him. He was going to find her again in two days. All at once Martin could feel his hands, cold and clammy about the icon. The gallows was out there, less than two hundred paces from where he stood. Why did the rope and the flash of eternity terrify him when he would be seeing Madeleine again?

Through the sleeve of his uniform, Martin could feel the warmth of de Lorimier's hand on his arm. The other man took the icon gently from his hand and placed it on the shelf beside a jar of pickled beets brought by Eugenie de Lorimier. "Don't be afraid Martin. We go to a better place. Now make your peace with God. Faith will carry us both beyond this valley of sorrow. Let us kneel and pray."

They went to their knees together. de Lorimier's eyes were closed and he was moving his lips, praying for strength for himself and for the errant prodigal beside him. Martin talked to Madeleine because there was no one else. God was still an idea; the icon was still pewter, and he was crying softly because he didn't want to die.

Rome, July 14, 1234

"It must be done, now," the old man said to himself.

"You spoke, your Holiness," replied the black-robed figure sitting at the small table.

"Nothing, Vittorio," Ugolino answered. "Just an old man's musings. It's something I just thought of . . . of no importance."

Father Vittorio Arguenti accepted the comment as he did most things, with the disinterest of the powerless. He fell back to his transcribing. Ugolino stared at his secretary's bowed head for a moment. He liked Vittorio well enough, and in a way, respected his unimaginative efficiency. He was not so sure of the man's loyalty. There was a yielding quality about the eyes, something akin to that of Honorius whom he had succeeded as Pope seven years earlier. Vittorio had been Honorius' secretary, too.

Frowning slightly, Ugolino picked up the nine depositions from the desk. He knew most of the authors personally, and believed beyond doubt their accounts attesting to the earthly sanctity of Dominic. As Pope Gregory IX, he had used them to justify the Papal Bull he had issued the day previously, officially proclaiming the devout friar a saint of the Catholic Church. Ignoring the pain in his arthritic knees, he walked to the window and stood, hands clasped behind his back. For a long time, the pale, watery eyes looked beyond the noise of Rome, to Bologna, and he thought about Dominic, Reginald, and what he had copied and kept to himself these past thirteen years. Its puzzle remained locked in his mind . . . Significance, secrecy, and meaning, all intertwined, wanting a key.

As he stood there unmoving, the young man's mind in an old man's body went over the reasoning which always led him to the same conclusion. This day would be no different, except now it was the time for him to let go. The names were clearly important. Dominic and Reginald were scarcely given to frivolities. If Reginald had written them, and Dominic had kept them for so long, they had to hold considerable significance for both of them. One thing, however, was puzzling. Despite their close kinship, Dominic and Reginald had actually spent little time together. Really, only in Rome that time Reginald was ill. This seemed to discount the notion that the names called out common acquaintances or experiences. Moreover, he was as well read as either of them, and the names were totally unfamiliar to him. Ugolino always came back to the one commonality shared by both.

Visitations! And from the same heavenly figure. The words could be related to these visions. A message from Mary? But what and why? It was all conjecture, and at that point, Ugolino always ended his analysis.

He watched the pigeons circling, landing, pecking at the ground and quarrelling with an intensity that Ugolino envied.

Strange, he thought, that we creatures made in God's image should have so many doubts.

His mind was still on the names. Thirteen years ago, he had consigned them to a proper haven. Render unto Caesar . . .

If they were linked spiritually with Reginald as he still believed, then they would re-appear in time through the grace of Reginald, himself, a man who felt that his earthly work for God had been too fleeting to be of any consequence.

But then he, Ugolino, man of God, had yielded to the temporal possibilities suggested by Reginald's names. His own copy, made in that cell so long ago with Rodolph on his knees in front of him, was, to quote one of his favourite phrases, "just in case." Now, thirteen years later, with the weight of the Papacy heavy on his shoulders, he faced reality. He knew that Reginald's names would not help him in his struggle with the Romans, or would protect the power of the Papacy itself against the clever and ambitious Holy Roman Emperor, Frederick II. Other enemies within his own ranks waited like carrion birds to claim him. Ugolino did not fear death. It waited on the edge of each coming season, collecting its harvest according to divine decree. He only hoped he would be given enough time to resolve his conflicts with the Romans, and most of all, Frederick.

Ugolino removed the piece of vellum from between the pages of his personal copy of St. Augustine's Confessions. His script leapt up at him. Three rows. Two words each in the first, and third rows. Names. Three names. Well, he thought they were names. The second was a single word only. He turned the vellum over in his hands as he pondered its future. Though there seemed to be three options, Ugolino's strong faith and practical instincts told him that there was but one. Yes, it was time.

The list of names could not be consigned to the flames. If Reginald and Dominic had not destroyed them, then neither could he. He was certain of that. It was potentially too volatile to be assigned as a holy relic, open to public scrutiny, or worse, private manipulation. Ugolino was equally convinced that its past should not be shared. Of course, the names may be meaningless. But in the papal turmoil that he was sure would follow upon his death, Ugolino could not risk jeopardizing the Order he loved. There were still far too many who resented the Dominicans, and the new spiritualism that they and the Franciscans represented. The mystery of the list, hidden for years by two saintly friars, had the potential for enormous misuse. Significance could be construed in infinite variety. The old cardinal, his political instincts honed over fifty years of dealing with men doing God's work, winced at the thought.

No! Like the original list, which had found its place with Reginald, Ugolino's copy belonged with Dominic, for the future to reveal. Quickly Ugolino pressed the parchment between the pages of Rodolph's deposition, and turned to his secretary.

"Vittorio. The depositions are finished. I have no further use for them. Take them to the library. Seal them carefully for, in law, no eye may behold them for many years. Time will honour Blessed Dominic's sanctity and make it more real among doubters."

He paused and joined his secretary's gaze outside the window.

"Yes, your Holiness," replied Vittorio. "When the rain stops?" He smiled questioningly.

Ugolino noticed for the first time that it was raining heavily. He could see the pigeons huddled together, warm and dry, under the stone colonnade that bordered the courtyard. Just then, two priests came forth, scurrying through puddles like black mice, robes held high in a futile defence against the rain. Ugolino shook his head, shrugged an inner grin, and turned his attention to another riddle that could not be assigned to the future. The Romans and Frederick. How could he utilize them both to strengthen the power of the Papacy?

~ ~ ~

An hour later, Vittorio Arguenti carefully created the last letter of script and leaned back to admire his work. He was proud of his artistry, the closest in Rome to the beautifully elegant Caroline script. Nothing like the bastardized styles that foreigners were bringing to Rome with increasing frequency. He rose, straightened his robe and glanced about the room. It was too untidy. Too disharmonious. Not like when Honorius was Pope. He spent the next few minutes fussing about the sparsely furnished room, arranging proper order and form before returning to his desk. When he was finished there, it showed no sign of former use, save for the pile of depositions. Muttering, he picked them up, and after closing the door softly behind him, entered the courtyard.

The leaden sky was still heavy with the smell of rain as he made his way across the loosely cobbled square. He would have paid more attention to the precarious footing had he not been so intent on sidestepping the puddles, raising his legs fastidiously like a huge black stork. Without warning, his foot gave way on a loose stone, and with a cry he fell headlong, the depositions flying out in front of him to lay strewn across the glistening stones. Muttering to himself, and appalled at the sight of his soiled surplice, he bent to retrieve the depositions when he noticed with horror that a page had torn itself loose to rest on the watery edge of a concave cobblestone. Then he saw the damage. No matter that the script was ugly and written by no artist. Probably a Dominican. Maybe one of those wretched fanatics who, even now, were preaching sedition in Germany, and who would turn the Christian world into a earthly paradise for paupers.

Vittorio scarcely glanced at the writing, for already tears of guilt and mortification were welling in the ingenuous brown eyes. The wet, slimy pigeon dung that clung to the paper was more than sacrilegious. It was a heinous act of defilement. The hand of the Evil One. Vittorio glanced about nervously, picked up the scattered papers, and then began running blindly, heedless of the mud that leapt up to despoil him.

Thankfully, the small scriptorium that adjoined the library was deserted. By the abundant, diffused light even on this gloomy afternoon, Vittorio could see that the damage was far worse than he first thought. The vile slime had partially defiled a whole line of script. What was he to do? This desecration could not be consigned among the holy codices in the library. Yet, omission or destruction of a companion in evidence to the sacred work of canonization was equally unacceptable, even if it was Dominican. His hands trembling, Vittorio sank to his knees and sought guidance.

The inspiration came to him in divine testimony. If thine eye offend thee . . .

He rose and looked about him to the desks, lecterns, inkhorns, fine quills, pumice stone, chalk, rulers, and . . . knives. He selected the sharpest, and, taking a ruler to guide his hand, carefully severed the defilement, including a whole line of script. A little work with the pumice stone, and the re-sized parchment showed no sign of violation. Vittorio looked guiltily at the dung-covered, written line staring back at him from the floor of the scriptorium.

His thoughts raced ahead of him encouragingly. God would understand. The reference wasn't important. It was the last, and therefore the least significant entry. Excreta did not belong with the works of divinity. It was surely just a minor association with some trouble-making Dominican. The last thought made him feel better. Now almost jaunty, he replaced the page in the deposition. He believed it fell from the testimony of a deceased friar named Rodolph. Two lines now instead of three. He then sealed the depositions, and placed them in the private spaces in the back of the library, beside those belonging to the beggar from Assisi. Gregory had canonized him, too. "Disturbers, fanatics," he muttered. "They belong together."

Outside in the courtyard, he dropped the foul evidence of his deed into a puddle. His small foot ground it to a soggy pulp.

CHAPTER XI

The Vatican, October 4, 1838

Some called the Sala Regia the inner sanctum of the Vatican. Beyond it were the Sistine and Pauline Chapels and one of the two private chapels reserved for his Holiness himself. This morning, however, Cardinal Luigi Lambruschini scarcely noticed its magnificence. Usually he lingered as long as possible before the mounted paintings, pausing longest before the passion and power of the Madonna painted by the incomparable Dominican, Fra Angelico, or the intricacy and colour of Vasari's frescoes. This morning he had been privileged to see what few others had ever seen. Tears had come to his eyes as he had watched his Holiness bless the wax medallions made by the Cistercian monks of the Basilica of the Holy Cross in Jerusalem. They would be distributed to the faithful, and blessed was the man who received one, for their like would not be seen again until another Agnus Dei ceremony came to pass.

Yes, he was a favoured man. Everywhere he turned in this wonderful place, he was touched by the hand of the masters. The majesty of Raphael and Michelangelo. The vision of Bernini, the brilliance of Botticelli and Roselli. As he emerged into the bright autumn sunlight and began walking to the Apostolic Palace he could see ahead and to his left several large sculptures soon to be housed in the almost completed Gregorian Pagan Museum. He recognized two of his favourites. The Apollo Belvedere, a second century sculpture depicting the ultimate beauty of the male form, and the 2,000 year old sculpture of Laocoon dying with his sons in the coils of serpents. He wrapped his arms about himself as he did when pleased and breathed deeply. This was a place where Christianity and antiquity merged to form a visual earthly paradise for lucky ones like himself. He loved the Vatican, and relished its aura as much as he did the daunting challenge of trying to further God's work among men.

Out of the corner of his eye, Lambruschini saw Alphonse Battiste. The fat priest was obviously in a hurry, moving about as gracefully as a grounded pelican. Lambruschini quickened his pace. The priesthood was sometimes a refuge for the ungodly: men of the cloth who were bent on designs of their own that had little to do with the good Shepherd. Lambruschini had almost broken into a run when he heard the thin wheedling voice.

"Eminence. Wait."

Grimacing with resignation, Lambruschini stopped and waited, his back to Battiste in cool contempt. He could hear the man approaching wheezing noisily, and then felt – no, smelled – the presence beside him. Battiste's forehead was glistening and he was already waving something at him. It was a letter.

"Your Eminence, I am glad I was able to reach you so soon. Cardinal Gamberini felt that you should receive this personally."

Battiste leered as he passed the envelope to Lambruschini who took it, noting that it had already been opened.

"The address, Eminence, will explain. As you can see it is addressed to the Papal Secretary of State. The writer apparently had no knowledge of the recent division of our Offices."

The piggy eyes never leaving Lambruschini's face, Battiste went on expansively. "We . . . His Eminence found the contents fascinating. If you will forgive my curiosity, Eminence. But was not your Office pursuing the matter of a possible visitation in Scandinavia. A former colleague at Santa Sabina. Father Bernard Blake . . ."

Lambruschini was annoyed, but let nothing show behind the façade that he employed so often since he had come to the Vatican.

"Thank you, Father. But I cannot discuss what I do not know." He smiled benignly. "You know what is in this envelope. I don't, yet. My best wishes to his Eminence, and to you of course." He extended his hand, and hoped that his eyes sufficiently chastised Battiste.

There was a pause. No head bowed to the ring, and Lambruschini was surprised to see Battiste meeting his gaze. He looked bigger, more imposing somehow, and there was a glint in the small eyes that he had not seen before.

"No, Eminence. Not quite yet. I am a simple man, humble and plain of body. But do not be misled. I am neither stupid nor foolish. I have something to say to you, Eminence. To refuse, or ignore me will be to imperil yourself." He shrugged his shoulders and waited.

Lambruschini was stunned. Battiste's voice was hard. The wheedling quality was gone, replaced by a resoluteness that made him wary. He stood for a couple of seconds in indecision before replying. "You sound serious, Father. I am intrigued enough to humour you. What is it you wish me to do?"

"Read the letter, Eminence. Here with me, and then listen to what I have to say. The decision then will be yours alone."

They walked to one of the many benches in the nearby gardens. Battiste sat with his hands across his stomach and his eyes closed against the sun as Lambruschini read. His voice broke the silence the instant the Cardinal put down the paper.

"Very interesting, Eminence, don't you think? A Protestant girl found dead by her own hand, or by that of another. Who knows? With a miraculous medal about her neck. Apparently spoken to by Our Holy Mother in words understandable to Catholics yet incomprehensible to her kind. The writer is convinced of this girl's extraordinarily sanctified presence. Puzzling, I should say."

Lambruschini's mind was spinning. There was so much that Bernard had not told him. He kept his voice level. "Hardly puzzling, Father. Interesting, even fascinating, but I do not see how it concerns me. Do you want an investigation?"

"You continue to underestimate me, Eminence. Now listen well." His voice was sharp with impatience. "I possess irrevocable proof. Proof I will use unhesitatingly if need be, that Father Bernard Blake was in Bergen at the time of these incidents, dressed not as a Dominican priest, but as a man of the world. The visitor Signor Hanson referred to. He was from Marseilles and played the flute. Bernard Blake is proficient in languages. He was born in Marseilles and he too plays the flute. You forget, Eminence. I know this man from Santa Sabina. I know what he is."

Battiste produced two letters and thrust them at Lambruschini. "Written by somebody who has been near him since he left Rome. Full of details. Damaging details."

Reading Lambruschini's thoughts, he added quickly. "It's not for you know the details of my knowledge. That is unless you don't believe me and want to test my intent."

"I still fail to see—" Lambruschini began, parrying for time.

"I am talking about a scandal, Eminence. Many of them hate you in this place." He paused for a moment "It is clear you have little respect for me. But do not deceive yourself. My persuasive powers are not wanting. Did you know that I preach very well? It was said in Santa Sabina that I was better than Rivarola, but more dangerous. I trust you understand me, Eminence. I have evidence that a Catholic priest in disguise was in the company of a young Protestant girl who was later found dead with a Catholic medal about her neck. This priest was under your orders and is therefore your responsibility. He has vanished and the Norwegian police are searching for the man who visited Olaf Hanson. Not all think he is at the bottom of the fjord. Many are crying 'murder.' We know all about this mystery priest, don't we, Eminence? Cardinal Agostini and the others will also be very interested. Yes, Eminence, I can and will bring you down over this."

"What do you want?" Lambruschini muttered thickly.

"Not you, Eminence. Oh, no, I do not want you. I want Bernard Blake."

Even as he paused for effect, Battiste felt the heaviness in his heart. It was the sadness and the anger which were fuelling his bravery before this most powerful of men. He had been so distraught these last few weeks. No word from Ignatius. His letters, faithful, full of love and promise had stopped suddenly and without warning. Just that one from Bergen. Then nothing. Olaf Hanson's reference to the missing lover at the bottom of the fjord should not have worried him. But it did. He knew deep down that his Ignatius was gone from him forever. Bernard had returned from Norway, but Ignatius had not, and there was a dead man in Bergen. Bernard Blake must pay.

"It's quite simple, Eminence. Your future or Bernard Blake's. I know him for what he is and my heart and body bear the scars of his evil. I want him where he can do no harm. Send him from the Vatican, far away to a place where he will labour long and hard in anonymity. I'm sure you can find such a place. Or by all that you revere in heaven, or hell for that matter, your future at the Vatican is as precarious as yonder leaves. I promise as much before God, our Judge."

Battiste bent to kiss the ring.

"My solicitations, Eminence. May God and His Blessed Mother be with you. Always."

Then he was gone, waddling off back towards St. Peter's. Lambruschini watched him until he had disappeared, and then made his way thoughtfully to his own offices in the Apostolic Palace.

Rome, October 5, 1838

She lay back in the bed, her long blonde hair heavy on her breasts. The bed was wide and finely quilted. The room itself was plain. Just the big bed. Two pictures of running deer on the walls, and a washbasin on a small table. There were no windows in the room, but a pair of drapes on one wall hinted of something beyond them. The girl scratched at her stockinged leg, yawned once, and after rearranging her hair settled back on the pillows.

She heard the knock, and then he was in the room. The girl's smile was matched by an inner feeling of satisfaction. At least this one was good looking. Dark hair, A little pale, but fine featured, and, according to her trained eye, of good breeding. He looked nervous as he approached the bed. Probably his first time.

Bernard Blake's mouth was dry. He had searched a long time for a girl who reminded him of Signy. This girl was the closest. Tall, blonde, and with a look of innocence. Now that he could see her closely, he realized she was not nearly as beautiful. There was a hardness about the mouth and eyes, but she was slim and her mouth was full-lipped. God, it was difficult. Where was the thrill in his loins? Why was there no longing? He had to be sure. The lingering doubt that had tormented him this last month had to be tested. He took off his coat and trousers and approached the bed.

~ ~ ~

It was well after two o'clock in the morning when Bernard Blake awoke from a fitful sleep. He was in his hotel room and he could smell the bitter odour of vomit. His head was throbbing so hard he wanted to run away into the darkness. He sat up in the bed and rubbed his eyes. Everything was wrong. The vile females continued to mock him. That girl in that hellhole of a place had looked like Signy but she had repelled him. Just like the rest of them. What was happening? Pain always. A destiny that withered on an impotent vine. No disciples. No future, and now this incessant feeling of longing. He had always listened to the soft one, had had certainty defined for him by forces that came to him in the quiet places when he had called upon them. He forced himself to think, to face the question that had been tormenting him since Bergen.

Signy had done what no other female could do. If she was an aberration, then how could it be explained? If she wasn't, then what did it all mean? Bernard closed his eyes and tried to block out the pain that threatened his sanity.

It was clear he could not go on like this. Purposelessness had replaced the certainty that had formerly guided his actions. Signy was the only variable that seemed to make a difference. She had made him happy. With her, there had been no pain. His destiny dissolved to nothingness, and in its place came a wild joy, and then fulfilment. What was here in Rome? Lambruschini was talking about intensive archival work and a future for him as a multilingual researcher. A glorified clerk. A lackey running errands, proffering assistance to others who took it as their due. He, Bernard Blake, the ablest of them all, reduced to a puppet on a string. Lambruschini was a nearsighted buffoon. There was even talk about Lambruschini's future at the Vatican. But without him, incompetent minion though he was, Bernard knew he was lost. They were all idiots. All of them. The despairing thoughts tumbled around in his mind until he wanted to cry out. He looked at his stained shirt, and recalled the horror of being sick on that girl's bed. She had suffocated him. He was sweating, and the moans of pain would not stay inside him.

Signy's face swam towards him, and he reached out for her. But she was gone.

He sat up in the bed, his senses suddenly clear. Could it be that simple? That wonderful? His destiny was with that girl, not away from her. He had been preserved for one woman by being repelled by all others. Why? Could it be associated with the visions? He had dismissed them as fanciful illusions, but he also recalled Signy's unwitting association of her Frigga with the image of the Virgin Mary. Coincidence? Possibly. He fingered the miraculous medal about his neck, and relived his strange meeting with the music teacher. Could that be what was bothering Olaf Hanson? The old cripple believed her, was obsessed by her chosen status, and wanted her for himself. It all made sense. Signy was his destiny. It had to be. There was no other answer. He had faced his truth and had abandoned it in Bergen. But it was not too late. He would go to her. Renounce the priesthood. Damn them all. His calling was of a higher nature. He felt invigorated. Quickly he cleansed his body and after putting on the white robe quietly left the room, hidden from curious eyes by the solitude of the early morning darkness.

The Vatican, October 7, 1838

From where he sat at the marble table tucked away in the Vatican Gardens, Bernard could hear the gentle rippling of water over stones. He counted the gold coins carefully before placing them in a leather pouch around his neck. Enough for him – them – to live comfortably for a year, maybe more. Yes, he was very glad he had been careful with his father's money over the years. He began walking unhurriedly along the fine gravel path which wound between shrubs and late-blooming flowers towards the Apostolic Palace, and the opulent room that the hypocritical Lambruschini referred to as his humble office.

One more encounter with this man who had so cruelly misled him, and then he would leave this shallow petty place forever. Everything was in readiness. Tomorrow he would be gone, vanished as the spring snow, leaving only the white robe of slavery as a mocking testimony to his renouncement. Lambruschini had summoned him today, probably to assign him another menial task fit only for fools and servile vassals. He would have ignored the directive except that he wanted one last confrontation with this bumbling procrastinator whose cautious ineptitude had stayed his hand while sending him unwittingly on the road to his destiny. He only hoped the pain in his head would allow him sufficient scornful vehemence.

~ ~ ~

The two men faced each other coolly across the oaken desk. If Lambruschini had noticed that Bernard Blake had not kissed his ring he gave no indication. For his part, Bernard was aware of the suspicion in the older man's eyes. He seethed with impatience, anticipating the battle.

Lambruschini was turning something over in his hands, and when he spoke his calm tone held a hint of menace.

"Father, I called you here today because I want to be sure about this girl in Bergen. As I understand it, you met and spoke with her twice, and found her vague, vacuous and entirely unreliable as a source of interest to Mother Church?"

Bernard's eyes flashed. His words were defiant. "I told you it was a waste of time. I wanted to go to Saxony. The choice was yours."

Lambruschini appeared unruffled. "You met the music teacher too. Is that correct?"

"A crippled idiot. A dreamer. He knows nothing."

"Then tell me, Father, how you explain this most interesting new development."

He waved the letter in the air. "This letter from the music teacher arrived recently. In it, Herr Hanson gives a most persuasive argument for the authenticity of this girl's vision. He also mentions a visitor who matches your description, but makes no mention of a priest. In fact, he deplored the fact that his original newspaper article did not excite the interests of the Church."

He leaned back in his chair. "Now, I find that very interesting, Father. Very interesting indeed."

Bernard returned his gaze evenly. He kept his voice challenging. "I did what I thought was best. The interests of truth had to be well served. As for what you think, it matters not a whit. I am weary of your crude interrogation. I have better things to do. Much better."

He rose to leave.

"Remain seated if you please, Father. There is more. The vision apparently spoke to this girl, a fact you either failed to discover, or if you did, decided on your own behest to conceal it from me."

"Another irrelevancy. Words may have been implied. They were never uttered. You bore me with your crude innuendo."

Lambruschini went on as if Bernard had not spoken. "According to Herr Hanson, the vision said words reminiscent of the Angel Gabriel at the Annunciation. He believes the girl misunderstood the words, and actually thought that the vision whom she assumed was the Goddess Frigga was telling her about another son, a brother of the mythological Balder."

Bernard's heart beat faster. It was all so real. He could hear Signy talking. It was as though Lambruschini was bringing her to him. But he stifled a yawn, and kept the contempt in his voice. "This is sounding more ludicrous by the minute. If you will excuse me."

"Stay." The words were sharp and biting. "Herr Hanson believes that the vision said, 'Blessed is the fruit of thy womb.' If it is as he says, the implications are profound, Father." He fingered the folds of his robe. "I find it very strange that you found none of this."

He continued plucking at his sleeve. "There can be but three explanations. One. Herr Hanson is demented and has fabricated a wild story. Two. You are completely inept in such investigative matters. Three. You are a liar who has knowingly concealed important information. Which is it, Father?"

Bernard could scarcely contain himself. This was beyond his wildest dreams. The idiot opposite him was reaffirming his destiny. She had tried to tell him but he had been disinterested. The thought of combat vanished in his delight. Signy was chosen. Just as he was. The fruit of thy womb.

He tried to be calm and conciliatory, "Eminence, I honestly believe that Herr Hanson possesses too fanciful an imagination. He rambles on so, and is full of accounts of mediaeval saints appearing to him in the night, promising him greatness. I believe he is probably obsessed with this girl, who some might say is quite comely."

A thrill course over his body at the thought of her.

"Should I be you, Eminence I would ignore Herr Hanson's ramblings. There is no harm done. Now I must go. I have a long day's archival work ahead of me."

He was almost at the door, having decided on a last gesture of defiance in ignoring the ring, when Lambruschini spoke again. The words froze him in his tracks.

"No, Father. You are wrong. There is harm done. Much harm which we cannot ignore, and since it concerns both of us, I suggest you forget whatever it is that you are trying to achieve through churlishness and sit down."

Bernard looked angry but the look in Lambruschini's eyes broached no argument. He took his place again and waited. Lambruschini continued, "Yes, Father we might be able to forget this whole affair were it not for two unpleasant details."

Bernard's eyebrows raised.

"First, Father, you were observed in Bergen. Alphonse Battiste has proof, and is prepared to use it against both of us."

Bernard cut in. "Battiste hates me bitterly. He is a petty vindictive man without courage or faith. Surely whatever proof he might have about my actions cannot be so damaging. I realize you have enemies, Eminence. But this is too flimsy. We could sustain it, I am sure."

"It is possible, but I must warn you, Father. We are on dangerous ground here." Lambruschini sounded worried. "Petty and vindictive as he may be, Battiste is also clever and ambitious. You may find this strange, Father, but this most unappealing of men has the ear of several of my enemies within this place. He could be dangerous, whereas you, Father, have either been too proud or too indifferent to cultivate useful friends. You have only me."

"And that might not be enough?" *I understand you fully, Eminence.* "I was under the impression, mistakenly it now seems, that your position here was more impregnable. Certainly secure enough to withstand a minor incident such as this."

"If we speak solely about your clandestine actions in Bergen, yes. I believe we could extricate ourselves without undue damage." He sighed and looked at the ceiling. "There is more, Father. Something you have not told me. Something that jeopardizes both our futures."

"I don't understand, Eminence."

He sounds genuinely surprised thought Lambruschini. *We'll soon see.*

"The girl, Father. The girl who saw the visions. The one you spoke to twice."

"Yes, what of her."

"She is dead."

Bernard's eyes widened. A sickening wave jolted his insides.

"She's dead?" he whispered.

"By her own hand, apparently, although Herr Hanson himself isn't convinced, and neither is the local constabulary. Her body was found on the rocks at low tide."

Lambruschini paused for a second or two looking hard at Bernard's face before continuing, "She had a miraculous medal about her neck."

Bernard instinctively felt at his collar. Unseeingly, he looked about him. The room was suddenly stifling. He had to get out. He couldn't move. It was as though he were rooted on the spot. He was conscious of Lambruschini's voice. "And that, Father, is what makes it very difficult for us. A girl dead, a priest there but not there. A vengeful father, a missing body. A miraculous medal. And something else I have not told you. Your Battiste also knows of all this, and vows to use it against us. As I have already said, I don't think you have told me everything, Father. But that is of little consequence now."

He handed Olaf's letter to Bernard. "Read it, Father, and decide for yourself."

Numbly, Bernard took the paper. The words blurred before him, and for five minutes he passed his eyes over every line, and read nothing.

He looked up at Lambruschini, who was watching him carefully. It was the cardinal who spoke. "Are you wearing your miraculous medal, Father? Show it to me." Then, reading Bernard's eyes, he made little attempt to keep the mockery out of his voice. "I thought not."

Bernard seemed not to have heard. He was staring vacantly at the wall opposite. "It doesn't matter now. I must go. There is nothing that can be done. Nothing anybody can do. It is finished."

He got to his feet, woodenly as if his legs were paralyzed, and ignoring Lambruschini, left the room.

The Cardinal looked at the door, and then murmured to himself. "Yes, Father Blake. It is indeed finished."

Then picking up pen and paper he began to write.

~ ~ ~

He didn't know where to go, or what to do, so he just walked. Aimless steps that took him slow miles away from naves and spires and back again until he stood in the Belvedere Courtyard that led to the museums and the archives. There had been no focus to the images seething in his mind. Memories and hopes blurring with visions of death and despair. The realities of yesterday blotted out by the certainty of no tomorrow. The ache was unbearable. He had never known the sorrow of loss. Now as he walked towards the building that housed the archives, his body ached for Signy, and his soul lamented the loss of his destiny. He had bound his Signy to him in a love so sweet, he thought it an aberration. He had turned away from her leaving the fruit in the womb, where it perished. Instead of reshaping the world in his own image through a child conceived of divine ordination, he was reduced to nothing. No present. No future. He could not stay here. He would go to his cave so far away, and after he had talked to the images who always listened sympathetically, he would swallow the pills. The two pains would go away, then. The one in his head and the other in his heart. Tiredly he entered the archives and made his way to the small working room and the drawer where he kept the pills.

The Secret Archives in the Vatican housed the most comprehensive manuscript collection in the world. No one knew its exact compilation, but it was well known that ancient manuscripts, some dating back to early antiquity lay everywhere in the labyrinthine cells and vaults which seemed to go on forever deep within the ground. Paulo Nunzatti had been the Archivist for over twenty years, and though he had grown old and fat, no one ever thought of replacing him, for who could replicate his prodigious memory? His knowledge of the collections was so formidable that it was said that he could put his hand on any document belonging to any year in any century. It was true, and Nunzatti liked it that way. He had resisted suggestions that the Archives be modernized and made more readily available to Church scholars. So he screened all visitors and made sure that they saw only what he wished them to see.

When he had been told personally by Cardinal Lambruschini to accord the young Dominican the utmost of cooperation, he had been resentful. That is until he found out that the young priest was uninquisitive and better yet, prone to long silences. Then he discovered that this Father Blake had an astounding facility with languages. His own ability with Latin, classical Greek and mediaeval French was quite good, but later manuscripts in Spanish, Portuguese and English sometimes made it difficult for him to assign true value. He could not ask for help, for then he might be required to admit an inadequacy – or worse yet, to take on an assistant. Father Blake had changed all that. He helped with translations, and while he could not bring himself to admitting a liking for the strange Dominican, he did feel a sort of kinship. After all, it wasn't as if they were going to be together permanently. Lambruschini had said that the Dominican's archival assignment would last only as long as the classification process, which, he had to admit to himself, might be some time yet judging by the amount of material he had acquired from far-flung monasteries. Some excellent manuscripts, and yes, he had been wise to insist that he see all of them and make the decision as to where they would be located. He had expected more opposition from the Dominican who, on the contrary, had seemed disinterested as to what happened to the priceless treasures of Mother Church he had brought here to add still more to the wonderful storehouse of knowledge that was his, Paulo Nunzatti's, domain.

Like this plan, for example, that had come with the Dominican from Bologna. He had known what it was immediately. The plan of the priory the early Dominicans were going to build in Bologna. The one which Dominic had disapproved of. But he had to be sure, and now that he was, it needed to be consigned to its proper place. Usually he had Father Blake first classify the material he brought, reserving for himself the option of deciding on its disposition, and though Father Blake had sometimes accompanied him to the vaults, Nunzatti always made sure that it was he alone who concealed it in its proper folder or unbound volume or parchment rack. But since this priceless plan belonged with the St. Dominic codices in the back vaults, it presented a problem. Nunzatti shrugged his shoulders as he approached Bernard Blake's working cell. If the Dominican was here working, he would ask him at once. There was no use prolonging matters. This document had to be properly filed, which meant he had to trust Father Blake.

Bernard didn't hear Nunzatti enter the room. He looked up startled to see the fat priest looming over him, a wrinkled white face sitting on top of a shapeless black expanse.

"Father Blake. It is fortunate that I find you here." Nunzatti's voice was high-pitched and nasal as if he had a bad head cold.

Without waiting for Bernard to reply, he went on leaning over the younger man confidentially, and dropping his voice to a whisper. "A favour, Father Blake. I ask a favour." He grinned conspiratorially. "A rewarding one for you, I might add."

Blake was silent. It was as if he wasn't listening.

"The records of your Order's saintly founder, Father. His and those of St. Francis occupy the top level of the recess I have classified as Mendicant XIII."

He went on obviously heedless of the other man's disinterest. "This plan you brought from Bologna. I won't tell what it is, but it belongs with St. Dominic." Nunzatti hesitated before blurting out the words. "I want you to take it there and consign it properly."

A look of puzzlement, then annoyance crossed Bernard Blake's face. What was the fat fool saying to him? Did he expect him to descend into that black pit where age was sacred and trivia divine. The whole place was suffocating him. He just wanted to leave. Go to another place. To another blackness, or to Signy. He turned to face Nunzatti, the scornful words of refusal hanging on his lips.

They were never uttered. His eyes turned cunning as the thought rippled through his mind. He scarcely heard Nunzatti's rambling explanation. He just wished his bladder were fuller.

"In sure truth, Father, I have not been to that recess for some time now." He patted his stomach. "A long time ago when I was thin I arranged the codices in proper form, and since then no other eyes have rested on them, not even my own. The space is small, Father, and I am now unable to gain access to them. Not that it matters, for they are safe, hidden from unworthy eyes."

He smiled. "And I still remain their guardian and protector. But you, Father, can easily traverse the space where they lie. The second folder from the bottom. It's leather-bound, and black. You will note that it contains references to the various priories established by St. Dominic. It rests just above the sealed depositions to St. Dominic's canonization. Of course you understand, Father. These holy papers are not to be touched."

Nunzatti didn't add that he was fairly certain that no one save himself and now this Dominican knew of their existence. The warning was therefore necessary.

He handed the plan to Bernard. "Place this plan in that folder, and return it to its proper place. I have lit the area for you, and will go with you to the space where I cannot enter and wait for you."

Bernard's mind was full of his visions. The final act of defilement. To urinate on the testimonies to sainthood would be the ultimate insult to the ignorant idol worshippers who had misled him while holding him in bondage for over six years. It was a delicious thought, and despite the pain in his head and the ache deep inside him, he smiled.

"I know the place, Father Nunzatti. You have shown it to me on one occasion and on several more have alluded to what was contained therein. But, Father, I will go alone. Or would you prefer me to tell someone else who will do your bidding in your presence?" He looked at Nunzatti guilelessly.

Nunzatti sighed. He shouldn't have asked. The Dominican was more astute than he had thought. He was trapped and he knew it."

"As you will, Father. I shall await your prompt return, and say prayers of thanks for your generosity and understanding." He licked his lips. If Blake took longer than five minutes he would come for him.

Bernard merely nodded, and taking the yellowed paper, made his way through the heavy wooden door which led to the staircase and to the long dimly lit dungeons where centuries of knowledge hid.

Once into the cavernous rows of shelves, stacks, recesses and vaults, Bernard quickened his steps. Nunzatti wouldn't wait long before coming after him. He was certain of that. It was dark and the illumination was poor, except directly under the yellowish glow of the oil lanterns. By the time he reached the section where Nunzatti kept the pre-Reformation manuscripts, Bernard was bending low to the ground, and somewhere above him he could hear the dripping of water. A solitary lamp lit the entrance to the recess marked "Mendicant XIII," and Bernard squeezed himself through the narrow space. A stone shelf set just above the level of his eyes was stacked tightly with assorted bound volumes, folders, and papers. With some difficulty, he removed the two bottom volumes, and without really knowing why, placed the priory plan where Nunzatti said it belonged in the black leather folder, and replaced it on top of the stack. He then turned his attention to the thicker, more elaborately bound folder. It was sealed with a reddish material that had barely cracked during its six-hundred-year repose. He noted Gregory's imprint before breaking the seal open along the entire length of the folder. Quickly he rifled through the depositions, seeking a suitable candidate for desecration. The heavy black printing of the name, Rodolph caught his eye in the gloom, and then he saw the piece of paper fall to the ground. Even in the poor light, he could make out the black writing, and with one hand already reaching beneath his robe, he bent to retrieve it.

His penis was out now and trained directly on the Rodolph deposition.

Nothing happened. The urine dried up in his bladder. His face blanched and he stumbled from the recess to the lighted lantern affixed to the stone wall at shoulder height just beyond the entrance. Trembling, he held the piece of vellum to the flickering light and read the words. The top line identified its age and origin. "St. Nicholas of the Vineyard, Bologna, August 19, 1221." Written below it were two more lines of the same writing. Not full lines, more like words, or names.

In the distance Bernard heard footsteps, slow, plodding, but becoming unmistakably closer. He looked about for a moment in indecision, and after closing the canonization depositions, quickly re-entered the recess and hurriedly replaced the volume with the broken seal facing inwards, on top of the one containing the priory plan. Then stuffing the piece of vellum beneath his stockings turned to meet the approaching footsteps.

The voice was breathless, and loud in its echo. "You are finished, Father. Good. We shall speak of this to no one, and I will take you to where I keep a copy of a letter written by St. Augustine before he was converted. You may read it. Alone if you like." He chuckled knowingly. "We scholars and keepers of antiquity share many obscure joys. Do we not?"

Bernard had heard not a word. He was gone long before Nunzatti had stopped speaking, striding, half trotting, and finally running into the bright sunlight to a bench in the gardens among the trees.

~ ~ ~

His hands were still shaking as he removed the piece of vellum from the stocking. It was already disintegrating from the careless handling, and flakes of yellow particles spilled onto the ground below the bench. The two lines of writing below the top inscription were browner, more faded, but unmistakably clear. Unmistakable and almost six hundred years old.

"Signy Vigeland," and below it, a single other word, "Lamar." Bernard's eyes locked onto Signy's name as his thoughts tried to arrange meaning from chaos. How? What? Why? Signy's name, reappearing on a piece of paper written by who knows, and found with depositions attesting to the sanctity of St. Dominic. It had to hold some significance. His eyes scanned the paper again. "August, 1221. Bologna." Dominic had died in Bologna in 1221, and he was sure it was August. The sixth, if his memory for feast days was correct. The names then had been written soon after Dominic's death. But by whom, and how had they found their way to the depositions? Clearly, somebody had thought they were important.

Bernard allowed the realization to come to him, savouring it as revelation, acknowledging it both in faith and reason as divine intervention. The eccentric Dominic had been canonized, not only because of his blatant beggar's life. He was also prone to visions which the Church readily accepted as reality. And the figure he had seen most often was the Madonna. The music teacher had believed that Signy, too, had had the same experience even though she hadn't known it. Here was proof positive, not only of Signy's chosen status, but also its origin and direction. Not only Signy, but himself as well, for had he not been preserved just for her? The perfection that had marked his life had had but one aberration, and now he knew why.

His thoughts raced on. Repelled by females. But drawn to one. It was all so simple. Clearly he was to father the new Messiah. The past images and voices were messages sent by God to lead him to his destiny. But evil forces were also afoot. They had misled him as they had Christ in the desert. He had listened to the false ones, and they had taken Signy away from him before he could fulfil his destiny, and guide the man, his son, who would bring about the new Renaissance. Yes indeed. He, Bernard Blake, was no ordinary man. Not slavish before a hollow Christianity, grown impotent and weak through time, and under the direction of weaklings. The new religion would be different, very different. Purification would be necessary. A new world in his own image. And what's more, God agreed with him. A mother had been selected, revealed possibly to Dominic by the Madonna. The Almighty One Himself, foreseeing this dreadful age of travail, had chosen him, Bernard Birous, to spawn a saviour. He thought of William Blake. He'd even had his own John the Baptist. It would all be realized one day. Bernard was breathing heavily, and drooling, and there were beads of sweat on his brow even though the sunlight lacked warmth.

The tears came suddenly. They were just there rolling down his cheeks. He had failed. Signy was gone. There would be no child. Agents of evil were aligned against them. He had been put in a favoured position, and he had been found wanting. He must be punished. Idly he reached for the vial and the pills. The piece of vellum fluttered to the ground, brushed by the hand that held the vial. Bernard looked down at it, at the word which bonded itself to his eyes.

Lamar.

Could the Madonna have foreseen the handiwork of the Evil Ones? Could this Lamar be a woman, also chosen, and out there somewhere, waiting for him? Yes, that must be it. God would never imperil such a Divine cause. He would be led to this Lamar just as he had been led to Signy. Through the workings of the very enfeebled institution through which his son and himself would re-make the world. He picked up the vellum, kissed it, and placed it carefully inside his shirt next to his skin. Then, half walking, half running he entered the small empty chapel near the archives. He knelt at the front, and for the first time in his life, Bernard Birous prayed sincerely. Prayers of contrition, thanks, and finally a promise shrieked hysterically at the statue of the Madonna who stared at him from her pedestal on the Gospel side of the altar near the rails.

"I must find Lamar, O Mother of God. Long have you wept, and longer have you been misunderstood. Your wishes are now known, and I will be your instrument. Lead me to her, and I will make her mine. From my loins will spring the new religion, and you will be pleased as I am, blessed. Show me her."

He rushed towards the statue, arms outstretched. She was spinning. Around and around. He followed with his eyes. Her small, white pointed feet rose to meet him. He fell on them and knew no more.

When he awoke it was dark in the chapel. He felt light headed and there was a strange buzzing in his ears. He genuflected low towards the Madonna and entered the darkening dusk. The cool air slapped at his burning cheeks as he made his way back to his quarters just off the Apostolic Palace.

~ ~ ~

The two men occupied the same seats in the same place. The Cardinal at his desk. The white-robed priest opposite.

"I have no other choice, Father. The Bergen matter. Your own, shall we say, lack of directness, and now others, dangerous ones, are ready to spring upon me like a lion on a deer. The price is clear, Father, and must be paid. I am troubled, but I would be more so had you not been the author of your own demise. You must leave this place. I have another placement for you."

Without waiting for a reply, Cardinal Luigi Lambruschini rose and taking a sealed letter from his desk came to where Bernard Blake was sitting. The young priest met his gaze calmly. Lambruschini noted the absence of anger, defiance, and even the pain he had discerned of late, and wondered.

Idly the Dominican took the letter from Lambruschini's hand, and after noting the title, set it down on his lap and waited for the Cardinal to continue. He endured the silence until he noticed that the Cardinal had gone to the window and was standing looking out at the square now covered in a cold grey rain.

"This place, Eminence. Where is it, and when do I go?" It didn't really matter to Bernard. Wherever it was, Lamar would be there. He was certain of that. He was just curious and Lambruschini clearly expected him to say something.

"Far away, Father. Across the sea to the bottom of the globe, to a colony on the edge of the earth. An English colony. A place for prisoners. Some call it a hell on earth, the farthest exile. The English call it New South Wales."

"The Great South Land? Terra Australis? It's English, and therefore Protestant, is it not?"

"It is, but many Irish are being sent there, and so our Church has become interested. My colleagues in England have sent me information on conditions there. The news is not good. There is much suffering, and dissoluteness is rife. Priests are sorely needed. I understand we are fortunate in that an excellent prelate resides there now. Monsignor Polding is an admirable emissary of God, and he has need of you. Go there, Bernard Blake, and through good works and tribulations endure the penance that will cleanse and temper you. Until . . ."

Lambruschini raised his eyebrows, and waited for the reaction. He was surprised at the response. Bernard Blake merely looked at him, and shining from those dark eyes was interest, not contempt.

"Thank you, Eminence. When do I leave?"

Was that a smile on his lips? Banished from the Vatican to the purgatory of a penal colony. The harshness of the missions without their nobility. A man impatient to move the earth, accepting exile with a smile. It didn't make sense.

"Aren't you going to ask me the duration of your stay? Or has resignation been added to the many talents of Father Bernard Blake?"

"The length of my sojourn is of no consequence. Purpose defines its own rules, Eminence, don't you agree?"

"What purpose? You don't know what awaits you in this wretched prison land, beyond the normal dictates of Christian charity and the priestly life."

"You are wrong, Eminence. Nothing substantial has changed since our first talk so long ago. Nothing, you understand. The arena perhaps. Different pages in the book of unfolding. But the resolution is as clear and sublime as when we first spoke. For a second time, Eminence, you send me to my destiny. I welcome it."

As the dark head bowed towards the ring, Lambruschini thought he heard him murmur, "But you and your like will not be part of it."

~ ~ ~

He raised the host high above his head. The bell chimed. He genuflected, still holding the holy wafer. Again the bell rang. Then he lifted the Son of God aloft towards the crucifix above the altar. Once more the sound of the gong penetrated the silence of awe and touched the ears of the kneeling congregation. Though his head was still pounding, Bernard Blake was able to push it aside. He had said countless Masses, but had uttered the words mostly hollowly, sometimes derisively, and when the pain was bad, in a tormented rage. Today was different. He was truly offering his first Mass. To the Madonna. The one that no one but he understood, and who had chosen him as the instrument by which the world would be re-made. As he returned the host to the golden chalice he saw his reflection in the cup's interior. It was where it should be, and soon he would be where he was meant. He waited a few seconds before he covered the chalice with its holy cloth, and prayed for Lamar.

Portsmouth, England, January 17, 1839

Bernard stood on the deck of the *Emma Eugenia* and watched the longboats making their way through Portsmouth Harbour. There were six of them, all crowded and sitting low in the choppy water. At the bow of each a single man stood, rifle at the ready. Behind the longboats and closer to shore were the vile-smelling hulks that were strung together stern to bow in an ugly line like floating slum tenements. There, a hundred more wretches, shackled in twos, some with a bundle of meagre belongings waited silently, morosely for the return of the longboats. An hour later they were all on board, one hundred and eighty-four, herded like cattle in the stinking darkness between decks, and stacked in berths four abreast, a foot and a half of space for each man. The only ventilation came through the grills on the padlocked hatchways at each end. Aside from the occasional moan or curse, few sounds broke the fetid silence. Bewilderment and hopelessness kept them cowering in the suffocating darkness. Transported to New South Wales. Hell on earth awaited them. A death sentence that stretched in misery across the ocean to a land more unforgiving than the unsmiling magistrates who had sent them there.

A few hours later the ship was underway. Bernard lay in his cabin oblivious to the creaking timbers and the sound of the heaving waters. The wretched mass of humanity that had boarded the ship had revulsed him. What he had seen were not men, but vile spectres. He would have to minister among rabble like this in Australia. Yet he had endured worse tribulations in Santa Sabina, and it would only last as long as his destiny demanded. No, what had disturbed him profoundly had been the sight of the score or so female prisoners who had come on board last. Hideous creatures, their clothes in tatters, filthy in appearance and louder than the men. More than one had gestured towards him lewdly, and even from the distance that separated them, he had felt the familiar nausea. If this wretched land was peopled solely by the garbage of England and Ireland, then what of Lamar? She could not be one of these dregs; how could a chosen one rise from seeds planted in human offal? Should he be wrong, then he was truly doomed, and the Madonna a bitch. Just like all of them. No, not all. He thought of Signy and smashed the demons in his head with the heel of his hand.

Chapter XII

"I don't understand, Excellency. You want to commute both sentences. Why? We agreed that all four would hang. Goyette is as guilty as any we have tried. Prieur too. He led the charge at Baker's field. The order has been signed. The coffins ordered." Clitherow knew he was overreacting, but this was too much. He would lose face before the tribunal.

Sir John Colborne put on his most placating tone. "Major General, I know your feelings, and I am aware of the embarrassment it might cause you among the tribunal. But hear me out for a minute. The Goyette family has influence in French commercial circles, the very ones we will want to cultivate. Commuting him will be viewed as a gesture of our magnanimity. We have hanged one Goyette. It's enough.

"Prieur, I have discovered, has relatives high up in the Roman Church. If he is spared, we may continue to enjoy its support." *Lies,* Colborne thought as he finished, but Clitherow would have to be in the country a long time before he would be able to disavow either.

After Clitherow had left to carry out his governor's pleasure, Colborne granted himself a moment alone before meeting the Upper Canada delegation now waiting in an adjoining apartment. Idly he picked the letter up from the desk again. Lady Jane Ellice had not requested action nor had she asked a favour; she had merely pointed out that a Patriote with a deformed lip and a François-Xavier Prieur had both rendered kindnesses to her family during their recent ordeal. She had heard they were on trial for their lives and would appreciate any consideration extended to them for their favourable actions towards the Ellice household.

Yes, Colborne told himself. So be it. For all his discipline and devotion to Queen and country, he was also no fool, and long ago had learned that one didn't hinder one's aspirations unnecessarily. His next posting would come soon, a peerage and a country house in the Ionian Islands. It was what he wanted. The powerful Ellice family and its affiliation through marriage with the even more formidable former Prime Minister, Earl Grey, made better friends than enemies. It was a small favour to grant and therefore an easy decision to make. He would write to Lady Jane Ellice privately this very evening, informing her of his actions and in guarded language soliciting her discretion. Two hangings instead of four. At least de Lorimier would hang. It would have been much worse had he had to take his head out of the noose. Carefully placing the letter in the desk drawer under lock, Colborne rearranged his uniform to its proper bearing and went out to meet the farmers from Upper Canada.

Le Pied du Courant Prison, Montreal, Friday, February 15, 1839

There was a moment of silence, then the clear voice of Joseph Dumouchelle, loud and firm in its vibrancy, carried its way down the length of the passage-way. The words were picked up by the others in the cells, and it was said later, testified to by a Catholic soldier who formed part of the gauntlet to the scaf-fold, that the glorious words of Dei Profundis were heard by everyone in the courtyard; that it sounded like it was coming from the sky; that the cold wind which was stinging his cheeks that day became soft and warm, and that a ring of light had circled the head of the noble Chevalier de Lorimer as he climbed the steps to his martyrdom.

September 26, 1839

The press had known the fate of the condemned several hours before the war-den did, and when morning broke over the grey prison, more than a hundred people, most carrying bundles of clothing and food, were waiting outside its iron gates.

They were allowed in at 8:00 AM and for two hours the exiles spent their last heartrending moments with their wives, parents and children. Then with weeping loved ones still clinging to them they were led into the assembly room where a pile of iron fetters lay on the floor. Shackled in pairs they were marched into the courtyard, and assembled and counted under a bright blue sky. When the number reached fifty-eight, the counting stopped and the armed detachment of regulars surrounded by a squad of cavalry fell into escort posi-tion. Someone barked the order to march, and at a lumbering half-trot, the prisoners passed out from the high dull walls to the noise and crowd of a city they had not known for almost a year. Once outside the gate, Martin found his eyes drawn to the big maples that in summer softened the grimness of the con-fining walls behind them. The sun caught them in a flash of gold against blue, and then they were gone, replaced by a wailing sea of faces and outstretched hands that threatened to engulf them in an anguished wave. One woman broke free from the crowd and with arms outstretched ran between the cavalry horses. A soldier grabbed her and threw her back towards the others who caught her as she collapsed in a heap. Beside him, a young man Martin didn't know was crying, trying to turn and wave, only to stumble and fall taking Martin with him. Martin felt the stony hardness of the ground and the pebbles that bit into his hands before he was jerked roughly to his feet and thrust back into the lurching formation.

"Shame!" yelled a female voice as a crying child was pulled away from the legs from a father he would never see again. At the dock, the soldiers closed ranks behind the cavalry and faced the crowd stolidly while the prisoners were herded up the gangplank. There was one final glimpse of loved ones; one last exposure to sympathies yelled in a familiar language before they were taken below. Five minutes later the steamer the British American entered the channel bound for Quebec.

Quebec, September 26, 1839

The naval stores ship H.M.S. Buffalo had seen better days. One of the few colonial-built ships to have seen battle action in defence of the realm, she held ports in her bulky sides for thirty guns. But it had been a long time since she had bristled with the defences of a British man o' war. When she was not carrying stores for distant outposts of the British Empire her holds were filled with the wretched human derelicts doomed to toil and die as convicts in the penal colonies of Australia. Now as she lay at anchor in Quebec Harbour below the guns of the mighty Citadel and within sight of the castle soon to be vacated by Sir John Colborne in favour of a more amiable governor, all she waited on were her human cargo. They were due before nightfall and all going well she would sail with the tide on the morrow.

The prisoners' quarters was named the third deck, an expansive term for such a space. Roughly twelve feet wide, and four and a half feet high except at the ends where it curved upwards to a height of five feet, it was a gloomy, foul-smelling place, airless save for the ventilation allowed by the iron grills in the two heavily padlocked doors that guarded each entrance. Two narrow passageways separated by stacked crates and boxes formed the only free space, the rest being taken up by the double row of bunks that ran down both sides. About seven feet long and less than six feet wide, each of these bunks would contain four men stacked tightly together in the fetid darkness. A shelf cut into the inside hull for storing personal effects provided the only other physical amenity. There was neither mess area nor utensils; the heads were on the deck above, as were the vomit buckets, and easily visible to the eye were the smudges of nits incubating in the thin mattress that each prisoner would take with him into his four-man open box.

It was to this squalid area that Alexander Black had taken himself this morning to perform the last of his duties before the convicts came on board.

His face crinkled at the smell as he knelt in the darkness throwing a thin dirty blanket into each dark recess. Next he checked the buckets and dipping cup, one for each mess of twelve. It would be one of his first duties: dividing the prisoners into lots of twelve for communal feeding purposes. He already had his exercise roster figured out. They would go on top daily, half in the morning and half in the afternoon but not equally balanced in time. That way he could reward his favourites and punish the Frenchmen he didn't like without incurring the ire of the Captain.

Alexander Black was a well-educated and shrewd businessman, fluent in both English and French, and energetic, who nonetheless had failed. A clothier by profession, he had plied his trade up and down the Richelieu and into New York and Vermont during the late twenties and early thirties. He had become reasonably successful although his clientele, particularly the French-speaking farmers, thought his prices were inflated and his manner overbearing. But then Black became greedy.

An avid, silent eavesdropper, he turned informer on his own customers. In the turbulent months preceding the insurrection of 1837, the British received information from Black on Patriote movements. He had continued his nefarious activities in 1838, and was almost responsible for the capture of a Patriote leader he had noticed moving through the southern parishes in the fall of 1838. If they had have caught that bastard, he wouldn't have been here now, that was certain. Ingratitude was not one of that arrogant Colborne's faults.

In the uprising that followed, Black found his English customers in Lower Canada to be dubious about a man so obviously tarred with the American brush of republicanism. The French farmers had other things on their minds and they didn't like him much anyway, but most important was the young entrepreneur from Pennsylvania who being much freer with his credit was able to undermine him among his American customers. In the spring of 1839, Black suddenly found his business on the wrong side of the balance sheet. Some imaginative juggling of the books brought a brief respite, but it was only temporary.

Sentenced to ten years in Montreal Gaol for fraud in July, he had called in his markers. The bastard Clitherow could have let him off for his service to the Queen. But no! Instead he had offered him this. Steward to a bunch of traitorous rebels in return for a passage to Sydney and permanent exile. He'd had no other choice. Any life would be preferable to the hell of prison. Now, caged in this hulk they called a ship, and soon to be surrounded by the refuse of the earth, he wondered. He might suffer on this hellish voyage, but not as much as the scum who had to do his bidding. Particularly, the French. Yes, especially the French.

~ ~ ~

On the first deck, Captain Paul Niblett was sitting in the small cramped cabin that was to be his home for God knew how long, and wallowing in self-pity. Clitherow didn't like him. He knew that. But this? It was something he never envisaged in his wildest imaginings. Months of hellish boredom and discomfort herding a miserable bunch of traitors to the bottom of the earth. He had been put in charge of the marine detachment that was to supervise the transportation of almost one hundred and fifty rebels to Van Diemen's Land and New South Wales. Clitherow had told him that he needed the experience; that the discipline and rigour of extended duty on board one of her Majesty's ships would temper his mind and body. Bloody idiot. Did Clitherow think he was stupid? It was a punishment, undeserved and unwarranted. He had already sampled the food. Abominable slop, and the captain seemed a quiet but waspish sort who had already angered Niblett by espousing his distaste for the demon drink and telling him that he ran a tight ship. Tight ship, indeed. A worm-eaten old man o' war, long past any semblance of usefulness. Ideal for carrying the scum of the earth, but for gentlemen like himself? A damnable vile-smelling insult like the Buffalo should never be foisted on men better fitted for nobler things. The brandy bottle was one fifth gone and he was already drunk enough to want to tell Clitherow what he could do with the Buffalo and its cargo of dregs when he heard the commotion outside. He adjusted his leather belt around his ample girth, breathed in and out heavily half a dozen times, and went out into the afternoon light.

They were coming aboard, scruffy, shackled and clutching their meagre belongings. They looked like a woebegone lot, thought Wood, standing on the bridge. But looks could be deceiving. He watched them clamber awkwardly aboard and assemble on the deck area. Then with his habitual shrug of dismissal, he went into the wheelhouse to confer with the tug captain who would tow them down the river at six bells on the morrow.

From just outside his cabin, Niblett felt the cool breeze at his cheeks. He recognized some from the tribunal, the more notable ones who had either bleated their innocence, or who had advertised their sublime stupidity in other ways. The young dark-haired fellow with the smile that almost had gotten him acquitted. Louis Bourdon was his name. Well, we'll soon see how much he liked to smile. There was the little bastard, Prieur, who had just stood there in the dock clutching his wretched beads. No attempt to defend himself. Just a fool's look. He'd felt like strangling him with his own beads. And talk about fools! The buffoon with the idiot's lip was climbing aboard. Look at the way he was gazing about him! What did he expect? A royal welcome? We'll have some fun with that simpleton. There were others he thought he recognized. Abruptly, he turned his head away. He'd seen enough. Any more and he would throw up. Remembering the brandy bottle, Niblett returned to more important things.

Alexander Black met the prisoners at the entrance to their quarters. He supervised the removal of the shackles, and for ten minutes enjoyed himself in a harangue which covered everything from mess groupings to the proper way to vomit. Then he watched and counted as they were filed into one of the two passageways. It was towards the end of the line that his eyes widened, then glittered with contempt. The one with the lip; the one they hadn't caught; the one that had caused Clitherow's rancour towards him. It was him. As he watched Martin's retreating back now bent double and quickly losing itself in the gloom, Black felt strangely at peace. Yes, justice would be done on this voyage.

October 4

Martin had never felt so sick in all his life. He lay in the darkness trying to quiet the nausea that seemed ready always to erupt in uncontrollable spasms, and listening to the noise of the ship as she fought the storm. She was like a leaf in a gale, rising then falling in a series of sickening lurches that threatened to tear her asunder. Most of the soldiers were sick; Alexander Black had not been seen for two days now, a welcome absence indeed had not the circumstances decreed an even worse scourge for the exiles. Weakened already by the rigours of confinement, and totally unused to sea travel, all but a fortunate few succumbed terribly when the gale hit. The sole vomit bucket was in the head above, but after a day, only the strongest were able to make the lurching staggering journey upwards. The others were forced to vomit onto their clothes, into their bedding and on the floor until their already foul quarters became a stench-filled pit. Now, into the third day and with no abatement in the lurching pounding of the ship, the debilitating nausea was giving way to a listless inertia the would bring death to the weaker.

Beside Martin, old Charles Huot moaned and tried to clamber towards the passageway. He had barely put his feet on the vomit-slicked planks when

Martin heard him retch violently, gagging then spewing until his whole body was shaking. François-Xavier Prieur came as quickly as he could, wiping Huot's face and easing him gently back towards the bunk. Then with a stinking sodden rag he began mopping up Huot's vomit.

Martin felt the gorge rising in his own throat. Covering his mouth with his hand, he clawed his way over Huot and along the passageway where he pounded as hard as he could on the barred door. A guard opened it and watched indifferently as Martin lurched past him to the iron ladder. He retched once before he reached the narrow space above where two tub-like vessels were fixed in place by chains. Even so, the steep pitching of the ship slopped some of the muck over the sides, excrement and vomit mixing together in a slimy stinking mess that covered the whole head area. Another man was at the bucket retching. Martin rushed headlong past him, slipping and falling until he was at the second bucket, tasting the bitter bile that added to the foul soup steaming just inches from his lips. After several minutes he lifted his head. The other prisoner was still there. Martin recognized him as the one they called Towell, the most quarrelsome of the Upper Canadians. He had heard him make uncouth comments towards his comrades on the deck during exercise time. He was looking at Martin belligerently, half staggering half swaying as he fought to keep his balance.

"Traitor," he mumbled through clenched teeth as he passed by. "You're the coward British-loving traitor. You'll be a dead man before we're through."

For an instant there was silence but for the creaking of the ship and the slopping sound of the buckets. Martin was lurching back to the ladder when he was hit from the side and he felt Towell's hands about his throat. Martin tried to kick but lost his balance instead, falling against his bigger, stronger assailant, who grunted and locked his hands tighter. He was snarling into Martin's face, "Die you mongrel cur, die." Red, then yellow, then red spots danced before Martin's eyes. Blackness enveloped him like a sweet blanket. There was no strength to his legs and he was sinking, sinking.

Outside in the rain and wind, the *Buffalo* rose on a wave, bow thrust upwards, higher, higher towards the starless black sky. She was half out of the water when a swell hit her broadsides. She keeled to her side and for a second teetered on the edge of capsizing completely. Then, still sideways, she plunged into the trough like a stricken bird, striking the bottom with a wrenching heaving motion that threatened to break her in half.

The force threw Martin and Towell against the hull. Towell's shoulders took the full brunt of the impact, driving him to his knees and then to the deck itself. Martin was on top of him and then they were both on the muck-coated planks sliding in a tangle of arms and legs. The pressure on Martin's neck relaxed. He lay stunned for a minute, pressed against the vomit tub, one leg caught up in the chain which secured it. Towell was prone. His head was against the metal bucket and blood oozed from his scalp. As Martin's senses returned, so did his panic. Without picking himself up, he crawled through the darkness, oblivious to the cold slime that met his palms. He clambered down the ladder, and past the guard who was chewing nauseously on a piece of cheese. Only when he got back to his bunk did Martin discover that he was shaking uncontrollably. An hour later when his stomach again heaved with nausea, he vomited into his own bedding, consciously if not gladly.

October 6

The thirty-six prisoners were herded onto the top deck slowly and arranged in loose ranks. As Martin breathed in the clean air, he found it difficult to believe that this was the same ocean that had foamed and boiled with a fury that had threatened them all but which had only taken one. The sun was warm and high in a cloudless sky and the gentle pitch of the ship was echoed by a brace of dolphins cavorting abreast of the bow. The armed guard formed itself in a square just behind a hatless Captain Wood, who was holding a worn open bible, the flat of his hand keeping the pages from turning in the breeze.

On the deck in front of him lay a body wrapped in sailcloth and weighted down with four cannonballs. Phillip Priest was one of the Upper Canadian prisoners, a small gentle man who had never recovered from the bout of seasickness that had racked his weakened body. As Wood began reading, the armed guard snapped to attention, and for less than thirty seconds the words of the Twenty-Third Psalm touched the ears of the exiles, the Catholic Patriotes among them invoking their own prayers to replace the unfamiliar English words. As the last words died away the shrouded shape was slid over the side. There was a soft splash and a moment more of silence. When Martin raised his head he felt Towell's eyes on him. He shivered and instinctively moved closer to François-Xavier Prieur. The little man, mistaking his fear for disquiet in the presence of death, smiled reassuringly and put his hand on his arm.

~ ~ ~

The days stretched into weeks with no interruption to the daily regimen imposed on the prisoners. Insults and verbal abuse from Paul Niblett and the vindictive pettiness of Alexander Black turned an already grim voyage into an endless nightmare. The diet was spare and unrelenting in its sameness. Salted pork, thin soup and dry biscuit repeated day after day in a communal pail with but a single utensil among twelve men kept the exiles alive but with little strength. Twice weekly and to the accompaniment of heavy proddings and scornful jeers they were sent to their knees to scrub out their quarters and clothes with lime. By the third week in October the intensifying heat of the tropics began to have its effects. The vermin in the prisoners' bedding proliferated and soon every man's body was a mass of angry red swellings, torn and bloodied further through frenzied scratching. When Black reported to Wood on November 6 that over thirty men were sick in the holds and that the scurvy outbreak was worsening, he was answered only with the now familiar shrug of the shoulders. Not that Alexander Black cared a whit. The more that died meant fewer scum and less duties.

But Captain John Wood had listened. Scurvy on his ship at this early stage of the voyage was not good, and since they would not be in Rio de Janeiro for at least another three weeks, some action would have to be taken. Yes, tomorrow was the day. He sent for Niblett and keeping his voice civil – for he could abide this fat fool even less than he could Black – Wood told Niblett of his change in plans. Niblett listened with mounting annoyance but since it was Wood in charge of such things and not him, there was little he could do about it. Indeed, as he left the captain's cabin, Niblett could already envision how some sort of fun could be made out of the whole thing.

~ ~ ~

The warmth of the tropics descended on the prisoners like a heavy damp blanket. Their foul hole was like an oven, and any fitful sleep was interrupted by bites from the vermin that infested their bedding. Yet lice were not their worst tormentor. Thirst became unbearable as the heat took its toll. Each man's daily pint of water was like a miser's treasure, every drop guarded, hoarded and savoured.

The evening of November 6 was particularly distressing. Outside, not a breath of wind rippled the *Buffalo's* sails. The ship seemed to hang motionless in a void. The prisoners lay in the stinking, stifling darkness, skin to skin, soaking in each other's sweat, the weaker not caring, the stronger mumbling prayers. Martin touched Charles Huot's forehead. It was burning hot, and there was nothing he could do. Nothing any of them could do. If Charles died, he hoped it would be quick.

November 7

Wonderfully, miraculously, a breeze had sprung up when the Patriotes were herded onto the top deck at ten bells. Black was nowhere to be seen, and it was the sneering Niblett who told them that they were all to go topsides and form eight rows facing the wheelhouse. Everyone, even the infirm.

Wondering, they obeyed, half-carrying the sick and then supporting them on the pitching deck. Niblett was waiting with some soldiers. The rest of the crew were milling around smiling and nudging one another. Captain Wood was standing on the bridge, gazing down at them interestedly. The prisoners were urged backwards towards the rail and away from the large barrel that was roped to the wheelhouse door. Niblett barked an order. The soldiers moved out of the way and leaned against the rail. The Patriotes looked at each other, fear more than wonderment in most of their eyes.

It came as a dancing sound, a high-pitched trill which became lively, then agitated. The prisoners turned their heads to seek out the player. They saw him in the rigging. One of the older sailors balanced himself like a cat, holding the reed in both hands and running up and down the notes in a wild melodic cadence. Higher, faster he went, the same melody repeated over and over again in a musical frenzy. To Martin it sounded untamed. He found himself thinking of Madeleine.

They smelled and heard him before they saw him. He must have been hanging over the side of the ship all the time, and as he clambered over the rail he was out of the Patriotes' sight, their eyes being glued to the player in the rigging. He gave a piercing yell and as fifty-eight startled pairs of eyes turned towards him, he began a series of squatting dancing steps which carried him around the prisoners to the secured barrel.

"King Neptune," bellowed one of the sailors. "It's King Neptune."

He was the mighty king, all right. Covered from head to foot in a porpoise skin, Neptune crouched before his assembled subjects. His face was painted gaudily. His beard was wild and unkempt and on his head he wore the horned helmet of a Viking warrior. In one hand he brandished a trident fashioned crudely from a pole and some cooking utensils, and in the other he held a wide cone-shaped shell which he put to his lips in a mock salute. He danced and pranced towards the Patriotes, his spear thrust menacingly towards them. He came so close that Martin could see the colour of his eyes and the beads of sweat that clung to his brow. The stench that rose from the skin that this macabre little Neptune wore was far more overpowering than the threat of his posturings.

"King Neptune comes," the little creature screamed, "to seek homage from those who would invade his domain. On this day of days when the two parts of the world meet for all my servants on this wretched craft."

It was Alexander Black, all right, thought Martin to himself. The thin whine was more poorly hidden in bluster than were features covered with paint and stinking under the sun.

"Bow, you miserable mortals," roared Neptune. "Bow and receive your smite of homage."

No one moved for a moment until Niblett came forward and pushed François-Xavier Prieur roughly to the deck. Seeing more soldiers coming forward, the rest followed hurriedly and when they were all prone, Neptune came among them striking each man with his trident. He poked hard, and Martin kneeling in the front heard more than one cry of pain. He could smell him coming nearer, could hear his wild curses in the name of the Gods. Then he felt the trident bite cruelly into the back of his neck. He winced in agony and fell prostrate on the deck. Another jab into his rear end brought a roar of approval from the watching sailors.

"Rise, servants, and receive your gift from the mighty Neptune. All who cross the line receive Neptune's favour." He pointed his trident at the barrel. "Good strong brew to nourish the guts and heal the scurves. My gift to you. But," the thin voice was wavering it was so high-pitched, "you will dance a dance of homage." Then he began to cavort wildly in a mock dance, prancing and swaying, stamping his feet and twisting about until he looked like a bizarre, foul-smelling parody in a pantomime. The Patriotes watched in incredulous fascination. When he got to the barrel he pulled out the silver ladle and waved it in the air. Neptune dipped it in the barrel and tipped it to his lips, drinking greedily. "Rum and lime," he chortled happily. "My gift to you. Now dance, you miserable subjects from nowhere. Dance."

Captain Wood had seen some wild Neptune ceremonies in his time, but Black was really overdoing it. It had been his idea to use the dance to give the Patriotes a much-needed tot of rum and lime, but he hadn't counted on Niblett and Black making it such a farce. Still, the crew wouldn't take it kindly if he stopped it now. They were laughing uproariously as the Patriotes, one by one, began their dance to the barrel. One tried a pirouette and collapsed in a heap. The weaker ones had to dance with a stronger and their stepping and kicking hopelessly out of unison was admittedly funny. Neptune would leap among them, prodding them and wrapping the decomposing porpoise skin about their heads, laughing and cackling like a demon.

Suddenly it was Martin's turn. A soldier pushed him forward. He began hesitatingly, not knowing what to do before a forceful slap in the middle of the back sent him prancing, sidestepping and hopping awkwardly in the direction of the barrel. He could feel his face reddening he was ridiculed with guffaws. Neptune was beside him, his painted face contorted, and a scaly arm pushing itself roughly across his face. A piece of rotting flesh dislodged itself and rested for a moment on his lips. He spat it out, gagging. The guffawing was louder, more strident, but still he danced, turning and twirling until the grinning faces gaped at him sideways, upside down in a blur of motion. As the deck rose to meet him, he straightened up trying to focus until the reek of fish and a jabbing trident drove him on. Even as he shuffled and quick-stepped forward, Martin could feel the sobbing sound welling within him, dragging the air from his tortured lungs. Oh God! The ship was spinning again, and he was falling. Something met his groping hands. The barrel! Desperately he grasped the protruding ladle and dipped it in the dark liquid. It was at his lips when a boot planted itself between his legs. A vicious side-ways kick sent him to his knees, the ladle flying from his hand and emptying itself uselessly into the air. Niblett was standing over him, his beefy face con-vulsing with laughter. "Don't you know, fool? 'Tis many a slip twixt cup and lip. For an idiot's lip on Neptune's ship."

The boot drove into his stomach. Martin could feel himself retching but only bile seeped between his teeth. He crawled towards his comrades, barely conscious of the jeering laughter and Neptune's frenzied cackling. "Who's next, shipmates? Neptune waits. Some he likes; some he hates."

On the bridge Wood stood, frowning. It must be the troublemaker that Niblett had told him about. The men were laughing and clapping, and yelling for Niblett who was bowing in mock appreciation. For an instant Wood brought the whistle to his lips. Then he shrugged and turned away.

November 28

It was dark in the hold and even if Martin had had a watch he could not have known the time. So he waited a while longer listening to the creak of the ship and the sounds of his sleeping comrades. Turning as best he could onto his side, he wiped the sweat from his face. The heat was still there but at least it was bearable. The stiffening east-south-east breezes that were driving the *Buffalo* on an even course for Rio had broken the airless, stifling grip of suffocation. Men who had hovered at death's door were now appreciably recovered. The dance to the rain barrel had become a formality with the daily tot of rum more than compensating for the comic parading it demanded. Hewitt, the friendliest of the guards, had informed them this morning that they would be in Rio within two days. He was sure that those with money would be allowed to purchase some fresh fruit there.

Martin felt Charles Huot's face. It was still hot to the touch and he was sleeping fitfully. As quietly as he could, Martin crawled from his space, tiptoed to the barred door and tapped softly. It opened and for a moment he could see Hewitt's face framed in the light of a hand-held lantern. Wordlessly he took the proffered boot replacing it with the glint of silver and crept back to his bunk. Seconds later he was forcing water from the boot between Huot's lips. He couldn't see the colour of the stuff but he knew it would be brown and brackish, vermin and dung filled, having accumulated in the open longboats through weeks of periodic downpours. But it was water nonetheless dearly bought with scarce coin and it would ease old Charles's suffering. He was mopping the lined face with the sodden sleeve of his shirt when Huot's eyes opened.

"Drink, Charles. There's plenty." He tipped the boot and let Huot gulp eagerly.

When the boot was empty, Huot lay back breathing shallowly. He looked at Martin and smiled in the dark. "Martin, my friend. You save me from the fishes."

November 30

After so many weeks of confinement at sea with nothing to break the eye's vision but foam-crested grey-green swells that flattened to a dull shimmer before becoming nothing on the horizon, the Buffalo had arrived at Guanabara Bay the previous evening but had been denied access by unfavourable winds. Now, under a blue sky and a slight breeze the ship entered Rio de Janeiro.

All the prisoners were allowed on deck, and they lined the rails as the ship nudged past the two heavily fortified stone fortresses that guarded the bay. The azure calm felt strange and still under their feet.

The shoreline was high and green, the tops of the mountains losing themselves in a wispy mist that might have been clouds. To starboard a narrow peninsula reached out into the bay with a high rocky hill protruding from it like a giant thumb. Dozens of ships lay at anchor in the calm blue water, several bearing the insignia of the British Navy. Around them scurried little crafts of assorted shapes and sizes tended by olive skinned natives who manoeuvred them deftly shouting all the time and waving what were obviously saleable objects in the air. Behind the ships at the bay's end the town seemed to cling to the green hills like a white fungus. Martin could make out the spires of churches, and on both sides of the town ran a ribbon of white sand that curved and foamed with the coastline in a graceful arc before disappearing into a hazy green horizon. Martin stood there gripping the rail and staring with all the wonderment of a child. He was conscious of the cry of the gulls, gracefully white against the blue canopy, and of the warm breath of wind touching his cheeks like a silken fan. All at once he could feel the emotion welling within him. He would remember this sight forever.

The *Buffalo* dropped anchor near a British Man-o'-war. The prisoners were still on deck when a boarding party of officers drew alongside. They looked at the prisoners curiously but none approached them with words, preferring instead to go below immediately. Later the prisoners were to learn from Hewitt that the visiting officers had been impressed with the kindnesses being allowed criminals, and that the exiles should count themselves fortunate at being transported to a penal colony in such fine fashion.

During the five days at anchor in Rio, the prisoners were allowed extra time on deck, and to purchase fresh fruits and other edibles from the boatside vendors. The days were warm and tranquil and the spirits of the men lifted. It was too good to last.

January 1, 1840

Pushed along by strong west winds, the *Buffalo* had rounded the Cape of Good Hope and into the Indian Ocean when the old year passed joylessly into the new. There was little time on the deck to marvel at the swarms of flying fish driving before the ship in a wondrous shimmer of gauze and silver, or to stand and watch the dolphins. The exiles were herded together on the deck in groups of twelve to stand silent for two hours, or, when it suited Black, to shave. He supervised while they shaved each other with a single blunt razor, laughing at the cries of pain and the free-flowing blood. Old Charles Huot had become sick again. It was difficult for Hewitt to get extra water to him but somehow he managed. Martin felt doubly grateful for he had nothing with which to pay the kind-hearted little Yorkshireman. He would make it up one day, he promised.

January 10

With the others, Martin climbed the ladder and out onto the deck. His first impression was not of the greyness of the day or of the bite of chill in the air, but of the calmness. The high winds that had slapped and whipped the rigging about had died to a murmur. Without the spray to sting his cheeks or to bite away at his vision, Martin could see clearly. The deck was clear in front of him for only a few feet. Then came the soldiers, and beyond them stood a brawny sailor with tattoos on his huge arms. He was holding a long thin cane loosely in one hand and picking at his nose with the other. Beside him a man was tied to the mast, his back bared whitely in the morning light. Martin stopped for a moment frozen in his tracks before being pushed forward by one of the guards. The man at the mast was Hewitt.

When all the prisoners were assembled on the deck, Captain John Wood descended from the bridge. He faced them, the peaked outline of his cap and his gaunt appearance reminding Martin strangely of some giant malevolent bird. As Niblett snapped the soldiers to attention, the bare-armed sailor took up his position, laying the birch rod slantwise across the back of the tied man.

"You are present today to bear witness of what happens when the discipline aboard my ship is mocked by disobedience. Some of you prisoners have doubtless profited by this man's greed and contempt for his duties, and now you shall watch him pay. That is, unless any of you want to join him. Bosun Cartwright has the arm, I assure you, to do you all justice." Wood paused for effect, scanning the ragged bunch who stood mutely, some shivering as the first flecks of rain began to fall.

Something inside Martin was twisting at his entrails. He willed the words that gathered in his throat. *He did what he did for the sick among us. He should not be punished. Let me take his place for it is I who am the more guilty.* But nothing came. His teeth remained clenched; he felt his own laboured breathing but there were no words.

"I thought not," said Wood. He stepped back a pace, and nodded towards Cartwright. "Do your duty, Bosun."

The sliver of birch raised towards the light, pausing for an instant and pointing towards the heavens. There was a swishing sound as it descended and then a sickening half thud, half crack as it sliced into Hewitt's back. He screamed in agony, a long high yelp of pain that had scarcely died when the cane again bit into his flesh. Again and again it ripped downwards until Hewitt's back was patterned with welts and covered with blood. His screams echoed back and forth, long penetrating cries of pain that gradually became sobs, heaving and loud, then quieter, muffling into soft moans before the head fell forward to rest against the mast. To Martin watching with eyes tightly closed, the searing tear of the cane seemed worse somehow without the sound. Like its futility was obvious and that Hewitt had paid his price.

Finally, Wood raised his hand. Two sailors came forward. One untied the ropes that bound Hewitt to the mast. The other cushioned his fall to the deck. Together they carried him past the prisoners. Hewitt's eyes were closed and the thin greying hair was matted to his scalp. He was bleeding from the mouth where he had bitten his lip to control the pain.

They stood mutely afterwards. Wood said, "Let that be a lesson to all of you. I should have hanged him."

January 13

The roaring forties picked up again, and the Buffalo made good time across the Indian Ocean. At the rate they were going, the shores of Van Diemen's Land would appear out of the eastern horizon in less than three weeks, or so the prisoners were told by the guard who had taken Hewitt's place. They hadn't seen Hewitt since the flogging but they were relieved to hear that his wounds were healing. He would not be returning to guard duty but would be assigned lesser tasks.

They were on the deck for exercise. The guards had relaxed their demands about talking during deck exercise, and when Charles Huot had to sit down, Martin squatted with him on the deck. For a few moments they looked out at the grey-green swells billowing, frothing to a head, and then rolling away. Finally Martin spoke. "Charles. Hewitt had been good to us. He saved you. With the water he gave. But before they flogged him and I had a chance to say something in his defence, I kept my piece and stood by while they cut his back to raw meat. It was horrible, and I did nothing. No wonder the rest of them think of me as a coward. I am a coward, Charles."

Huot stared at the waves. "You must not be harsh with yourself, my young friend. Your heart is good. You would not have stopped the flogging."

"You would have not stood by, Charles. I know you wouldn't."

"We all have regrets, Martin. Do not berate yourself. I would probably have done exactly as you did even though it was my lot that Hewitt's water eased. Let me tell you a story."

Martin had to listen hard to hear Huot's soft words above the wind. "It was during the rebellion. We were at Odelltown and we had the British pinned down in a church, or so we thought. We were all behind a stone wall and were readying ourselves to cut them down when they emerged with cannons and turned them on us. We scattered like sheep. Some of us tried to stay, but soon there was just myself and another. It was a woman."

Martin started forward. "A woman. Are you certain, Charles?"

"Yes! It was a woman, and what a woman!" He gripped Martin's arm. "She was fearless, Martin. She stood erect, firing into the British lines. I knew we had no chance, that we had to run. I called out to her, but she didn't heed me. She just kept firing. I stood transfixed for a moment, wanting to flee, but feeling that I should go to her and drag her away with me. It was then that I heard her voice. She was loading her rifle, but her eyes were lifted beyond the British to something else, and she was calling out to someone. Words I couldn't understand. Then I ran. I left her. So you see, Martin I too am a coward. I might have saved her. I think about it often."

Martin sat silent for a long time, Hewitt forgotten, his head whirling with memories. She had died just as he had imagined: nobly, seeing the vision that inspired her. He wished he could have done that at Caughnawaga or at Baker's Field. He half closed his eyes and stared out over the heaving waters, and after pausing for a moment to steady his voice finally spoke. "Don't feel bad, Charles. I have had some experience with a woman like that. She would not have gone with you. Her destiny was to die that day. She was a chosen one going the road of the chosen."

February 13

The hazy shoreline emerged out of the horizon in a long low line. Over the next three hours it loomed larger, and by dusk, the *Buffalo* was at the mouth of the Derwent River in Van Diemen's Land.

As the *Buffalo* made her way to anchorage at Hobart town the next morning, there was a strange air of quiet finality among the prisoners. They had arrived. It was not New Holland, which lay north across a channel separating Van Diemen's land from the mainland, but it was part of the Great South Land. For the Upper Canadians, Hobart marked the end of their long voyage. They were herded on deck, and under a cloudy sky with a slight breeze blowing in from the sea, the exiles took their first glimpse of their new land. The bay was wide and large and there were several ships at anchorage. Many bore flags that were not English, and it was the first time Martin had seen the squat, fierce outline of the whalers' ships, with their harpoon guns mounted on the bow like a giant insect's sting. The town itself appeared small and well kept, but there was a loneliness about it. The bush seemed to hem it in, and looming directly above the cluster of white buildings that formed the village was a single mountain so high that its peak was lost in mist.

The stay in Hobart town was pleasant enough for the Patriotes. Their diet improved considerably with the addition of fresh meat and vegetables. It was also uneventful except for the day the Upper Canadians were taken away. Special instructions had been issued by the Captain himself, much to the chagrin of both Black and Niblett, for the Patriotes to bid farewell to their fellows.

It was a strangely emotional scene. Separated by the gulfs of language, religion, and customs the two groups of exiles met on the deck to say goodbye. Martin found himself hugging men he had never spoken to, listening to their farewells, sometimes uttered in poor French. At the end of the group came Towell. No Patriote spoke to him, and Martin was quick to notice that he stood apart from his own kind. Towell stopped before Martin, who stood his ground forcing his eyes to take in this man who had tried to kill him, this man whom he had come to fear. No words were uttered, but as Martin watched him walk away he felt a sense of relief mixed with satisfaction. One nemesis was gone. He had survived. He didn't know why, but he also felt vindicated, as if there was an unspoken understanding among them all that he might have been misjudged.

February 25

For an hour the Patriotes had stood on the deck watching the shoreline pass by their eyes. There was the same wildness about it as Van Diemen's land. The cliffs were high and rugged, and below them ran the sandy beaches curving and ending in a series of wide white sweeps. The Patriotes were now visibly excited. They would be in Sydney town within a few hours. Like the others, Martin could hardly wait. For five long months they had endured their travail with a numbed patience that knew no future, but now that they were almost here, the anntication was unbearable.

It was mid-morning when the *Buffalo* entered a wide break in the coastline. A lighthouse sat on its southern extremity, a solitary beacon perched hundreds of feet above the sea with nothing but a grey-brown jumble of rocks for company. The northern head was even more formidable. Rising out of the sea, a vertical wall of rock seemed to defy the breakers that smashed and sprayed futilely against its base. Inside the bay the sea became calm and still, and the Patriotes craned their necks for their first glimpse of Port Jackson. It was magnificent; the olive-green water reached into wide bays and narrow inlets, meeting beaches, cliffs and shoreline in a wild display of Nature's caprice. It was though a giant had uprooted a chunk of the coastline, breaking it along faults and tearing it at whim.

The port seemed to go on forever as more bays and inlets slipped by the ship, and gradually an occasional house was visible and soon ships could be seen at anchor. Nowhere near the number in Rio, or even Hobart town for that matter, but enough to remind the Patriotes that this was indeed a place of habitation. The shoreline was closer now and Martin heard for the first time a steady high-pitched sound coming from the tall trees that reached almost to the water's edge. They were strange trees, twisted with mottled white trunks and leaves that seemed to be no definite colour at all. Nothing like the brilliant greens of spring or the rich deep hue of summer foliage familiar to the Patriotes. It was a muted green expanse that stretched up and on unchangingly. As for the noise, it filled the air, insistent, loud, and in a strange way, musical. Martin was wondering what it was when he heard the strangled frightened cry from someone standing near him. Leandre Ducharme was pointing ahead of the ship towards the shore. "Look!"

All eyes turned to follow his pointing finger. A gash in the trees ahead gave evidence of a new road under construction. There were soldiers there guarding what looked like a work gang. The bush was broken by jumbles of piled rocks, and a line of grey smoke and a few crude huts indicated the presence of a camp. Martin gasped when he saw what had caught Ducharme's attention. Four men hitched together in harness were straining to move a giant rock. A guard was yelling at them, and in his hands he held a whip. The Patriotes watched in fearful fascination as one fell stumbling to the ground. The guards were on him in a second, beating and berating him until his bare shoulders were again straining with the others.

There was silence aboard the Buffalo after that. Each man was with his own thoughts. They scarcely noticed when the ship dropped anchor off shore just beyond Sydney Cove. When Martin finally did take the time to look, the squalid-looking assemblage of buildings that nestled at the end of a small inlet. He turned his eyes away to the north side where at least the never-ending green forest and the high-pitched singing sound bespoke a solitude he could understand.

February 27

The excitement in the prisoners' quarters was intense. The boxes and crates had been stacked together in the high end of the passageway, arranged carefully so they formed a platform. Joseph Marceau's small crucifix was affixed to the wall through the kindness of a guard who had provided some twine and a small nail. Just off the centre of the platform, beside and back from where the veiled chalice would rest, stood Martin's little pewter Madonna. She looked small and insignificant there in the gloom but she was the only piece the exiles had that would be fitting enough to adorn God's altar of the holy sacrifice.

Monsignor Bede Polding, Bishop of Sydney, had visited yesterday and had talked reassuringly with them in excellent French, even hearing some confessions and promising to return the next day to say Mass and administer the blessed Eucharist. Captain Wood had been most co-operative, he had explained. The prisoners were overjoyed at seeing a man of God after so long in misery. After he had gone, they had talked excitedly, all agreeing how fortunate they were to have such an excellent prelate in this dismal land.

As he followed his secretary up the ladder to the deck of the *Buffalo*, Monsignor Bede Polding had less positive feelings, for he knew of matters still concealed from the exiles. He was about to say Mass for fifty-eight good Catholics, peaceable men who had merely sought to lift what they believed was the yoke of foreign oppression from their shoulders. Misled and misdirected, they were the victims of their own idealism. The infernal Protestant press in this place was less sanguine and there seemed to be little he could do about it. If the *Sydney Gazette* could be believed, they were nothing but revolutionary insurgents who would simply add another dangerous element into an already volatile pit of Papist ne'er-do-wells and lawbreakers. They should not stay, the Tories had trumpeted. Norfolk Island was a better place for them. The hellhole of the earth. Polding winced at the thought as he pulled himself over the rail onto the deck. It was in the Governor's hands now. He would try, but Governor George Gipps was not a man easily suaded once his mind was made up.

The exiles were already kneeling in the passageway when Polding arrived. Quickly he laid a white cloth over the altar and added the missal, four candles, and a large crucifix on a stand. Next he placed the veiled chalice right where the tabernacle would normally be, moving the small Madonna well to the gospel side where she seemed to fade into the darkness. Five minutes later, dressed in the red vestments of martyrdom, he mounted the altar and began the opening verses. The secretary acted as acolyte, answering Polding in a rich voice that strangely lacked lustre. The contrast made Martin look up from his own reverie. The acolyte was dressed in the garb of a Dominican but with an unshaven head. After the Mass when the Dominican filed past his place, Martin noted the fine profile and strong jawline etched against a pale skin. For an instant their eyes met. There was a sadness there, and something else. The white-robed figure had passed him when realization dawned. Martin turned and followed the retreating back, the name forming involuntarily on his lips. *Madeleine*. He had just looked into the eyes of Madeleine.

Paris, 1673

Father Basil Thibeault surveyed the open, metal trunk in the centre of the room, and turned to the elderly nun beside him. "Have you taken note of its contents, Sister?"

"Yes, Father," replied the nun. "Mostly statues, stone and metal, a few crucifixes and some candlesticks. They look so old. I wonder how long they've been there."

Sister Martha Mary was the Mother Superior of St. Sebastien's Orphanage for Girls, operated by the Ursuline Nuns in Paris. A small, nervous woman, she reminded Thibeault of an agitated bird. She was especially agitated this morning. Some workmen preparing the foundations for a new dormitory on the east wing of the orphanage had uncovered a small, stone cellar, empty save for the metal trunk that now stood before them.

Thibeault bent down and picked up a crucifix. "A long time, Sister. This crucifix is centuries old. Look at the Christ figure. Fourteenth-century, or even earlier. Must be Dominican. The friars had a priory here, right on this very spot, before they moved across the river. The first in Paris, I am told. If I recall, they found some other things here when this building was first constructed. Did you know that, Sister?"

"No, Father," answered the nun, eyeing the begrimed objects, and very conscious of the odour of age and dampness filling the room.

She turned to the priest.

"What will we do with them, Father?"

"Like they did with the others. Return them to the Dominicans," replied Thibeault, his mind already on more important things. "Some of them surely can be made inspirational again, although I do not envy the worthy Dominicans their cleaning task."

Thibeault left the room after promising Sister Martha Mary that the unsightly box would be gone by the morrow. The old nun was clearly disappointed. She had hoped for more from the trunk. Maybe some gem-encrusted monstrances, exquisitely wrought gold-inlaid chalices, or ivory-embellished crucifixes. Even her untrained eye could see that this blackened assemblage contained no such treasures from Christian antiquity. In the bright morning light, the objects seemed drab and unholy. Her reflections over, the nun turned to more practical matters. The room would have to be aired, and the floor cleansed of mud and mildew.

~ ~ ~

At that moment, Cecilia Montellan was in church hearing Mass. Her thoughts, however, were not on the holy sacrifice, but of the great adventure awaiting her. Very soon she would leave this place and sail across the sea to a land which she had been told was full of sky and woods. A husband awaited her who would be a good man, a lover of the Lord, and diligent. She would have children. She had already decided on a name for her first born. Dominic! After the saint who had received the holy rosary from the Virgin Mary herself, and who never did an evil thing in all his time on earth. Her son too, would be good and strong.

231

The little girl beside her rose and moved to the aisle of the church to join the procession towards the altar. Cecilia stood, her lips touching the tips of her fingers pressed together in supplication. At the altar rail, she took the host, and lost herself in that instant of rhapsodic oneness with the Lord. Then she followed the line of smaller girls back to her place. Her lips moved wordlessly through the joyful mysteries of the rosary, and for a moment she could taste the salt of tears.

Cecilia Montellan was seventeen years old and had lived at the orphanage as long as she could remember. She had been left in the church as a baby. Sister Catherine had taught her to read a little, and she now worked at the orphanage cleaning, and helping with the younger girls. Cecilia knew why she had not been adopted, or allowed to leave like the older girls. It was her deformity, the one the nuns said was her cross in life to be borne in the name of Jesus and His Blessed Mother. The lip which marred her comeliness, and which twisted her speech. Sister Catherine had told her to say three *Aves* whenever she heard scornful words about her ugliness. After that, the pointing and laughter never bothered her.

But this day in her tiny room under the staircase, she felt like a princess — which she indeed, was. The King of France, Louis XIV, had chosen her to be his daughter, and go to a new land across the sea called New France. The man who visited the orphanage had told her that New France was a young place that would grow mightily to become one of France's brightest jewels. But there were few Christian women there to plant the Catholic families, so the land could become steadfast in the faith. Good men there would vie for her hand. There would be a small dowry, and even a modest trousseau. Cecilia had accepted eagerly, and it had all come to pass in a very short time.

Cecilia was mending a bonnet for a seven-year-old waif new to the orphanage when she was joined by Sister Catherine. A shrewd woman with a sensitivity born of years of witness to human suffering, she knew what awaited Cecilia and the other "filles de Roi" in New France. Ignorant town girls suddenly thrust in an alien and harsh new land, cut off from everything they knew. One did not create a peasant girl by merely providing her with a husband and a new land. Most would not make the change well. The King's experiment would produce far more failures than successes. Yet, Sister Catherine had few illusions about her Cecilia. Where others saw plumpness of body, plainness of mind, and physical deformity, the nun beheld faith, strength, and a beauty that glowed from within. She would be a dutiful wife, and loving mother, and would survive where others more comely and cunning would not.

She took the needle from Cecilia, and continued the neat line of stitches. "Cecilia, my child, I shall miss you. You go so soon. The journey, they say, is not difficult, and though I fear the winters are cold in New France, the climate is agreeable during other times of the year."

Cecilia did not answer. She used her eyes when she was with Sister Catherine.

"I'll complete this, child. Sister Martha Mary wants you to air the community room, and clean it well, A trunk found in the earth, and brought there, has left mud and unsightliness on the floor."

Ten minutes later, Cecilia was in the community room with cloth and pail. The air was dank and heavy. She opened the windows, and washed the mud and earth from the wooden floor. She was returning a blackened crucifix to the trunk when she noticed the small statue of the Virgin. Without knowing why, she reached down, picked it up, and held it to the light. Even through the tarnish and grime, Cecilia could sense the rapture it conveyed. Still clutching the little icon, she looked again at the trunk with its assorted ugliness, and pondered an act that before this minute, she would have considered a vile sacrilege. Her trousseau contained nothing of the Mother Mary. Except for her rosary, which had lost beads and which lacked a proper crucifix, she had nothing sacred to take with her to a strange new place. Nothing of God to protect her, or to give her succour in times of travail. Sister Catherine had told her that the ways of God were to be known through signs. She shut her eyes, and holding the statue tightly in her hand, waited for her sign. It happened miraculously. The icon slithered through her wet fingers, and fell into her pail, concealing itself in the muddy water, and the traces of the metal case which had held it prisoner. When she removed it half an hour later in the privacy of her room, she noticed happily that Mary's features were clearer, all without the rubbing of cloth and lye. It was another sign. Her act was approved. Cecilia knelt for a short time in silent prayer, and then placed the statue carefully in her trousseau between folds of the woollen blanket given to her by Sister Catherine.

~ ~ ~

Only Sister Catherine came to bid Cecelia a last farewell. As the carriage approached, the girl and the nun embraced, Cecilia's broken speech lost further in tear-filled sobs. When her meagre possessions were loaded, she climbed awkwardly into the carriage to join three others; like her, young, solemn, and frightened. Sister Catherine watched the carriage move away, her hand held in a final wave as she re-lived Cecilia's last words to her. She had understood only two. "Mary" and "forgiveness." She wondered what it was that Cecilia was trying to tell her. Then the carriage was out of sight.

Part 2

CHAPTER I

Though scarcely forty miles west of Sydney Harbour, the mountains are barely visible to the naked eye. Shrouded in a blue haze, and undulating gently in a low line on the horizon, they appear innocuous, even benign. Yet it took a quarter of a century to conquer their crags and to discover the river-fed western slopes and the unforgiving outback beyond. On their eastern side, the mountains contain the coastal plain, a much gentler place, but for the most part more beautiful than productive, except around the Hawkesbury River flats. This river emerges suddenly from the mountains where it was born in deep gloomy gorges in raindrops caught in fern clusters; from rivulets which trickled across forested valley floors, or out of thin silver waterfalls spraying down from some damp rocky prominence. Once free from its confines it sweeps north as the Nepean, then east as the Hawkesbury, meandering through ever widening arcs before meeting the sea at Broken Bay. The early bush towns marked its course: Camden, Campbelltown, Penrith, Richmond and Windsor, with their heavy stone buildings and bridges, were links in a tenuous chain, held together by marginal roads, circuit-riding priests and officials, and the ever-present convict work gangs.

The people of the dreamtime, the Dharug, did not resist the white man, but nor were they impressed by him. They played with his gifts for a while, and then discarded them for they were not part of the land. Afterwards, they shrank from his violent depredations, retaliating only little, moving back into the bush to the wild country beyond Barrakee Mountain, and abandoning the scrublands around Sydney and the fertile pasturelands of the Hawkesbury River flats. Soon they were gone, leaving no reminder of their presence. No evidence of habitation. Nothing, save for middens of oyster shells and some marks on trees.

The white man was not drawn to the blue mountains nor to the wild upland areas that formed their eastern vanguard from Warragamba to Kurrajong. So the dreamtime people went there. Carrying everything they owned with them, they passed easily through the thick scrub, and cut across rocky gorges and forested valley floors until they were deep in the bushland fortress that guarded them from the guns and the settlers' huts along the Hawkesbury. Life was instantly familiar among the banksia and eucalyptus; old totems instantly recognized. Gogolongo, the white cockatoo was there. So was ngungurda, the turkey, and kalabara, the kangaroo. Still, some re-affirmation was necessary, and when the Dharug whirled the tjurungas that made the sacred noises, and hid others in secret places, they were call-ing on their totemic ancestors of the dreamtime to be at peace with them in this new place.

The Upper Colo River Area, northwest of Sydney, Summer, 1838

When Lamar bled for the first time, she went away alone so that the great Rainbow Snake would not see her and claim the children she would have as his own. When the bleeding stopped and she emerged from the shadows of the bush, the older women bathed her in the shallow waters of the billabong that backed off the creek where the trees were tall and where the large green frogs croaked, and when her body was clean she was led to the ritual clear-ing ground. Curved lines of red ochre were painted on her arms and shoul-ders, and below her breasts a white crescent moon was placed so that her menses would be regulated. Then she was put on the food mound while the totemic leaders of the clan danced about her, waving the secret-sacred daragi boards before her eyes so that she may catch a fleeting glimpse of their power, and all the time whirling the sacred tjurungas that called loud to the spirits of the Dreaming. Afterwards she ate at the mididi feast from the very food that had been dug from the mound, and when it was over, the dancing and the hooting of the didgeridoos at last spent and silent, and there was only the sound of the soft night wind moaning through the gum trees, Lamar hugged her legs in the dark and dreamed of the spirit world. She was now woman. Her totem was Water, and Water's assistant was Crow.

~ ~ ~

Lamar had listened well when Nagerna had told her special stories about the Dreaming, stories that the men did not like to hear. About the spirit women called the Ganabuda who possessed magical powers and who had knowledge denied to men. Nagerna did not believe the elders when they said that the Ganabuda had lost their power to men, and in the bush when she and Lamar collected berries or gathered the sweet wild honey, she would whisper often about the min-min, the flash of light in the sky which pointed the way to where the Ganabuda had come to earth bringing with them the most hidden secrets of the daragi. Lamar asked if Nagerna had ever seen a min-min. Nagerna had looked sad. No, she had never seen a min-min. But, and she had dropped her voice low though only a kookaburra was nearby laughing in a tree, and she told Lamar about Crow and Kurikuta's messenger that had caused her own spe-cial quickening so long ago.

Summer, 1839

As the famine of the dryness ravaged the Dharug, the people of the dreamtime, the elders became increasingly solemn. Their numbers were less and food was not as easy to find. There was no place to go except higher into the mountains, and their white enemies were quick with their firesticks should the Dharug go to their dwellings and take the animals that meant food. So they danced to make rain; they danced to bring kalabara back; they danced so that their numbers might be great again. But nothing happened. Just more dryness and fewer kalabara. Nagerna looked at her daughter. So few warriors to give her children. Only old men, older even than Awur.

~ ~ ~

Though the less knowledgeable in the Sydney press reported it as a comet, it was commonly agreed upon by the more scientific that the disturbance in the night sky that January evening was probably a meteor burning up as it entered the earth's atmosphere. It appeared to fall west and north of the city, probably in the Wiseman's Ferry area. When no one reported the sudden appearance of a chunk of material in a crater, it was concluded that it had burned up completely before coming into contact with the earth, or had fallen in the bush somewhere and would be found in time. Whatever its fate, it was averred to by those lucky enough that night to view the sky lit up in a blaze of flashing light that it was a spectacle well worth seeing.

~ ~ ~

The camp of the Dharug was quiet. The night was dark but warm and few slept beneath the boughs of their gunyahs and none under the robes of kangaroo or wallaby hide. There was no moon that night, and Lamar lying wide awake in the darkness could barely discern the sleeping forms of her mother, father and brothers curled up on the earth around the now dead ashes of their camp fire. Usually she slept well, undisturbed by the sounds of the night. Yet, this night her eyes had snapped open just a short time ago, strangely, unaccountably, and now she lay there gazing at the stars that twinkled like the dew drops on the morning ground. The Dreamtime was up there behind the lights in the sky. At Wantanggangura, the place inhabited by Daramulun, Kurikuta, the Ganabu, the Great Rainbow Snake and the other spirits of the sky world.

Then she saw it. The min-min! It appeared above like a path of fire, burning bright with a light that dropped from the sky to the ground. Fascinated, she stood up and tried to follow the arch of the light. She saw it come to earth in the area away from the hills and bush and down where the people with the firesticks built their gunyahs that were all closed up.

She spoke about it to Nagerna the next day when they were out gathering wood for the fire. Nagerna expressed no surprise, merely the grunt of satisfaction. "It is good that you were the one to see the min-min. You must follow its light. To the Ganabu."

"Yes, my mother. To the Ganabuda, and to Kurikuta."

"The mother of Crow? The wife of Daramulun?" Nagerna looked pleased and nodded approvingly. "I have heard the elders speak of the times that Kurikuta has come among us. She may dwell among the Ganabuda. My own mother says it is so"

"Does she come as Crow?"

"No, she comes in strange forms. Always in a light so bright that it is like the sun only the colour of the moon. You must follow the min-min. Seek out Kurikuta and ask her to save our people."

Lamar left the next day She passed easily through the bush always heading downwards towards the wide river. Occasionally she saw white people. One was felling a tree; another was running blindly and looking over his shoulder; another squatted by the water shaking dirt from a flat vessel. But they didn't see her. Her feet were like the wings of owl in the night, and on the third day when they cooled themselves in the soft mud by the banks of the wide river, she could feel the spirits calling her. As if led by unseen hands she began following the murky green waters.

~ ~ ~

Tall forest red gums and grey box trees ringed the water forming a giant mottled green canopy that reached endlessly back into the bush. Patches of orange and yellow dotted themselves among the she-oak and banksia, and occasionally the climbing indigo entwined itself thirty feet from the ground to hang suspended like a brilliant violet wreath. The water itself was like a dark still flat space. Not a ripple broke its perfect mirror, nothing beneath its warm shallow depths rose to meet the sun. No insect buzzed or flitted about its surface. It was one of those breathless burning summer days that blurred and rippled its heat in limpid waves, and which showed the bush in its still-life survival pose. Everything hiding, turning in on itself, waiting out the heat. All except the cicadas. High above the ground in their green canopies, they drummed out their song from serrated cavities under their abdomens. Black, gold, red or green, and bedecked by exquisitely formed large gauzy wings, these harbingers of summer sang endlessly in a loud, persistent, musical eulogy that stretched between the sky and the earth, in a high-pitched crescendo. So energetic was their singing that the cicadas could not keep still. It was as if the energy of their noise-making had to be accompanied by other movement. Even when they flew they sang. Slow-moving and possessed with no natural evasive tactics, they fell easy prey to even the most undignified of avian hunters. So they developed an alternative strategy. They would crawl backwards down the branches and trunks of the trees, singing lustily until they had reached a point low enough for the journey to be reversed. They rarely allowed their downward journey to bring them really close to the ground, but occasionally a particularly preoccupied singer got carried away.

The crow was watching one such wayward singer, his black beady eyes fixed intently on the lime-green cicada who was now only about ten feet from the ground and still crawling. One easy jump and he would have had the tasty morsel in a second. Had he been able to fly, that is. His right wing dragged below his body. He had injured it escaping from a wedge-tailed eagle, falling from the sky in a tumbling black heap. Now he limped around the billabong catching what he could – which was not a great deal, given the competition for food and his own immobility. He eyed the cicada hungrily. The crow's anxiety overcame his patience when his quarry was still four feet above him. With a squawk and a leap, the crow lunged for the cicada, missing it with his long beak but knocking the startled creature to the ground. Then just as he was about to seize it, the cicada took off, flying low and erratically towards the water. Infuriated, the crow chased after it, heedlessly splashing into the water in his eagerness. Before he knew it, it was too late. His feet sank into the mud; both wings flapped uselessly cascading water over his feathers until his whole body was saturated. Then, inevitably, the uneven flapping of his wings tipped him over until he was lying sideways in the water. The thrashing became feebler, then ceased completely. The crow's beak opened slightly, one black eye looked towards the sky, and then the long ebony head slipped below the surface.

Lamar stood on the bank, frozen for a moment into stillness as she watched her own totem claiming Crow. It was a sign. Kurikuta's son must be saved. She splashed out into the water and placed her two hands under Crow just as he was sinking to the bottom. She was suddenly frightened. Cradling the sodden, limp form close to her body, she rushed headlong towards the water's edge. She didn't see the sunken log until her shin struck it. With a cry, she fell forwards, throwing out her arms to protect herself and releasing the crow. The large flat stone was half buried in the mud just above the waterline and with a sickening thud, the side of Lamar's head struck it with the full force of her plunging fall. She lay still for hours until the sun was low in the sky, long after the Crow's feathers had dried and he had recovered enough to sit on a moss-covered log where he remained watching the bleeding figure on the sand.

Lamar awoke slowly feeling the blinding flash of pain at her temples. Everything seemed strange and new and there was a tingling ringing feeling at the back of her head. Where was she? Ah, there was Crow looking at her from a log, so she must be close to Kurikuta. Where could she be? Lamar got to her feet unsteadily and leaned against a tree while she fought for her balance. The crow was still watching her. His black beady eyes were fixed on her and his head was cocked slightly, inquiringly as if he too was looking for Kurikuta. Why shouldn't he, she thought? After all, she was his mother. At last when the pain in her head died down enough to allow her to walk, Lamar stepped back into the tepid water and walked out until she was knee-deep. Above her, the cicadas were screaming their chorus to the sky. For a moment the noise was deafening and as she put her hands to her ears she felt herself spinning. The trees were turning, blurring, upside down, and weaving in and out of her vision like a spirit from the Dreamtime. She was going to fall. But she didn't. The light held her up, kept her feet planted in the soft mud. It was right in front of her rising from the water accompanied by what seemed to be a fine mist. "Kurikuta," she breathed.

The Mother of Crow was before her in the mist above the water, but she was not wet. A white light beamed out from her and she sparkled like the wet grass with the sun upon it. Her skin was white and she was adorned in the colour of the sky. Her head was covered and around her waist she wore a string of sacred tjurunga attached to a form of Daramulun on two pieces of black crossed sticks.

"Kurikuta." The words tumbled from Lamar's lips. "O, mother of Crow. Hear me. We have become the wretched. The Dharug have not eaten emu. They have performed the dances to Daramulun and of Ngalabal with much reverence. But still our numbers grow small even as our bellies rumble with hunger and our tongues thirst for the rains that do not come. Help us Kurikuta. Help us, your people."

Kurikuta spread her hands, but she said nothing. Was she going away? Lamar felt an urgency. "Speak to me, O Kurikuta, so that I may tell my people."

Kurikuta raised her face. It shone like the sun itself. Then she spoke in a voice so low yet so wonderful that Lamar would hear its message over and over again in the days of terror, and through the nights of loneliness that were to come. "Go now, for it is not yet time. My son will be with you and then in you after I come again by the water and the rushes where the duck flies. Prepare yourself. Walk in fresh tracks, and speak only to my son."

"Yes, Kurikuta, and then will my people be saved?"

Wonderfully, Lamar saw Kurikuta smile. It was like a flood of joy, and for a moment she was in the Dreamtime among the spirits that breathed life into man and tree and flower. "Yes! All will be saved."

Then she dissolved into the mist. Lamar stretched out her hand but felt nothing. For an instant she thought she saw two other figures standing behind where Kurikuta had been. The Ganabuda, she thought to herself. Then she was standing alone in the water. Her head was still ringing, and again she had to put her hands to her ears to dull the throbbing songs of the cicadas.

~ ~ ~

Three weeks later a group of riders returning with some stray cattle found Lamar, wandering up along the riverbank upstream from Wiseman's Ferry in the Wilberforce area. She was very thin and her body was scratched in several places. She made no attempt to run away but faced her discoverers with a look of detachment in her strangely-flecked brown eyes, the look that told them she was mentally enfeebled. Telling the story in a Windsor hotel a day later Roy Barnes, one of the search party, went over again and again the most interesting aspect of the whole strange bizarre episode. A naked abo wandering around the Hawkesbury so close to settlement was unusual; so was the fact that they couldn't get her to say a word even in Windsor when they brought a couple of civilized abos in to talk to her. It was the bird that had intrigued them. "She had a bloody crow. It sat on her shoulder and wouldn't leave."

"So why didn't you piss the bloody thing off, chase it away, wring its friggin' neck?" It seemed like a reasonable thing to do, they all agreed.

"We tried," admitted Barnes. "She went mad. Attacked us. Growled and snarled like a mad dog."

"So what did you do?"

"What could we friggin do? We let the bloody thing stay with her."

"Where is she now?"

"Pat took her to his house. The Mons is coming in tomorrow. He'll know what to do with her. He'll probably take her back to Parramatta."

"To the orphanage, probably."

"Or the nut house. She'll get her share of cock bird there." They all snickered. The new Lunatic Asylum in Parramatta was a rumourmonger's delight.

"Then she won't need the crow?"

They all laughed uproariously and went back to some steady drinking.

~ ~ ~

For Monsignor Bede Polding, saddling his horse in the warm light of the early morning sun, it was to be a totally new experience. He had ridden into Windsor yesterday morning and rather than say Mass immediately in the tiny church, he had conducted one of his popular bell-ringing ceremonies, followed by a public penance offering and a cavalcade through town. He was aware of his nefarious reputation among the Protestants and even some of the more orthodox Catholics. It was said that he would sooner invent a Pontifical ritual than go without one. But it worked.

The Church had suffered terrible setbacks already in this colony. It had been maligned, even banned. But now, after four years here, he could discern some changes for the better. Why, even at this moment a Dominican priest was on his way from Rome to help him. And the people flocked to his sermons; they gathered at the side of the mud-filled roads gazing with awe as he paraded past, dressed in the glorious vestments that pronounced ritual and pomp to a populace ground down with ordinariness and the hopelessness that accompanied it. Yes, he was a missionary and proud of it. He smiled as a willy wagtail cocked its inquisitive head towards him. The bird reminded him of this land. It didn't seem to know its place. The rules were different here. He, Bede Polding, a Benedictine monk over forty years of age and old enough to know better, carrying two pistols tucked into his belt while he conveyed God's word to a rootless people. Who would have believed it back in the monastery?

The horse was saddled now, and everything was packed into two saddlebags. Vestments, holy vessels, missal. He was going to have to give Richmond a miss this time. He had to get the girl back to Parramatta. Once on the horse and heading out through bush, he began to recite his daily Office. He stopped after only a few moments. The words seemed hollow and misplaced. Instead he found himself thinking about what Pat Treacy had whispered urgently to him the previous morning during the time the public penance brought people to his ear. "Father, you must come tonight. An aboriginal girl had been found wandering by the river. No one knows who she is. She cannot talk and suffers from dementia. But she is comely and I fear for her fate should she be set free or indentured. I do not know what to do, Father. I cannot keep her, but in God's name I also cannot cast her loose. Come tonight and see for yourself."

So, late that afternoon, he had gone to Treacy's house by the river. Treacy's sister had dressed the girl in a simple dress. She had been washed and her hair combed and smoothed. Polding had gasped inwardly when he saw her. The girl was indeed beautiful, with eyes that seemed to look through and beyond him. She didn't speak but reached continuously for the crow that sat on her shoulder, patting its sleek neck and stroking its leg. He had tried to speak to her, using the coaxing reassuring tone that brought him success when dealing with the terrified or insensitive creatures that inhabited the Rookeries just off the wharves of Sydney, and who lived off the avails of licentiousness. But the girl had simply looked through him as if he wasn't there. Demented. Out of her mind. She was a child-animal, Pat Treacy had said originally, but now he wasn't sure. Polding wasn't either. There was something there behind those eyes. He wished he knew what it was.

Afterwards, he and Pat Treacy had talked. A kind-hearted Irishman with sandy hair and blue eyes, Treacy had come out from Ireland with his sister as a free settler in the early 1830s. A strong back and a knowledge of horses enabled him to land some government contracts hauling trees out of the bush, and within five years he was able to build his own small house by the river just outside Windsor. The arrival of this strange girl had upset him greatly.

"I expected her to leave, Father. Throw the dress off, run away and become someone else's problem."

"But she hasn't, Pat. So now what?" Polding was hoping that Treacy would volunteer to keep the girl; train her as a servant girl or try to locate her people and send her back to them, if that was where she belonged.

"Well, she can't stay here."

"Not even after you built the cage for her crow?" Polding's eyes were smiling.

"She just walks about with that crow on her shoulder. I'm sure she talks to it."

"Have you heard her? Speak, I mean."

"No, but she sure enough loves that crow. Look, Father. She can't stay here. She can't be simply let go back to the bush. I don't think she'd survive. You've got to take her back with you. They've moved the orphanage for girls from Sydney to Parramatta, haven't they? Why couldn't she stay there? At least she could be looked after until . . ." Pat broke off, and reached for his pipe, leaving Polding to pick up the conversation.

"The orphanage. Yes. It's not in Sydney anymore. It's run by good people. Many of the girls are as pitiful as this poor child. You know, I think you're right, Pat. I just wish I knew the full story. I think there's more to her than some mute abo wandering the bush."

"But what if she can talk, Father? What if we're wrong about her being a simpleton? You may find out everything in time."

Polding seemed to relax somewhat now that his mind was made up. He got up and walked around the small veranda. "How do we get her there? She won't know how to sit on a horse and I doubt whether she will want to ride behind me. You've got to come with me, Pat."

Treacy nodded his head, surprising Polding, who had been prepared to be more persuasive. "Yes, Father. I'll come. I think she trusts me, and she'll be frightened."

"Thank you, Pat. You're a good man." He rose to leave. "Tomorrow all right with you? Around nine? Maybe she'll be gone," he added.

Pat didn't reply at first. He was looking down past his vegetable garden to where the girl was walking vacantly. "No. She'll be here." Then he went on. "Father, what about her crow?"

Polding hesitated for just a second. "Leave it here. Let it go. She can't take it with her."

Treacy's pale blue eyes were suddenly moist. "But she has to, Father. It's the only thing she has. Isn't it?"

For once, John Bede Polding was at a loss for words.

~ ~ ~

Treacy's hut was built a little bit back from the banks of the river, obscured by trees and bushes. The sun was just setting and the flat mirror-like surface was tinged with a golden hue, disturbed and then rippling when Lamar splashed in and walked out until the hem of her dress was sodden. She looked around. She could see no reeds and the voice of duck was not among those whose throaty calls heralded the coming of night. The pain in her head was still there but the strange noises were not as loud. Kurikuta would not come here tonight. It would be in another time when more new tracks had been made. Dreamily she thought of her people. All in the spirit world. Away, up and gone to the Dreamtime. She would ask Kurikuta to send them back; to make them all rise out of her totem; to come out of the water where reeds grew and duck sang, as eagle, lizard, snake, possum, wombat, galah. She giggled a girlish giggle and raised her arms above her head pointing her slender long hands at the puffy pinkness that was hiding the sun. Lizard! Yes! She would ask Kurikuta to make Nagerna lizard. She wished she could remember if Nagerna liked lizard. But she couldn't see Nagerna's face. The shadows danced in front of her eyes, holding up daragi that she couldn't see. Her head was hurting. Lamar reached urgently for Crow. His feathers were warm and soft, and she rubbed the bird's sleek neck for a long time before she left the water and lay down in the darkness on the ground near the gunyah of the man with eyes like the flower that grew high in the trees, and hair like grass in the sun.

~ ~ ~

The trip to Parramatta went off better than Bede Polding anticipated. The girl seemed relaxed around Treacy. Even the crow didn't seem to resent the red-faced Irishman's presence. He put her on the horse first and when she was settled climbed on in front of her, talking all the while in a matter-of-fact tone that managed somehow to sound reassuring. They were riding a horse, he told her, and were going to a place where she would be looked after, and where she would learn many new things. Polding was surprised at her reaction. Her eyes opened wide and she grabbed onto Treacy's arm. My God thought Polding, she understands. She knows he won't be there. Treacy was laughing and patting the girl's cheek. He'd visit her when he came to Parramatta.

They rode all day along the well-worn road that passed through bush interspersed only occasionally by cleared fields and settlers' huts. Polding felt the pistols at his belt. Bushrangers. That's all they'd need. The ruffians would only too willing to take the girl off their hands. But there was no sudden emergence from the bush; no strident sound of "Bail up"; no ring of prancing horses or the hot desperate eyes of men already doomed to welcome the hangman should they be caught. There were just the bird sounds and the infernal cicadas. Polding wished his congregations sang with a fraction as much gusto as the cicadas. Strange! He'd never seen one. Idly he found himself wondering what they looked like.

Treacy kept up the banter as long as he could, saying anything, and laughing and pointing. Once, at a kookaburra with a snake in his beak. They stopped the horses and watched the bird wheeling in the sky, dropping the reptile and retrieving it in a series of repetitions that effectively did what the bird's beak couldn't. Only when the snake's body was sufficiently pummelled did the kookaburra consider his quarry a fitting meal. Throughout the whole spectacle, Lamar said nothing. There was no release of pressure from the arm around his waist and when Treacy turned to look at her, she wasn't even watching the kookaburra. She was staring straight ahead with those strange light-brown eyes that seemed empty and all-seeing at the same time, and all the while, her left hand stroked the side of the crow's neck.

~ ~ ~

They were ushered inside the orphanage that evening by a small woman in a uniform too big for her, and led to a large community room. Matron Edwards joined them soon after. A large formidable looking woman whose imposing presence hid a gentle kindly nature, she kept clucking sympathetically and casting sidelong glances at Lamar while Polding explained their circumstances. Then it was Treacy's turn to speak. Matron Edwards gave his advice the same level of credence as she had the priest's, nodding approvingly and making notes in a small black book. She did not have to be pressured into taking the silver that Polding offered her to help with the girl's upkeep.

It was agreed. The girl would stay at the orphanage indefinitely. Until such time as she could be released to find work, or to return to her people if that was her choice, or alternatively to be committed to the asylum for the insane should her mental condition so demand. Since she didn't seem fit or able to receive lessons in the custom of the orphanage, possibly she could be assigned simple tasks. And yes, she would be allowed to keep her crow. Providing it slept outdoors, of course.

Once outside, the two men parted, each back to his own world. Pat Treacy's last glimpse of the girl was of a shadowy figure standing in front of the matron. The crow was on her shoulder but there was a solitude about her as if she was all alone in the world. He thought he saw sadness in the vacant eyes, and for an instant Treacy wanted to go back and take her with him, back to his farm and a life that wouldn't be as frightening as this.

Usually when he visited Parramatta, he'd go to the General Bourke for a few drinks and later a meal and a warm bed. But not tonight. He just wanted to get home even if he had to travel all night. Back at the chapel, Bede Polding felt a sense of relief mixed with the misgivings of incompleteness. Something was not quite right. It must be the Protestant orphanage. Yes, that was it. He would consign her to the Catholic orphanage when he got it organized. Unlike Treacy who kept the girl's face with him through the blackness of the night and beyond into the bush trails and among the felled trees, Polding quickly lost her memory, a wilted flower to be forgotten and gone among the forest of problems that beset him from all sides.

~ ~ ~

It was fortunate that Matron Edwards was such a charitable soul. Having quickly concluded that the girl was a simple wild imbecile, she left her alone to wander the grounds of the orphanage at will. After all, she always came back. Even when she didn't one day in May, Matron Edwards did not worry. She merely assumed that Mary — for that was the name given to her — had simply gone back into the bush where she probably belonged. But there she was three days later, feeding the chickens in the back sheds. It was then that Matron Edwards had had her inspiration.

The child was good with animals. It was impossible to keep her in a dormitory and the other girls made fun of her behind her back, not that Mary seemed to notice or care. There was a presence about her which made even the coarsest of the girls leave her alone. Why not allow her to feed the animals and look after them permanently? And so it was. Mary was given a small room in the cow barns. One of the other girls checked on her daily, bringing her meals to her, and even these were scarcely needed, for Mary seemed to survive on nothing. The farmer from Windsor, Pat Treacy, visited her whenever he could, but even he could get no response from her. He did bring coin, however, and that always got Matron Edwards' response. The girl was no trouble, kept to herself and was far more self-reliant than any of the other orphans. Abandoned waifs for the most part, and illegitimate unwanted offspring from convict mothers, her girls needed all the attention and money she and her poorly maintained staff could give them. And so, Mary stayed, with her crow. She came and went like a brown ghost, unnoticed and unheeded, except for the animals in the barn who had come to love her.

Spring, 1839

The newly green rushes that choked the side of the creek hid the places where water met land, the taller older shoots standing brown-tipped and straight in the brisk south wind. Toongabbie Creek spread slowly out in a wide expanse of shallow swamplands that seemed to go nowhere. Even after the rains of winter it resembled more a swollen floodplain than it did a flowing creek. No tall trees surrounded or protected it. It just went on. Water becoming reeds, reeds becoming bush and scrub until all moisture gave way to dryness. In time, burnt and ravaged by summer, the flowing creek would shrink, fading away into disconnected waterholes. But for now it exuded a lethargic vitality, meandering northeast to empty itself into the headwaters of the Parramatta River.

Abruptly, the early afternoon was broken by the sound of wings thrashing as the marsh fowl rose from the reeds in great flocks, retreating into the scrub where they waited watchfully. The creek was cold and silent, the only sign of movement being the ripples that spread themselves before the wind.

Lamar came from nowhere, moving unhurriedly through the reeds. Her eyes were fixed on some point in front of her. On her shoulder the black crow sat as if he were carved in stone. The water was cold. So was the mud that squelched between the girl's toes as she moved knee-deep into the centre of the water's open expanse. Suddenly she stopped and gazed around as if taking in the scene for the first time. This could be the place. The reeds were there, and she had seen duck rise into the air quacking his departure to the wind.

Her head was spinning hurtfully and for a second she thought she would fall. But she mustn't. She spoke the words as firmly as she could. "O Kurikuta, mother of Crow. Where are you? I have waited long for you to come again as you promised. With new tracks and a tongue that talks only to Crow, I have done as you asked. Where goes the Ganabuda? Where goes Kurikuta?"

But there was no sound beyond the fading tones of her voice. Out in the scrub, the birds sat silent. Lamar patted the crow's neck and turning her head whispered to it. "Kurikuta does not come today, Atha. This is not the place."

There was a sudden freshening in the wind, and Lamar cocked her head listening intently. Her voice quickened in urgency. "Atha, listen! She is calling to us on the wind. 'Where the reeds grow and the duck flies, there will I come'."

Trancelike, she turned in the water until she was facing east away from the blue hills and from creeks that grew false rushes and ducks that spoke hollowly. Her eyes widened and she smiled. "That is the way, Atha. Kurikuta will come in the direction of the morning sun. Next time we will go farther into places where the tracks of the Dharug have been forgotten. Kurikuta will wait for us there."

She was gone as silently as she had come. The birds came back and within minutes the ducks had recommenced building their nests among the reeds, the wind rippling their mottled feathers and catching the yellow grasses that hung from their bills.

CHAPTER II

Sydney, March 11, 1840

The Patriotes emerged from the holds in a single ragged line and though the day was dull and heavy with the residue of rain, the frailer ones were still forced to shield their eyes from the unaccustomed light. Most were able to carry everything they owned on their backs, but a few had satchels and trunks which were taken from them and thrown into a heap on the deck of the *Buffalo*. Less than ten minutes later, three longboats were making their way towards a small dock at the western edge of the main cove. They sat low in the water, their huddled occupants making them look like floating shapeless blobs. Watching from the shore with his sandaled feet almost touching the incoming ripples, Father Bernard Blake felt a sense of satisfaction. It was all so easy and so predictable. He had little sympathy for the miserable lot of French peasants whose lives he had undoubtedly saved. They would be as worthless in the place they were now going as they would have been in Norfolk Island. It didn't matter to him.

The longboats had reached their destination and Bernard could scarcely see them as they disgorged their human cargo into a long flat-bottomed barge. A half an hour later when the unwieldy craft began its sputtering journey up the river that fed into Sydney Harbour, Bernard Blake was gone.

~ ~ ~

It was around noon when the barge swept slowly into a wide, shallow bay. The tide was out, exposing dark brown mud flats and naked mangrove swamps, twisted, stinking and impenetrable. A long, rather primitive jetty jutted into the bay, and just beyond it waited a detachment of British troops, together with a cart drawn by two large bullocks. The Patriotes clambered ashore awkwardly and several blessed themselves as their feet touched for the first time the land of their exile. There was no way out. On all sides, and across the river to the north a dark green sameness met their eyes. Stark, inhospitable, unfamiliar, save for the hated red uniforms and the truculent men who wore them.

When the Patriotes' effects were loaded onto the cart, they fell in behind it, and under the watchful eyes of the guards followed the rough track that led inland from the mud flats and the jetty. Martin's legs felt unsteady and he stumbled over hidden roots, falling more than once to his knees in the yielding brown earth. There was no breeze and the air was stiflingly hot. They were all sweating freely when they emerged from the bush into a large square compound. Martin cringed at the four crude sheds that passed for huts, squatting there in the mud like dreary sentinels. A pungent muddy fishy odour hung in the air. It was like a new world, a thousand miles from anywhere, with its own smell and all around a mottled wall of green that hung damp and listless in the heavy air. Longbottom Stockade! Martin shuddered. The land of a thousand sorrows! At the time it was coined on the ship, he had thought it somewhat of an overstatement, but the description the Patriotes had given to this land seemed all at once to jump out at him with its own awful truth. He blinked rapidly fighting back the tears, scarcely conscious of the rain that had begun to fall again.

~ ~ ~

Sydney Cove was a jumble of old and new buildings, constructed seemingly at random. Recently built warehouses, new docks, makeshift jetties and squalid buildings competed for space along the water's edge. Bernard Blake had been standing on a protrusion of rocks between two wharves just east of the Cove, and as he retraced his steps towards the old Tank Stream, he stepped around two aboriginal women squatting on the ground roasting some fish in hot white coals on the damp earth. Clothed pathetically in dirty long dresses that reached down to the ankles of their bare feet, they looked incuriously at him as he passed.

Soon the tall masts of the ships were behind him and he was in lower George Street, heading back towards the priests' residence beside the new church which rose beyond the abomination they called the botanical gardens. Latterly a dust bowl, it was now a quagmire. The notion of sun-shrivelled specimens drowning in a surfeit of water appealed to Bernard. It was typical of this country. Just like the aboriginal women. Filthy stone-age creatures, black and simple, eking out an existence within sight of respectable English houses where tea and muffins in the afternoon bespoke proper British tradition. Blake stopped and took in the confusion of buildings that sprawled to the blue waters of the harbour. Yes, it was truly a land of extremes. It allowed man-made ugliness to foreshadow a wild and wonderful natural beauty; it postured refinement while wallowing in a turgid shameless ignorance. But most of all, this place sustained an unmoulded pliancy, stirred accidentally into raw anarchy by the very idiots sent out to impose order. And that was why, despite his abhorrence and disgust, Bernard Blake was at home in Sydney Town.

When he arrived in the late summer of 1839, he had been dismayed by Sydney's primitiveness. Unpaved alleys passed as streets, meandering aimlessly just like the infernal goats that plagued the settlement with their voracious appetites. Though the Royal Hotel, two Protestant churches and the new Government House were beginning to give the place some sort of civilized flavour, it still lacked any sense of permanence. The military barracks with their low roofs and open verandas was a vulgar colonial announcement, and even the burial grounds beside the Post Office with the domed synagogue hovering above them reminded him of a forlorn cemetery in a Moorish country. Polding had once told him that Sydney resembled a typical English seaport town. If that was the case, then he was glad he had never lived in England.

There was nothing to remind him of Genoa. No old gentility nor even a sense of potential refinement. Sydney was a dirty place, squalid to the extreme once you got past the newer brick houses with their geranium hedges. The dens of vice known as the Rookeries stretched from Sydney Cove to Darling Harbour, a strip of hovels and filth that made the poor quarters of Rome respectable by comparison. The only place he ever found interesting in Sydney Town was the market. The great array of flowers, fruits, vegetables and other produce, advertised in half a dozen accents and languages gave an indication not only of vitality, but also of the potential fecundity of this place. Sydney was coarse. It was ugly. It harboured no respect and little honour. Yet it roiled with a restless energy. It was a veritable desert out of which Lamar would come. Every time the barrenness of his own life tormented him in the night like the black flies, he thought of Lamar. The new order would begin here. Where errors had not yet been made; where rawness could be moulded; where libertines could be made into martyrs.

He spent the rest of the morning in the Rookeries visiting its gaunt denizens: felons; freed men without money or hope; husbandless women and their bastard impoverished children, the Currency lads and lasses who hated their own native-born status almost as much as they despised the Englishmen who posed as their betters. Bernard Blake loathed the place, but he kept looking, sometimes at perfumed sluts, but more often beyond them at the ragged, reed-thin creatures in tattered skirts who melted away whenever he came. He endured the frightened silences, the thinly-veiled suspicions and even the pathetic gestures of gratitude as evidence only of the torpor of survival, worth neither fear nor sympathy. They were at best slaves of right-minded idiots, misled and untempered by hope. Yet his Lamar could be born out of such despair, just as the beautiful butterfly rose from a grub in the dirt. Or so he had hoped when he first visited the hovels of the wretched and met their daughters. But he had found nothing save lewdness, fright, and most of all, vacuousness. He knew he frightened them, but he didn't care. He was aware that they fell before his white robe and avoided his dark eyes. Fear always engendered the highest level of respect.

But time had to be spent there, mouthing words and ministering meaningless rites. In the Rookeries, as everywhere else in this anarchical land, Bernard Blake practised his own blend of prayerful glibness. He would juxtapose liturgies and evoke nonsensical Latin phrases. He once absolved a petty thief's confession by quoting directly in Arabic from the Koran. His entire set of religious duties became creative exercises in contrivance. He daydreamed during confessions; he spoke quietly but hollowly of the curative powers of miracle waters to men who couldn't walk; he equated fecundity with piety to sick women heavy with child, and talked about celestial feasts to families whose stomachs rumbled with hunger.

This day was no different. It was noon before he made his last call, picking his way among the tangle of ramshackle buildings, and stepping over still-prone bodies and the half empty bottles that lay beside them. He stopped outside Phillip Branston's crumbling wattle shack, pausing for a moment before entering. The room was dark and smelled of stale urine. The sole occupant lay on a filthy cot breathing shallowly. But as close to death as he was, and though he might welcome Bernard with relief in his eyes Phillip Branston would still die alone.

It should have taken Bernard Blake half an hour. Instead, it took him five minutes. It was the fastest Extreme Unction he had ever administered. He had left out most of it and had perfunctorily gone through the crucial anointment rites. He couldn't bear to touch the dying man's skin. But he knew Polding would ask. Not that Bernard couldn't have lied, but you never knew with these people. Someone with wayward eyes and a loose tongue might have noticed his absence. Oh God, he hated the rookeries. But he would have gone there despite Polding, just like he would continue to go to the place he hated most of all. The Factory for Female Convicts in Parramatta almost made him physically ill, so much so that he had almost convinced himself that Lamar could never be found there. But there were so few women in this place and she had to be somewhere. If not, only madness awaited him.

~ ~ ~

Bernard spoke to few people as he made his way up King Street. The passers-by touched their hats and bowed slightly. Some even smiled and a few greeted him by name. A terse word in reply and a flash of the eyes were all that they got in return. The shops in this place were a ghastly agglomeration, festooned with everything from hanging meats and glassy-eyed fish to female finery and its cosmetic accoutrements. The grinding whir of a potter's wheel, a stack of mutton pies smoking hot and flaky brown, the smell of beer and the laughter that went with it, and worst of all, the vacuous looks in the eyes of those who rummaged and sniffed and who rustled their skirts like pale serpents. There was no merit, no solace in such squalid peddling. And he had been inside every one, searching.

Soon he was crossing the open field, avoiding the mud puddles, and quickening his steps as the first raindrops began to fall. The small church that Polding dreamed would one day be a cathedral was barely discernible as the rain began to fall more heavily. Bernard Blake broke into a run. He had never seen rain fall like it did in New South Wales: heavy and thick, like a cloud had burst directly above. Only there was no cloud, just a grey canopy and a wall of wetness. He was thoroughly soaked by the time he reached the humble stone house where he and Polding resided when they were in Sydney. He had a bed-room and a place to work and nothing else. There was only one decent room in the whole house, a semi-library and community room where Polding received his guests and where he met with Bernard Blake every second day at one o'clock to discuss church business. Bernard Blake noted the time. It was two minutes to one, and Polding was a punctilious man. But he hated being awry far more than he feared the ire of a monk-turned-administrator.

Not that he despised Polding. On the contrary. The man was sincere and dedicated. He was just misguided, like the rest. Bernard sighed as he changed his robe. Polding was the irritating type. Incapable of seeing – let alone grasp-ing – his destiny, but serious and confident enough to believe he could make a difference. Such peasants held enormous nuisance value to superior men. Bernard Blake was changed by ten minutes past one. He read a book for another ten minutes. Then after straightening a robe that needed no adjust-ment, he made his way unhurriedly to where he knew Polding would be fum-ing impatiently.

But Bishop John Bede Polding had far weightier matters on his mind that day than the tardiness of his Dominican secretary. He sat at his desk heedless of the rain drumming against the windows. Prematurely grey and with a strong broad ruddy face and a robust sense of humour that belied his former monas-tic life, he had not had an easy time bringing the faith to a land ruled by a reli-giously unsympathetic nation, a country that had only recently embraced what it fancifully called "Catholic Emancipation." Exacerbated by the presence of so many Irish, whether as felons or freed men, the Church in New South Wales was viewed as a haven for subversives. The editorial on his desk from the Catholic-baiting rag, *The Sydney Gazette*, was a case in point. It accused his six Sisters of Charity of propagating Papist doctrines in the Female Factory in Parramatta. It was all nonsense, of course. The good sisters were merely practising charitable acts among the prisoners. But with the watchful eye of the government and the Church of England fixed malevolently on him, he would have to do something about it.

Polding scarcely heard Bernard's knock. A quick glance at his watch and he remembered his secretary. "Come in, Bernard. It's not locked."

A few seconds later, Bernard stood in front of his superior. He was scowling slightly, a look that Polding had come to recognize and understand. He was annoyed at being called Bernard instead of Bernard Blake, but to Polding it was such a mouthful. It couldn't be helped. "Good to see you, Bernard. I trust the Patriotes were disembarked without incident."

Bernard nodded. It was obvious that he didn't want to say more, but Polding pressed on regardless. He knew that Bernard liked to use terseness, like most other things, as a goad. He mocked you with indifference. He challenged with sarcasm. Terseness was his substitution for contempt. So Polding countered him by feigning obliviousness, a sentiment which if secretly scorned had to be openly tolerated.

"They should be at Longbottom by now." Polding slapped his leg. "By all that's truthful, Bernard, but that was a masterful stroke you employed. Gipps was bound and determined to send them to Norfolk Island."

Bernard shrugged. "He was afraid of the *Gazette*. They all are."

"But an appeal made to one of Her Majesty's governors by invoking his very own words! Marvellous, Bernard, Marvellous."

Bernard's eyes held a familiar mocking look. He smiled slightly. "You didn't know, Monsignor? About Gipps, I mean?"

Polding recognized the taunt and ignored it. Two could play the game, wearisome though it was. Like many men of enormous intelligence and ability, Bernard was vulnerable through his own pride. Polding had had to deal with it often in others, both in years past in the monastery, and now here in Sydney. Sometimes it could be assuaged through flattery. Verbal bullying or the exercise of rank was occasionally in order. Frankness, too, had worked well for him. The first two were useless with Bernard. He had known that after their first conversation. The best thing to do with Bernard was to outline the situation or circumstance and then allow him to define his own options within them.

Thankfully for Polding, Bernard usually chose the wisest course, although occasionally he would suggest an alternative of his own. Since Polding had no difficulty in demurring to a wiser man – and, he had to admit, Bernard was right far more often than he was wrong – there had been little friction between them. On the occasions where he disagreed with the Dominican he found that evincing uncertainty was an excellent palliative. To Polding, Bernard's subsequent supercilious smile was proof positive that one man's uncertainty meant the other man's moral victory. All of which was fine to John Bede Polding, a man of God with a worldly view of God's work. Let the Dominican have his head as long as he didn't recognize the harness.

Polding went on effusively. "I knew, of course, that Gipps had spent some time in Canada, but had no idea of his work there. I am amazed, but he knows as much about the Patriotes as they do themselves. But how did you find out? About the Royal Commission, I mean? His recommendations?"

"It's in the library. I came across it when we called upon him in Government House last week."

"But how?" Polding's incredulity showed.

"Remember when Gipps wanted to show you his new hound? I stayed while you went out to the kennels with him."

"Yes, but we were away such a short time. The animal was being walked. You would have had to find the book and discover the information in less than five minutes."

"You had mentioned once that Gipps had visited Canada. I also possess an affinity with books. Even on the shelf they can tell you much. It was thin, too thin, and looked out of place, displayed so prominently among other obviously significant historical tomes. So I examined it. *The Gosford Commission: A Royal Commission into the Political Problems of the Canadas*, prepared by George Gipps and George Grey. It was all so simple. Since I read very quickly, I discovered what was needed in a short time."

"That Gipps and Grey had sympathy with the plight of the farming class and that of the artisans. That their political and economic grievances were real. It was a fine stroke of fortune for us, Bernard. The good governor had no choice but to agree after you confronted him so coolly and with such convincing words." Polding was clearly excited.

Bernard continued as if he hadn't heard the other man. "But they also saw no real solution to the problem. Beyond independence, and that, the British would never agree to give. It is a manifestation of their utter haplessness that the peasant farmers went about it the wrong way."

"You excite my curiosity, Bernard. You might tell me more some day. The main thing now is that our good governor agreed that banishing these men to Norfolk Island was inconsistent with the tone of his own Royal Commission. Gipps had no choice. Persuaded by the righteousness of his own words. It was brilliant, Bernard, the way you coaxed the final nod of that finely manicured head. 'Right-minded men with legitimate grievances, easily led astray by more devious and dangerous anarchists. None with a prison record. Many of them artisans with skilled hands, and bound by the doctrines of a church they love.' Yes, Bernard, you were masterful. As for Longbottom, they tell me is not a disagreeable place and the new superintendent is a reasonable man. With the last nails about to be driven into the foul coffin of convict bondage, our French-speaking friends should not have to languish long in confinement."

Polding rubbed his hands together in satisfaction and leaned back in his chair looking out at the grey sky, seemingly oblivious to his companion's disinterest. There was no shared joy. Bernard Blake's eyes were clouded, as if he were seeing other things, and the corner of his mouth was twisted in a slight curl.

"But on to other things, Bernard. We have a problem."

Bernard's eyebrows raised imperceptibly.

"It's the Female Factory, I'm afraid. Over a hundred more women have been added since our last visit and the confounded *Gazette* is accusing us of proselytizing among them." Polding waved his hand impatiently, even though Bernard had said nothing. "Oh, I don't mean that our sisters have become overly zealous. That dreadful Bell woman hates us and has probably fed a few evil rumours to the press."

"The Matron is vile carrion. I'll aver that."

Polding looked up, surprised. Agreement from Bernard was a rarity. He wondered what the ample Mrs Bell had done.

"I want you to leave next week. For the Hawkesbury towns. I realize it's premature but they need us more often, and God knows the English Church is like a vulture preying on our flock. Do the full circuit. A fortnight, no less, possibly more. But before you do, you should visit Longbottom and satisfy yourself on the state of matters there. Doubtless, Gipps will hold you as much accountable as he will me for the Patriotes' behaviour. After all, you were most forthright, and according to the *Gazette*, the word 'Patriote' is a synonym for 'cutthroat'." Polding laughed.

Bernard shrugged, despising Polding for manipulating him. He knew he'd welcome the chance to throw the stink of Sydney off his shoulders and ride the countryside and explore for more plant specimens. The Longbottom thing was his way of stating the price. He'd suggest a visit to the Female Factory next. The idiot. He didn't have to make that bribe. The bit about the new female prisoners made it necessary anyway. So he decided to give Polding his scrap of meat. "Perhaps you're right, my Bishop. A visit to Longbottom at this early juncture might be seen as politically judicious." Bernard rose to leave. "I'll take my leave now, Monsignor. I have a sermon to prepare." He raised his brows questioningly. "There is nothing else, is there?"

Polding looked startled for a second, then recovered himself. "Now that I come to think of it, yes. Maybe it would also be wise for you also to visit the Female Factory and reassure the authorities that we have no intention of spreading our word among their inmates. It will be on your way."

"But of course, Monsignor. Do I lather Mrs Bell in syrup or in acid?"

Polding swallowed and forced a grin. It always came to this. The challenge! And now his response. Bernard had shifted the balance. He always did. Now he had to restore it. He measured his words carefully. "Do what you have to do, Bernard. With the end result always in mind. And while you are in Richmond, try and establish a census. We really do need a priest there permanently. Before too long, I imagine."

Bernard received the barb with a smile of his own. The old fool. Threatening him with tenure at the new Richmond parish. He knew how he hated the place. How dare he! Polding would be just another chattel one day. They'd all be.

"Then more syrup than acid it will be, Monsignor." He paused for a moment. "The Rookeries. I was there today. I visited old man Branston. He was already dead. It was unfortunate that he was not able to receive the last sacraments. It must have been God's will."

Polding's reply was still on his lips when he heard the door close, forcibly like in a sudden breeze. Then he was alone with his thoughts.

~ ~ ~

If it hadn't been such a transparent fabrication, Polding might have taken offence. As it was, it was amusing. Preparing a sermon. What a joke! Bernard had never prepared a sermon in his life and they both knew it. What he was really going to do was work some more on their major report on convict conditions for presentation to authorities in London. But he was not prepared to admit as much, all of which induced more puzzlement than annoyance in Polding. Of all vices, Polding detested laziness the most, and irritating though he may be, Bernard was not slothful. Headstrong, unpredictable, even aristocratic in his tastes, but not lazy. There was much to observe about his young Dominican secretary, but very little to understand. Polding had been with him for almost a year now, yet knew nothing about him beyond the inescapable fact that his was easily the most brilliant and disturbing mind he had ever encountered.

Polding was no stranger to introspection. The monastery, if nothing else, had taught him that. The aloof, taciturn even unfriendly Dominican had not upset him, and at first he had presumed it to be but a residue of a monastic mould he himself well understood. The fact that he kept to himself and made light of Polding's initial attempts at conversation were of no consequence to a man like himself who had so little time and so much to do. As long as the Dominican filled his priestly role, how he behaved privately was a matter for his own conscience. Bernard was strong, energetic and capable. He worked efficiently and purposefully. He argued well and was not afraid of the British nor their posturings. True, the faithful were not drawn to him as Polding might have liked. Instead, they seemed afraid of him. Even the other priests seemed afraid of him. As far as Polding knew, the innkeeper at the Bath Arms Hotel on the Parramatta Road near Longbottom Stockade was the only person with whom Bernard had any familiarity. Probably because they were both Genoans.

No, what bothered Polding most of all, and even then it was a gnawing uncertainty more than a fearful dread, was the paradox within the man. He had eyes of fire like a volcano lurked within him, a restless suppressed energy even anger, that was mocked by an outward passivity. How could eyes that flashed like that reside in a body that ran through the day like tomorrow was here already? Then there was the other thing. For some reason crowds seemed to interest him. At first, that is. He would walk among them receiving new introductions enthusiastically. Polding recalled how Bernard would look intently at them, women as well as men, as if he thought he might recognize them. Then suddenly, unaccountably, he would walk away towards another throng. Polding had even asked him about it. Was he searching for lost kin? But all he had gotten was a curious look and a shake of the head that told him to mind his own business. Bernard Blake was an enigma, a man who probably wouldn't be here much longer. Rome would want him back in time. He wished it was soon. Sydney and John Bede Polding would lose little when that proud arrogant body took its unlit furnace elsewhere. Polding sighed. Would that it were different. But he knew it never would be. Not with a man like that. Irritably he pushed the Dominican from his mind and began reviewing the specifications for the Windsor church.

Bath Arms Hotel, Parramatta Road, Concord. March 18, 1840

Bernard took his time, riding easily through the Newtown settlement and the flats at Gippstown until the afternoon sun and the increased traffic told him that his destination was just ahead. The Bath Arms Hotel sat where the Liverpool and Parramatta Roads converged, a most popular place known for its cold ale, fine liquors and excellent food. The interiors were dim and cool, the bar finely polished, and a drinker would not sit long before being welcomed in a most gentlemanly manner by the proprietor himself, Mr. Emmanuel Neitch, himself a Genoan, and if he could play chess or perchance had read a good book lately, chances are a free drink would come his way.

The Bath Arms was a two-storey cream coloured brick building. An ornate lantern overhung the arched leaded main door, itself framed by two large rectangular windows also leaded in their upper panels. Three smaller windows on the second floor indicated the best rooms in the hotel, being far more impressive and expensive than the four smaller, windowless rooms behind. Flanked on both sides by the squat kitchen and stables and the bar proper, the Bath Arms exuded respectability and refinement. Emmanuel Neitch had gone so far as to try and trim the line of gum trees that backed away from the hotel. Even the two horse troughs out front boasted their own elegance, being curved upward at both ends to resemble a canoe.

Bernard endured the fond greeting from a delighted Emmanuel Neitch and, feigning fatigue, managed to escape to his room instead of taking tea in the parlour. As he was climbing the stairs he saw the red-headed maid back out of one of the other rooms, her arms full of folded linen. Bernard had encountered her several times usually on the stairs or with Neitch, and occasionally in his room when she was working, but they had never spoken beyond nods and polite formalities. But he loathed her with all his being. She was like the others who made his flesh crawl with their evil. But this slut didn't know enough to be afraid of him. Just like the other filth who had jeered at him on that monstrous night. He continued to look at her coolly, fighting the twisting churning feeling in his stomach and willing hostility to his rage. The green eyes looked back at him. Damn it! They wouldn't drop. Terrible eyes! Not cold, not hot. Not wide, but narrowed slightly and turned up like an oriental doll. An assassin doll! The ones he had seen in the curio stores in Rome wielding their daggers and smiling like fiends. For a moment he shivered, suddenly afraid. He was still looking at her when she brushed past him. Bernard flinched. Her hair was like a red wave and he watched it fascinated as she descended the stairs. Halfway down, she turned and spoke. "Your room is ready, Father. Mr. Neitch had your books moved back in. He said to be sure to tell you that no one has used them in your absence."

Bernard found himself nodding dumbly. He didn't know what else to do, and behind his eyes, deep in his head he felt the echoes of a familiar pounding, quieted these past months except when on occasions like this when he was challenged by slime. Oh God, he hoped the pain wouldn't stay. Ten minutes later, Bernard lay with both arms across his face. He was writhing, screwing his perspiring face into the blue embroidered quilt and staining it damp. His lips were moving "Bitch. You will die. You will all die."

Longbottom Stockade, March 19, 1840

The Longbottom area was a seven-hundred-acre parcel of government land between Parramatta Road and the river. Originally envisaged as a government supply centre maintained by convict labour, the stockade had gradually fallen into disuse. Governor George Gipps' subsequent decision to use it to house the Patriotes was linked as much to its availability as it was to its suitability for political prisoners who, not being obliged to wear irons, must also be relied upon not to escape. The Stockade itself was within view of the Bath Arms Hotel. It was marked by an ornamental gate beside which was a crude sentry hut made from boughs. It was empty this fine Saturday afternoon as Bernard Blake rode through, past the superintendent's modest house and on about a hundred yards to the stockade itself which consisted of four barrack huts, a mess shed and an open fireplace.

It was the first time Bernard had been there and he was struck by the marked contrast it bore to the other convict camps he had visited. There were no rifle-wielding guards. There was not even a palisade. Longbottom Stockade was a clearing in the bush, surrounded by red gum, stringybark and blackbutt trees, and beyond them the marshy flats that eventually became mangrove swamps by the river. A rough track known as Wharf Road stretched the mile or so to the water, passing several crude huts utilized by the families of guards and the policemen whose forays into the bush after the bushrangers often kept them away for weeks on end. A place for breaking stone, a small poorly-made kiln, open-boughed stabling for about five horses, and an unfinished well were the only other evidence of human habitation.

As Bernard dismounted in front of the crude long rail that stretched between two gum trees, he smelled the acrid fragrance of the bush. Then when he faced north to tie his mount he caught the other odour, a muddy, fishy dampness, soured by something he couldn't place. The trees were high and he couldn't see far into the green thickness. Yes, it would not take long for the bush to reclaim Longbottom. It was already moulding away in the heat in spite of the men who worked there. He could feel it.

The Patriotes must have seen him coming, for they came spilling out of their huts to greet him. Soon they were all around him talking excitedly in their crude, strange French. Bernard listened patiently to the litany of complaints. The spokesman was a fiery little man scarcely over five feet tall but whose voice and emotional intensity lent stature to his remarks. Why were they forced to wear branded uniforms? Why were they not allowed to attend Mass? Was it true that their letters were to be censored? How long would they be here? When would they be going home? Breaking stone was labour fit only for criminals. François-Xavier Prieur was still talking animatedly – "You don't starve to death but you're always hungry" – when they were joined by a second, smaller group.

The elevated status of this new group was immediately discernible to Bernard. Prieur's eyes blazed and he fell into a sullen silence. One of the five not in prison uniform introduced himself importantly as Louis Bourdon, the general overseer and spokesman for all the Patriotes, answerable solely to Superintendent Baddely. The other four were his hut captains: Charles Huot, François-Maurice Lepailleur, Pierre-Hector Morin and Charles-Guillaume Bouc. All were literate and all spoke English, Bourdon explained airily. He hoped that Bernard would hear confession this afternoon, and return to say Mass tomorrow in the hut that was even now being prepared in hopeful anticipation of the holy sacrifice. Bernard could hear the muttered tensions as Bourdon expounded on how their miserable lot was being eased by a humane and honourable superintendent. The Sabbath totally work-free, and Saturday afternoon as well. Liberal supervision, and endurable if unchallenging work. Bourdon also talked about a rosier future. The promise of regular attendance at Sunday Mass in Parramatta; the prospects of improved food and additional free time after the evening meal. It had also been hinted by Superintendent Baddely that the coveted ticket-of-leave status, the prelude to a pardon and eventual return to Canada, might be only a few short months away. By the time Bourdon had finished, Bernard noticed that some of the Patriotes had drifted away. This Bourdon was scarcely a popular man, he decided. Not that it mattered. They all could rot here forever as far as he cared. He'd only interceded on their behalf to make Polding beholden to him.

~ ~ ~

Martin did not go to confession. Instead he wandered about the stockade area flexing his right hand, and thinking. It was strange, but he had felt detached listening to François-Xavier and the others tell the Dominican about their misery. François-Xavier, who desperately needed to go to Mass. Toussaint, who wanted to get out so he could earn his passage back to Canada. The others who longed for their farms and families. It was different with him; he had nothing. A father who hated him, a mother he couldn't acknowledge, and Madeleine lying in a churchyard, gone forever. The Patriotes cried; he mourned. They yearned for a life that had been taken from them; he . . . what did he feel? He looked up past the tall gums to the blue sky above. Could he ever accept this land? Then he saw the priest. He was walking towards him. Martin felt the urge to escape. But it was no use. The trenched perimeter of the stockade yard was just in front of him. He could not cross it. So he turned to face the Dominican.

"Good afternoon, Father." Oh my God. The eyes. So much like Madeleine's. Dark, intense, wild. "I'm just out for a walk," he added lamely.

The priest was closer now and Martin caught the sweet fragrance of lavender. Then the unsmiling face filled his vision, so close that Martin could discern the pulsating blue vein angling above the left eye, and the dull sheen in the black hair that reached in an unpriestly length about his shoulders.

"I noticed you on the ship, and back there." Bernard gestured towards the huts. "You always hang back. What is it? Boredom, timidity, indifference?" The voice was mocking.

Martin swallowed then shrugged. "Talking doesn't help things, Father. Not when the issue under discussion is already resolved. If we've learned one thing, it's that struggling is futile."

Bernard nodded inwardly to himself. "The first candid comment I have heard here today. Pessimistic perhaps but understandable. Everything is ultimately resolved. It's called destiny. Know your destiny and you know yourself."

The tone. The message. He had heard it before. For a second Madeleine swam before his eyes. His eyes welled even as he replied. "It is easy for you to talk, Father. You have your faith, your destiny as you call it. I have nothing."

A strange smile creased Bernard's lips. "Why, my sad young friend? Why have you nothing?"

Martin felt foolish but went on anyway. "It's not just this place, Father. I imagine we'll all get out one day. And God knows we've been through worse. Condemned to die. Waiting for the hangman's call. No, there's more, much more. I've lost someone I love. She died in the rebellion and now I have nothing. I find solace nowhere. Not in friends." He paused before continuing, "or in the church." He lifted his right hand towards Bernard. "My hand. I can't use it. An accident. I was going to be a painter. Now I can't. I don't know if I care any more, Father."

Martin's eyes were down and he didn't see the priest smile and nod. He did however suddenly feel his hand being examined, the fingers being moved about. The priest's hands were warm and surprisingly strong. "Flexibility seems all right. Are you sure you can no longer draw? Have you tried?"

"A doctor gave me some exercises. But no, I have never tried. I'm afraid to, Father."

Bernard looked grim for a moment, then pulled some paper and a pencil from the deep pocket in his robe. "Draw!"

Martin was startled. Uncle Antoine had said the very same thing, so long ago. "I can't, Father."

The Dominican's voice was rasping and Martin was suddenly afraid. "Draw! That plant there. Draw it, damn you, draw it."

The eyes. They were boring into him, moving his tongue and his hand. "Yes, Father."

For five minutes Martin forced his hand to guide the pencil, fearful and acutely conscious of the priest breathing heavily at his shoulder.

Bernard grunted as he took the sketch from Martin. The drawing was rough and inelegant. But the form and the perspective were both there. And something else. Life! This plant could live.

"Practice! All you need is practice. Mr. . . . ?" Bernard raised his eyes questioningly.

Martin was looking at the drawing. It was better than he expected. For a moment his heart leapt. Why hadn't he had the courage before? The priest was still looking at him.

The words tumbled from his lips. "Goyette, Father. My name is Martin Goyette. Do you really think I can paint again? Well enough to be good, I mean?"

There was an edge of scorn in Bernard's reply, but Martin was too excited to notice. "It's not what I think, Martin Goyette, but rather, what will be made to be."

"I don't understand, Father."

But Bernard did not reply. Instead, he was looking back across the cleared ground to the road that led to the gate. Abruptly, he turned and when he spoke, it was like it was a new conversation. "Do you speak English, Mr. Goyette?"

Martin was surprised. "Yes, my uncle taught me."

"As well as Louis Bourdon?"

"Yes, I think so."

"Then our destinies are about to converge."

Martin watched him walk away. What a strange reply! What a strange Priest! What a good day! He flexed his hand. It felt loose, relaxed.

The Bath Arms Hotel, March 20, 1840

Colleen Somerville hummed to herself as she cleaned the priest's room. Father Blake might not be a nice man, but he was a neat one. Nothing was out of place. He had packed his clothes away carefully and except for the unmade bed and the scent of lavender in the air there was no sign of his presence. The sheets on the bed were twisted, though, as if he had had a restless night. She wondered if priests usually slept well. What did they think about when they went to bed? She was sure that some of them thought about women. Not Father Blake, though. He hated women; she could see it in his eyes. Though she did her best not to show it, she was afraid of him, which was not like her at all.

She was afraid of nothing. Not the snakes and lizards that her younger brother brought home and which terrified her poor mother. Not of men, even when they got drunk like her father did often. Mr. Neitch had spoken to her more than once about the need to be very polite to all the Bath Arms patrons. She had not listened though, and continued to be quick with her tongue and whatever else was at hand when an unwanted hand caressed her bum or poked at her breasts. Mr. Neitch understood. Besides she was very good at her work. She could pull beer quickly, and could compute the prices in her head faster and more accurately than any of the men. Why else would Mr. Neitch pay her twenty pounds a year, two pounds more than the top wage for publicans' maids?

She had finished making the bed and turned her attention to the mirror above the bookcase. For a moment she examined herself critically. Her mother said she was too thin, and that refined ladies did not allow the sun to turn their skin brown. She liked being tall, having men look up at her. She wondered if she was too tall. No, she didn't think so. Her nose might be a trifle long but her green eyes more than made up for that blemish. They were slightly tilted up at the ends, and she wasn't afraid to smile and show her white, even teeth. She twirled about, watching her hair swing and cascade back over her shoulders. Mr. Neitch had once introduced her to a friend as the best-looking maid in New South Wales. Well, he was wrong. Colleen Somerville was not going to be a maid for much longer. She thought of the bottle of coins under her bed.

She would soon have enough. Twenty-five guineas for room, board and singing lessons at Isaac Nathan's Singing Academy in Parramatta. And when she was a trained singer she would perform at the lavish parties the rich men had in their big homes in Glebe. Then it was off to Europe and maybe even America.

Yes, Mr. Neitch was wrong. Very wrong. Except about the "best looking" part. He might have a point there. She giggled to herself and pirouetted just for the spinning sensation. Once, twice, three times. On the fourth turn her leg hit the book shelf. When she recovered her balance she noticed the book on the floor. Idly she picked it up and rifled through the pages. The illustrations leapt out at her. Demons dancing around blazing fires; humans with animal heads; sorcerers concocting potions. The text was in French. She recognized that much. The title on the inside front leaf meant nothing to her. *De Philosophie Occulte*. It was only when she closed it to replace it on the shelf that she noticed the large gold lettering on the outside spine, *Acts of the Apostles*. Curious now, she removed others from their shelves. They were all the same. Religious titles on the outside and different ones on the inside leaves. None but a book of poetry in English and all by authors she didn't recognize. It didn't make sense.

She made a mental note of the names of several of the authors. She would ask someone. But who? Certainly not Mr. Neitch. However, the mystery of the mixed titles did not stay long with Colleen. By the time she had finished cleaning the room the title *De Philosophie Occulte* was gone from her memory. Later when she thought about it in bed, the only author she could recall was Raimon Lull, and then only because she had liked the name Raimon.

Longbottom Stockade, March 20, 1840. 11:00 AM

Henry Clinton Baddely examined himself in the full-length mirror. It had been a while since he had worn a uniform, and now that he was dressed in one again, he remembered how much pride an official ensignia had given him. It had hurt, being drummed out of the army so many years ago for a deed not nearly as vile as what went on here daily. It was a dark memory that he never discussed, and in fact no one in the colony knew that he had ever been in His Majesty's forces. He sucked in his paunch and looked sideways over his shoulder at his figure. The cap covered his thinning hair nicely. The blue uniform itself had just arrived this morning from the tailor's, and he couldn't wait to try it on. He would wear it proudly tonight when he addressed the prisoners. His future looked promising indeed, and it would only get better when he was able to move among the ladies. Even the proud ones were often curious about the man under the uniform. Well, they would soon find out.

When Governor Gipps had asked him about the superintendent's position at Longbottom, he had jumped at the chance. From an Assistant Engineer supervising convict chain gangs to an administrative position of authority and respect was a major step indeed. It hadn't meant an increase in pay, but after all, prestige and freedom were far more important than mere remuneration. There was no doubt about it. Henry Clinton Baddely had done well. While he recognized the fact that his ability to speak French hadn't done him any harm, Baddely had no doubt that his governor's faith in him rested on a proper awareness of his exceptional ability. All of which he would prove with ease, for handling these ignorant and docile Frenchmen would be no problem at all.

Baddely was not insensitive to the realities of his new situation. He was convinced that his French-speaking charges would respond positively to fair treatment. How liberal that might be was, of course, dependent on their behaviour and respect. But like many a man before him thrust into a superior position through exigency, he could not discern between the right of authority and its enabling licence. Lust and greed, two of the seven deadly sins, loomed large on Baddely's list of priorities. Walking across the clearing to the superintendent's new house that bright Sunday forenoon, Bernard Blake was well aware of Henry Clinton Baddely's frailties. He made it his business to know such things about the people with whom he dealt. Not that he always exploited this knowledge. He would today, though. He had good reason.

~ ~ ~

Baddely had already decided how he would control this meeting with the priest. He once had a captain in the army who used the term "cordially affirmative" as the most effective way of handling men. In this case it would mean being friendly but firm. There was to be no doubt at all over who was in charge at Longbottom. The priest would go away happy that Henry Clinton Baddely was a reasonable man. After all, he knew how much the Patriotes looked up to their clergy and what a calming effect that men of the cloth had on them. Their frequent visits to Longbottom could only aid him, but priests could be meddlesome and he didn't want that.

Yet as soon as Baddely opened the door and was confronted with those dark penetrating eyes, any thought of dullness vanished from his mind, along with any plans he had to be cordially affirmative. He found himself doing all the talking as he told the priest how he had organized the Patriotes into self-appointed hut groupings under a captain who spoke English; how he had arranged the work parties as equitably as possible; how he was negotiating with the Governor to allow the prisoners the privilege of attending Sunday Mass in Parramatta; how he found them to be gentle and God-fearing men. All the time he talked he avoided the eyes, and eventually when he ran out of things to say he finally looked at the Dominican in a kind of helpless fascination. There was a faint smile on the priest's lips, and Baddely was acutely aware of the scent of lavender. Then he heard the words coming from his own mouth but he could not believe he was uttering them. "I trust you approve of my actions, Father. Have you any suggestions?"

The priest held up three fingers, shaking his head and smiling condescendingly. "I have but little time, Superintendent Baddely, and I will not be coming back for some weeks. Listen well for you have much to gain."

Baddely leaned forward, his face straining intently to adopt a businesslike, professional pose.

Bernard went on. "The first piece of information is for your personal interest only. I understand you are an acquaintance of a Molly MacGuigan."

Baddely's face blanched. He opened his mouth but no words came out.

"Do not concern yourself, Superintendent. Your dalliances are of no consequence to me."

"But she is. I mean, I thought she—"

"Was in the Female Factory. She was. For stealing jewellery from her employer. Naughty naughty girl. But take heart, Superintendent. I have some favourable news for you. As I understand it, Mrs Bell, the Matron, will be asking me my opinion of her mental competence when I visit the Factory later this week. She believes me to be something of an expert. And since your Miss MacGuigan has apparently been a source of some concern to the good Matron, she will be hoping that I lend my support to her recommendation that our affectionate Molly be transferred to the Lunatic Asylum. You know what that means, don't you?"

Baddely knew, all right. Visiting privileges! The Lunatic Asylum was the cheapest and best whorehouse in New South Wales. And God, how he loved Molly's tits. He could go up there twice a week for the best fucks he had ever had in his life. Stay the whole night if he wanted. He couldn't believe his good fortune. But he must proceed cautiously, and not let the priest see that he was too eager. He tried give his words the tone of polite interest. "She was employed as a cook in the household of an acquaintance. Still, she is an agreeable sort, if dim witted. Your suggestion sounds most charitable, Father. The Asylum is a far better place for a wretched soul like her than the Factory."

Bernard noticed the beads of excited sweat on Baddely's brow and above his thick lips. The man was an idiot who ought to be crushed like the pathetic vermin he was. When he replied, the contempt in his voice was not lost on Baddely, who flushed noticeably. "Yes, Superintendent. We shall just have to make that recommendation, won't we?"

Bernard got up and walked to the window. Baddely was glad of the respite from those eyes. "There are a couple of other things you might find interesting, Superintendent. More on the business side. On the way from Sydney I noticed a convict gang making those new road blocks. The workmanship was abominable."

Baddely nodded, feeling for the first time on secure ground. "Yes, Father, I agree. It's difficult to procure suitable artisans among the scum they send us."

"But Superintendent. These Patriotes. Many are artisans, carpenters. Why not use them for building the blocks? Your ingenuity would be noticed."

Baddely nodded. Of course. It was a fine suggestion, But before he could reply, the priest went on.

"It also appears to me, Superintendent that the presence of these industrious and skilled workmen may be used in other, more profitable ways."

"I don't understand, Father?" Baddely was intrigued.

"They are builders, carvers, craftsmen. Think of all the things they could be making in their spare time. Saleable items. Experts using government equipment and materials to produce fine products for ultimate use or disposal . . ." Bernard shrugged his shoulders and held Baddely's eyes before continuing, "at your whim. A canoe, perhaps. Some carved boxes. Now, they would bring a healthy price. The possibilities are endless."

Baddely's mind was racing. It was true. Already some of them were beginning small projects of their own. With the tools and the time, think of what they could do. For him.

"And I have another suggestion for you. The unskilled men. They too can be made useful."

Baddely didn't even try to reply. He just looked at Bernard with his mouth open. He could scarcely believe what he was hearing. He could already see the money piling up.

"The mud flats in the bay. I was down there yesterday. Oysters, Superintendent, Oysters."

"Oysters?"

"Yes, Superintendent, oysters. They are lying in the mud by the thousands."

"You mean, the prisoners should collect them and eat them, and in that way we can save money on food?" Baddely sounded pleased.

Bernard could scarcely contain his laughter. The buffoon! "No, Superintendent! Eat as many as you want, but the shells! Load them on a barge and send them to Parramatta. They are used to make lime. The market is excellent, I understand. 10d a bushel in Parramatta, a little less in Sydney. Let the Patriotes keep a major portion, say 5 or 6d, and the rest you assign to yourself for the privilege of allowing the venture. At ten bushels a day, you could make yourself up to fifty guineas a year."

Bernard scribbled a name on a piece of paper and handed it to Baddely. "The name of a man in Parramatta whom you might wish to contact regarding the sale of these oysters. Ah yes, Superintendent, there is much that an enterprising man like yourself could accrue. Of course, it would mean allowing the Patriotes time after the evening meal. Time well spent, I imagine."

"Of course, Father." Baddely was in a daze.

"And now, Superintendent, I shall take my leave with the full assurance that the interests of the Patriotes are being well served."

Bernard rose to leave. He did not shake Baddely's hand. He was at the door when he paused. "Superintendent?" He waited until he had Baddely's full attention before continuing. "One other thing. You have no sentry at the gate. That is most careless."

"I know, Father. It will be attended to immediately. There has been so little time."

"Give the task to the boy with the deformed lip, Martin Goyette. He is intelligent and speaks excellent English. If I were you I would give the assignment to him on a permanent basis. It's best that one man only perform the function. It assures continuity, accountability. Don't you agree, Superintendent?"

"Of course, Father." He met the priest's eyes and swallowed. "I will assign Martin Goyette there tomorrow. It will be his sole function."

"Excellent, Superintendent. It is good that we are able to accommodate each other." The next words came like an order. "Make sure that Goyette has all the paper and writing materials that he wishes. There is other work that he has to do."

"What might that be, Father?"

"Such is neither of interest nor importance to you, Superintendent. Put him on the gate. Inform him of his responsibilities and leave him alone. Do I make myself clear?"

"Yes, Father." Something told Baddely that he had been bested, but he didn't care. All he could see was Molly MacGuigan sprawled naked on a bed, and golden coins jingling in the pockets of his trousers as he threw them off to mount her.

The Government Factory for Female Convicts, Parramatta, March 23, 1840, 2:00 PM

Bernard left his horse at the visitors' hitch and approached the large heavy wrought iron gates of the Female Factory. They were high and narrow, and absurdly misplaced. Too imposing to be ornamental but hardly formidable enough to guard a jail, they looked like something that might grace a child's picture book. The turnkey on duty greeted him curtly and motioned him in. As he crossed the cobbled space between the wall and the main door he glanced upwards at the sun. It was still high in the northern sky. Good! He would have time to visit the orphanage as well before nightfall.

As he clattered the brass knocker on the big black door, Bernard felt the sweat on his palms. He loathed this place, and only the knowledge that a newly-arrived female convict ship had disgorged its cargo to the Factory induced this visit, despite Polding's wishes or the threat of his disapproval. But he had to confront their vileness, and if Lamar should be there then he might well be surmounting the most telling test demanded of his destiny.

He could hear the heavy footsteps. The old cow was answering the door herself. At least the Edwards woman at the orphanage had the sense to be afraid of him. This fat idiot was too stupid. The door opened and Matron Bell stood before him frowning heavily, her pink jowls bobbing up and down in time with her forced pleasantries. He got it over with quickly, standing in the vestibule and angry again with Polding for forcing a conciliatory conversation with this heap of human refuse.

He informed her politely that the good sisters were interested only in alleviating the prisoners' misery and had no intention of wreaking mischief among them. Matron Webb smiled her agreement but all the time her hard eyes watched him. She was just filth. Harmless filth. Then she led him to the Third and Second Class Sections, never straying far from his side, never dreaming that her gesture of mistrust in the hated priest was in actuality a comfort to him. Bernard mightn't have had the courage to face them all alone.

He said some prayers. He offered blessings and heard several confessions. He saw the dirty emaciated faces and the wretched fearful ignorance in their eyes; the infant heads that sucked on the pendulous mounds of flesh that hung outside the coarse prison calico. He heard them cry and whine and ask for his forgiveness, and in spite of himself he recoiled at the insults that the

Protestants spat in his direction. When his sweating hands began to shake uncontrollably he put them inside his robe. And now afterwards, sitting in Matron Bell's office with an untouched cup of tea in front of him, he waited for the tremors inside him to subside. The old bitch was watching him, her eyes as benign as they could be. She was going to ask him for something. Probably about the MacGuigan woman. She couldn't know that the approval she sought was already assured. He had no intention of seeing the criminal slut. All he wanted to do was leave. Lamar was not here, and as the back of his head began to ache, Bernard knew that he wouldn't be able to come here for much longer.

"Father. I need your opinion."

She sounded so unctuous, the old cow, but Bernard could not muster the inclination to play her game, even one as pathetically obvious as hers. He closed his eyes and listened to her drone on. "She has been nothing but trouble, Father. Violent towards the other prisoners. Unmanageable in her speech. She is surely demented. She can't remain here, Father. Will you look at her, and tell me if I am not right? And afterwards . . . Well, the Chief Magistrate. He always listens to you."

He could take it no longer. He got to his feet. Misreading his intention, Matron Bell moving surprisingly fast for a big woman was at the door before him. "If you'll come this way, Father. She's in the end cell upstairs."

The pain was worse now. He had to leave. "I do not care to see the MacGuigan woman, Matron. I have good reason to believe that her condition is as you say it is. I will speak to the Chief Magistrate on the morrow. Now if you'll excuse me."

"Father. There's something else. I think you should visit her."

For the first time Bernard noticed that the Matron had something in her hands. She proffered it to him and he took it wonderingly, turning it over in his hands. It was a crudely stitched sketch of a figure on a piece of calico. A triangle for a robe, single stitches for the arms and legs, and what appeared to be a circle above the head which was also superimposed with a triangle. The matron's words suddenly cut to his consciousness. "She says its the Virgin Mary. She talks to her all the time. She says she sees her in the darkness, and I can hear her myself, calling and moaning in the night like a lost soul. You've got to see her, Father. You must make urgent recommendation. I'd sooner Molly MacGuigan stay than this woman. She is not of this world." Matron Bell's lips were twitching and there were beads of sweat above her brow.

Could it be? Was it possible? Lamar? Bernard could feel his whole body tense with excitement. The pain was suddenly gone and he was alive with a feeling that he couldn't describe. He tried to remain calm. "This woman, Matron. Where is she from? And her name. What is it?"

"She came but last week on the boat. She has no name, Father. The list said, Name unknown, so they called her Jessie L." She grimaced before continuing, "but the other prisoners call her 'the witch.'" Her arm was on Bernard's. "Come, Father I'll take you to her."

~ ~ ~

It was silent outside the barred cell, and when the Matron opened the door, Bernard could make out nothing in the gloom. His whole body was tingling. "You leave, Matron. It's better that I confront her alone."

"Yes, Father."

Bernard stepped into the cell. He could make out the form now, huddled in the corner. She had long dark hair that covered her shoulders. As long as Signy's, Bernard noted. He moved closer towards her. He was close enough to touch her now but still she didn't move

"Lamar?" He knew his voice sounded strained but he could not conceal his excitement. "Is your name Lamar?"

The dark head stirred, slightly at first. Then still crouching and with her hands held close to her chest, the woman turned to face him. Bernard gasped, drawing one hand to his mouth in disbelief. She was hideous. Pockmarked and grotesquely disfigured with what seemed to be a burn scar or a birthmark, she was like a creature from a child's nightmare. Her two mad eyes rolled in her head; a slit of a mouth opened to reveal blackened teeth and bloody gum spaces in between. Stupefied, Bernard watched as she fumbled at her breast, reaching inside her prison uniform for something wrapped in a dirty shawl. Then, as the blood-chilling sound of her mad cackling filled the cell, she thrust the bundle towards him. A sweet sickly smell assailed Bernard's nose. Oh God, he could see it now. He wanted to run, but it was like he was frozen in time, an image now only inches from his face etched in his consciousness forever. The lolling head of the dead infant on top of a naked discoloured body was like a wizened broken doll, and the wisps of down on the top of the skull were stained with a dark redness.

Bernard's scream swelled from his lungs in a long loud cry of sheer terror. He bolted from the room, down the stairs and outside to his horse. Once astride, he spurred it recklessly hearing all the time the mad cackling rever-berating through his brain.

The Orphanage for Girls, Parramatta, 5:00 PM

Matron Edwards had never seen Father Bernard Blake so agitated. He was pale but his eyes were unnaturally bright. He had barely spoken to her, which was not surprising, but asked immediately if he might tell all the girls a story. That was unusual, especially the bit about having all the girls there. Usually he had to be persuaded to tell a story and then he always selected a few of the smaller girls. Today was different. So was his story. The girls had sat open-mouthed as he told them a tale about monsters who tortured young maidens before eating them alive. His voice was so intense and his eyes blazed like fire. It was no wonder that several of the girls were terrified, even crying. There was no doubt about it. There would be bad dreams aplenty this evening. And he would have told more had she not contrived an excuse and intervened.

Yes, she was glad that he was leaving. They were at the back door and he was about to fetch his horse with not so much as a goodbye when she remembered. Mary! She had forgotten to tell him about Mary.

"Father. Before you go. I know how you like to see all our girls every time you come. There's a girl you haven't met. An aboriginal girl. Mary is her name. She was brought in here a few months back. Some farmers found her somewhere on the Hawkesbury. She tends the animals."

"Where is she, Matron? I have but a few minutes." Bernard's voice was dull. One more wouldn't make any difference.

Matron Edwards pointed down towards the river to the barn area. "She is down there, Father. It's not far. I can see her now. There she is. Right on the bank of the river."

They began walking down the dirt path with Matron Edwards continuing her breathless monologue. "I'm afraid the poor child's demented, Father. She won't speak except maybe to her crow, and there is a wildness in her eyes that frightens me. If she doesn't get better we will have to transfer her to the asylum."

Bernard stopped in his tracks. Another madwoman. With a bird! He shuddered. How he hated birds. And the girl. Would she cackle? Would she make his guts writhe in disgust? He couldn't take it. Not today.

"On second thought, Matron. I see it is dusk, and another urgent appointment awaits me elsewhere. Possibly I or another priest will see the mad girl at a future time."

"As you wish, Father." For some reason Matron Edwards was pleased. She liked Mary and found her far less strange than this wild-eyed priest who seemed to dislike everyone. He would probably have just frightened her further.

CHAPTER III

Longbottom Stockade, May 15, 1840

Martin looked about the empty hut and then at the pile of unopened oysters on the plain wooden table. They were as big as plates and would taste delicious. The trouble was opening the things, a task he hated, but it was his turn and the other five members of his hut were still down in the bay loading the day's haul onto a barge. He sighed and got to work, using the large communal knife as both wedge and lever, and for a half an hour he worked patiently until all but one lay open on the table, gleaming transparently and smelling wonderful. The Patriotes had come to relish their oysters, all except Toussaint, who disgustingly likened them to cold mucous. Old Charles Huot would fry them whenever he could get the flour. Now that was a real treat.

For five minutes Martin grunted in frustration. This last one wouldn't open. It was sealed too tightly to insert the knife. For an instant Martin thought of throwing it away but it was such a big one and he disliked the idea of being beaten by a mussel. He searched about the hut for something else. The Virgin looked back at him from her place above his cot. She would be nice and heavy, and certainly solid enough to smash an oyster shell. She shouldn't mind, and even if she did, Martin didn't. She hadn't helped Joseph-Narcisse or the Chevalier. As he brought the heavy base down on the shell, Martin thought of Madeleine. He pounded harder, harder. The shell shattered and the pewter sank into the fishy smelling moisture. Then he saw something else: a darkened silver substance on top of the shell. The Virgin had broken. Suddenly feeling guilty, he turned the figurine over in his hand.

Her left hand had broken off, and some softer filling had dislodged itself from the base revealing a space the depth of a single finger joint. As Martin examined it he could see there was something inside. Curious now, he worked to free it and seconds later was examining the piece of yellowed paper. It was very old and contained three names and below them another three lines of different writing. The language was unfamiliar but he could make out the words *Bologna, Dominic* and *Reginald*. The writer had also signed his name and written the date. *Ugo of Segni, Bishop of Ostia, the twentieth of August, 1221*. His eyes travelled up again to the three lines of words written in heavier ink. The top two had stood the test of time better than the third. The first line had two words, Signy and . . . It looked like Vigelard or Vigeland; the second line had one word only. It was quite clear. Lamar. The third was faded in places. Martin had raised it to the light to see better when he heard the others coming. They must not see that he had abused the Virgin. He could not risk incurring his companions' disfavour just when he was beginning to feel a greater level of kinship with them. Quickly he stuffed the piece of paper back into the figurine and replaced her on the shelf above his bed. Afterwards in his own time he filled in the bottom with some clay, sealing in the paper again. It was a mystery that he might concern himself with it at a later date. It was only when he had sealed the base to his satisfaction that he realized that he had never looked properly at the faded third name. He thought for a moment of breaking the seal but was dissuaded as much by his own incuriosity as he was by the effort needed to satisfy it.

June 25, 1840

It was one of those beautiful early winter days typical of Sydney in June. The sun had burnt away the morning fog and now there was just the lulling comforting warmth that made you glad you were alive. Martin moved his chair farther into the sun so that it was half in and half out of the space that served as the entrance to his sentry hut. The road in front of him was quiet. Even the noisy wren that habitually kept him company with its insistent chirping was silent. He was suddenly very sleepy, his eyes so heavy he couldn't keep them open. He let the collected drawings on his lap to slip to the earthen floor and sliding down farther in his chair allowed the sun to lull him into a reverie.

Not having yet experienced the burning inertia of a Sydney summer, Martin might be excused for thinking that this place had to have the best climate in the world. Now that things seemed to going so much better for him, he had begun to allow himself the latitude of contentment. In bondage? It puzzled him and induced feelings of guilt in the quietness of the night, for in God's truth he could scarcely believe his good fortune. Now that their lives were much better, the Patriotes played and sang and told stories at night. After the day's labour – and to be truthful even the working days were not that onerous – each man was free to do his own thing. How had Lepailleur put it? "We are all our own bosses." The soldiers who had originally guarded them had been withdrawn and now there was only Baddely and the two resident policemen, William Lane and Sam Gorman – and they were gone most of the time chasing bushrangers. After working hours the Patriotes in effect supervised themselves through the direction of the hut captains and under the leadership of Louis Bourdon, who, even if he did take himself and his position too seriously was infinitely preferable to any Englishman.

Longbottom had become a veritable hive of industry as the Patriotes pursued a variety of activities. Some were making canoes; others, trinket boxes.

Joseph Paré was designing fish traps. The unfinished well was almost completed and Superintendent Baddely's quarters had been made much more commodious and pleasant. But if the superintendent often had tasks for them, he was also grateful and saw to it that the Patriotes' pockets jingled with cash well earned. And if that were not enough, everyone was making money on oyster gathering. It was like a grand conspiracy that involved them all. Every Patriote knew about Baddely's supply of secret government stores hidden under the wharf. No one told. What would be the point? Why spoil a good thing? Yet, despite the ease of their new existence, it was not enough for most of the Patriotes. Martin knew that. Their real lives lay across the sea. Longbottom was bondage pure and simple despite the recent ameliorations.

Martin moved in his chair so that the sun fell fully on the side of his face. His own life was better here than it had been in St. Clement. It had been bondage there as well. At least here, he was spending the great part of his day in solitude away from vexation, doing the one thing he enjoyed most: working on his art. He had never had that in St. Clement. He flexed his fingers. Yes, his hand was definitely healing. His drawings were getting much better. He could hardly wait to show this latest lot to Father Blake. Maybe the priest would take him with him on his next overland trip. He had hinted as much when he had last passed by and had seen how well his drawings had progressed. The thought of escaping from Longbottom for a little while, even if it was in the company of a priest, had excited him immeasurably. Soon he would be getting away from Longbottom often. He was to be Baddeley's driver, and the superintendent usually visited Parramatta two and sometimes three times a week, with at least one overnight stop thrown in.

Martin's backside was sore from sitting slouched for too long. Then he heard the sound. A rustling behind him. He froze in his chair, afraid to open his eyes. It was a bushranger, he was sure. Those cutthroats would kill you as soon as look at you. He sat still, willing the sound away. It was coming nearer, nearer. Oh, God, he was going to die.

"Martin? Are you the one they call Martin?"

It was a woman's voice. Martin opened his eyes and turned his head. She was right behind him, having approached his shelter through the trees that backed up to the road. The first thing he noticed about her was her eyes. They were green and her hair was the colour of maple leaves in fall. It was tied back in a white ribbon, the same colour as the dress she wore. She must have recognized the shock on his face for she suddenly began to laugh, a warm musical sound that took away his trepidation like a leaf in the wind.

"Yes, you're Martin. My brother said that your lip reminded him of what a pirate would look like. I think you look like a poet." She had a newspaper in her hand. "Here's your paper. Thomas says he always brings you Wednesday's paper on Thursdays when he delivers eggs to old man Rose." She thrust out her hand like a man. "My name's Colleen. Colleen Somerville. Thomas is ailing. Ate too many apples yesterday."

Her hand was warm and Martin held it a trifle longer than he should have. "I'm pleased to make your acquaintance, Colleen." He took the paper and put it on the rough boards that served as his table, and gestured to the single chair. "Do sit down. How is Thomas? He has been good to me."

It was true. The ragged thin Somerville boy had been a periodic visitor to his hut and latterly had been bringing him a Sydney newspaper whenever he could. He was a furtive boy who didn't talk much but who came and went like a startled fawn.

Martin didn't know what to say. She was looking at him with those large beautiful green eyes. He didn't want her to leave. "I didn't see you coming. Thomas comes up the road. I'm sorry if I appeared startled."

"Then Thomas is foolish, and so are you. He could be seen. He would be chased away and you would be punished."

It was true. His duties were to stop all visitors and demand proof of their business before allowing them entry to the stockade. Under no circumstance was he to fraternize with civilians. He had forgotten. Possibly because Thomas was only a child.

She was glancing around the shelter smiling conspiratorially. "Let me sit on the floor. You take the chair. No one passing will know I am here."

She stayed for over an hour, content to talk, but in a manner that told Martin that she was not used to having people listen to her. He asked her first about her family. There were just the two children. Her parents were both former convicts. Her father was caught poaching in Lincolnshire. Her mother was Irish who never spoke about her early life. It was she who had taught Colleen and Thomas to read. Her father farmed just down the road and helped old man Rose with his carting business. He worked hard but drank harder. So did her mum. There was not much else to do. Martin was amazed at her matter-of-fact tone. No bitterness, or even the placidity of resignation. It was just the way it was.

She had brightened when he had asked about herself. She was going to be a singer. When she was sixteen she had sung one of her mother's Irish songs at Mr. Neitch's picnic at the Homebush race track. Afterwards a fine gentleman had approached her and told her she should take singing lessons. From that day onwards she had begun saving as much as she could, and by next year would have enough to go to Isaac Nathan's Singing Academy in Parramatta for a whole year.

She had suddenly stopped in mid sentence. Martin's sketch of the road and the Bath Arms had caught her eye. "It's beautiful, Martin. You're not a poet. You're an artist."

Martin reddened. He felt like he was floating on air. She liked his work and she had called him, Martin. He desperately didn't want her to leave so he asked her more questions.

She worked at the Bath Arms Hotel, the one in the drawing. Mr. Neitch was kind and good to his workers and often asked her to meet his guests. She didn't know why. Maybe it was because some men found her attractive. She had looked archly at Martin who was too busy fighting the churning feeling in his stomach to notice. The only thing she couldn't understand about Mr. Neitch was his fondness for an evil-looking priest.

Seeing Martin's surprised look she went on. "It's his eyes. There's madness in them. And he hates me. I can tell. He comes here some times. You must know of him. Father Blake?"

The eyes swam before Martin. Just like Madeleine's. Madness! No, it couldn't be. It was conviction, intensity, a seeing something beyond. It couldn't be madness. Colleen was wrong. She was too young.

He shook his head, but Colleen was not to be dissuaded. "He's mad, Martin, I know he is. And I am not sure that he is the right kind of priest."

"What do you mean, Colleen?" asked Martin, curious now that his composure was somewhat restored.

She told him about the books and the wrong titles. She couldn't remember them. They were all in different languages. She could recall only one author. Raimon Lull. The name meant nothing to Martin, who made a mental note to ask Charles Huot. He would likely know.

Martin asked her about her likes and dislikes; her father's farm. He even asked her to sing for him. She refused, remarking simply that it would be too dangerous. Someone might hear. At last and very hesitantly he asked her the question he had wanted to right from the start. Had she a serious gentleman friend? Her answer shocked him at first. Then they both had laughed. Loudly, until she had put a finger to her lips. There were only two types of men. Those who wanted to bed her and those who wanted to marry her which was the same thing only it was permanent. How had her mother put it? Men were interested in two things only: Their stomach and what hung beneath it. No, men were the farthest thing from her mind. Only when she was rich and famous would she consider marriage, and then only to a gentleman.

A cloud passed across the sun and the hut was suddenly cool. Martin was conscious that she wasn't talking. The silence wasn't uncomfortable but her steady gaze was drawing him towards her like he was in a trance. Then she rose and straightened her skirt. She was leaving. Martin's mind was racing. He had to get her to come back.

"Would you like to learn to speak French? It might be helpful to you in your singing. I understand they have fine concert halls in France. I could teach you."

"When, where?" The reply was quick, immediate.

"Here. I am here every day, even Sunday if you want. It's a wonderful language."

She was at the entrance, but had not turned away from him. Martin pressed his urgency. "I would like to teach you, Colleen. Please."

Then she smiled. It was like the sun had come out again.

"Tomorrow."

Martin watched her disappear into the bush. He held his hand in a wave. The last he saw was a shimmer of red and then she was lost in the trees.

~ ~ ~

Colleen came the next day and the next for two weeks, except for two successive days when Mr. Neitch needed her all day. They were the worst two days Martin could recall. The Montreal jail hadn't been as desolate as his sentry hut among the trees and the birds. She was an excellent pupil with a fine ear for the nuances of sound and accent. After the third day she had begun to ask him about himself. It was like the dam of his suppressed feelings had spilled over. He found himself telling her everything. Everything. About his mother, Uncle Antoine, the father who didn't want him, the rebellion, Joseph-Narcisse, the Chevalier. He told her about a God he couldn't understand and the fear that condemned him to cowardice. She was an empathetic listener. She laughed at his stories of Uncle Antoine; she cried when he recounted his last meeting with his mother and fumed in fury at Theodore Brown. She hadn't seemed too upset over his lack of bravery.

"It's to with need," she had said. Fear was often no more than the inactivity of commonsense, just as bravery was simply doing what you had to do. She had patted his arm and said simply, "Martin Goyette is no coward." He had closed his own hand tightly over hers and for a moment rested his head on her shoulder. "Ssh," she had whispered. "It'll be all right."

He was not going to tell her about Madeleine but he did anyway. He had to. About meeting her, being with her, her altar and the visions, and finally recounting her death through the eyes of Charles Huot. Colleen had listened impassively. When he had finished she had shook her head. "Poor girl. She didn't have to do it that way. Your cause could have used her in better ways."

"But she had to, Colleen. Don't you see. She was driven."

Colleen looked at him. The soft gentle blue eyes were moist with emotion. The eyes that couldn't see the madness in the passionate twisted face of a white-robed priest was certainly unable to recognize it in the flaming zeal of a tortured woman. But she couldn't say it. Instead she had tried to use her French to soften the impact of her words.

"Madeleine wasn't for you, Martin. I know you loved her but . . ."

"What?" he had replied dully.

"She didn't love you. She couldn't."

~ ~ ~

It just happened. It was in August. The sixth, because François-Xavier had made them all kneel beside their cots for an extra five minutes in honour of the feast of Christ's Transfiguration. It was a beautiful sunny late afternoon and Colleen was getting ready to return to the Bath Arms. Mr. Neitch, who loved a secret, approved of her French lessons and had agreed to give her an hour off in the slack part of the afternoon providing she began work an hour early.

As Martin put her shawl over her shoulders, his hands fell to her arms turning her towards him. Her eyes were calm, unquestioning. He tilted her chin and kissed her softly on the lips. He felt their warmth and softness. His hands slipped to her waist and he held her tightly. Their kiss seemed to last forever. When he finally lifted his head he felt her arms around his neck. Then he dropped his head into the crook of her neck, pressing his lips against her warm skin. Beneath her heavy woollen jumper he could feel her heart beating fast, and all the time she was stroking the back of neck whispering muffled words he couldn't understand. They stayed like that for a long time. He didn't release her and she didn't disengage herself but then he was alone with the fragrance of her body clinging to his skin like a perfumed drug.

Tarban Creek just outside Parramatta, Saturday September 19, 1840

Martin Goyette examined his sheets of paper and checked his pencil case. Satisfied that all was in order he let himself out of the small room in the servant quarters and began walking towards the creek which lay just beyond sight of the Lunatic Asylum less than a league from Parramatta. After consulting a small notebook, he picked his way along the bank for a while until he found what he was looking for: a purplish orchid growing in the shade where the earth retained surface moisture. He recognized it by the column of metallic coloured hairs on the labellum and by the two eye-like glands on either side of the base. He got to work quickly, sketching first the configuration of the plant itself, then the narrow deeply channelled leaf, and finally the flower.

It was his second trip to Parramatta as Baddely's driver, the first just three days ago following the superintendent's not-so-apparent recovery from an illness that seemed to be wasting him daily. He had looked terrible this morning, spending most of the drive huddled under two thick blankets even though the day was mild. The sores on his legs were not healing, and, according to old Samuel Newcombe, he had contracted a filthy disease carried by vile women. Doubtless from one of the creatures that inhabited the asylum, said François-Xavier, who had not envied Martin for his onerous task of escorting Baddely and therefore placing himself in close proximity to the filth-ridden sluts.

Martin didn't mind, for once ensconced in the asylum, Baddely had no need for him until the following morning. His time was his own within the grounds encompassed by the asylum until sundown when he had to return to his assigned quarters in the servants' building. The asylum grounds proper covered several acres including Tarban Creek, so there was plenty of room to walk and sketch. Plant life was abundant and he was eager to get as much as possible to show Father Blake who would be returning to the Bath Arms sometime in October.

He didn't know what made him look up for she had made no sound. But there she was right behind him, the same girl he had seen three days ago. She had been standing then on the other side of the creek at a fair distance. He had waved once, and when he had looked again she was gone. Now she was back, standing silently just feet away from him. A native girl, she was tall and slim. Not as tall as Colleen but much slenderer, like a reed in the wind. She wore a plain blue dress which had been ripped away above the knees. Her thighs were lean and muscled and as he looked closer Martin could sense a lithe strength. She had the most amazing eyes he had ever seen. Light brown with flecks of yellow, they seemed to see everything and nothing at the same time. Her hair had a dull yellow sheen and it was thick and curly, bending itself under and over her neck.

Martin found his voice at last. "Good afternoon. I saw you last time I was here. I waved. My name is Martin."

He stopped for he was sounding foolish. The girl just looked at him, her right hand resting on her shoulder touching the claws of the black bird which crouched silently watching his every move.

Martin blundered on. "See. I am drawing this plant." He took the back of his pencil and began making marks in the bare earth. "See. Drawing. I am drawing." He made a quick sketch to resemble the bird crouching on a torso-less head and shoulder. Motioning to the sketch he said, "Your bird. This is your bird."

No response. Just the steady gaze of those brown-yellow eyes and the glittering stare of the black statue on her shoulder. Martin had never felt so embarrassed or absurd in his life. Standing there babbling to this strange silent girl with a bird on her shoulder. The whole thing was ridiculous. So he did the only thing he could do: Continue his sketching. He bent to his work, forcing himself to concentrate not knowing whether or not she had gone away. At last he could bear it no longer. He turned around. She took a small step towards him. My God, she was beautiful in a wild and untamed way. Her eyes burned into his and he caught the scent of honey. Then he felt it, an emptiness in his head like he was going to fall, a sense not of foreboding but an acute awareness that something was happening inside him, around him, around this girl. He closed his eyes and waited for the wave of anxiety to pass. When he opened them, she was gone.

~ ~ ~

In the month that followed Martin visited Parramatta a dozen times, and every time the strange silent girl came out of the trees like a dark ghost. Though he went to different places along the creek to sketch, she was always there, as though she knew where he would be. He always talked to her and drew something in the earth, trying to avoid her unnerving eyes. She had come a half dozen times before he stroked the crow. The bird frightened him but he felt that contact with it might help him with the girl. The black feathers were surprisingly soft and warm, and the bird had not flinched from his touch. After that she seemed less wary, though she still did not speak.

October 20, 1840

Martin placed the Virgin in his bag that warm October day when Baddely made what he imagined was possibly his last trip to Parramatta. The superintendent had deteriorated terribly, lapsing into fits of uncontrollable rage and irrationality. The Patriotes were calling him "the devil" and even Martin's former favoured status was now punctuated by tense silences and more frequently of late by vicious tirades. He was becoming suspicious of everybody, and up until this morning had been going to take Lepailleur as his driver. He had changed his mind at the last minute and that was when Martin had thought of the Virgin. The sores on Baddely's legs had not gone away and now he usually called in at the hospital for treatment before he visited the asylum. Though apparently undiminished in his capacity to fulfil his duties as superintendent at Longbottom, Henry Clinton Baddely was anything but a well man.

They arrived in Parramatta shortly after noon. Time was short, as the superintendent had indicated his desire to return to Longbottom that very evening. Martin felt an unfamiliar sense of urgency. He had to find the girl. After leaving the carriage in its usual place at the asylum stables, he trotted the quarter mile to the creek. He stopped at a place where a large sandstone rock jutted over the placid water and waited. The Virgin glinted in the sunlight. Why was he doing this? Giving a Catholic icon and a legacy of his mother to a mute aboriginal girl. From a mother he couldn't have to a girl he couldn't know. Martin turned her over in his hands rubbing his finger across the sharpness where the left hand had been. Though they hadn't spoken, there was kinship there. He could feel it. And since he mightn't be seeing her again, why not a gift? Then his eyes caught the clay seal and he was reminded of the paper inside. Yes, the figurine was a mystery. A family heirloom with its own secret. Just like this girl. Her mystery showed in the eyes, those powerful eyes that could evoke sensations like he had never before experienced. He wondered what she would do when he gave it to her.

He felt her presence and turned his head. She was there, less than five feet away. She wore a different dress, white and diaphanous. She came closer and let Martin stroke the crow on her shoulder.

"I might not be coming here again. I've brought you something. A present." Martin held out the Virgin towards the girl. "It was my mother's, but I want you to have it. Isn't she pretty?"

The girl's eyes were fixed on the Virgin and in them was a look Martin had never seen before: Excitement. Her brown hand reached out and took the icon. Her other hand left the crow's claws and both encompassed the Virgin holding her at eye level so that Mary's face was only inches from her own.

Then the most radiant smile Martin had ever seen transformed the girl's features. Delight came to those fathomless eyes and joy burst forth in the sparkle of perfect white teeth. And then she spoke. It was only one word, a word Martin didn't understand, but one breathed in a tone of reverential awe.

"Kurikuta."

The Banks of the Georges River, the Bankstown Area, Sydney, October 30, 1840

The late-afternoon sun glinted off the wide calm reaches of the river as two men sat by the bank. One, dark-haired and dressed in the white robe of the cloth, was busily writing in a large brown covered book; the other man, taller, fairer and younger, was sketching the strange yellow flowers growing on a stiff erect shrub. They were hardly flowers at all but more like clusters of thin yellow tubes protruding from a hard central cone. In the clearing behind them a small tent was pitched. A tin can was suspended by a stick supported by two others over a smoking fireplace. Nearby were cooking utensils, a slab of brown bread, some potatoes and meat, and a container of water. Beyond this small open space the bush stretched away on all sides; vast, seemingly empty, and, to the superficial eye, featureless.

The two men were lost in their own thoughts although both would have been most surprised had they known how congruent they were. Bernard Blake was as close to happiness as he could be. Only with Thomas had he ever felt this content. He really liked this boy. Martin Goyette was an avid intelligent listener. He didn't intrude, was deferential but happily lacked Neitch's obsequiousness. He asked excellent questions and was malleable without being easily influenced. Yes, he was glad that he had employed a rarely used charm with Bede Polding to enlist his intercession to Governor George Gipps. The result was the issuance of special two-day tickets enabling Martin Goyette to leave the stockade on a temporary work permit basis. Both Polding and Gipps, it appeared, were impressed with his plans for an illustrated compendium of native flora. He was aware that it would lend stature to their mutual goal of utilizing educated residents to elevate the colony from its present wretched penal status. After all as he had reminded both men, it had worked with Francis Greenway, once a convict, now a noted architect. Certainly, the fact that the boy was a fine artist with an incredible eye for colour and detail meant that what was originally a diversionary project now had the potential to become a worthwhile scientific contribution. And while Lamar was never far from his consciousness, the excitement of his compendium and the sudden emergence of a disciple in the making all seemed to point to a coming together of a destiny distorted by Lambruschini, unheeded by Thomas albeit unwittingly, and almost destroyed by Signy's death. He paused for a moment as the print blurred before his eyes. If he didn't know better, he would think they were failing him. It was Signy, not his eyes. She still made him cry sometimes in the night, or now when her memory forced itself upon him and made things dance out of focus. Bernard looked westward towards the rolling hills sheathed if only temporarily in their brilliant pre-summer green. Lamar was out there somewhere waiting for him, them. He looked at the fair head just a few yards away and smiled. The soft one was whispering at his shoulder. Yes, he will follow you anywhere. Then he turned to the words in front of him. He needed to finish these notes before the sun went down.

For Martin, the easiest and in a way the most luxurious part of his art was filling in the colour tones. It enabled busyness while allowing the latitude of reflection. As the varied-hued yellows of the plant Father Blake had laughingly named "drumsticks" came to life on his sketchpad here in this beautiful place, he could not help but dwell on his good fortune. It was difficult to believe the change in his life over the past few months. In fact he felt guilty when transcribing letters to loved ones for his illiterate comrades. They told of an existence filled with anguish and loneliness whereas his was ripe with the promise of love and creativity.

Colleen had already changed his life. He loved her with an emotion that frightened him. The feel of her lips and the smell of her body inflamed him beyond imagination even though he recoiled at the notion of loving her dishonourably. She was beautiful in both body and mind. To her, life was not a mystery or a mission towards something beyond. It was there to be grasped and lived with joy and confidence. She was so different from Madeleine. He realized it now. With Madeleine there was a draining of body and soul. She had been like a whirlpool, numbing his senses and sucking him into places he didn't understand. Colleen just made him feel happy. When he was with her he felt good about everything. Himself, his art. Everything. Well almost everything.

Martin looked up from his pad. Father Blake was busy writing. The sun had caught his face, and for a moment the strong nose and jaw and the dark intense eyes were bathed in a golden glow. Martin was reminded of an early saint. Christ might have looked like this man. It was the only thing that he and Colleen ever disagreed about.

She said that Father Blake frightened her with his dark looks of hatred. Charles Huot didn't like him either. Said that he was sure there was something ungodly about him. But that had been after Martin had recounted Colleen's story about the wrong-titled books, and the name Raimon Lull. Charles had looked strange and had said that Raimon Lull was a name not to be uttered by any Catholic. No, Charles was wrong. So was Colleen. Those eyes could never flash hatred; it was intensity and it frightened some people. He knew all about that. Father Blake was different from other men, that much was true. But it was a difference that drew Martin in while repelling Colleen, Charles and several of the other Patriotes. The Dominican knew so much about the world, yet possessed a spirituality greater than any priest.

He thought suddenly of the native girl. There was a spirituality there, too. He wondered if Father Blake knew about her. He was on the point of mentioning her when he remembered what it was that he was going to ask his new friend about. He needed to resolve something about Madeleine. The Chevalier's words about chosen ones, and the unforgettable sight of a wild-eyed girl he had loved in communion with something she saw above her altar spoke of another and more disturbing spirituality. Colleen said that Madeleine's vision was just her imagination. If indeed it was, it would make it that much easier to forget her. No, not forget her, but relegate her to a proper place in his memory and his new life. If anyone could help him, it was Father Blake. He stopped his sketching and put the pad at his knees.

"Father! I have need to ask you something."

There was a look of polite interest in the dark eyes. Martin went on. "What do you think of visions? I mean people seeing God, the saints, the Virgin Mary."

Bernard frowned slightly as if he was annoyed. Martin caught his breath. "Why do you ask, Martin?"

He sounds annoyed, thought Martin. Though somewhat discouraged, he pressed on. "Before I was sent here, in Canada I knew a girl who talked to the Virgin Mary. I saw her eyes, Father. They held neither dementia nor a desire for attention. She had an altar and when she knelt before it she raised her eyes and spoke to the air like I would to you. Though I saw nothing, I remain uncertain. She was not a nun or even a holy person. She was brave and beautiful and she died nobly fighting the British. Did she? Could she have seen the Virgin?"

"Her name, Martin. What was her name?" There was urgency in the tone and Martin wondered.

"Madeleine, Father. Her name was Madeleine. I . . . I knew her well."

The priest was murmuring and Martin had to strain to catch his words. "It's the same scene repeated many times over. The woman believed she saw the Virgin. But did you believe she saw her?"

"That's what I am asking you, Father. I don't know."

"But you have to know." The words were sharp and Martin was taken aback

"I don't follow, Father."

"Listen to me Martin, and listen well, for what I am about to say to you I have said to no other." The voice was calm now, mesmerizing, and Martin found himself caught by the dark eyes.

Bernard Blake was feeling the excitement in his breast. The soft one at his shoulder was whispering encouragingly, affirmatively. He had given much time to his thoughts since that wonderful day in Rome; had offered many masses to the misunderstood, betrayed Holy Mother. He had also spoken frequently and at length to the soft one which had travelled with him to this place on the path to his destiny. Neither cave nor wall now hid the soft one. Not now that the false ones had been found out and banished. It was time to capture this bright-eyed apostle.

"She did not see the Virgin. She couldn't have. Her miserable experience and much more in the church, is nothing but a testimony to falsehood."

"Miserable, falsehood. I don't . . ."

"A house built on unsound foundations is bound to fall. The Church, Martin has been built on falsehood. Hundreds of years of decay; of misplaced ardour. And all because of Christ. It was he who misled us. He was a chosen one, but he was seduced by false ones. He saw and heard the things denied to mortal man; he gathered unto himself the twelve who would be his worldly testimonials; he began his work with the unwashed, the preaching which was but the prelude to his destiny. But he failed. He allowed the false ones to seduce him."

"How Father?" Martin could scarcely believe his ears.

"He listened to a soft one at his shoulder and it was false. It led him to the foul embraces of the Magdalene slut and to the whorish John. And then he went to the desert because he was ashamed and after that they came and killed him. He thought he'd vanquished the false one in the desert but even then it was too late. Don't you see, Martin? His destiny was never completed. A church so constructed is as false as if Christ had not been a chosen one. The false voice was sent and Christ listened to it. Your misplaced faith has alarmed you. Do not be so disquieted, for you were merely divining the truth. For centuries, others less enlightened followed falsity, building lies upon lies until we wallow now in myth, icon worship, and in platitudes to metaphysical voids." He gripped Martin's arm. "It is about to change. Soon. And you, my new believer, will be a part of it."

Martin's thoughts were racing. The Dominican reminded him of Uncle Antoine. Except that Uncle Antoine had merely doubted. It was one thing for Uncle Antoine or himself to doubt, and indeed the priest's words had brought their own measure of clear vindication. But the fact remained that this was a priest belying the very creeds he had vowed to uphold. It didn't make sense.

"But why, how, Father? You are a priest."

"I became a priest because I could feel my destiny drawing me to the monastery. A search for truth, if you will. For a long time I didn't understand until the day I was allowed revelation."

Bernard leaned forward so that his face was close to Martin. His eyes were blazing and his breath was hot on Martin's cheek. "One day, Martin, I will tell you. For now, this is enough. A new destiny. Paths reforged. Here, Martin. Here in this place. It has been foretold. To me and now I to you. You have had your own harbingers. Good things have happened to you since we met. Your hand has healed and your painting skills are much more manifest. And it will go on. You will be out of your prison in a short time."

Martin could feel the excitement coursing through him. No one he had ever met had had the courage to call a whole accepted way of belief into question. It made Uncle Antoine seem timid by comparison. Christ misled, an impostor? It was too much. But he also knew there was definitely something wrong with a church that promised a bloodless joy for an equally bloodless commitment that posed as passion. And, if that long espoused as finality in gloomy churches was not finality, then he was in some way being released from a bondage that had plagued him for so long. "Good things have happened to you." Yes, they had. He thought of Colleen. Father Blake did not know of the very best thing that had happened to him. He would tell him soon.

The priest was on his feet now, walking about the downtrodden grass circling Martin who kept following him with his eyes. "Destiny imposes itself Martin. I know mine. I ask for your alignment in its unfolding. You will be enlightened when the time is right. When the path is ordained your way will also be made clear." Bernard's eyes were still hot and Martin didn't detect the sudden craftiness creep into them. Instead he was feeling the urge to wipe away a fleck of spittle which had lodged itself at the corner of the priest's mouth. "You give me loyalty. I give you freedom, and a place in destiny."

As he thought about it afterwards, it was an easy choice. It didn't matter that fundamental creeds were being arbitrarily juxtaposed through one man's revelation about a wayward Christ. What did matter was the promise of shedding forever a mindless allegiance to mere concepts and shadowy wraiths in the sky. He was not being asked to pledge fealty to a cause he didn't espouse or to a mission that was foreordained to failure. There was no vision to inspire him. There was just this strange wonderful courageous man who dared to question the unquestionable. His friend asking, no entreating, a commitment that had never before given. He could commit to flesh and blood if inspired by it. Yes, he admired this man like none on earth. He could give his loyalty to

Father Blake just as he had given his love to Colleen. It was a moment of his own becoming, an instant when choice and happening were the same thing. Commitment and faith were all about wanting to give, and for him, want spent itself on people, not ideas.

Martin held out his hand. "You speak of destiny and loyalty, Father. Destiny I do not understand. Loyalty is something that only lately I have come to appreciate. You have mine."

It was done.

Bernard took the outstretched hand. The tone of his reply surprised Martin for it was not that they were suddenly strangers, but more like teacher and pupil instead of comrades. "Destiny is bestowed. It has no master. Loyalty will exact its own price. Each is equally certain."

A kookaburra broke the ensuing silence. Martin was the first to laugh. Then Bernard broke into a grin. "It's your turn to get the fire, my young artist friend. I shall prepare the wine. We didn't drink it all last night, did we?"

Sydney, November 3, 1840

Bishop Polding listened to his young priest with more than his usual interest. Politically the proposal made good sense but only if it succeeded. The convict system was in its death throes, but there were many in the colony who believed that no healthy society could ever rise from debased humanity. With land and occupations at a premium, and the economy in a deplorable state, every convict granted a ticket of leave was usurping a prospective free settler. Instinct told him that the Patriotes' interests would be best served by prolonging their internment until a pardon could be guaranteed with return passage to Canada. Their language difficulty alone would make it difficult for most of them to secure gainful employment in Sydney, even though their skills were far superior to most residents, convict or otherwise. An intercession to the Governor for ticket-of-leave status to one of the Patriotes would not in all probability be received favourably. However, there were extenuating circumstances. The convict that Bernard had in mind could speak excellent English, but more importantly was a fine artist.

It was the same one on whose behalf he had already interceded for the temporary work permits, the one that Bernard seemed to have befriended. He looked at the young Dominican sitting opposite him. He looks nervous, Polding thought. Bernard had changed, not a great deal but enough for Polding to notice. He seemed happier, his step had a little more jaunt, but most important was an increased relish for his priestly duties. If ticket-of-leave status for a harmless but talented political prisoner would make Father Bernard Blake a better priest, then it was well worth it.

"Yes, Bernard, I agree. I'll do what I can. The young man is most promising and given his talent, I feel confident of the Governor's favourable ear. There are fifty-eight in incarceration. Let's see how one handles liberty. I trust he has employment."

Bernard smiled. "Thank you, Monsignor, for your consideration. The compendium will be completed much sooner now. And yes, I have arranged for him to work at the Bath Arms Hotel. Mr. Neitch has need of both interior and exterior painting on his premises. There will be much for Martin Goyette to do. With the stockade so near, the public impact of the ticket of leave status will be greatly lessened."

Bernard rose. His ears were ringing but it was like a melody. Yes, he was happy. For a moment he even felt a surge of gratitude towards Polding.

Longbottom Stockade, November 9, 1840

As soon as the news arrived, the letter delivered personally by a most official looking Superintendent Baddely, the scene dissolved into joyful confusion. The Patriotes poured into Martin's hut shouting and yelling. François-Xavier threw his hat in the air with joy. They slapped Martin's back and rumpled his hair, and afterwards carried him aloft around the square. Then the questions came. When would he leave? Had he a job? Where would he live? Did this mean that they all would be freed soon? Instead of trying to answer them all, Martin passed the letter around. His ticket-of-leave status was effective the day following receipt of the letter. He would be working for Mr. Neitch at the Bath Arms Hotel and would be staying there as well.

"You'll be able to visit us often," said Toussaint happily.

"And bring us food and news."

"But most of all you can show them that we can be trusted and can work hard and live honestly." The words belonged to Charles Huot. He gripped Martin's hand. "Much will depend on you my friend. They will be watching you. Do us all proud, Martin."

"What if he doesn't?" Charles Roy asked the question that many were thinking.

It was Louis Bourdon who replied. "Then we'll rot in this place for years."

It became quiet. Martin could feel his comrades sudden concern. "I don't know whether or not my early release may help you. I will promise you one thing, though."

Their eyes waited for him to continue.

"I will not be the cause of any disfavour towards us."

François-Xavier broke the silence. "Three cheers for Martin Goyette, the first Patriote to be released in the land of a thousand sorrows."

As the loud cheers rent the air, Martin smiled and thought. *No, François-Xavier. A land of a thousand joys.*

December 19, 1840

The Australian summer had arrived and as Martin stepped out into the morning sunlight the heat hit him like a warm blanket. It wasn't even mid-morning and already the heat was stifling. It had been like this for the past three weeks, the sun burning his back and his head as he painted. It was hard work, particularly difficult on the neck and he still found himself falling into bed at an early hour, dead tired. He looked up at the cream walls and dark brown window frames and smiled approvingly. Yes, it looked good, and more importantly for him, Mr. Neitch thought it did too. He'd be finished in another two days and then it was on to the inside. Considering the fact that he had another three months of this heat he was looking forward to the cooler if more exacting task of painting the inside of the hotel. It was hard to believe he had been here for over a month. Mr. Neitch was an excellent employer. He rarely interfered and appreciated Martin not only for his work but for his ideas as well. Why, he had been enthusiastic about Martin's suggestion to paint murals on some of the walls. They would start with Father Blake's room, of course, but Mr. Neitch would have to approve the motif first. Something appropriately Renaissance he had said. Martin hadn't been quite sure what the older man had meant. They could work it out later.

The worst part about his new life was something Martin had not anticipated. In fact he had thought precisely the opposite. He had not been able to enjoy Colleen's company as often as he had expected. Even less than when he had been the gate sentry. She worked all day, had duties at home in the evening, while he was only too happy to fall into bed. The weekends were not a great deal better. He did errands for Mr. Neitch on Saturday; Colleen worked. Sunday was not a great deal better. He felt it wise to accommodate Mr. Neitch's offer to attend mass with him on Sunday. That took up most of the day and what little time he and Colleen had for themselves was confined to the late afternoon and evening. They took long walks hand in hand, and when night fell they held each other close and talked about the future. Still, if he couldn't be with her he saw her often around the hotel. They loved each other with their eyes, and every time he passed her he made sure that their bodies touched.

It was different today. Mr. Neitch had given them both the day off. Well, almost the whole day. It was Homebush Races day. Everyone was going, even Governor Gipps. The first race was at noon, the last at four. Then it was back to the Bath Arms for a night of revelry. They were to be ready to work at six, Colleen to wait on patrons, him to do the extra odd jobs needed on busy nights. But until then the time was their own. When he had asked Colleen what she wanted to do her answer was swift and definite.

"Go to the races, of course."

~ ~ ~

Martin patted his pocket. His purse was there with all the money he had in the world. Eight guineas nine shillings and sixpence represented his entire savings from transcribing and oyster gathering at Longbottom, his month's wages from Mr. Neitch and the coins that Father Blake had given him for his flower drawings. His decision to take all his money was not made easily. Certainly he didn't intend to gamble it away on some racehorse. He did want to impress Colleen, however. His clothes, while presentable thanks to Mr. Neitch's generosity, were hardly those of a gentleman. If he took all his money he would not feel so inferior. Besides he wanted Colleen to pay for nothing. Who knows what things cost at the races? He wondered what it would be like. He had never been to the races, not even in Canada.

He waited for Colleen in the shade on the south side of the hotel. He saw her coming from a distance and watched her approach. She walked like she did everything else: with purpose and that other quality he couldn't put a word to. Practical elegance? No, that wasn't it, but it was the closest he could come to.

"Sorry I'm late, Martin. I came as quick as I could. My mum wanted me to do her hair."

"Is she going to the races too? Can I meet her?"

"Lordy no. There's a party at old man Rose's. He always has a race party. They'll drink and bet there."

"On what?" Martin was puzzled.

"Oh, anything." She took his arm

Her hand was warm and brown on his arm. Martin turned to look at her as they walked. The thick tresses of auburn hair fell across the white dress, shiny and burnished. Martin reached to touch them, and she turned to smile at him brushing her lips across his cheek. He thrilled to her smile and the dancing joy in her eyes. At that moment, he was the happiest man on earth.

The carriage was crowded with people going to the races. Most had picnic baskets and all along the four-mile road west they joked about the sums of gold they were going to win. Then the carriage turned north towards the river and the conversation quieted, replaced by the jolting sounds of the wheels as they traversed the pitted track that took them into the Homebush flats and the racecourse. Soon they were there. As he climbed down from the carriage, Martin gasped at the sight. There were people everywhere, many bedecked in a finery that he had never seen before. He counted at least thirty parasols in the steady stream of elegantly dressed couples wending their way along the dusty track that led to the river and the ferry dock. They looked comical, picking their way fastidiously through the dirt. Others were filing in through a narrow gate to the grandstand. A hundred or so milled about on the grassy area just inside the entrance gate. Rough rails separated the spectators from the track, a worn grass oval about twenty-five yards wide and about a half mile around. Behind the stand Martin could make out a long row of stables.

Colleen's excitement showed. Grasping Martin by the hand she propelled him through a narrow gate and onto a grassy flat area, past the food and ale stands to where a series of umbrellas were set up by the rails of the track itself. Beneath each one stood a single figure, bag slung about his neck and stub of pencil in hand. A crude board was affixed to the umbrella pole.

"That's where you make your bets," Colleen said. "But not yet. I'm hungry and I saw some sugar apples for sale over there. Let's get one each and some lemonade. I hope it's cold this year."

He gave her the money and while she was gone wandered over to a table set on two barrels. It was covered with sheets of paper.

"It'll cost you a penny," said a voice from behind him.

"I don't understand," Martin felt embarrassed.

"How yer to bet ifn you don't know whose racing," The short fat man shoved a sheet at him. "A penny me young bucko. Just a penny."

Martin took the sheet and handed over a penny. He was scanning it when Colleen approached. Two toffee apples were in one hand and a pair of dull green bottles were in the other.

"Here. Eat it quick, but careful. You don't want to be spilling on yourself. When's the first race?" she said between mouthfuls."

The name jumped out at him and Martin could scarcely believe his eyes. "Look, Colleen. Uncle Antoine. There's a horse called Uncle Antoine and he's in the third race.'

"Let's go see him. They let you, you know. If he looks good we'll wager a shilling on him." Colleen immediately felt a little guilty. A shilling was a lot to bet.

"The first race begins in ten minutes. Shall we wait and watch it? We could sit in the grandstand if you want."

Martin was inwardly glad at Colleen's reply. For some reason the money was suddenly burning a hole in his pocket. Uncle Antoine! What a coincidence! He had to see him.

"No, Martin. Let's see Uncle Antoine. I'm as curious as you are."

When they reached the barns they had to wait as the entrants in the first race entered the saddling paddock. Martin didn't know a great deal about racing but he was surprised at both the range and quality of the horses. Some were obviously very well bred animals; others had a mulish cart horse look about them. It wasn't difficult to tell the favourites.

They found Uncle Antoine at the end of the stables beside a stall where a magnificent grey was being tended to by two grooms. The contrast between the two animals was startling. Uncle Antoine was a smallish nondescript bay with a large inelegant head. His ribs were clearly visible and he appeared elongated, his longish awkward-looking body sitting on top of legs that seemed too short and strangely malformed. Marin's heart sank.

"He's beautiful, Martin," Colleen squealed. "He's so ugly, he's beautiful. We have to bet on him."

Martin could not follow her logic, let alone agree with it. Uncle Antoine's sad eyes looked at him. He reached out to stroke the lowered head when he felt a bump at his shoulder. A small man with a fork and watering pail in hand had backed into him from the opposite stall.

"Excuse me, Sir. Sorry."

There was something familiar about the voice. The tone. And the bearing too. Martin peered closer trying to focus more closely in the dim light. The balding head, the grey watery eyes.

"Hewitt. It's you isn't it?"

The little man looked hard at Martin. A look of recognition dawned in his eyes.

"Mister Martin. I'll be blessed. You're out already?"
He extended his hand.

The old feelings of shame; of wanting to explain rose in him but Martin fought it down. He took the proffered hand and shook it warmly.

"It's good to see you, Hewitt. But what are you doing here. I thought you'd be . . ."

"Back on a ship. Not bloody likely. Niblett and Wood saw to that. I'm finished." He looked at the floor before continuing. "My wife's sick back in Portsmouth. I'm needing money to get a ship home. I work when I can. With horses." He shrugged. "It's not easy these days."

Mercifully, Hewitt saved Martin from further anguish. He seemed to recover a measure of good humour and inquired about Charles Huot and some of the other Patriotes. He had heard that the *Buffalo* had gone down in the Tasman Sea, and muttered darkly that he hoped both Niblett and Wood were on board which was not bloody likely, to use his favourite expression. Martin wanted to introduce Colleen but felt awkward. She saved him by introducing herself and thrusting her hand at Hewitt who took it looking surprised.

"Pleased to make your acquaintance. Missy." He must have seen her eyeing the grey because he went on without missing a beat. "You like the grey, eh, Missy? He's a beauty. Mr. Thompson owns him. Says he's the best in the country over a mile. Hasn't been beaten in ten starts. Not much use backing him in the next race. He'll be odds on."

Martin saw Colleen nodding and made a point to ask her what *odds on* meant. His own eyes were still on Uncle Antoine standing mournfully, a sprig of hay hanging out one side of his mouth.

"It's this one I'm interested in, Hewitt. He has the same name as a dear friend of mine and I thought I'd place a small wager for sentiment's sake. By the looks of him, though, I'd be wasting my money."

Hewitt flicked a practised eye at Uncle Antoine and spat on the ground. "You know, Mr. Martin. People here think they know horses but most of them don't know hay from straw. This bay could be better than he looks. Take his head. It only looks too big because he's so thin. He looks stretched. Out of shape. Legs too short." He poked towards the outline of Uncle Antoine's ribs. "He's thin. But that don't mean he can't run."

Martin opened his mouth but Hewitt went on speaking even as he lifted one of Uncle Antoine's forelegs. "They say his legs are no good. Look at these swellings. Spavins. Bone and bog, both." He pressed a softer indentation near the hock. "He's got thoroughpin too. But that don't mean a damn. Excuse me lady, but it don't. He could still run like the wind for all I know. I talked to the freed man who owns him. Says he's been running well at his place at Wilberforce. He might be worth a shilling, Sir. He'll go long. Twenty-five to one I'd say." He turned to Colleen before continuing, "I hear old Jonesy's taken the grey off his book and is giving odds on second. Seven or eight to one at least, Miss, if you get my meaning."

A hoarse voice at the end of the barns called Hewitt away and soon Martin and Colleen were standing outside in the hot sun. Colleen explained that odds on meant that you had to wager more than you would expect to win, and that old Jonesy was a bookmaker who was prepared to offer odds on who would finish second. They watched as the horses were led out to the saddling enclosure. Uncle Antoine followed the grey out. They looked incongruous. How could Uncle Antoine ever beat a horse like that? Colleen broke his thoughts.

"David and Goliath. That's what it is, Martin. David and Goliath." She fumbled in her purse and produced a shilling. "I am going to back him," she said forcefully and headed over to where a knot of betters was clustered around one of the umbrellas. Martin followed her uncertainly.

The bookmaker saw her immediately and pointed in her direction. "What'll it be, Missy?"

"A shilling on Uncle Antoine."

"Twenty five shillings to one, Uncle Antoine."

A hand scribbled something on a piece of paper and handed it to her. Colleen took it and looked at Martin questioningly. "Are you going to put a shilling on him too, Martin? He is Uncle Antoine isn't he? Our very own David."

Just as if it had never gone away, Antoine Cousineau's face was before him again, wrinkled and brown from the sea. For a moment he heard the rollicking laugh and felt the big callused hand slapping his shoulder affectionately. He recalled something Uncle Antoine had said not long before his death. Something about trust, not hope being eternal. Trust went beyond hope. Hope was easy; trust was sacred. Then he saw again the little bay in his stall standing beside the magnificent grey, the thin malformed body begging the trust that made hope real. He grabbed Colleen's arm.

"No, Colleen. Not a shilling. Everything. The whole eight guineas."

She watched fascinated as he extracted the eight gold coins from his purse. "All eight! To win? You're sure, Martin?"

He nodded.

"Then let's do it.

Martin edged his way uncertainly to the same bookmaker. He said the words slowly feeling embarrassed at speaking aloud in English in public. "Eight guineas on Uncle Antoine."

There was a slight hum from the dozen or so who were clamouring to place their last-minute bets but Martin didn't notice. All he could see was his life's savings disappearing into a black bag and a voice pronouncing its departure. "Two hundred guineas to eight, Uncle Antoine."

Then the slip of paper was in Martin's hand. He looked at it incuriously, not even noticing that it said two hundred and eight instead of two hundred. It was done.

Colleen took his hand and nudged her head into his shoulder. "Don't you fret, Martin. Uncle Antoine'll do us proud. Now let's go and watch him beat that grey."

~ ~ ~

The horses were at the post, milling about as the starter tried to arrange them in a straight line. Martin couldn't see Uncle Antoine. Then there was a cloud of dust and they were off. A little more than twice around the track, Colleen told him. As they passed the stand for the first time, the grey was a length in front. His rider had him on a very short rein and the grey was fighting him, wanting his head. Uncle Antoine was on the outside second from last and already four lengths behind the leader. Martin's heart sank. He tried to follow them around the back straight. Uncle Antoine was moving forward but was falling farther behind the grey. At the finish line the second time with a little under half a mile to go the grey had increased his lead to eight lengths. The crowd was cheering wildly. Colleen was jumping up and down yelling, "Go, Uncle Antoine, go." Martin was whispering, "Please! Please Uncle Antoine, Please!"

No one saw him make his move. The dust was thick in the air now on the back straight, but when they turned the corner for home, the little bay had moved into second place chasing the grey whose rider now had his whip out. It was fascinating, marvellous like a drama unfolding before his eyes. Martin was screaming, forming words he would never remember as he watched Uncle Antoine, head low to the ground, lessen the gap. They were less than fifty yards from the finish line when Uncle Antoine joined the grey in a final battle of speed. Martin didn't know it, but it was to be a battle of wills not of speed. The result would surely have been different otherwise, for like many a racing animal before him and countless more since, the grey was a front runner who would not, could not meet the challenge no matter how hard the whip flailed. He gave up, and Uncle Antoine crossed the light a full head in front.

It was a moment he would never forget. Colleen's arms were around his neck and she was kissing him, half laughing half crying. They danced and jumped around like two children, and no one seemed to notice or care. He didn't want to stop. It was like a piece of time standing still just for them. At last when the rush of excitement finally subsided and Martin could get his breath, he rasped at the air. "Thank you Uncle Antoine."

Colleen was quick to reply. Her face was flushed, her green eyes alive with excitement and she bore a grin from ear to ear. "Which one, Martin?"

"Why, both of course."

She gave him her betting paper. "Then you talk to yours while you go and collect our money, and I'll go watch mine while they unsaddle him. Wasn't he wonderful, Martin?"

"Yes, he was. He truly was."

"One other thing, Martin." Colleen came close and looked about her warily. "You're going to collect a lot of money. We could lose it all a dozen times over between here and the Bath Arms. There's people here who would cut your throat for a shilling let alone two hundred guineas. When you get the money, take it over there." She pointed to a small tent set up just behind the grandstand. "It's a bondsman's tent. For half a crown, they'll keep your money in a strongbox and deliver it to the Bath Arms tomorrow. Oh don't look so doubtful. All the big winners do it."

Martin nodded. Then he stood there holding the two betting slips as he watched Colleen run towards the saddling paddock. His thoughts were strangely far away. To a wide river, russet leaves that crackled underfoot, and a pipe-smoking old friend whose memory had come with him.

"Yes you truly were wonderful, Uncle Antoine. Trust is more real than hope."

~ ~ ~

He collected Colleen's money and his own two hundred and eight guineas, aware of the envious eyes of other betters. In the shade of one of the several high gums he counted out fifty guineas, wrapped them in the entrants' sheet he had bought for a penny and headed back towards the stables continually glancing over his shoulder. No one pursued him and soon he was back in gloom of the stables. He found Hewitt mucking out one of the stalls. The little man's face broke into a wide grin when he saw Martin.

"Put a shilling or two on him, Master Martin, I trust. That grey was nothing but a speedy squib." He chuckled leaning on his fork. "Had a feeling about the grey. I've seen too many of them. No guts in the straight. Anyways, it's your good fortune, Sir. You did back him, didn't you?"

"Yes, Hewitt. I backed him." He fumbled at the paper. "I've got something for you, Hewitt. Your share. It'll help you get home."

For a few seconds Hewitt stared at the glittering pile in Martin's hand. "My share? I don't understand, Sir."

It was one of the best feelings in his life, and Martin relished it. He placed the money in Hewitt's hand. It was rough and smelled like horse. "Fifty guineas, my good Samaritan friend. Fifty guineas. It's yours, Hewitt. All of it. Your voyage home." His left hand fell on Hewitt's shoulders. "My way of thanks for your bravery, and . . . your pain."

Hewitt looked at him like a startled animal, the tears welling in his eyes. "My God, sir, any decent God-fearing man would have done the same. I've been treated worse by meaner scum."

There was nothing more to say. Hewitt shook his hand. "I'll never forget you, Master Martin. You're a saint you are, a blessed saint."

~ ~ ~

Outside, he made his way to the bondsman's tent. *My God*, were those two men following him? They were a rough pair and he was certain they had been there when he was collecting his money. They were right behind him now and moving closer. He could hear their footfalls. His steps quickened and soon he was running. The tent was just ahead. Then he was inside. Now, blessing Colleen for her practical common sense, he saw his money placed in a heavy vault and secured safely. His hands were still cold and clammy when he returned to the crowd and the sun, glancing nervously about. The two men were gone.

Then, out of the corner of his eye, he saw Colleen. She was backing away from a man who was reaching for her, goaded on by his companions. Colleen suddenly stood her ground and the man grabbed her arm. Martin felt the gorge rise into his throat. My God! He recognized him. The drunken man was Alexander Black.

Martin broke into a run. He had to do something. Without thinking he reached out and shoved Black. The man lurched backwards, startled.

"Leave her alone, you swine. Get away."

Martin heard the jeers from around him. Black's friends were pressing forward. Black himself had recovered somewhat and Martin could see recognition in his eyes.

"You," he breathed. "The *Buffalo*. The bloody idiot with the lip." He cackled drunkenly, "A bit brave are you? Well, nitwit, we'll soon see about that."

Black started forward, fists clenched and pawing wildly at the air. Martin waited. He could feel the gorge of fear rise into his throat.

It was Colleen who stepped between them. A crowd had gathered and there were angry murmurings behind them.

"Leave her alone," yelled a voice.

Two of the young toughs with Black eyed each other nervously and began to back away. But if Colleen noticed, she gave no sign. Her face was flushed and she was looking directly at her tormentor. Her voice was firm and unafraid.

"You're drunk, Sir, and no gentleman. We'll have no more to do with you and your kind." Her hand tightened on Martin's arm as her eyes blazed at the lurching pantomime figure in front of them. "Come, Martin. We have better things to do than dally with drunken fools."

It must have been her courage that had done it, but Martin saw his fists in front of his face. They were clenched and waving towards Black. He must have said the words because Colleen told him about it afterwards, but he didn't remember.

"Come on, whelp. We're not on the *Buffalo* now. Come on."

Martin waited, feeling the churning in his gut and watching Black's fists. How would it feel? He'd never been hit by a punch before. It would hurt a lot and there would be blood. His blood. He'd close his eyes and swing. Yes, that's what he would do. Close his eyes.

He held his breath, waiting as Black came closer. He could see the serpent on the ring on his adversary's right index finger. It was big and swayed like a cobra in the menacing circling fist. It was time. He closed his eyes tightly and swung wildly from the waist, his fist cutting the air. He swung again and again, waiting for the crack against his face. Nothing happened. He braved a look. Wonder of wonders! Black had stopped and his hands were by his sides. There was a muted tone to the bravado in his voice.

"Have it your way, nitwit. If she's with you, she can't be worth much, can she boys?" He gestured over his shoulders towards the already thinning knot of onlookers. Then he moved forward until Martin could smell his reeking breath.

"You'll pay for this, bastard. By all in hell you'll pay. Alexander Black never forgets."

Black was lumbering away when Martin felt Colleen's hand guide him away to a rough plank bench under the gums. She held his trembling hands in hers and talked softly. About the money they had won and how she had fondled Uncle Antoine's ear while he was being unsaddled. Then she became adamant. It was a great day and they were not going to let a drunken idiot spoil it for them. What they needed was a cool drink and another visit to the stalls. She had talked to Hewitt about a dappled horse called Brother Mick. Hewitt said he was worth a shilling. But they would have to hurry. Then she took his hand and as her lips brushed his cheek, she whispered, "You were wonderful, Martin. I've never loved you as much as I did back there."

It was like a release, there in the heat on the rough boards; in their own solitude with people all around them. Though his heart was still pounding wildly, he thrilled at her words. He, too, had never loved her as much as he had back there when she had faced down his nemesis.

As they returned towards the stables and the stall that held Brother Mick, Martin squeezed her hand, rubbing his forefinger gently up and down her wrist. He could feel the sweat on his back and the sky above him was like a blue oven. Hewitt, Black and Uncle Antoine! A visit from a guardian angel, and two burdens laid down in this dry dusty place. He looked at Colleen, at the clean line of her jaw and the swell of her breasts. It was strange that it should all be happening here in this place his friends in bondage called the land of a thousand sorrows. Yes, this was a good day. The best, if he really thought about it.

CHAPTER IV

The Orphanage for Girls, Parramatta, December 23, 1840

The room was oppressively hot as Matron Nance Edwards laboured over the letter. The faded yellow drapes behind her head hung still and listless, and through the wide-open windows the sound of the cicadas drowned out the ticking of the huge mahogany clock in the corner. But Matron Edwards was used to them by now and didn't hear them any more. She was clicking her tongue as the pen moved laboriously across the paper. Though she had a hundred things to do just before Christmas and the idea of letter-writing always daunted her, she felt she had no choice. Bishop Polding was Mary's last chance.

Against all her protests they wanted to get rid of Mary. They always had. Her own superior because he thought Mary cost the orphanage too much and that she didn't belong there anyway. "Why feed an abo girl who's just going to disappear into the bush one day?" he had said. The Chief Magistrate because he thought she was a danger to the good people of Parramatta. He had had complaints, he had told her. And worst of all, Doctor Armitage who believed she was quite mad. If he had his way, Mary would be locked away in the lunatic asylum. Just yesterday he had told her that it was going to be done after Christmas. All of which had led to this letter of desperation. She knew what would happen to Mary in the Asylum. She didn't belong there. She was such a pure simple child. You didn't lock children up in asylums. You protected them. If she would go back to the bush all and good. But she hadn't. She liked it here and this was where she would stay if Nance Edwards had any say in the matter.

Though she was writing to Bishop Polding, it was Father Blake that Nance Edwards was interested in. To be sure, she didn't like him. Not at all. He had such wild strange eyes, but the little girls did seem to like him, and goodness knows, they loved his stories even if Nance herself did not approve of all of them. But it was what he could do that interested her. Father Blake did seem to get his own way with people of importance. If he would talk to Mary. If he would even advise her what the best course of action was. But best of all, if he would intercede with the chief Magistrate, then all would be all right. She knew it. Nance Edwards' own Catholicism was a well kept secret. She wouldn't have gotten this job otherwise. And though she hadn't said a prayer in years she still held priests in a kind of awe. Particularly priests like Father Blake who seemed so apart from everyone. So alone, like he wasn't of this earth. Her mother telling her how awful God's wrath was. Father Blake reminded her of what God's wrath must be like. Yes, he was the man to save Mary from those who would do her harm.

Parramatta, January 4, 1841

Kookaburra woke Lamar with his morning laughter. She was dizzier than usual; she wondered if that meant that this might be the day. Fighting nausea, she stirred from her bed among the trees and bathed her face in the cool waters of the river. She wished it would wash the hurting away. Atha watched her from a low branch and when she had finished, hopped to her shoulder where he sat waiting to be stroked. His wing had healed and he could fly again. He rarely did, preferring instead to spend most of his time perched on her shoulder.

Rubbing her fingers along the the bird's black neck, Lamar picked her way along the riverbank to her totem tree. She scarcely saw her friend, the small frill-necked lizard, scurry across her path, and twice she stumbled because of her head. She remembered the pain last time, when her head had ached so much she had almost fallen in the river. Kurikuta had come then.

The gum's roots were in water and it was dying, but Lamar didn't know that. A tall tree with its roots in her totem was a good sign and she had hidden her sacred tjurungas there. She would call to Kurikuta here today though she knew she would not come, for neither duck nor reed lived in this place.

"When comes Kurikuta?" she called to the sky. "When come the Ganabuda?"

The cicadas were silent in the morning air and there were only the bird songs in the gums above. Lamar waited until the sun shone through the higher leaves of her totem tree. Then, reaching into the forked hollow just within the height of her reach, she extracted the Virgin Mary figurine. She held it close to her and whispered softly.

"You do not guide me, Kurikuta. Are the spirits angry? Has Lamar displeased them?"

Suddenly Atha left her shoulder, soaring into the air like a spirit going to the dreamtime. Holding on to the tree for support and cradling the Virgin with her free hand, Lamar watched him as he dipped towards the morning sun. Then he was gone. She waited patiently, biting her lip as the sky turned over and over. The sun had climbed a fingernail higher before he reappeared as a speck, then as a black form and finally as Atha to settle on her shoulder again. His beak was slightly open and his eyes glittered like black rain in the sun. Lamar stroked his back and whispered her thanks. Kurikuta had told her which way to go. She would travel at night towards the morning sun when no one could see her, and when she found reeds and duck she would stop and wait for Kurikuta. Carefully she placed the Madonna back among the other tjurungas and went back to feed the animals. As the sun sank lower towards the blue hills of the Dharug, Lamar's eyes became clearer and the spirits inside her head were quiet. She knew then that she was right. Kurikuta would come soon.

She stole through the night silently past yellow-lit farm houses and black paddocks, and found the water in the darkness. It was warm and still and smelled like frog. She lay beside it and waited for the light to come.

It was duck that made the noise of morning, not kookaburra. He filled the air with his song and all along the banks of the small watercourse the reeds grew thick and straight. Lamar smiled as she stretched her arms in the dawn's light. She had been on this river of the duck before, but not so far from where it joined its mother. She looked about. There was no sign of the strange ones' houses. The strange ones didn't like places that smelled of frog and where sharp grasses cut their soft hands. They would not come to this place.

Lamar waited as the sun climbed high in the sky, and, until from far away in some wooded place beyond the reeds, she could hear the faint songs of the cicadas. And when she began hearing the noises within, like the soft sounds of the night birds in flight, she took off her white dress and stepped into the warm water. As the soft mud squeezed between her toes she realized it was like last time. Instinctively she reached for Atha but he was gone. She shuddered as a sharp pain bit into her head forcing her to shut her eyes tightly, and for a moment she swayed forward towards the still brown water.

Light glowed like the moon's, only brighter, much brighter, and Lamar could feel Kurikuta all around her. The light was coming out of the brown depths and Kurikuta was suddenly there, standing on top of the water. Lamar could not see her face at first. It was hidden in a kind of misty cloud. Shielding her eyes from the light, Lamar splashed forwards.

"Kurikuta, Mother of Crow. You have come at last."

Kurikuta was silent but the mist was suddenly gone, and Lamar could see her long pale fingers reaching towards her. She wanted to clutch them but her own hands would not move. She spoke again.

"I have done as you asked, Kurikuta. I want to go back to the Dharug but I have stayed with the strange ones. When, Kurikuta? When? When will the Ganabuda come among us to drive the Kalabara back? When will the Ganabuda make the rains fall again?"

But Kurikuta said nothing, and her pale sad eyes did not seem to belong to the Dreamtime.

"Speak, Kurikuta. Speak of the Ganabuda." For a moment Lamar saw Atha's wings in the sky above her. She looked up and heard Kurikuta. Her words were low, soft but clear. Far away like in sleep, like the Dreamtime.

"It will be as is. Go and wait for him to come. He has been given to you."

"Who, Kurikuta? Who has been given to me?"

"Wait for him. He will come. With the rainbow."

Lamar was exhilarated. "The Great Rainbow Snake?"

Kurikuta smiled a slow sad smile and Lamar thought she saw a slight shake of the head. "It will be as is when it wasn't to be."

"I do not understand, Kurikuta. When come the Ganabuda?"

"It will be by the water when the rainbow comes."

The Ganabuda. She saw them. They were standing behind Kurikuta. Three of them. She could see them clearly. It couldn't be, but she was one of them. Then they began to sing, a loud sweet sound that silenced duck and the slow-moving ones in the far away trees.

Using her mother's voice, they were singing about a great quickening; someone to be born. Of whom? Her! By whom? The Rainbow Snake?

No! This couldn't be. But the Ganabuda wouldn't lie to one made in their image. And all the time Kurikuta was standing on the water, her sad eyes dull and colourless.

The voices were louder now and Lamar had to put her hands to her ears to try and stop them from hurting her head.

"By the rainbow. A great quickening. Wait for him."

She had to close her eyes, the pain in her ears was so bad.

Suddenly the singing stopped. Lamar kept her eyes closed. Only when she heard the distant insects again did she open them.

Except for duck she was alone.

The Orphanage for Girls, Parramatta. Thursday, January 7, 1841

Nance Edwards re-read the letter and gave thanks to God. Bishop Polding understood. He would send Father Blake to talk with the girl and give the matron his feelings about her sanity. She could expect Father Blake this very Sunday. He would be saying Mass for the French prisoners at Longbottom Stockade in the morning and would proceed to Parramatta afterwards and should be at the orphanage by mid-afternoon. If Matron Edwards could see to it that the girl was there then Father Blake could speak with her at that time. Bishop Polding had heard how she was wont to wander at will and there would be no sense in having Father Blake make the trip for nothing.

Nance Edwards went to the window and looked out to the hedged pathway that led to the river and the barns. She could see Mary tending to one of the lambs, and her crow in a nearby tree watching her. She had a blue dress on and the sun on her hair made it look like burnished gold. She was such a beautiful child in her own wild strange way. Nance Edwards wished she would talk. Goodness knows she herself had tried hard enough. But she had gotten nothing. No expression; no semblance of understanding. They said you only had to look at her to know she was mad. Nance didn't think so. There was something there in those strange yellow-flecked eyes. Something different, unfathomable. But it was not madness. Well, she'd soon have an answer. If anyone could tell it was Father Blake. It was funny now that she thought of it. Father Blake's eyes also had a special look of their own. And he certainly wasn't mad.

The Parramatta Road, January 9, 1841
Bernard rode his horse tiredly. The pain had returned. Quiet, subdued for a time by plants and things of the earth, the demons were back summoned by thoughts of foul ones, and shrieking now inside his head. First it was Neitch telling him about his cousin's daughter from Spezio, a serving girl who was coming to better her life in Sydney. It was the whore. He knew it. Then that idiot Polding had commanded him to go to the orphanage to examine the mad girl, and worse, minister more frequently to the vermin in the Female Factory. Oh they loved that, the cesspit dwellers that rose from hell itself to assail him once more, laughing and dancing like a whirlwind inside his skull. He ground his hands into his eyes, and bit his lip until it bled, but the demons wouldn't leave him alone. The road in front of him blurred into shapeless images. His sight was going. They were taking his vision. He moaned amid the bile that had spilled into his throat and lowered his head to the formless brown mane beneath him.

The Bath Arms Hotel. January 10, 1841
It was one of those close overcast days that kept the sweat on your face no matter many times you wiped it. Martin straightened his back and for the thousandth time pulled out his handkerchief. He'd be very surprised if they didn't get a good storm later in the day. Repairing a fence was not his idea of the best way to spend a Sunday but at least it was preferable to going to Mass. In fact he had been quite pleased when Mr. Neitch had suggested two days ago that he work on the fence until it was done. It wasn't a big job and he would probably finish it today in time to spend an hour or two with Colleen. It was not like Mr. Neitch to forget about Mass but he always forgot things when he was excited or

upset, and nothing made Mr. Neitch more excited than a visit from Father Blake. Martin was pleased, too, when he had been told that Father Blake would be staying overnight on Saturday and Sunday. Maybe they could talk; possibly take a short sketching trip. Martin had found an interesting-looking fern by the river just a half hour's walk away. Possibly they could go there. At least that was his idea at the time.

Father Blake had arrived soon after lunch on Saturday. Colleen said he looked sick. He had lain down immediately and did not dine that night with Mr. Neitch who, according to Colleen, was terribly upset. Martin had tried to visit Father Blake in his room later in the evening but Mr. Neitch had been adamant. Father was sleeping and must not be disturbed. And this morning, he hadn't gone to Longbottom to say Mass. Priests rarely failed to say Mass unless they were really ill. It was quite distressing. What if his friend was seriously sick? No, it was probably just one of those summer ailments that seemed to happen often in Sydney.

He was taking his noonday break under a tree when he saw Mr. Neitch. He was hurrying and looked worried. Martin got up and approached his employer.

"Good day to you Mr. Neitch." He pointed to the fence. "Do you like it? I'm almost done."

Emmanuel Neitch did not even glance at the fence. "Martin. Father Blake is still not well. He could not even say Mass this morning."

"Does he need a doctor?"

"He says, no, but he is asleep now. He was to go to Parramatta this afternoon, and I do not know what to do. He has to go to the Girls' Orphanage. He told me so last evening."

"Can I help?" asked Martin.

"Father is not a man to forego his duties." Neitch paused before continuing. "Yes, that is what we will do. We must pass his regrets on to the matron at the orphanage."

Emmanuel Neitch was still speaking. "It will have to be you, Martin. I cannot leave Father. Go see the matron. Explain that Father Blake is very ill and most distressed over missing his appointment with her. Leave the fence. Dress. I will have the chestnut saddled. I want you gone within fifteen minutes."

Martin groaned inwardly. There would be no time with Colleen now. He wouldn't be back until very late. But he was happy to help Father Blake.

He nodded his head, "Yes, Mr. Neitch. I'll be ready in ten minutes."

Emmanuel Neitch did not answer. He was already heading back to the hotel.

~ ~ ~

It began raining about mid-afternoon and for an hour the water fell in grey sheets until the ground was awash with muddy rivulets. Then as suddenly as it had begun, it stopped. The sun showed itself, bringing a cloying heat that drew the moisture from the ground and left it hanging in the air like an invisible cloud. And then the rainbow appeared. Even long-time Parramatta residents, used to the ribbons of colour stretching across the sky after a summer storm, stood to marvel at its perfection. Each of the distinctly hued bands stood out clearly against an unusually blue sky. It was brilliant, perfect; a coloured arch shining in the sun like it had been polished.

When she saw the rainbow Lamar smiled and whispered to Atha. Then leaving him on a gum branch she made her way along the riverbank to the tree where her tjurungas were hidden. She extracted the Madonna and talked to it softly while pointing upwards to the rainbow that came out of water and which entered the earth again in the land of the Dharug. Later, when the sun began to slip behind the blue hills, she put on the white dress. She looked up once at Atha now wheeling silently in the sky above. Then, still clutching the Madonna she knelt on the still damp grass, and spreading the folds of her dress out about her faced the limpid water, and waited.

~ ~ ~

Matron Edwards closed the door behind him and Martin was in the open again, squinting into the sun. His damp clothes clung to his back and he did not relish the thought of the ride home. Nothing had seemed to go right. It had started raining before he reached Parramatta and he was soaked to the skin. The Matron had been quite upset that Father Blake had not been able to come. Mr. Neitch had said that she was a kind soul who would feed Martin, but she hadn't, and now he had to ride all the way back to the Bath Arms without even a bite.

Martin's empty stomach made him think of the *Buffalo* and he was re-living some painful memories when he saw her. He was almost at the tree where his horse was tethered when the flash of white caught his eye. It was someone sitting on the grass near the barn. It was the native girl, the one he had given the Madonna to. It had been so long since he had seen her and though he thought about her from time to time he had never thought that he would meet her again. For some reason he had expected her to disappear; vanish into thin air as suddenly as she had come. But there she was as big as life sitting there in the sun like a figure in a painting.

As he hurried down the track towards her, Martin felt an anticipation he couldn't explain. Did she still have the Madonna? Would she speak this time? At least he knew her name now. It had been Colleen who had known about her. Something to do with a friend of her mum's who worked at the orphanage. Mary! The native girl's name was Mary. She just might speak if he called her by name.

Lamar was awake but she saw him coming as though she were asleep; like the visions in the night that went away with the light. It was real and not real at the same time. It was as if the Dreamtime had opened up the sky and the Great Rainbow Snake had pushed him down the rainbow to her. She was expecting Kurikuta to send someone of the Dharug. But Kurikuta was wise and would know that there might have been those among the Dharug who had eaten emu in their hunger. But when she saw him clearly she was glad. It was the Strange One who made painted marks and who had eyes as blue as the sky. Lamar felt the Virgin in her hands. It was as it should be. Had not this Strange One given her the Kurikuta tjurunga? Something surged inside her and she rose to meet him.

Martin saw the girl get to her feet just as he approached her. My God, she was smiling. She looked happy to see him. He tried to make himself look as friendly as possible.

"I am glad to see you. I thought you might have gone away. I see you still have my present." The girl seemed terribly excited. She pointed to the water and spoke the same word over and over again, the same word she had said when he had given her the Virgin.

"Kurikuta, Kurikuta."

She continued to point at the water and then to the statue.

"Kurikuta, Kurikuta." Over and over again.

He finally understood. That was her name for the Virgin. Martin pointed to the icon. "Kurikuta?" he questioned.

She nodded fiercely, then after making a motion with her two arms to embrace an invisible figure, she pointed again to the water. "Kurikuta, Kurikuta."

Martin smiled, not knowing what else to do.

The Strange One was smiling at her. Lamar's face and body flushed hot. For an instant she swayed and then reached forwards. She felt his arm. Then her own arms were on his shoulders and she could smell his odour as she rubbed against him.

Martin was stupefied, then panic-stricken. What was wrong with her? What did she want? They said she was mad. Was this proof positive? As gently as possible he disengaged her arms. He had to do, say something. "Mary, Mary. What's wrong. Are you ill?"

The name they all called her. She hated it because it was not of the Dreamtime. Then she under-stood. Why should the Strange One know of the quickening if he did not know by what name she was called? That must have been why he had taken her arms away. She pointed to herself.

"Lamar, Lamar, Lamar." Then shaking her head vigorously, "Mary, Mary. No."

It was the first English word Martin had ever heard her speak. She was telling him that her name was not Mary. It was Lamar. At least, that is what he thought. Well, he'd soon know. He pointed to her. "Lamar, Lamar. Your name is Lamar."

Martin saw her smile and nod approvingly. Both hands circled her face. "Lamar, Lamar."

It was time. She was tingling and she could feel the spirit child wanting to enter her. She lay down in the grass and hitched her dress up about her waist. Her legs parted and she held out her arms to him.

Oh my God, this was not happening to him. Fascinated, then suddenly embarrassed Martin turned his head away from her exposed crotch. He had to get away. He began walking, then running up the track towards the orphanage.

Where was he? Was Kurikuta displeased? Lamar looked at the rainbow above her and at Atha still circling in the sky, staying away like he should. Then she felt the anger burning inside her. Long had she waited to do the bidding of Kurikuta so she could save the Dharug. How the special quickening would do this she did not know. Only that she trusted Kurikuta and the Ganabudu. The tears came suddenly to her eyes. She had been so happy to see the Strange One, and warm about the quickening he would give her. And now he was going away. She would catch him and they would fall down together. She stood up and ran, conscious only of his retreating back and the sudden kaarks of Atha above her.

Martin heard her running feet behind him and then feeling the clasp of her hands at his waist. As he turned, her arms moved up his body to encircle him tightly. Her head buried into his neck and he could smell the scent of wild honey. She was saying something about Kurikuta and another word, "Ganabuda." Then she lifted her head to look at him and he caught the full intensity of her eyes. They were wild and hot like Madeleine's. Light brown with strange yellow flecks, their meaning unmistakable.

He should have calmed the girl down; sat and talked with her; drawn pictures in the damp earth. Anything but what he did.

"No! Stop it!"

He grabbed her arms firmly and pulled them away. She fought hard against him and Martin was aware of her strength. She was hanging on and crying, a muffled sound like a distressed animal. Panic-stricken now, he pushed at her chest. Once, twice. She lurched backwards and fell to the ground. She got to her feet slowly and faced him, her eyes filled with bewilderment and pain. She was saying something. Unintelligible save for a pleading desperation that froze him to the spot. He was thinking of what to say when she turned and ran. Unable to move he watched as she ran to the water's edge and splashed in. She was waist-deep when the crow lighted on her shoulders. Then they turned to look at him. Both of them. Martin ran.

~ ~ ~

Hidden from view behind the yellow curtains, Matron Nance Edwards watched incredulously. She had gone to the window for a breath of air to see the young man who had just left the orphanage push poor Mary to the ground. She watched them both run away. Mary towards the water; the young man to his horse. Puzzled, she had stood there uncertain of what to do until a knock at the door distracted her. When she returned they were both gone.

~ ~ ~

The water lay still about Lamar's waist, tepid and brown in the gathering dusk. She waded downstream to her totem tree and all the time her body heaved with sounds that came from deep within her belly. The tears just wouldn't stop but she knew why. The Strange One promised to her by Kurikuta herself had gone away. He did not want her as Kurikuta and the Ganabuda said he would. There had been no quickening; no spirit child had entered her body. She had returned to her totem and then to the tree for protection against Kurikuta's anger. She was surprised when Atha had come. She thought that Kurikuta might have called him back. Was this a sign that she might have been wrong about the Strange One being the one spoken about? She did not think so; did not wish for anyone else, so she would wait until another rainbow, and hope that he would come back.

The Bath Arms Hotel, January 11, 1841

Martin tightened the cinches on the two horses, checked once more that everything was loaded and went to get Father Blake. He had been relieved this morning when Mr. Neitch told him that Father was much better, and over-joyed when he saw his friend after breakfast. Father looked thin and pale but his eyes were startlingly bright. He had greeted Martin in a friendly manner and had suggested that they take an overnight sketching trip west and north of Liverpool to find the red plants that were shaped like cleaning brushes. Martin was glad of the opportunity to be with Father Blake again. He had to talk to someone about yesterday. He couldn't get it out of his mind. If anyone could ease his burden of guilt it was Father Blake.

~ ~ ~

He had ridden hard and had gotten back to the Bath Arms Hotel around ten in time to meet Colleen before she went home. He had poured out the whole story to her. She had listened quietly as she always did but when he was fin-ished she seemed upset. She said that he'd be wise to stay away from native girls. They were loose with their bodies. And when he had tried to tell her that Mary was not like that, that what happened yesterday was something strange-ly frightening and that he felt sorry for the poor girl, Colleen had become agi-tated. No, angry was more like it. She had tossed her hair back and said that she had things to do at home and that she'd better be leaving. He had tried to stop her; had pleaded with her to stay but she had been adamant. She closed the door firmly behind her but not before Martin heard her mutter, loud enough for him to hear, "Slut."

~ ~ ~

They left the Bath Arms Hotel around nine and travelled along the Liverpool Road, passing Irishtown and veering west a mile or so north of Liverpool. Around three they found what they were looking for. As usual Martin sketched and Father took notes. Then Martin built a fire and heated water for tea and for cooking potatoes. As he peeled the potatoes Martin was thinking when he would talk to Father Blake about the aboriginal girl. Father Blake had been unusually quiet all day. Martin assumed it was because he was still not feeling well, but even so he was determined to bring up the matter of the girl after they had eaten.

Their meal was silent, not awkward but somehow different. The silence itself did not concern Martin; Father Blake would often stay quiet for long periods. However, it was a different kind of silence tonight. Father Blake seemed agitated, like there was something bothering him terribly. For a moment Martin considered keeping the matter of Mary to himself. But he couldn't. He was too upset. He got up to stoke the fire. Father Blake was lying down with his head on his coat. Martin could just make out the outline of his face in the firelight. His eyes were closed as though he were dozing. Then they snapped open and Martin felt them looking at him. Nervously he swallowed.

"Father I have something I wish to speak to you about. I cannot get it out of my mind. I have to talk to someone."

Father Blake did not reply but Martin knew he was hearing him.

"There's a native girl in Parramatta. When I travelled there with Superintendent Baddely I used to see her by the river. She used to watch me when I painted. I spoke to her but she never answered me. People in Parramatta said she was demented, but I did not think so. Her eyes, Father. They were strange and flecked with yellow. But I saw no madness."

Martin saw Father Blake shudder. "Did she ever speak?"

"Only once when I gave her the Virgin."

"Oh."

"It was my mother's. A pewter statue of the Virgin. Very old. I didn't value it except as a gift from my mother. I even used it to open the oysters at Longbottom. Still, I don't know why I gave it to the native girl. I didn't think I would see her again and I wanted to give her a present. You know how I feel about the church," he ended lamely.

"And?"

Father sounded like he was interested. Martin pressed on.

"When I gave it to her she seemed very happy and said 'Kurikuta'. Nothing more. Just that word. Just yesterday I found out that this was her name for the Virgin."

"How would she know . . . ?"

"Exactly Father. How would she know? As I understand it, Father, they found her in the bush almost a year ago. She speaks no English. She could not know of the Virgin, unless."

"Unless what?"

"That's one of the things that I want to talk to you about. I think this girl might have seen a vision of the Virgin."

"Like the other girl you told me about?"

"No. Madeleine was different. She was a Catholic. This girl knows nothing of the Virgin. Yet when I saw her yesterday she kept saying the word, 'Kurikuta' and pointing to the water and making a human shape with her hands."

Bernard could feel his quickening pulse. *Careful*, he told himself, remembering the foul madwoman at the jail.

"Are you sure you're not allowing your imagination to take its own flights of fancy? She could have meant anything by the word she used."

Martin pondered the priest's words before replying. He remained unconvinced that the vision thing could be dismissed so easily but the last thing he wanted to do was to argue with Father Blake and after all it was not that which had really upset him. "Yes, you're probably right, but it was something else which really bothered me." He paused before continuing. "I don't know how to say this to you, Father."

Bernard Blake said nothing.

"She proffered herself to me Father. She lay down on the grass and offered me her body. I was . . ."

Bernard tried to keep calm, though every nerve in his body was alive. He kept his voice calm, solicitous. "You're sure, Martin. This native girl indicated to you that she had seen the Virgin and then proffered you her body."

"Yes, I'm sorry to have upset you with such a terrible account but it happened as I said. In my shock I behaved badly. I pushed her away, Father. She fell to the ground. I cannot banish it from my mind. Her shock! A look that told me I had done something terrible. Did I do something terrible, Father? Afterwards I told my own love, Colleen Somerville, about my disquiet. You know her Father, the beautiful girl with the red hair that works at the Bath Arms, the one I took to the races when I saw that bully from the *Buffalo* I told you about. Anyway, she will be my wife one day, I hope. But I think Colleen might have been jealous, though she had no cause. I have no one to talk to but you. Was I right, Father? I am not an animal. I abhor violence, and towards a woman! Should I go back and see her? Should I inform the Matron? I don't think she is mad and such behaviour can only end in . . ."

"But I heard that her name was Mary," Father Blake said in strangled tones. Martin, wrapped in confusion, didn't notice the oddity of the question.

"That's another strange thing, Father. If I am right, she has another name she prefers to be called by. She seemed very upset when I called her Mary."

"And that name?"

"Lamar, Father. She calls herself Lamar."

~ ~ ~

The world fell away from Bernard in that instant. The canopy of stars vanished and there was just himself there in the dark, filling all space. This was the penultimate instant of his own becoming. There was only one more thing to do now and it was inevitable, pre-ordained. He had become suddenly calm.

The noises had gone away, replaced by the serenity of certainty. He waved farewell to the demons, contempt guiding the movement of his fingers. His soul formed the words he could never utter. *Thank you maligned Mother. Thank you.*

And to the world that was soon to be his. "What an incredible story, Martin! Quite incredible."

Martin wanted to talk more. What should he do about the native girl? Talking to Father had made it better but he had given neither priestly advice nor friendly solace.

"Father, what should I do?"

Silence. Father had gone to sleep, but Martin resigned himself to it. After all, he was not well.

In the Hills northwest of Liverpool, January 12, 1841

When Martin awoke around seven, he was surprised to see Father Blake up and dressed. His horse was saddled.

"Are we leaving so soon, Father? I thought we were staying here another day. Let's at least have breakfast."

Though he was disappointed at the thought of leaving a day early, Martin was pleased at Father Blake's answering laugh. It seemed such a long time since he had last heard him laugh. It must mean that he was feeling better.

"Martin, you won't believe what I have done. In my illness I had forgotten a settler who lies near death ten miles from here along the Dog Trap Road. I must go and administer Extreme Unction. Today. Now. Before he dies." He smiled conspiratorially. "After all, he believes in its efficacy even if you and I are less than certain. I'll be back by dark and should perchance prohibit such, then by the forenoon tomorrow. I would like for us to ride back together. You have sufficient sketch work."

Martin nodded, hiding his unhappiness. With Father in such a good mood it had promised to be a most enjoyable day. "Yes, Father I understand. I have much to do. The yellow flowers as well as the red ones."

"You mean the bottle brush and the wattle. When will you learn to name them properly?"

Martin smiled ruefully and for a long time watched the priest as he disappeared along the rough bush track. He hadn't seen his friend in such a fine mood. No, not for a long time.

~ ~ ~

Bernard pushed his mount hard through the heat, only stopping to avoid the possibility of recognition. Remembering the scum who had trailed him through Europe, he was determined that any actions he might perform today would go unobserved. Now he was closer to Parramatta he rested and waited for traffic to abate on the Dog Trap Road. Sitting there in the shade of a big gum, he was able to be with his thoughts. He was going to Lamar. She would not be beautiful like Signy but she had been chosen for him and would bear the one who would change the world under his direction. He had not made up his mind what he would do with her after the child's birth. The maligned Mother would guide him there. He would have to acquire more apostles. He would begin cultivating those immediately. He would need Thomas, of course. He'd also steal Neitch's money (drunk one night, the idiot had told him where he kept it), and the Church's as well (a contrived burglary). Then he'd leave the priesthood, and when the time was right they would lay the foundations of the new order. Here!

It would begin with a revolt against the British and Polding, if the misguided idiot lived that long. Then they would purge mightily. He'd execute the sluts first. All of them. And the birds. He would have strangling contests. The thought made him warm inside and he smiled. Oh yes it would spread and all of them who had dared question his abilities would perish. Tettrini, Battiste, Lambruschini, Gregory. All of them. He was angry now. He stood up and grasping a heavy stone threw it at a black crow picking at something on the ground. He missed and the bird flew *kaarking* into the air. For some reason the sound infuriated him further. Then he heard them. The demons inside his head. By the time he reached the outskirts of Parramatta a half hour later they were back. He was sweating when the orphanage swam into his blurred vision.

He tethered his horse among some trees and made his way towards the barn near the river. If he recalled correctly the girl had been there the day the orphanage woman had asked him to meet her. He had been thwarted then. Just like they had killed his Signy, they had also sent the lunatic slime that day to keep him from his destiny. Not today. No, not today. It was time. He wiped the perspiration from his forehead and cursing the demons within, moved as quietly as he could through the trees.

He did not find her in the barn. Yet Bernard Blake was not worried. She would be there somewhere, waiting. He stepped outside and walked to the water's edge. And, as he knew she would, she entered his vision. Suddenly, like a surprise gift. Only this was no surprise. It was his encounter with destiny. She was on the opposite riverbank. For a long moment he stood looking at her before moving towards the small boat tied to a makeshift dock below the barn.

Lamar was washing the berries she had collected when she saw him standing on the other side watching her. A Strange One. A ripple ran through her body and she glanced up at the sky. It was already darkening with the fading light but it was clear like an undisturbed crayfish pool. Behind her on a branch Atha gave a soft startled squark. She watched him get into the boat and row towards her.

He could see her more clearly now standing straight and slim in the gathering dusk, silhouetted against the mottled green of the trees.

The boat grounded itself in the mud and he stepped ashore. She didn't move and then he was with her facing her across a metre of space. His destiny. His becoming. Here in this strange place. He closed his eyes savouring the moment, and for an instant he was back in the meadow near the big rock with Signy. He moved closer until her face was inches from his own, and he caught the scent of honey. Her eyes were wide and the most amazing colour he had ever seen. Honey-brown with flecks of yellow, they drew him towards her. He kissed her lips, feeling the hot urgency of his own arousal. Her body was firm beneath the faded torn blue dress, and pliant as he put both hands on her hips. He rubbed hard against her before taking her hand and leading her into the trees.

This was not the one Kurikuta had spoken about. There was no rainbow and she could sense Atha's displeasure. But it was like she was a tree. Her feet wouldn't move. The Strange One had eyes that burned like a dying fire. He had a strange scent. Not of the morning like the other Strange One but more like the heat of a distressed animal. He was touching her, rubbing against her. She wanted to run away but she couldn't. His hands were soft like a baby, but cold and wet with sweat.

Bernard tore the dress down over her shoulders until it lay in a blue heap at her feet. He bent her backwards to the ground and fumbled at his belt, leaving his trousers about his knees as he pushed her legs apart. Now, he thought as he loomed over her, not seeing her face, his hands on the bare earth as he forced his mastery. He probed hard with his penis but found resistance. His hand was moving down to guide it when he heard the flapping of wings and then felt the infernal hell of the beast at his back. He turned his head to fight it.

It was Atha that moved her body. He flew onto the back of the Strange One and suddenly she had the power to fight against him. She lashed out at him, scratching and clawing with all her might. He was shielding his head against Atha and she raked her nails across his face. The Strange One was screaming his anger. He grabbed Atha by one leg and flung him into the bushes. She picked up the heavy rock and lunged at him.

It was a rage he had never imagined. He loathed and feared the black devil screaming its anger at him. He flailed at it, wanting to destroy it. Then he felt the raking sensation across his cheeks. But he had the bird now. He flung it away, and turned to face the girl. She had a stone in her hands and as her arm drew back to throw it, he lunged forward. He wrenched it from her hand and smashed it against the side of her head. Then his hands were about her throat pressing tighter, tighter.

Oh, God. The bird was back. Snarling, he drew back from the crumpled limp form at his feet to face it. It flapped away and he chased it heedlessly until he could run no more. It was almost dark before he found his way back to the girl.

She lay where he had left her. The right side of her face was a mass of blood and her head was twisted awkwardly to one side. Bernard sat down beside her body and tried to collect his thoughts. The sobs came gradually and when they did they had the controlled quietness of finality. The Evil Ones had won. It was all over. Finished.

He sat there until he could control the dizziness buzzing in his head, and, leaving the girl where she lay, climbed into the boat and took himself across the river to the barn where she lived. He found some rope in the stables but the rafters were too high, so he went the place where she slept. A pewter statue of the Virgin was on her cot. He picked it up and turned it over in his hands. The maligned Mother, fashioned, misunderstood, and now broken by fools. She had tried to bring him his destiny but the Evil Ones had thwarted them both. He would die with her. That much was right.

When the noose was secure around his neck he climbed onto the stool, holding the Madonna in his hands. Standing there in the dark he could see the rising moon through the window. One step, one launch and it would be all over.

His feet would not move. They stayed still while his brain raced. The soft one was there and the demons quieted. He listened until the urge to die was left behind, replaced by a new rage that urged him forward, down from this pedestal of destruction. It had not been his fault. The offal he had befriended, trusted, on whom he bestowed an apostle's honour had betrayed him; had tried to steal his destiny; all the time conniving while averring friendship. Martin Goyette, the spawn of Satan, would have justice meted out to him. Dreadful justice. Furious now, he tore the rope from his neck, and after placing the Maligned Mother carefully back on the cot, he lay the rope in coils about his neck, returned outside to the boat, and rowed back to the girl.

~ ~ ~

As he tied the blue dress with the big rock inside it to the girl's body, Bernard Blake hummed, then chanted his thoughts.

"Though all is lost, all will die,
Tettrini, Polding and Lambruschini.
The sluts, the whores and best yet,
The vile scum that is Martin Goyette."

The body was light and still warm. He lifted it easily even with the big rock tied to it. He rowed downstream to where steep banks indicated the deepening of the river channel. Then he pushed it over the side, hearing the soft splash but not seeing the ripples breaking towards the shore. He rowed away. He had much to do.

~ ~ ~

The water was dark and free-moving. The stone and the dress came away from the body, leaving the rope trailing like a giant tail to rest at the muddy bottom. Deep in her consciousness Lamar saw her spirit going to the Dreamtime. She saw Kurikuta and she swam to meet her.

January 13, 1841

Martin was appalled at Father's appearance when he rode up around eleven. He looked grey and haggard and his face was scratched from where he had ridden into a branch. One wound was red and angry and might be infected. He said he had been too late; the man was already dead. His poor widow was in an abject state however, and he had to spend a great deal of time with her. He was up most of the night with her.

They had tea and Father listened understandingly as Martin told him about his wasted day yesterday. He had done very little work on the flowers but had spent most of the day doing a portrait of Colleen to surprise her. He had thrown it away because he hadn't liked it. Father Blake said that was wise. It wasn't sensible holding onto something when it was not good enough for you. About the flowers. It didn't matter. One should take a day to oneself whenever need demanded it.

~ ~ ~

Father Blake brought the matter of the native girl after the teacups were washed and placed into the saddlebags.

"Martin, I have been thinking about what you told me about the native girl. I can understand your disquiet. I didn't realize. About your violence, I mean."

"But I'm not violent." Martin felt frustrated.

"No, I'm sure you aren't. But considering what happened between you both, it is probably best that you go and see her. Apologize. Explain to her that you didn't mean to do what you did. She will understand, I'm sure. We all do things for which we are ashamed afterwards. Only the most hard-hearted of men would say that it is all in the nature of the beast. For myself I think that remedy is contained in trial by error. You erred; you are sorry. That's all that matters." He smiled and Martin felt better. He knew Father Blake would understand.

The General Bourke Hotel, Parramatta, January 15, 1841

The well-dressed middle aged man left the hotel bar and disappeared into the sunshine of Church Street leaving only one man at the corner table in front of the two empty plates and unfinished wine bottle. Alexander Black's eyes never left the leather bag lying on the table in front of him. It was the most money he had ever seen in his life. Enough to get him out of this hellhole and back to Canada. Enough to buy a new business when he got there, with some left over. He sipped his glass of expensive cabernet appreciatively, and although still somewhat unnerved by his former companion's parting remarks, could not believe his good fortune. He glanced at the wall clock. Damn it. He was late for work. Then he grinned as the realization struck him. He didn't need the bloody job any more. He re-filled his glass and fell to reading the instructions he had just been left. When he had finished he nodded and placed the paper in his pocket. Then he called for more wine and settled in for an afternoon of steady drinking.

It had been a most interesting day. He had been cleaning the windows in the store he worked at when this well-dressed gentleman came in. He looked about forty-five, had the stomach of a man who lived too well and unblinking eyes that peered through blue-tinted spectacles. He only spoke French and was having trouble with his English so the store owner had asked for Black's help. They fell to talking afterwards and the stranger asked him to lunch. It was over the excellent roast beef and dumplings that the stranger had delivered the shock that Alexander Black was still recovering from. Their meeting was not by chance. The stranger knew a great deal about him. His experiences in Canada, the *Buffalo*, and his present wretched situation. He had a proposition, one he had added that would be difficult to reject both morally and monetarily.

Though they might be strangers, they were nonetheless united by a common bond. They had both been wronged by the same man. Him through heinous deeds done to his family in Montreal, and Black by public humiliation at the Homebush Races. Martin Goyette, the idiot with the lip, had cursed them both and now he was here partly on business but also to seek his atonement. Would Black like to help him?

He was wondering whether the man was serious when he had produced the money. A lot of money for a simple enough task. There was little risk involved. The stranger had heard that Black was a courageous man with, how had he put it, "nerves as steady as a Queen's Hussar." If he hated Goyette as much as he did, the stranger had said, and had the nerve then he could do two things: Settle the score with Goyette and make himself a rich man at the same time.

With the money, the stranger had also produced a set of what he called instructions, which he read to Black in hushed guarded tones. Though surprised at the scope of what the stranger had in mind, Black had nodded in hearty agreement. It was no more than the bastard deserved in the first place. It didn't take him long to make up his mind, not with all that money sitting there a foot away from his nose. He would do it.

As the stranger was getting up to leave, he had called Black's honesty into question. At first he had been annoyed but that had quickly changed. His companion's friendly eyes suddenly became cold and though his voice remained pleasant, the stranger merely said, "You try to trick me over this and I'll gut you like a fish."

Then he was gone. Alexander Black had never felt so frightened in all his life.

By the time Black was drunk enough to buy drinks for the Friday afternoon crowd, Bernard Blake was back in Sydney and a priest again.

The Bath Arms Hotel, January 18, 1841

Martin had never seen Mr. Neitch in such a sorry state. First, someone stole his last fortnight's takings last Thursday, and if that was not bad enough he had just discovered that his secret hoard was gone as well. Well over a thousand crowns. There had to be spies in his hotel. He should fire all of them. If he ever caught the bastards he'd wring their necks. Hanging was too good for scum like that. These were difficult times and if he couldn't get co-operation from the banks he could be ruined. It was a blow to Martin. It could mean revocation of his special ticket-of-leave status. He would have to see Father Blake. To make things doubly worse, Colleen had avoided Martin completely since the night he told her about the native girl. He was so heartsick he could die. He had to see her; explain that he loved her more than anything in life. He'd go to her house after dinner, if Mr. Neitch would give him permission. He decided to wait until later in the day to ask him.

Martin was mixing paint in the hotel storage room when he heard the familiar hated sound of marching feet. He put the stirring stick down and went out into the hallway. Four soldiers carrying rifles snapped to a halt and Martin could see an anguished-looking Mr. Neitch behind them.

"You're Martin Goyette?"

The same imperious tone. Officious and threatening.

"Yes,"

"You're under arrest."

"Arrest? Why?" Martin looked disbelievingly at Neitch, who appeared stricken.

"You'll know soon enough," replied the captain who had already moved to the front of the soldiers. The order was barked. "Prisoner to escort position. Forward march."

Emmanuel Neitch stepped aside to allow them to pass.

"I'm so sorry, Martin. So sorry.

They didn't stop until they reached Parramatta and the barracks, where in a large white room, cool even in the afternoon heat Martin Goyette was charged with the murder of the aboriginal girl known only as Mary.

CHAPTER V

Government House in Parramatta was an elegant two-storeyed white stone building with long vertically rectangular latticed windows, and an impressive portico supported by four square columns. Built in 1816 by Lachlan Macquarie as a second governor's residence, it sat surrounded by native trees a few rods from the river. Yet designed as it was as a reminder of genteel respectability, the house resembled more a speck of colonial refinement, and, with its low two railed fence guarding a strip of ragged lawn from the browsing sheep beyond, scarcely British. But it was private and for that alone Governor George Gipps especially liked it. Though hotter than in Sydney, here he could walk his dogs undisturbed by the vagrants that seemed to be everywhere in Sydney. And the river! He loved it. So much like an English stream. Still and serene with that kind of green that seemed so deep you were almost afraid to swim there. But now as he watched the two men dash from the carriage drawn up at the entrance he felt very much the harassed governor. This had not been a good week and it only promised to get worse.

First he had arrived on Monday with the rain and it was still pouring. The river was angry and flooded and he hadn't been able to do anything except business. And it had been business with a vengeance. Problems! Horrendous problems. "An extremely delicate situation," as his secretary had put it. But for all Gipps' concern over the rain and the interruption of what was to have been a leisure week in Parramatta, no one would have known had they seen him greet his two visitors and entertain them with tea and light conversation. Only afterwards in the closed privacy of his study with the sound of the rain drumming on the roof was he ready to receive the matter that had brought the Chief Justice and the Chief Protector of Aborigines through the rain.

~ ~ ~

Gipps addressed his Chief Justice first, aware of the man's discomfort as much as he was of his loquaciousness. "Well, Sir James. It appears we have a real problem here. The details, please, and keep them brief."

James Dowling cleared his voice and straightened an imaginary crease in his judicial robes. Gipps could never understand why but the man liked to wear the trappings of his office out of doors. Still, with it on, Dowling looked every bit the fine jurist that he was. He might be long-winded but he was also very astute.

"I'll start at the beginning, Excellency. Last week, a free man reported to the chief magistrate in Parramatta that he had witnessed a murder. A young aboriginal woman apparently was bludgeoned to death and her body thrown into in the river just downstream from the girls' orphanage. The witness also identified the murderer as a dangerous man whom he had helped to escort here from Canada on the ship *Buffalo* in 1838. He thought he was interned at Longbottom Stockade, and had no idea that he had been released. The chief magistrate received the information but took no action until he had made further enquiries on the activities of a young simpleton native woman known to reside at the orphanage. He was informed by the matron that the girl had indeed disappeared, and though she was prone to doing so, the matron expressed her surprise at its duration since the girl had been very attentive to her assigned task of feeding the orphanage animals."

The man beside him muttered something under his breath but Dowling ignored him. "What was also learned from the matron was that the identified murderer was indeed known to the girl."

"Tell him the rest." It was the other man who spoke. His face was set in anger.

Dowling paused in annoyance before continuing. "As I was about to add, Excellency, we were informed by the matron that she had witnessed a scene in which she saw the girl violently attacked by this same man."

"Have we a name for this person?"

"His name is Martin Goyette, one of the French political malcontents languishing in Longbottom Stockade, and who was only recently and surprisingly granted ticket of leave status." Dowling raised his eyebrows towards Gipps who stared back impassively.

"Go on Sir James."

"The man is a political prisoner, a revolutionary. He was assigned to the innkeeper, Emmanuel Neitch. Apparently, and I have learned this afterwards, Excellency, he has a history of violence. In his own land; on the ship that brought him here. Indeed, one of the recommendations that secured his ticket of leave involved a violent altercation in which some drunken policemen attempted bodily harm against Superintendent Baddely at Longbottom. This Goyette was prominent in the resistance which assured Baddely's safety."

"Hardly lamentable behaviour, Sir James. But please get to the point."

It was the other man who replied. Arthur Cripps, Chief Protector of Aborigines, a man not known for his meekness, was clearly not impressed with his companion. "The point is, Excellency is that this man has a penchant for violence. He's a murderer who thinks he can carry his dastardly ways from Canada to this place."

Gipps' expression did not change. Only those who knew him might have sensed just a slight annoyance. "You'll get your chance Mr. Cripps. Please go on, Sir James."

"After we had ascertained that a native girl might be missing and that there was some credence for the witness's story, we began searching for the body. Then the rains came. Now we'll probably never find it. Still, even without the body we felt we had no choice in our subsequent actions. The aboriginal girl is known to the Parramatta constabulary. She was brought in from the bush some time ago and lives at the girls' orphanage. She is young and quite savage. Some of the ladies have seen her naked. One needed smelling salts afterwards. Suffice it to say that the church elders as well as the chief magistrate have not been happy about her presence among us. With savage dim-witted heathen like that and with the type of scum that live among us in this place it was just a matter of time before the lusts of the flesh led to more evil."

"It was that reasoning which led you to the arrest?"

It was Cripps who again interjected. "The girl is a halfwit. He's said that already. She couldn't go back to the bush so Matron Edwards allowed her to stay. She was not much more than an animal when it came to thinking. Harmless, trusting. Easy prey for a bastard like Goyette."

Again Dowling went on, ignoring the other man. "We made the arrest a week ago today at the Bath Arms Hotel where Goyette is employed." Dowling stopped to consider his next words before continuing. "If I might add, Excellency, I might not have charged the man with murder. Not at the time. Not until I was more certain. But what's done's done."

"Not if it was a white girl," Cripps growled. "The Matron saw him strike the girl, and a day later she disappears. Then someone comes forwards and tells you he saw her done in. What sort of case do you need, man?"

Dowling glared at Cripps who stared back defiantly. When he couldn't break the other man's gaze, Dowling turned again to Gipps. "So the chief magistrate has Goyette interned here at Parramatta. No visitors, no lawyer. Nothing. We can't hold him indefinitely. We have to try him."

Gipps sounded resigned. "And your problem is, Sir James you are loath to try him. Why?"

The Chief Justice spread his hands. His thin lips quivered slightly. "This is not a simple case. An eyewitness and no body. A halfwit woman. And an educated political prisoner, not some worthless Irish dreg. Justice may not be as forthcoming as one might think."

"Cock and Bull, Sir," snarled Cripps. "We have two bloody witnesses. One an eyewitness. The girl's dead. Murdered. If it had have been some white girl, the trial would be over by now and the hangman ready. No, Excellency. Our Chief Justice is reluctant to pursue this matter for other reasons."

For the first time Gipps accorded Cripps his full attention. "Go on, Mr. Cripps. Say your piece."

Arthur Cripps was a big man and he looked even bigger as he shifted his bulk in the chair. The anger fairly oozed out of him. He had a Londoner's accent. "Five hundred pound a year they pay me, Excellency to see that these people are treated fairly. Treated fairly. What a joke! They're hard to find; they understand nothing and trust nobody. And if that's not enough, most people around here think they're no more than animals." Cripps was excited, his already florid face reddening further "I got this job less than two years ago Excellency. Forty years. Over forty years we've been killing these people. Treeing them like animals and then shooting them; poisoning their flour. I've seen their bodies fallen down from trees where they had been shot; I've seen children with burns on their backs. Ever seen the face of someone who's eaten poison, Sir James? No, I bet you haven't. Even the bloody church stood by. Some churchmen even approved." He waved his arms around. "A lot of them around here think I'm a joke. I'm only in it for the bloody money, they say."

Gipps' eyebrows raised but he said nothing.

"Oh, to be sure we did something after Myall Creek. Twenty eight of them butchered by a bunch of bloodthirsty idiots. You yourself stuck your neck out to go after the bastards that did it. But its just a start. We have to make some examples. My God, Excellency. The convict system is over. It'll be free people who'll be coming to this country now. Do you think they'll come if it's to a place where murder is allowed to go unpunished? They think we're a hell hole already. Letting murderous scum roam the streets as free men is no way to entice decent people. All we'll get is more scum."

Cripps leaned forward, carried away by the excitement of his own words. "Sir James Dowling here doesn't want to try Goyette, and personally I don't want him to either. He's scared. For his own popularity which has been suffering a little. If he hangs the Frenchman without a body, he's a hanging judge with no concern over rights. The liberals and the reformers, and there are more of all the time now, will howl for his head; if he acquits him he's an abo hater and more importantly a French lover and not the sort of man we want to look after the legal rights of free English settlers. I mean, releasing political revolutionaries into streets that will soon be as free as those in the Mother Country. Come on now, Excellency. The conservatives in this place will eat our Sir James without salt. Ah yes, our good Chief Justice is afraid of the papers and the talk that will follow in the toffy places where it will do him harm. Go to a trial and Sir James here's as shorn as one of Sam Marsden's sheep."

Gipps got up and went to the window. For a long minute he pondered the driving rain outside. When he spoke his voice lacked certainty. "I still don't see an insurmountable problem. His status means that he has no right to trial by jury. We try him with a civil bench and abide by its verdict. There need be no death penalty. He serves ten years. That's enough. Is it not, Mr. Cripps?

Arthur Cripps leapt to his feet. "No, Governor. It's not. Not this time. A civil bench'll send him laughing out of the courtroom in two days. The Frenchman is as guilty as hell and hanging is too good for him. I'm going to go to every liberal paper in this colony. I'll take it to back to London and Whitehall if I have to. And I'll talk to people in this colony. As I've heard it I can name two Legislative Councillors who think what we've done to these people is nothing short of barbarism. I'll stir up so much shit in this place you'll both wonder if you've ever smelled anything else."

Cripps stopped in mid sentence as if suddenly conscious that he had overreached himself. "I'm sorry, Excellency. I take back that last remark. It's just that I care for these people. It's gone on too long. It has to stop. We cannot let Goyette escape the consequences of his foul deed. They'll let him go. I know they will. I won't do it; I won't do it." He fell back mumbling to himself obviously drained by his outburst.

Gipps' reply was quick and even. He looked at Cripps all the time. "What you're saying, Mr. Cripps is that civilians would never convict Goyette. You're requesting . . ."

"The military," Cripps interrupted. "Yes, Excellency, a tribunal. A small one. I'd suggest three good officers. No more. Private, without the interference and comments of the press. I know it's not done much any more, but you have the right, and the extraordinary nature of this prisoner's status seems to warrant special measures. I mean a revolutionary. A traitor. A man who has taken up arms against the realm."

Gipps was aware of Dowling nodding affirmatively.

"And what if the tribunal's verdict is favourable towards the prisoner, Mr. Cripps? What then? Will you still be assured that justice has been done?"

A hint of a smile crossed Cripps' face. "But of course, Excellency. Won't you?"

~ ~ ~

Afterwards Dowling and Gipps sat alone. Cripps had left with an umbrella for an appointment with one of his Assistants in Parramatta. This time they drank rum. Gipps swilled the dark liquid about in his glass studying it morosely.

"I don't like it, Sir James. This should be dealt with through the courts. I could be hung up myself over this."

"True," replied Dowling. "But you could be anyway if Cripps goes to the press."

Gipps said nothing. Dowling continued. "You gave this man a ticket-of-leave even though it violated your own regulations. My God, Excellency. He hadn't served his time and is a political prisoner. You should have known better."

"Damn Polding and his favours, Gipps thought. Aloud he said lamely. "I was told he was gentle, harmless. An artist. One of those ignorant souls easily swayed into an insurrection they didn't want."

Dowling was speaking again. "You obviously didn't know about his record of violence. You can be sure the papers will. Look, Excellency. Cripps is squeezing you, us. I know him. He believes a military tribunal will have more chance of convicting Goyette than a civil bench. He thinks that because the man is a revolutionary, the aboriginal girl doesn't matter. To Cripps, the tribunal'll be after a foreigner who shed the blood of the empire. He'll get his verdict. He won't care how. Just as long as he gets it."

"But what do you think, Sir James? Would you try Goyette by tribunal even though our present court system dictates otherwise? Is Cripps right?"

"Yes, Excellency, I believe he is. I honestly believe that in this instance justice has a better chance of being served with a tribunal."

"They could acquit could they not?"

"Most definitely. But there are other things involved here too, Excellency. You know the problems we've been having over the wanton killing of natives. It can't go on. You know that. You've already placed yourself in an unpopular position because of your support of the aboriginals. And while I might dislike Cripps' overbearing demeanour, I also believe he is right. A civil bench probably would throw this case out, and, given the evidence, be right in doing so.

But what wider damage might we be doing? Particularly if the girl is later found dead. We have to be seen to be willing to redress former wrongs. Yes, Excellency. For yours, mine, expediency's, and, in all honesty, for the good of the colony's sake, I would authorize the tribunal and then let it run its course however unpalatable. We can no longer be perceived by the world as a lawless place. We have a reputation to undo. In this instance British justice will be better served in the hands of a British tribunal rather than in those of more capricious civilians. The latter could be ruinous, a circus, with no guarantee of justice being served."

George Gipps found himself thinking of his hunting dogs. No, more like the quarry they ran down. "I see what you mean. If we're right we don't have much choice. I just wished I liked it more. Any names you'd like to recommend?"

Dowling's brow puckered. "I can think of two who have had experience in matters of this seriousness and sensitivity. Both in the twenty-eighth here in Parramatta. Major James Cowling and Captain Archibald Weir would be my choice. I don't know about the third if you only go with three, nor the prosecutor for that matter. It's all up to Sir Edward Pagett. He's the Colonel of the regiment. But then again you might want to call on the 50th, The Queen's Own. They've got some excellent officers."

"The defence?" Gipps was scribbling.

"Greg Mahony," said Lowe without hesitation.

"I don't know the man."

"Former convict. Irishman. Drinks too much and ekes out a living defending petty thieves. Good astute mind though. He'd do his best." Lowe chuckled. "An Irishman defending a Frenchman. If they win who can ever doubt the impartiality of British justice?"

"And what if they lose?"

"Then British justice will still have been served."

For some reason Gipps did not want to finish his rum. Instead he wanted to wash himself in the rain.

Parramatta, January 25, 1841

Greg Mahony had a hangover. His head ached like it was about to split open and his tongue felt like it was coated with chalk dust. The trouble with hangovers was not so much the headache or the burning thirst but the feeling of complete lethargy that made you want to shut out the world. He hadn't remembered leaving the hotel last evening and not much more about the whore. Only that it had cost him three crowns. He wasn't even going to come in this morning but he had hoped there might have been an unpaid fee waiting for him, but there hadn't been. Instead there had been a delivery boy with a message from the chief magistrate Thomas Pruett. An hour later he still had the hangover and a new client as well. A French lad facing a murder charge while on a ticket of leave. A three man military tribunal set for opening, Thursday, three days from now. His fee was guaranteed, Pruett had said handing him the envelope containing details of the case. After all, every man deserved a fair trial.

Mahony stopped reading, pushed his glasses up on his forehead and rested his face against the paper. It smelled like his mother's dried flowers. He thought about her. Saw, as if it was yesterday, her work-lined face break into the joy of pride. The youngest graduating lawyer in his class.

He hadn't told her about the movement, the crusade against the British that stirred every young Irishman's heart. And so she had been more shocked than heartbroken when they had arrested him. At first, that is. Then when he was sentenced to transportation to New South Wales, she lapsed into an anguish he would never forget. They carried her crying out of the courtroom and that was the last he had ever seen of her. He had been in bondage three years when the letter came from his uncle telling him that she had died. Of a broken heart, the uncle had written. Another martyr to the cause, the words said. The grave would be tended until he returned. But he hadn't gone back. Not after his pardon. He had nothing to go back to. It was strange how seven years of degradation destroyed the will more than the body. And so he drank and played at law to pay the drinking bills. He had a group of friends as hopeless as he, and when they drank they talked a lot of changing the future. Then in the morning when they were sober they went back to doing what they did to pay the bills and buy more whisky.

Mahony forced his eyes back to the papers Pruett had given him. He knew why he had been offered him the case. They thought it was hopeless. A done deed. They obviously believed that the Canadian boy (he wasn't French at all but Pruett was either too lazy or stupid to appreciate the difference) was doomed. And they were probably right. His appointment as defence merely confirmed it. The bastards knew to offer him a fairly generous fee knowing he would accept it because he couldn't afford not to. He looked in vain for mention of the members of the tribunal. Not that it mattered.

He would have to go and see the boy today. Pruett had said that he had been allowed no visitors except his confessor, and his lawyer of course. Pruett had thought that was funny and had laughed, showing his yellowing horsy teeth. For a moment Mahony had been reminded of the ass that the meat vendor had used in the village he had lived in County Clare.

It was late afternoon before Mahony closed the folder. He thought for a while, his still aching head resting in the palms of his two hands. He wrote laboriously for two minutes, scrawling more illegibly than usual on a scrap of paper retrieved from his wastepaper box. Then placing the folder in an ageing tattered satchel, he began walking bareheaded through the hot damp air to the courthouse and to the squat grey prison block which adjoined it.

~ ~ ~

It was still light in the cell and Martin sat in the darkest corner where it was coolest and watched the flies buzzing in and out between the bars set in a small window just within the reach of his raised arms. He didn't know what day it was and he didn't care, but it seemed like he had been here for months though he knew he hadn't. He spent his time either tossing fitfully on the thin pallet which lay on the stone floor, or doing what he was doing now. Hugging his knees and rocking back and forth, first in a state of fearful bewilderment, and after two nights ago, not caring. He had told them everything they wanted to know. All he knew was that they thought he had killed Mary. No one came to visit him. No one except Father Blake, and he didn't seem to know anything about the charges against him. It was different here to the jail in Montreal. He had been with friends there, and at least he knew why they were punishing him. He also had wanted to live, then. He smiled to himself as he remembered how afraid he had been to die. Now the ache dulled the fear. Poor Father Blake was not to know of course, but it would have been better had he not come to visit him the night before last.

His dear friend had been solicitous and they had talked about the good times they had had together and how they would do them all again when he was free. Friends were so important Father Blake had said, and then he had put his arm around him and told him that he had some disquieting things to say but they were best said because they both knew that truth was always better than illusion. The man he thought was his friend, Mr. Neitch, wanted nothing more to do with him. Father Blake had tried to explain that Mr. Neitch was upset and didn't mean the things he had said. Then came the blow that brought with it the ache that would not go away. Father Blake had seen Colleen at the Bath Arms Hotel laughing and being very familiar with a dark-haired British officer. Father Blake was gentle. He was aware of his feelings for the lass, but she had proven herself fallible like most of her kind and in that sense was more to be pitied than blamed. Father Blake must have divined his deep disquiet for he left soon afterwards. He had cried. For a long time. Now his eyes were dry. But the wrench in his stomach was tighter. Oh God. What went wrong?

The sound of the footsteps on the stone floor was replaced by the jangling of keys and then a clang as the heavy iron door slammed. Martin looked up to see a sandy haired man still dripping from the rain. Not young, not old with a face that looked like it didn't like the sun. The jaw was gaunt and the tired eyes and pot belly advertised a man who drank more than he ate. He didn't come close but stood back as if he was unsure what to do. Martin didn't help him. Whoever it was, he couldn't be a friend. Not in this place. He turned back to his rocking staring ahead at the grey wall.

"Either you've got no friends or else no one knows you're here." The voice was rich and musical; the words rolled with a kind of slur that Martin had never heard before. He looked up.

"I would have thought that your comrades at Longbottom might have written to you. You lot are able to read, I'm told."

"I'm not allowed mail," Martin mumbled.

"Oh, yes you are. At least that's what they told me."

"Who are you?" Martin said disinterestedly still looking at the floor.

"Greg Mahony. I'm your defence, the miracle-making Irishman." He laughed without being funny. "Martin is it? They do call you Martin don't they?"

"I didn't do it if that's what you mean. I don't need a defence. I've done nothing wrong."

Mahony sat on the floor beside Martin. "That's where you're wrong, lad. You need me all right. They're going after you on a murder charge. And you're going to need all the help you can get." Mahony spread his hands and grinned a boyish smile. "And it won't cost you a penny. So why don't you tell me your side. Who was this Mary? How did you happen to know her? What happened? Take your time, Martin. Though we haven't much of it. It's a military tribunal." Mahony's voice became bitter, "And those bloody things have a habit of running their own course."

Martin started haltingly at first and then only because he thought talking would make him feel better. He told Mahony everything he could remember about his time with Mary. No it was Lamar but he kept referring to her as Mary. He told him about Longbottom, Baddely, Father Blake, and Mr. Neitch and the Bath Arms. The only thing he left out was Colleen. He couldn't bear to speak about her and for some reason wanted to keep his thoughts about her, private. It hurt that much.

Mahony listened patiently pausing to take notes and sometimes interjecting with questions. When Martin had finished Mahony got up and stretched his cramped legs.

"Good, Martin. You speak excellent English. They told me you spoke French. I thought we might have some trouble talking." His tone suddenly became serious as he sat down again, this time closer to Martin who had resumed his rocking. "Now listen to me. I don't know why they're going after you on a murder charge. A twelve man civilian bench would acquit you in a day. No body; flimsy evidence. In a civilian trial this case would be a farce. A military tribunal is different, however. Especially a three man one like this is. Anything can happen. And that's another thing. For the life of me I can't imagine why they're going away from standard procedures in favour of a military tribunal. They haven't had those for years. Look, I'm going to be honest with you, Martin. I think it means they're going after you. For whatever reason. And that's not good. Their whole case rests on an eyewitness who says he saw you kill the girl. He knows you apparently, and you know him. You can't verify any of your actions on the day in question. You were in close enough proximity to have committed the murder and gotten back to your camp before your priest friend." Mahony studied his fingers for a second. "Still, when it all comes down to it, it's going to be whether they believe you or their eyewitness. Three men who'll either believe you or the witness."

"Alexander Black," mumbled Martin. It was more a statement than a question.

Mahony's surprise showed. "My God, man. How did you know? What are you saying?"

Martin told him. All about Black. On the ship and then the scene at the races. He left out Colleen again, just describing the encounter as a provocation.

When Martin was through, Mahony whistled through his teeth. "Now that changes things a great deal, me bucko. A great deal indeed."

He got up again from the floor and this time straightened out his trousers and coat. "I'll be going now, Martin. I have a lot to do. I'll see you again tomorrow. Get some rest. Things may not be as bad as you think. We just might be able to beat this thing."

Martin didn't reply, so after calling for the guard, Mahony leaned over and patted Martin on the shoulder. A minute later, the night guard, a big burly soldier with an affable face, let him out and soon he was back into the fresh air and to the smell of a damp humid evening. The rain had stopped and a few stars showed above, and away to the west the cicadas were singing again.

~ ~ ~

Mahony tossed and turned until his sheets were crumpled damp. The case was absurdly simple and for that reason fraught with risk. All he had to do was to discredit Black's testimony and find character witnesses to testify on behalf of Goyette. If he could do both and impress the tribunal, and no body turned up, he stood a real chance. If he couldn't then who knows? He'd seen men hang on much weaker charges. At two he was still awake. He thought of a drink but something made him ignore the half full bottle just inches from his head. When finally he fell into a fitful sleep he dreamed. About his mother. They were in court and he was defending her. But he didn't know the charges. He was talking silly and laughing at the judge who was an aboriginal. When he woke the sun was streaming through the open window and half the morning was gone. An hour later, unshaven and his head light with hunger, he was on a Sydney-bound ferry. He had much to do and less than two days to do it.

The Bath Arms Hotel, January 26, 1841

Bernard said his farewells to Emmanuel Neitch and mounted his horse for Sydney. Thankfully the rain had stopped and already the mud was drying in the heat. The journey would be that much easier. He had just finished saying Mass at Longbottom and in his saddlebags were three letters for Martin Goyette that he had promised to deliver. One from that absurd little man called Prieur; another from a husky young farmer type and another from an old fool who spoke like he was someone special. What a joke! He'd destroy their pathetic gestures of loyalty; watch them burn as soon as he got back to Sydney. Yes, he'd had a very successful stay with Neitch, not to mention the excellent food and drink he had been served. All of which was only to be expected. However, he'd been a little surprised at the intensity he had to produce to convince Neitch that Martin had stolen his money. Neitch really seemed to like Goyette which just went to show how guileful the Frenchman was. Well, he'd succeeded and now Neitch shared his hatred of the treacherous scum. Bernard's head was pounding and his brow furrowed as he rode. It was the slut who had presented the most difficulty. Not that wasn't to be expected from dirt like that. She wanted to visit the Frenchman in jail even though he had persuaded Neitch to dissuade her. What had he told Neitch? It would only serve to sully the name of the Bath Arms. So Neitch had asked her not to go and had increased her workload so she didn't have time anyway. Bernard Blake had secured her letters too by telling Neitch to inform her that he could deliver them faster than the notoriously slow mail service. And so she had. (He'd wipe his arse on those) But the slut remained obstinate, threatening to go to Parramatta and to her lover, regardless. She had to be stopped. Goyette must believe he was totally isolated. When he did, it would be that much easier to destroy his will; his capacity for rational thought. Think of it. The idiot would die thinking he was a martyr, rapturous yet in his martyrdom and to the cause of Bernard Blake. It was so beautiful, so justified. Swine dying happily because of him. The first of many. But back to the slut. Yes, stopping her would be easy. And afterwards she would be one of the first to die. He'd probably use Black again. It all depended on how he performed before the tribunal. He should do well. He had the eyes of a rat and the disposition to match it. All he had to do was adhere to the lines he had been given.

~ ~ ~

Bishop Polding summoned his secretary as soon as had heard of his arrival from Longbottom. He wasn't convinced that the French Patriotes needed Father Blake specifically, as his secretary would have him believe, but still it had been a small price to pay to secure a greater level of co-operation from the moody Dominican. But that was some time ago when he believed that he had a war of wills to win. Now he wasn't at all certain that there was a war to win any more. The Dominican had retreated into himself. His body was wasting away and now the fine features were gaunt like a skull with burning orbs for eyes; eyes, always intense but which now mirrored an inner anguish. Polding had already made up his mind to send the Dominican back to Rome before winter. In the meantime it would mean a reduced workload and close scrutiny. Now as he watched the haggard stooped form enter the room, the black eyes blinking owlishly at him like they were not seeing clearly, Bishop Polding felt sad inside. So much ability; so much to give; so unable to give it. Maybe it was the Canadian lad Bernard had befriended that had caused this more noticeable recent deterioration. Facing a military tribunal for murder! An act committed while on a ticket of leave that he had prevailed on Gipps to grant at the request of Bernard Blake. A mistake. He was now regretting his magnanimity, probably just as much as Gipps since he had probably used up a lot of valuable and often scarce good will. As he rose to greet the Dominican, Polding was wondering whether this wild-eyed grave-faced young man held similar sentiments over his protégé now languishing in jail facing God knows what.

~ ~ ~

"Ah, Bernard, you're back. A fruitful trip, I trust." Polding gripped Bernard's hand noticing its coldness as much as the unyielding grip. "All went well, I trust. The Patriotes' disposition over the arrest of their compatriot, your friend, will cause us no concern? You did dispel any disquiet did you not? The last thing we want is trouble from political prisoners. Not when the whole system is so close to its own death."

"There will be no trouble, your lordship."

He sounds like he's not really here, thought Polding.

"Indeed, the prisoners are as malevolent towards Goyette as the rest of the populace seems to be. They fear he will have retarded their chances of pardon." He failed to mention the staunch support of Prieur, Rochon, Huot and others.

"Good," replied Polding sounding pleased. "One other thing, Bernard. Did you happen to encounter a man who goes by the name of Greg Mahony? He was here looking for you earlier and has gone to Longbottom and to Neitch's hotel in search of you. Your paths may have crossed."

"No," answered Bernard, his voice guarded. "What is his business?"

"He's the lawyer of the Goyette prisoner. He said he wished to talk with you. Perhaps he thinks you might know of matters which would help his case."

Bernard laughed derisively. "Help his case? It's lost already. He can find me if he wants."

There was a moment of silence. Then Bernard left without pleasantries, striding out of the room as though his superior weren't even there. Not that Polding minded. The man was unfathomable, and, beneath the arrogant posture, was anything but well. It was like he was teetering on a precipice. The last remark proved his confusion. Given the request that had secured Goyette's release it was hardly the sort of statement Polding would have anticipated. Neither sorrow, disappointment nor disillusionment. It was anger. No, more like rage. Well, he'd be gone soon. But he'd have to be watched. One push and . . . Polding shook his head at the thought.

January 27, 1841

As the ferry chugged its way down the river towards Sydney, Greg Mahony fumed impatiently. Another hour at least and what if the priest wasn't there. He'd have nothing. With the tribunal beginning the next day, he was in a state of near panic. His trip to Longbottom and the Bath Arms had been a disaster. Superintendent Clinton Baddely was not only dying, he was stark raving mad. No chance of a character witness there. Half the Patriotes did not like Goyette. Said he was a traitor and a coward, and deserved the worst. Not that Goyette didn't have friends among his countrymen. Several swore by his gentle nature, declaring him incapable of the crime of which he stood accused. They would be only too happy to testify on his behalf if possible. Which it wasn't, them being political prisoners and all, and even if it was, the prosecutor could just as easily line up as many or more of the exiles who would proclaim the opposite.

He had hoped for more from the innkeeper, Emmanuel Neitch, whom he had heard was an honest and steadfast man. After all it had been he who had been prepared to take Goyette into his employ and so enable the ticket of leave. To Mahony's surprise however, Neitch was anything but co-operative. He had been betrayed, he had said. Goyette was nothing but an ungrateful thief who had used his employer's friendship and good will to divest him of a goodly sum of coin. (Mahony made a mental note to ask Goyette about what Neitch had said about him). As for the accusation against Goyette, Neitch had had become confidential and somewhat guarded. Yes, he was very surprised that the boy was capable of such a foul deed. But, and he had waved a long bony finger in Mahony's face, most definitely testimony proclaiming such was out of the question. Surely Mahony could see that. Mahony didn't pursue the matter further. He might anger Neitch, and he certainly didn't need a hostile prosecution witness. That just left the priest. As the ferry passed Cockatoo Island and approached Sydney Cove, Mahony fell to studying his notes scribbled in Goyette's cell under the printed heading, "Priest."

~ ~ ~

Bernard Blake was finishing the second of the two letters when he heard the knock on the door. Even before he opened it he knew who it would be. He was not surprised by what he saw. An insignificant looking man with thinning hair, a large nose and a flabby belly. The candid grey eyes, though, were astute. Bernard resolved to be careful.

"Yes, may I help you?"

"Father Blake? I'm looking for Father Blake. Is he here?"

"You're looking at him. I'm Father Blake. How may I help you?"

Mahony extended his hand. "I'm Greg Mahony. From Parramatta." He nodded towards the inside of the presbytery. "May I come in?"

Bernard led Mahony to the small room that served as his office and indicated a chair facing the window. Mahony sat down and while Bernard settled himself, opened his satchel and began arranging some papers on his lap. "I'm a lawyer, Father. Assigned the task of defending a friend of yours."

"Poor Martin. Of course." Bernard kept his voice sympathetic. "I'll do anything I can to help. It's a sad sad thing. We were such good friends. I had no idea."

Mahony was still fumbling in his satchel. "He says he didn't do it, Father. Do you believe him?"

"Do you?"

The intonation irritated Mahony as much as it surprised him. It was like he was playing a word game. For the first time he met the priest's eyes. They bore at him and he found it difficult to meet them. He kept his voice cordial as if he hadn't noticed anything. "It's not what I believe, Father. It's what I must do to defend him. The thoughts and opinions of his friends are of course of interest to me. Hence the question." He shrugged.

Bernard furrowed his brow as if in deep concentration. "I tried to talk to him about it when I visited him. He was most upset. I learned but little. I tried to help him as best I could."

"Well, you can certainly help him now. Let me be frank with you, Father. Your friend's facing a three man military tribunal not a standard civilian bench as is custom in this land, and that's not good. Our main hope is to rely on character witnesses."

Bernard's thoughts were racing. The hurting was there. He fought to keep his voice even. "But as I understand it, the military have an eyewitness. A reliable one, I am told. Does this not make it terribly difficult for poor Martin?"

"But no body, Father. One man's word against another. In all good faith any decent civilian bench would throw this case out. I think the tribunal will too, if the eyewitness can be proven unreliable or prejudiced. That's my intention anyway. But I still need character witnesses to press any doubt the tribunal may have."

Bernard's eyes narrowed. He spoke carefully and for the first time Mahony detected real feeling in the voice. "You want me to testify to Martin's good character. That's it isn't it?"

"Yes," interjected Mahony quickly. "A good boy. Misguided politically perhaps, but in your opinion not capable of murder. It might be enough."

There was a long pause. Mahony waited for the priest to speak. There was something strange about him. His calm seemed forced. He was looking at his hands. At last he spoke. "May I be honest, Mr. Mahony. Candidly honest?"

"Of course, Father," replied Mahony.

"I can't testify. I won't."

"Why?"

"You asked what I believed. Now I'll tell you. Mr. Mahony, I believe he's guilty. I pray at night for forgiveness. For the silence I'm keeping. Before God in heaven I could not under pain of hell's fire do otherwise."

"You mean you know he's guilty?"

Bernard smiled a slow sad smile. "There are some things I can say. Some I can't. On the day in question, when we were in the hills south and west of Parramatta, I assigned Martin some sketching while I attended a dying man. Martin is an excellent, diligent worker. Yet when I returned the next morning he had achieved nothing. He had nothing to show me, Mr. Mahony. The previous evening he had discussed the girl with me, telling me about his disquiet over his actions towards her. A violence he couldn't understand. That much I can tell you, Mr. Mahony." Bernard spread his hands helplessly. "Anything else has to be between Martin and myself. You understand."

Mahony suddenly felt weary. This was not what he wanted to hear. He forced his reply. "Thank you, Father. You've been very helpful. Can I contact you during the trial if need be?"

The priest was suddenly solicitous.

"Yes, Mr. Mahony. I am Martin's confessor and he will need me now in his hour of travail." He bent lower towards Mahony. "You will keep our discussion today confidential, won't you?"

Mahony caught his meaning. "Yes, Father. There's no need. But if he asks, then what?"

"A contrivance of some sort. Tell him that the tribunal is avowedly anti-Catholic – which it probably is anyway – and that I'd do his cause more harm than good by testifying."

Mahony nodded, then rose to leave. "It starts tomorrow. With what we've got it won't take long. Two days probably."

Bernard reached the door before Mahony and held it open for him. "I'm sure you'll do your best Mr. Mahony. It's all in God's hands now. My prayers will be with you both."

~ ~ ~

Walking back to the ferry, Mahony thought about the priest. There was something about him. His posture, his words. Pride? Arrogance? No! More like mockery. Mahony thought of the priests back in County Clare. With them it had been the kindness of the well-intentioned doing their best to sustain hope in a miserable land.

The gulls were screaming above him and he could smell the sea.

Mockery, and something else which reached terrifyingly at him. A shell of a man with coals for eyes; the eyes of the pitiless. He couldn't be sure, of course, but convict life had taught Mahony to trust his instincts.

He stumbled over a fallen drunken form, cursing at the prostrate man who didn't stir. The water ahead was shimmering blue in the afternoon sun and he could see the ferry being boarded. He broke into a trot.

Maybe it was best that the priest didn't testify. It was then that Mahony realized that he feared the mocking Father Blake. He didn't fear Martin at all, and he had just been assured that he was a murderer.

The Courthouse, Parramatta. January 28, 1841

This morning as the murder trial of Martin Goyette was poised to start the empty jury bench looked strangely out of place. The judge's place occupied by a military man. Major James Cowling, a twenty-year veteran in Her Majesty's army with service in Egypt and the Peninsular and now second in command of the 28th Regiment stationed in Parramatta, had set his spectacles on his nose and was studying the neat row of papers lying before him. As the President of the tribunal it was Cowling's task to direct the proceedings. A large man with a kind ageing face, Cowling had served on many tribunals, both minor and major, to the point where he accepted them as part of a senior officer's lot. Secretly, he also took satisfaction in his own acquired expertise. Indeed, if the practice of law did not encompass as much banality as it did nobility, he might have enjoyed a lawyer's life. But that would have meant not being a soldier. No, it was better this way, where sitting on tribunals gave him the best of both worlds.

Beside Cowling and to his right was a tall polished oaken table with two ornately carved chairs occupied by the other two members of the tribunal. Captain Duncan Weir who also wore the red and yellow facings of the 28th was nearest to his superior but unlike Cowling he was not reading. His thin face betrayed no emotion as he took in his surroundings, his gaze resting more often than not on the manacled prisoner who was whispering to his lawyer at a less imposing table about five yards to the right. Weir's eyes were narrow, more like glittering slits and today their habitual resentment was offset by the unsurpassed joy that came only with vindication. Duncan Weir was happy. He was going to enjoy this. Revenge at last. A measure of retribution for that terrible day in 1837 when the bastards had beaten his brother to a pulp in the mud and snow outside some rebel French village in Lower Canada. Lieutenant Jock Weir, dashing, fun-loving, and the 32nd Regiment's favourite officer, cut down at twenty nine, bayoneted, mutilated and ripped apart by a bunch of civilian savages. He had died honourably, his life blood spilling onto the soil of treachery. A messenger he was, not even wearing his uniform, or the scarlet sash and sword. They said he was a shapeless mass of blood and flesh, and when the last bastard ran his dead body through with a sword, he had held the bloodied weapon high in triumph. The murdering scum. And "Radical Jack" Durham had let them all off. Sent them to Bermuda. What a laugh! It was no wonder the French pricks had tried the same thing in 1838. Weir was feeling warm inside. He could hardly wait for it to start. No one knew, of course. It was a shame he had not shared with his fellow officers. And now, the fates had smiled on him. There would be justice at last.

It was the third member of the tribunal that had induced Goyette's urgent whispering, and now Greg Mahony's face was set with a look of indecision. Martin's heart had sunk when he had seen him. It was like an omen warning him that he was lost. The pink soft face, the bloated body and most of all the malicious close-set eyes that followed him across the room. Paul Niblett. His life was once more in the hands of Paul Niblett now swaggering across the polished floor, the proud red and blue of the Queens Own Regiment looking as ill-fitting as ever. He heard the Captain's insults like it was yesterday; felt the sickening thud of Niblett's boot in his stomach on a heaving deck. His shock must have showed because Mahony had asked him what was the matter. He had told him as briefly as possible, not wanting to and not even caring. Mahony had listened and now he was drumming his pen lightly on the desk. Maybe Mahony now realized what he, Martin Goyette, knew for a fact. He would be condemned in this room. Nothing could be surer.

Martin was right. The revelation had jolted Mahony. Clearly they didn't know about the beating on board the ship. Mahony could protest the appointment but only on legal grounds since there was no verification for Niblett's antipathy towards Martin. He pondered his options, even rising to his feet to approach Cowling before sitting back down again. His instincts told him it wouldn't do any good. It was simply not worth the price of failure.

The only other people in the room besides the military clerks were the two prosecutors, Major Frederick Andrews and Captain Peter Gibling, both of the 28th, and the uniformed guards, armed and alert at both entrances to the courtroom. Then on the tick of ten, Major James Cowling opened proceedings. Andrews read out the details of the Crown's charges against the prisoner, dwelling on the fact that while there was no corpse, Martin Goyette's guilt rested on the presence of reasonable doubt, a doubt that simply did not exist in this particular instance. Andrews then brought his companion forward and begged the tribunal's indulgence in hearing background information which would show beyond doubt the type of violent milieu from which the prisoner came. Then, for over an hour and a half Gibling detailed the events of 1838 including the trials and commuted death sentences. For the first part of Gibling's address Niblett listened knowingly, winking and nodding affirmatively, then fell to yawning and picking his nose. Cowling followed Gibling interestedly while Weir's face displayed no emotion.

It was almost noon when Mahony addressed the tribunal. Reasonable doubt did exist, so much so that he was saddened that the colony's legal system had allowed the matter to proceed as it had. As for Gibling's comments on the uprising, Mahony deferred to them, but noted the seemingly random lottery of acquittals. From accounts he had read, the punishment had rested more on the intent of the leaders than it did in individual culpable behaviour. He wasn't close enough to hear Weir's sharp intake of breath or see the open hostility in the eyes.

~ ~ ~

Matron Nance Edwards was the first witness called. She detailed how he had come to the orphanage to inform her that a visitor she was expecting was ill and unable to come. She told what she had seen through the window answering in the affirmative to Andrews' question as to whether or not the native girl seemed frightened of the defendant.

Mahony asked four questions. Did the defendant chase the girl after she ran towards the water? Matron Edwards shook her head. No, he hadn't. Then what had he done, Mahony wanted to know? He had run the other way. Towards his horse she had supposed. Could the matron tell whether the defendant had seemed furious or startled or shocked? No, she couldn't tell. She hadn't really looked. The whole thing had been such a shock. Poor Mary. Nance Edwards had looked surprised when Mahony asked the colour of the girl's eyes. They were the strangest eyes she had ever seen. Light brown with a sort of yellowishness about them, they seemed to look right through you. But she didn't think they were mad eyes.

Andrews called Dr Armitage next, drawing from the medical man his opinion of the girl's mental condition. A child simpleton, Armitage called her. Was she attractive, Andrews wanted to know? Armitage thought, possibly in a heathenish savage way. She went about half naked and if she was like some others of her kind, was likely to be wanton in her favours if the tribunal got his meaning.

Mahony declined to cross examine.

~ ~ ~

After lunch Andrews called Alexander Black. Martin watched his longtime tormentor take the oath and settle down in the witness box after smoothing out what was clearly a new suit. Black's eyes lingered on his own for an instant before facing Andrews. There was an air of jaunty confidence about him.

Andrews led Black through his testimony. He had been taking his usual walk after work when he had noticed something blue across the river. Then he had seen them. The defendant wrestling with a woman. He had hidden behind a tree and watched. It was a native woman and he recognized her from having encountered her on other walks. The man, he knew at once. The deformity of the lip was unmistakeable. The dangerous rebel he had escorted here from Canada and who had incited a mutiny on board ship. Horrified he had seen the defendant hit the girl across the head several times with a large rock. She fell on the ground and did not move. Then the defendant had dragged her into a boat which he then rowed downstream away from his hiding spot but not so far that he had not seen him push her body into the water. He had been terrified. Martin Goyette, he knew, was a dangerous and violent man. Had he interfered he was sure he would have met the same fate as the native woman. So he waited until Goyette left. The rest they knew.

Andrews then asked Black if he really understood the seriousness of what he was saying; that a man's future, even his life, hung on the truth of his words. There was no room for error or doubt. Was Black certain about what he had seen, and, if so, was the perpetrator of the crime as witnessed positively identifiable as Martin Goyette, the defendant? Black had nodded affirmatively before repeating in tones a touch too self righteous for Mahony, that before all in heaven, the painful events had transpired exactly as he had said. Andrews then thanked Black for his co-operation and deferred his witness to Greg Mahony.

Mahony got to his feet slowly and approached Black, who was gazing at him incuriously, casually as if bored. The glint of perspiration on the forehead and a suppressed tension told Mahony that his witness was not as relaxed as he was making out. He decided to keep his stance confrontational. He pushed his face as close to Black as he could, smelling the dank odour of the man's body. His voice was louder than usual, and challenging.

"Very fine suit, Mr. Black. Very fine indeed. Tell me, Mr. Black. Where is your place of employ?"

"Grierson's Haberdashery Supplies. I'm the senior clerk."

Mahony's eyebrows raised. "'Am?' But Mr. Grierson said that you had left his employ. As of last Friday, he said."

"Yes, that's true. I had forgotten." Black smiled weakly.

"And you intend now to return to your native land. You have purchased your passage on the *Emma Eugenia*? Just this week I understand." Mahony made a pretence of consulting his notes. "Sailing date, two weeks today. Is that not correct?"

"Yes."

"How fortunate and how sudden. Mr. Grierson was very surprised when I told him. He didn't think you had the money."

"Well, he thought wrong, didn't he?"

Mahony's face was back close to Black's again. "These events you witnessed, Mr. Black. They occurred on Tuesday January twelfth. Late afternoon if I am correct?"

Black's brow furrowed for a moment. "Yes, I think so. I will have to think."

"You needn't bother Mr. Black. It was the twelfth. It's in your statement."

"Yes, the 12th. It was a fine afternoon, I recall now. A Tuesday."

"But you failed to report the matter until the fifteenth. Three days later. You witness a murder on the Tuesday and only get around to bringing it to the attention of the police three days later. I find that rather strange Mr. Black. Could you tell the tribunal why?"

Black swallowed. "I was going to, when the body was found and information sought. And," His eyes rested on Martin before turning again to Mahony. "I was afraid. I thought if the police did not believe me and Martin Goyette found out he would do me harm. He is a dangerous man."

"So you waited. I see. What made you change your mind, Mr. Black? Why did you rediscover your bravery and your conscience?"

"Easy, Mr. Mahony. The witness is not on trial. Temper your remarks." James Cowling's tone was only mildly rebuking.

"Though I had heard of no body being found, I had witnessed a murder, sir. I had to report it. It was my duty."

"Three days later?"

"Yes." Black's eyes were defiant.

"Mr. Black, in your testimony you referred to encountering the girl on previous occasions during your walks in the bush. Did she ever speak to you?"

"No, she never did. She was an imbecile you know."

"You saw her from a distance. Or up close?"

"Up close. Close enough to know that it was the same girl I saw killed. I'd see her on my walks. She was there fishing or picking blackberries or just walking. Three or four times I seen her.

Mahony scratched his head as if in puzzlement. "Strange. I've never known any of the dark people to allow themselves to be seen in the bush when they didn't want to be seen. This girl must be an exception. Still, if you saw her up close then you saw her. Tell the tribunal then, what was the colour of her eyes?"

"Her eyes! How should I know. Brown I suppose."

"Dark like your own."

"Yes."

Mahony glanced towards the tribunal but made no comment. Instead, he went on. "When you did see her was there anything strange or unusual about her? Anything you noticed particularly?"

"No. Only that she was usually half naked.

"The bird, Mr. Black. The crow. What about the crow?"

"I don't understand." Black was clearly confused.

"As I understand it, she had a tame bird that never left her shoulder. You say you didn't see it."

Black caught himself. "Yes, yes, I remember now. She did have a bird."

Cowling broke in. "You're under oath Mr. Black. Please keep that in mind."

"This bird," Mahony continued, "did you notice it when you saw the girl being attacked?"

The bastard was trying to trap him. *Keep your presence*, Black told himself. *If I say 'yes' and if he knows for a fact that the bird is dead, I could be in trouble. But, say 'no' and the bird could be anywhere.* He looked levelly at Mahony. "I saw no bird. Just the events I have described."

"Two other things Mr. Black. According to the defendant it was you who performed the crossing ceremonies on board the *Buffalo*."

"Yes."

"And during that ceremony, the defendant says he was mistreated by you far in excess of that normally permitted in such circumstances."

"It's a lie. There were no excesses."

"You have no real liking for the defendant, have you Mr. Black."

Black shrugged. "I don't like rebels. Other than that Goyette means nothing to me."

"Even though the two of you had an altercation at the Homebush races a little over a month ago?" Mahony's voice cut like a whip.

Black swallowed nervously and reached for his handkerchief. "He exaggerates. We had words, that's all. He was drunk and abusive. I chose to ignore him."

"That's not what he says, Mr. Black, and doubtless a corroborative witness can be found, eh?"

Black shrugged indifferently.

Mahony grinned mockingly at Black before turning to Cowling. "No further questions, Mr. President."

As he was escorted from the room, Black had trouble keeping steady. His legs felt like water.

~ ~ ~

It being past three, Cowling adjourned the tribunal till ten the next morning. Mahony accompanied Martin to his cell.

"It went better than I hoped," said Mahony. "The bastard's lying. Why, I don't know, but he's lying. Yet, I think we sowed enough reasonable doubt. Enough for a jury to acquit there and then." He rubbed his hands together. "Yes, I'd feel real happy if I had a jury. But these bloody three man tribunals. Cowling's a good man. He knows how things are around here. But the other two. I don't know about Weir. He hasn't been here that long. Cold fish so my sources say, who keeps to himself. Who knows with people like that? And this Niblett, if he's anything like you say he is, we've got one against us before we start."

Mahony got up and walked about the cell. "We can't afford to rely on what we did to Black today. I've got a feeling that Andrews has something else in store for us. He's a smart devil. We've got to do something else."

"What?" asked Martin feeling his spirits dip again.

For a short time in the courtroom listening to Mahony expose Black for the liar he was, he had allowed himself the luxury of a shred of hope and the generous optimism which accompanied it. If he was acquitted, he would go to Colleen and hear it from her own lips. Father Blake might have been misreading things. There could be all sorts of reasons. But now he was hearing from Mahony that in spite of Black's weakened testimony he was very far from out of this mess.

"You've dealt Black a savage blow. Is that not enough. Can there be anything else.?"

"Yes, I think so," said Mahony sitting down again. "Tell me something honestly. I have to know for certain."

Martin nodded.

"Did you kill that girl? Please Martin. I have to know. Whether you go free or not may depend on the truth of the answer you give me."

"No, it happened exactly as I told you. I have left out one thing only in my words to you and it has nothing to do with the charges against me."

Mahony looked curiously at him but said nothing.

"That's what I expected to hear. You know, Martin I've never really believed you were guilty. Not even after . . ." He caught his breath and looked at Martin. Thankfully he was rocking again and looking at the floor. "You possess a presence. It's in your eyes, your whole demeanour. Honesty drips out of you."

"You're wrong," thought Martin remembering Brown, Baker's field, the tribunals, the *Buffalo*.

Mahony was continuing. "I'm going to put you on the witness stand tomorrow. Just tell your story like it happened. I'll be gentle. Andrews will go after you. But you'll be all right. Just tell the truth. One word of caution. Leave Niblett out of it completely. We can't take the chance."

"And you think?"

"I think the tribunal will know it. I certainly believe Cowling will. The key is Weir. I just wish I knew more about him. If he's anything like Cowling, things just could go our way. We can't lose anything by you testifying on your own behalf and we could gain a great deal."

His fate in his own hands. It had never been that way before. He could face them with honest words. Let Martin Goyette tell his own story. He had to do it for Colleen

"I'll do what you think is best, Mr. Mahony."

Mahony slapped him on the shoulder. "That's me boy. Now you get some rest. Me, I've got some things to do before tomorrow. Remember. On that stand. Just be yourself."

A wave. A whistle for the guard. Receding footsteps, and Martin was alone with his thoughts. He tried not to dwell on his misery. He tried to be optimistic, to share in Mahony's faith in him. The plate of cold food came soon after sundown, slid in and untouched between the lower bar and the stone floor. Martin Goyette was asleep.

~ ~ ~

Father Bernard Blake watched the guard depart leaving him in the cell with the sleeping prisoner. He made no attempt to rouse Martin but stood there in the gloom fingering the letter. For a moment he swayed before catching himself. The pains were worsening. He had stumbled twice outside on the street. It was a tribute to his magnificent strength, he told himself, that he was able to concentrate at all with the evil vile ones screaming their hatred at him. Out to destroy him they were. But he'd best them all yet. Chosen ones like himself seized their opportunities. Like just now when he had encountered Mahony in his office. He had shown nothing but solicitousness to the cunning worm and he had learned things. Important things. Alexander Black had performed less than convincingly. He might have known that. Slime like that could be nothing else.

Mahony was also going to seek Martin's testimony. It was their best chance, he had said. Bernard Blake had agreed. A most wise choice. Martin's honesty knew no bounds. It would shine through like a beacon.

Yes, you worthless lump of shit. It most certainly would. But not in the way you think. Bernard smiled in the gloom, and placing the letter in the folds of his robe went forward to wake the prisoner.

~ ~ ~

It was the lavender. He smelled it first and then saw the pale face above him. Martin pushed himself onto his side facing the priest.

"Father. You came. I'm glad Father, really glad."

"I would have come earlier if I was allowed. In the courtroom."

"No visitors, Father. They were letting in no one. Mr. Mahony says not to worry. But I do. All that secrecy."

Bernard's eyes narrowed, but his voice showed pleasure. "You sound much better than when I last saw you. It must have gone well today. You don't know how happy that makes me. I had felt badly about not testifying on your behalf."

"It doesn't matter Father. You could not risk it."

"Oh, but I would have, Martin. I would die for you. You know that. It's the tribunal. Violently anti-Catholic. All of them. They've been here many years and have nursed much resentments against our faith. Not that it should worry us. But it could have done harm. So I refrained. You understand."

Martin nodded. It was so good to hear his friend again.

"I did find out something which may help you, Martin."

"What is that, Father. A pardon?" Martin laughed.

Again Bernard Blake felt the lash of hatred burn into him.

"No, but I found out some things about these native people. Simple things which put all in its place."

"I don't understand."

"Listen to me, Martin." Bernard gripped Martin's shoulders until it hurt. "When the girl proffered herself to you and you rightly refused her, she was already dead."

"How . . . ?"

"A gift. You gave her a gift. The Virgin icon. Nothing to you perhaps, broken as it was. But to her it was a special sign. To do with the Dreamtime spirits.

Possibly she thought it resembled one of them. To her, you were someone sent by the spirits, and when you spurned her, it as if she had been found unworthy. She had to die. They do that, these people. They just die."

"But that's terrible. I caused her death."

"Inadvertently, Martin. Inadvertently. My point is that regardless of how she died she was already dead. Inadvertent culpability is no culpability at all even . . ."

Bernard stopped. His head was screaming but he had timed it perfectly.

"My God, Father. You think I killed her."

"No, Martin. That is not the issue. But she is dead. She has to be. That is the issue."

"Then it doesn't matter any more. They'll hang me."

Bernard sat down beside Martin. It was time. He thought of the letter. No, not quite. It was like the soft ones were talking over a storm. But he could still hear them. *Send him where he belongs, Bernard Blake. Let his ignominy be our triumph. Do it now and do it sublimely. We have no equals. Only our destiny.*

"Martin, listen to me. What I have just told you is good. It removes all design from you. There can be no shame now. No remorse. All that is lacking now for the fear of death to disappear completely like a chimera in the certain knowledge that it only seals something far greater. Death is nothing without that. Remember your brother, and the other brave man who died and who was your friend?"

"Yes."

"The real tragedy was not their deaths but the gnawing doubt that they might have died for nothing. Your brother did not want to live any more and the chevalier believed he was simply going to a better place. But what if they both could have been certain that their deaths opened the gates to a far better world. Then what?"

"Joseph-Narcisse would have smiled. So would have the Chevalier. They were not afraid."

"Exactly, Martin. Exactly."

Bernard could feel the urgency. Concentrate. The foul ones were screaming in his ear and he wanted to run away. Out of this place. He was whispering, his hand resting affectionately on the arm of the man he hated. "Out there, Martin. Out beyond the squalid confines of this hellish town they are waiting. Beaten, bruised and cast out by a society that despised them."

"You mean, the blacks? Like Lamar?"

"No, Martin. Not the blacks. They are but animals. I mean the wretched souls who have escaped their bondage in this place. Hundreds of them, thousands and more joining them all the time."

Martin thought François-Xavier that day when Uncle Antoine had died. He had said the same thing. They all had. Robert Nelson would save them all.

"They are ready to rise, Martin. We can take this place and begin the new order we talked about. Remember. That day when you pledged your loyalty."

Martin nodded. Father Blake was nothing like Robert Nelson.

"What we need is a martyr. Someone whose death will be seen as so foul, so heinous that it will become its own battle cry. They are talking. The newspapers. Everyone knows you're innocent. There are rumblings that if you should hang, the British will have more than an execution to account for. And the newspapers don't even know about the others in the hills beyond the Nepean."

Father's eyes were pleading, and there were specks of saliva around the corners of his mouth. Suddenly Martin knew. "Do you know what you're saying Father? What you're asking?"

"A martyr, Martin. We need a martyr. A symbol of liberty in the midst of oppression. Your innocence becomes its own sanctification. Don't you see? Death is nothing when there is no fear. It's your name. It will live forever in glory. Your brother, the Chevalier. They didn't know that. You do. I pledge my word. Please, Martin. For me."

He could see the look of uncertainty on the idiot's face. He would do it. For him. Paying the ultimate price for nobility's sake; not knowing that it was merely to serve the man who hated him. What could be sweeter? Bernard grimaced as the pain bit into him. *Soon, O maligned Mother soon. You will have the dog that took our destiny. I will join you then, Mother and we will both torment his soul. Together, Mother. We will do it together.*

Martin felt a strange detachment. His friend was asking him to die. And what was strange was that the thought did not inspire the craven fear he had experienced in Montreal. Why was that? Was it because he was not convinced that the tribunal would find him guilty? Possibly. But if he was not afraid any more, and if indeed he had pledged his loyalty to his friend, then why was he not prepared to entertain his friend's request? Was it because in spite of the love he bore for his friend, the words he uttered were the same ones he had questioned in the farcical sequence of events which had seen two close ones hanged, and the rest of them exiled to this place? No. That was not it. It was Colleen. He had to see her again. He had to hear her say she did not love him. And until he knew that he would not, could not embrace the sort of request his friend was asking of him. But as he looked into those desperate eyes, the eyes of the man he admired most on earth, the face of his loyal and kind friend, he could not deny him completely. Instead he just said, "I will think on what you have said, Father. The trial is not yet over and we still have time to talk."

Bernard looked at his enemy, trying to keep his incredulous rage under control. The imbecile. The ungrateful whelp. No wonder he deserved to die. He possessed no graciousness. Vermin! Well, he'd soon change his tune. Bernard fought to keep the understanding in his words. "Of course, Martin. We shall talk later. But, as you and I both know, destiny will not be denied. Now I must leave. The hour is late. Until tomorrow, then."

"Thank you for coming, Father. You have given me much to think about." The lie sounded all right and Martin knew it was what Father would want to hear. He couldn't know that all he could think about was Colleen.

Bernard had called for the guard and was at the door of the cell when he turned and reached into his robe. "Oh, Martin. Forgive me. I almost forgot. The serving girl at the Bath Arms Hotel. I was there today. She asked me to give you this."

~ ~ ~

Martin took the letter with trembling hands. Then he was tearing it open, all thought of the priest gone.

A large round immature hand had written the name *Martin Goyette* across the plain white envelope. The letter itself was a single page with the same writing on both sides. The ink had been blotted in several places as if the writer was having difficulty in composition. The words leapt out at Martin.

> Dear Martin
>
> This is not easy for me to say. I would tell you myself with my own words, but I am afraid you would have been to angrey or upset. When you were put in prison and acuysed of that terable crime I did not know what to think. Most people think you are gilty but I just felt alone and disapointed. I thought a lot about what we would do if you were found not gilty. My mum tells me I would be disgraced and that we would have to go somwhere else to live.
>
> I have also met a British officer. He came to the Bath Arms one night and was very gentle to me. He told me about his family in England and the lands that are theirs. We have taken long walks and picnics. We love each other Martin and plan to

mary so we can never see each other again. I had to tell you this so you would know and understand. I am sorry very sorry but I dont love you anymore I love Phillip. I wish you well Martin and may God go with you.

Colleen

For hours Martin sat there in the dark, the letter lying on the stone floor. He couldn't cry. It was like his eyes had dried up like everything else inside him. Uncle Antoine had once told him that some things were too sad to cry over. He had cried over Uncle Antoine, over Joseph-Narcisse and Chevalier, over Madeleine, and when death hovered at his shoulder in the Pied du Courant. But now there were no tears. Just a lump. A dried shrivelled lump like his life. Around midnight he rolled himself into a ball and began rocking back and forth mumbling himself into a fitful sleep where images of Colleen paraded by, there, and then gone when he reached out for her.

January 29, 1841

The moment Mahony saw Martin he knew something was wrong. Dark circles under red-rimmed eyes told him that Martin had not slept. But what had disturbed Mahony was a noticeable difference in demeanour. Martin's eyes were flat and withdrawn; his shoulders were stooped and he seemed detached, as Mahony had often seen in men who had given up. His questions were answered with a blank silence and Mahony learned nothing beyond the fact that the priest had visited the prisoner after he had left the previous evening, a fact he found interesting nonetheless. Martin had clearly not wanted to elaborate further so Mahony contented himself with instructing him on the importance of his own testimony and the dire necessity of conveying his innocence and honesty to the tribunal.

"This is it, me bucko," he said as they were escorted to the courtroom. "Do your best, boy and tell it like it was."

~ ~ ~

Andrews opened the proceedings by producing two pieces of evidence, both of which, he noted, proved with a fair degree of certainty that the aboriginal girl was dead. The first was a rock retrieved on the Thursday following Black's report of the murder from the riverbank where he had witnessed the crime. The stains on it had been verified as probable blood stains. Andrews pressed his point to the tribunal that the presence of this possible murder weapon properly removed Black as a suspect for why would a man who had committed a murder also direct police to potential implicating evidence. The second piece of evidence was a blue dress found a few miles downstream from the crime scene, and left by receding floodwaters. Matron Edwards had already identified it as a dress she had given the aboriginal girl, and, if Black's testimony was to be believed, which also corresponded to the colour of the garment worn by the girl on the fateful day in question.

Mahony then assured the tribunal that the worst that the two pieces of evidence could suggest was that an accident may have occurred. The point of criminality was not proven nor was the accused's guilt affirmed in any way. Mahony felt a twinge of relief when he thought he noticed Cowling nod in agreement.

Mahony called Martin to the stand. "Walk as if you're innocent," he had hissed. Martin however approached the stand like he was already condemned and did not care. It was unsettling and Mahony felt more than a twinge of uneasiness.

Mahony led Martin through an account of how he had come to meet the girl, leaving out reference to the gift of the icon. He had Martin recount the events of the sketching trip with Father Blake and his day's activities on the day in question. And long before he was through he realized that he had made a mistake. Martin was unconvincing, halting and terse in his answers and conveying anything but the confidence of an innocent man.

When Andrews got up to cross-examine, he had already decided on his strategy. His original intention had been to destroy any credibility the prisoner might have built up, but after listening to Martin's confused responses to Mahony's questions, Andrews felt that any attempt to attack the prisoner might lead to a re-focussing and to the believability that Mahony was obviously relying on. So Andrews had decided to try and lead the prisoner on. Who knows, he might even condemn himself further.

"Mr. Goyette. You have testified that you had seen the native woman on several occasions. Did she ever speak to you?"

"Yes."

"But the court has been told she was mute. You say she spoke? What did she say?"

"She said a word when I gave her a present. I do not remember the word"

"A present. You gave her a present? What?"

"A figurine of the Virgin Mary. I wanted her to have it. I . . . I had no further need of it."

"I see." Andrews glanced at the tribunal before continuing. "Tell me, Mr. Goyette. When your friend the priest left you alone that day he had instructions for you, did he not?"

"Yes he told me to sketch the golden flowers and the red brush-like ones."

"And what did you have to show when he returned?"

"Nothing."

"Nothing? Had you done nothing all day? No spoiled sketches. Nothing?"

Colleen's face swam before his eyes. She was gone. Gone forever. He had sketched her that day. It was to have been his present to her. But he hadn't liked what he had done and had thrown the sketches away. Now it didn't matter.

"Nothing. I did nothing that day."

Andrews rubbed his chin thoughtfully and turned away from the witness stand. For a long time, it seemed to Mahony, he gazed at the painted ships on the wall. Then he turned abruptly back to the witness stand. "She's dead isn't she, Mr. Goyette? You killed her didn't you?"

Mahony had leapt to his feet to protest the question when he heard Martin already replying. He stood open-mouthed for an instant and then sank back into his chair.

"Yes. She's dead."

The boy was crying. The words were slurred, pain-filled, the voice tight with the hollow tones of resignation.

"I caused her death. I didn't mean to, but I did."

"You killed her, didn't you? You killed her?"

Mahony had never seen such anguish. A gentle soul ripped apart by something beyond his control. Knowing more than he had ever told Mahony. But innocent. An innocent man destroying himself and Mahony didn't know why.

"She is dead because of me. I suppose that means I killed her."

"No further questions." Andrews' triumph was obvious.

Martin was sobbing louder now. Cowling adjourned proceedings until after lunch when both sides would present their summations.

~ ~ ~

Thirty minutes later Mahony left Martin's cell for his office to prepare his closing remarks. It was lost, and he didn't know why. Martin refused to talk to him; he just sat in his cell rocking back and forth. Damn it. Something had happened last night. It had to do with the priest and there was no way he could find out.

~ ~ ~

Andrews began his summation at 2:00 PM with the assurance of a man who knew he had things his own way. Reasonable doubt had been removed totally in this case. The motive was probably rooted in the relationship between the defendant and the native girl, a relationship that before today no one had known existed. The defendant could not corroborate his actions the day in question. The eyewitness testimony of Alexander Black was damning.

Clearly if the tribunal believed Black, then the case was closed. But it had been the defendant who had condemned himself. The tribunal members had heard it from his own lips. The verdict was clear. Guilty as charged. The death penalty as the only punishment.

~ ~ ~

Mahony did his best. Bitterness between the defendant and the witness Black was longstanding. Threats had been uttered by Black at the Homebush Races which regardless of direst impact on the case in question did show that the defendant at least considered that Black believed he was the defendant's enemy.

Black's testimony, too, was flawed. Though he claimed to have seen the girl on several occasions he did not know the colour of her eyes, a colour which had been averred to as most striking and remarkable. He claimed ignorance of the girl's crow though it never left her shoulder. Could the evidence of such a witness be possibly used to condemn a man, let alone send him to the gallows? Furthermore, there was no real proof that the girl was indeed dead.

Regarding what the prosecution presented as a witness box confession, Mahony did not see it that way. The defendant believed that the girl was dead and that in some way he was responsible. That much was admitted, but only that much. "Be that as it may," Mahony had said, pounding on the witness stand, "that did not mean that he himself killed her. He could have meant anything." And since the prosecution had not followed up with more incriminating questions, the tribunal was obliged to view the defendant's statement as those of an innocent man. Mahony concluded by referring to Andrews' reasonable doubt. Reasonable doubt had not been removed, and since that was so a Not Guilty verdict had to be reached.

~ ~ ~

The shadows were lengthening in the courtroom when Mahony at last sat down beside Martin Goyette, who smiled wanly at him and laid his hand on his arm. Cowling brought the Tribunal to a close. A decision would be handed down at noon tomorrow. After charging both Andrews and Mahony to refrain from any contact with the newspapers over the trial, Cowling ordered the prisoner back to his cell. Mahony wanted to return with him, but Martin shook his head. Half an hour later Mahony was at the General Bourke downing but not enjoying his first drink in a week.

CHAPTER VI

The Courthouse, Parramatta. January 29, 1841

Major James Cowling looked at the clock on the wall. It was just past seven and not yet dark. He stuffed some notes inside his briefcase. The other two members of the tribunal were doing the same. He had thought a decision might have taken much longer. But here they were finished in time to dine properly, and though he didn't particularly relish having to deliver the judgement the next day, his military mind told him that it was fair and just given the circumstances.

Cowling himself had not been prepared for his colleagues' vehemence. To Niblett and Weir, the facts were clear and unequivocal. Niblett because he believed strongly in the testimony of the eyewitness; Weir because, given the girl's sudden and unusual disappearance and the incriminating circumstances surrounding it, there could be no other explanation. Cowling originally had not been so certain. It was virtually one man's word against another's, and certainly Black's testimony had not stood up well under Mahony's cross-examination.

But then the defendant had condemned himself, virtually admitting the crime openly. No, the defendant's guilt had not been in question. The sentence, however, had. To Cowling, it seemed that prison would be an appropriate sentence. But then Weir had reminded him that the press were howling for a guilty verdict, saying that if New South Wales persisted in mocking the concept of equality of justice before the law, then it would remain a lawless hellhole. Niblett had agreed. A jail term for a man already branded a dangerous revolutionary, a man who had probably killed an innocent farmer in his native land, was an insult to justice. And so Cowling had been persuaded.

Martin Goyette was found guilty as charged. The penalty: death.

January 31, 1841. 11:00 AM

Colleen took one last look at her sleeping mother and stepped out into the hot sunshine. Her mother's fever had broken during the night and all she needed now was lots of rest. Her father was home all day and sober, and had promised to look after her. Which left Colleen free to do what she had wanted to do so much over the past week and a half. She would go to Parramatta and find out about Martin. There had been no letters from him. No word. Nothing except Father Blake's words to Mr. Neitch that he was being tried by the army for murder.

It was ridiculous, she had told Mr. Neitch. Martin was no murderer. He couldn't hurt a fly. But Mr. Neitch had said that he had trusted Martin and he had stolen from him so maybe she, Colleen, should not be so certain of this man. She knew her employer didn't believe her when she told him that Martin didn't need to steal; that he had won lots of money at the races. But Mr. Neitch had just smiled and Colleen had cursed herself for persuading Martin to keep their winnings a secret.

As she walked towards the Bath Arms, she went over things again; what had happened, and now what she had to do. She had been a petty jealous fool. Sulking all that time after Martin had told her about the native girl. And just when she had been going to hold him and kiss him and say she was sorry for behaving poorly, they had come and taken him away. She had written many letters and had given them to Father Blake because she knew he was seeing Martin. And every time she had tried to find things out from Father Blake when he was at the Bath Arms, he had always been too busy. Mr. Neitch had given her more work to do, and then her Mum had gotten sick.

But now she was getting better, and Colleen Somerville was not going to cry herself to sleep any more. She was going to do something about it. She was going to Parramatta, Mr. Neitch and anyone else be damned.

~ ~ ~

Mr. Neitch had gone to an earlier Mass so Colleen was denied her resolve to tell him that he either give her time off to go to Parramatta or she would leave his employ. A letter was waiting for her. She had never seen Martin's writing but she knew it would be from him. She took it outside into the sun below the hill where she and Martin used to walk and read it rapidly, frowning at first, then shaking her head.

When she had finished she put it down on the grass and began pacing. Something was wrong. Terribly wrong. Words from Martin, yet not Martin's words. Telling her to forget about him; that he wasn't worthy of her love; that he was facing retribution; that he didn't love her anymore. Martin would never write that. He would say other things. He loved her. She knew he did. He might want to save her from public humiliation, but he would tell her himself. He would write with the love of a broken man. He would not write like he was talking to a stone. Something was not right. She went back to the letter and re-read it.

It came to her after ten minutes. The open letter g. She had seen those same gs before. Father Blake left notes to the servants rather than talking to them. They were his gs. The letter was his. At Martin's request? No, Martin would never do that, no matter how poor his English or how good a friend Father Blake was. She thought more of Father Blake and his wild mad eyes. This was a bad priest and now he was trying to destroy them both.

She had to go to Parramatta.

Colleen was running now, down Parramatta Road to the track that led north to the river and the Parramatta ferry dock. She didn't stop until she was there, heedless of her flushed face and the sweat that moulded her dress to her body like a sodden statue.

Parramatta, 2:00 PM

Greg Mahony was alone in his office, writing. It was hot, and breathing was difficult despite the open window. Every now and then he sucked on his pen while he pondered the next sentence. The appeal must be rational, based on the necessity rather than the desirability of clemency. Governor George Gipps had a reputation for being fair and humane, but he also had a passion for justice.

Mahony had not been surprised at the guilty verdict. Martin had done that to himself on the stand. But they had sentenced Martin to death. Impossible! Could they be that afraid of the press, which, judging by the approval in the front-page headlines, clearly felt that the verdict was fair and just? Worse yet, the bastards were going to hang him a little over eighteen hours from now, all of which left little time for an appeal and no time at all for any favourable public opinion to arouse itself. That tribunal sure must have had it in for him. Niblett, yes. He could understand that. But Weir and Cowling? The unanimity of a death sentence was something he hadn't anticipated in his wildest dreams.

Mahony went back to the appeal. He would finish it within an hour and could have it in Sydney at the Governor's residence by nightfall. Gipps was his last chance. He wouldn't even be able to see Martin again, but he had no choice.

~ ~ ~

Mahony sensed her presence before he turned to look, and there she was, framed in the open door. A tall striking girl with dark red hair and green eyes. She was wearing a light green cotton dress, and her only adornment was a ribbon of the same colour tying back her hair. Mahony rose to his feet awkwardly.

"Can I be of any help, Miss . . . ?"

"Are you Mr. Mahony, the lawyer?" Her voice was deeper than Mahony would have imagined, with a musical lilt. He wondered what her laugh would be like.

"Yes, I am he."

"The lawyer who defended Martin Goyette?"

"Yes."

"I'm Colleen Somerville. From the Bath Arms."

She paused waiting for the recognition that did not come. "I'm Martin's love. We are to be wed. Where is he? Can you take me to him?"

My God, thought Mahony. *So that's what he was hiding. Didn't want anyone to know. Protecting his girl from shame.*

Then it hit him. She didn't know. The girl didn't know. Mahony kept his words as gentle as possible. "Sit down, Miss Somerville. A glass of water?"

She must have read his disquiet. "Where is he? They are going to let him go, aren't they?"

Without thinking, Mahony reached for her hand. She stared at him with a level, unblinking gaze that somehow made it easier instead of harder.

"No, Miss Somerville. They are not going to let him go. He was found guilty."

"Guilty?" She breathed the word but Mahony heard it like a scream.

"I'm afraid so." He paused for a long second. "There's worse. Much worse. I'm sorry, Miss Somerville. They're going to hang him tomorrow morning."

Colleen's hand flew to her mouth. Mahony watched her bite on her finger. Hard. But when she spoke her voice was level and controlled. "He's innocent. He didn't kill anyone. You know that, don't you?"

"Yes, Miss Somerville. I know he is. The tragedy is that the tribunal didn't think so."

"What can we do?"

Mahony pointed to the paper on the desk. "I'm taking this appeal to Governor Gipps tonight. It's our only chance."

"Can I do anything? There must be something."

Mahony shook his head. "No. Not now. It's all in Gipps' hands."

"Then I will be with him. To the end." She grabbed his arm. "You will take me to him."

"I can't. No visitors. Just me and his confessor, and I have to go to Sydney. I won't be able to see Martin again, myself."

"Father Blake. It's his fault. I know it is."

Mahony was taken aback by the pure hatred in her voice. "Until you, . . . I mean, I thought that aside from his comrades in prison, Father Blake was the only friend Martin had."

"If you can call a snake a friend. Mr. Mahony, has Martin been receiving any letters in prison?"

"No. He used to ask me if there was mail for him. I presumed he must have had friends at the Bath Arms. Of course, I had no idea about you."

"I've written Martin six or more letters. And do you know who I was told to give them to? Who would gladly deliver them?"

"Father Blake? He visits often."

"You are right, Mr. Mahony. Only the letters never got to him. And yesterday I got a letter from Martin telling me that he doesn't love me any more and that I am to forget about him."

"I don't understand. I thought you said. . . ."

"That Martin loves me. He does. The letter was not written by Martin, Mr. Mahony. Father Blake wrote it. He thinks he is so clever. He forgets that I've seen his writing on notes at the hotel. He hates me. I know that. He must also hate Martin."

Mahony's mind was racing. Not that it mattered anymore but if Colleen was right, the priest could be involved in the whole ugly mess. His mind recoiled from the implications of the thought, for if Martin was innocent, and the girl had indeed come to some harm as Martin believed she had, then someone had to be guilty. And if Martin believed he was in some way responsible and if he wasn't, then who could have persuaded him that he was? His good friend the priest. Who else?

But it was all conjecture, and even if it wasn't, he couldn't prove a thing. No, regardless, the appeal was his only chance.

He said as much to Colleen, who seemed to read his mind. "I know," she said. "Do what you can Mr. Mahony." She rose to leave.

"Where will you go? Do you want to accompany me to Sydney with the appeal?"

"Will it make a difference?"

"Probably not. The Governor will make up his own mind."

"Then I shall see Martin. Where is he?"

"The cells at the barracks. But you can't go there. They won't let you in."

"We'll see about that. Thank you Mr. Mahony. God speed." She took a step towards him and Mahony could see her fighting for control. "You're a good man. I can tell that. Martin will understand. We'll thank you when it's all over."

"I hope so." He turned away, his eyes wet. When he looked back towards her, she was gone.

The scaffold now stood ready, the noose already in place, the five steps which led to the platform less than thirty paces from the cot where Martin Goyette lay in his warm cell, the stone walls still radiating heat left by the afternoon sun. He listened to the cicadas droning in the distance. It was such a pleasant sound and it reminded him of this place, a place he was coming to love but which he would never see after tomorrow. It was strange, how good things could change to bad so suddenly.

In Canada he had seen the bad hovering on the horizon, ignored by mis-guided zealots like his brother and the Chevalier. He had wittingly become involved even though he knew they couldn't win. The death penalty had been handed down, only to be lifted by fortune which had smiled down on him for reasons he hadn't even tried to understand. Possibly he had deserved to die then; he had done no worse than poor Joseph-Narcisse. Where was the need to rec-oncile what had happened with what was understandable? He hadn't tried back in Canada. Not really. He had just been afraid and sorry for himself.

But now, when he didn't deserve to die, he was not even afraid. Sorry for himself? No, not sorrow. Just a gnawing emptiness. He had been rejected by Colleen and by the land he had thought might be his. He didn't understand. He wanted so much to understand. He turned over on his side and listened through the noise of the cicadas. He desperately wanted Father Blake to come. He would help Martin understand. For when morning came and the clock ticked forward towards nine, there would be just himself.

For some reason Lamar came into his mind. He saw again the slim brown figure with the black bird perched on her shoulder, and the strange yellow eyes that seemed to look right through him. But it was not madness in those eyes. It was something else. His thoughts drifted to that day when she had proffered herself to him like she was driven by something else than the lusts of her own body. And his rejection of her. His cruelty and the shock on her face. It should have all been so different. And as he kept her in his thoughts, he remembered where he had heard – no, had read – her name before.

~ ~ ~

Colleen knew he would come. Even a priest like Father Blake would have to hon-our the needs of a condemned man. Cramped from sitting concealed for so long, she got awkwardly to her feet and stepped out in front of the priest. Though she hated and feared him, she knew she had no other recourse. Not if she wanted to see Martin.

"Father Blake. You've got to help me. Please take me with you to see Martin. I have to see him. Please Father, please." She reached for his sleeve.

The slime was reaching for him. He had to get away. He broke into a run.

Colleen pursued him. She was crying now. "Please, Father, please." She caught him and grabbed at his arm.

Rage overcame his terror. He couldn't allow scum like her to defile him in any way. He wheeled to face her, the fury burning in his eyes. "Leave me be, miserable wretch. We have no need of you and your slatternly kind. Go back to your own hell." Before she could reply he resumed his rush towards the sentry gate just a hundred yards ahead.

Colleen watched him. She couldn't let him get away with it. She yelled at his retreating back. "You're a liar, priest. You wrote the letter, not Martin. You're destroying him. Martin thinks you are good but you are evil. You read evil books. You lie. It was you that stole Mr. Neitch's money. It was you that killed the girl wasn't it? It was you. You're a thief, a murderer."

The fiend was shrieking at him, hurling words at him like barbs of fire. He began to run blindly, lurching from side to side, but not falling, half stumbling through the gate, his hands held tightly to his ears to ward off the terror.

~ ~ ~

Martin's relief at seeing Father Blake was mixed with shock at his good friend's appearance. His face was white and his hands were shaking, as if he had seen a ghost. Martin greeted him, the relief obvious in his voice. But Father Blake did not reply. He ignored Martin. He spoke not a word; he just sat on the cot and seemed to lose himself. Martin left him alone, wondering at first and then feeling more wretched than ever. What was wrong with Father? He wasn't the one who was going to die.

Martin had to talk, say something, if only to make himself feel better. Being with a man he believed was so strong, a man who would comfort him in need only to find a ashen-faced shaking silent figure was too much. So he began talking.

"I'm glad you could come, Father." He forced a laugh. "I know it's upsetting but you said it will be over in seconds and what will happen afterwards will make it all worthwhile. A martyr, you said. Well, a martyr I am going to be. My destiny awaits." He put his hand on his friend's arm. "Help me, Father. Help me understand why. Tell me about my destiny."

There was no reply. Father was mumbling to himself but Martin could not catch the words. He was drooling and for an instant Martin felt frightened. "Please, Father. Help me."

Father Blake turned his eyes to look at him. My God, his eyes were more like Madeleine's than ever. He remembered holding her shaking body and listening to her humming to herself. Father's eyes were not seeing him. Neither had Madeleine's. Then Father looked away and fell back to a mumbling. Martin kept on talking – anything to break the spell that had overcome his friend.

"Father, there is something I want to ask you. Remember when I told you about the native girl's name, Lamar? It is a strange name but I knew I had heard it before. I did. I had. Remember the icon I gave the native girl? It was very old and had been in my mother's family for centuries. Well, when I was in Longbottom I discovered a piece of paper in the icon with some writing on it. There was a date. Twelve hundred something, and the name Lamar. There was another name above it. I do not recall the second word in the name but I am sure the first word was Signy. Isn't that strange, Father? Lamar's name being found on an old piece of paper in an icon of the Virgin and then me thinking later that maybe that native girl had a vision of the Virgin. Isn't that strange?"

Suddenly Father Blake lurched to his feet and grabbed Martin by the shoulders, snarling. "It belongs to me. It belongs to me. It's mine. It was Signy Vigeland, you fool. It was Signy Vigeland." Then he began to weep, loud mad sobs like Martin had never heard before. Martin held his friend close until the sobbing had subsided. Then Father spoke. This time his tones were quiet, subdued. "They were my destiny. Both of them, and the foul ones destroyed them They used you, Martin Goyette. You were their agent in Lamar's destruction. You, Martin. You were their agent. Now you die in atonement. It's your destiny now."

It was then that Martin first realized that his friend was sick. Possibly really sick. Martin also knew for a fact that there was no martyrdom facing him, only death. His friend had misled him. First a martyr; now a sinner, dying in atonement. But Father was sick and now it didn't matter. Martin kept on talking, remembering something more, speaking for the sake of speaking, yet knowing somehow that it should be said.

"Father. These names I saw. There was a third one below Lamar's name. I didn't read it but it looked like two words. It was probably another name, but I didn't have a chance to look. I was going to, but then I re-sealed the paper in the icon and I forgot all about it. Until now, when I remembered Lamar's name."

Father Blake was suddenly standing, swaying like he was drunk except that his eyes were wild like fire. The Maligned Mother had again shown her wisdom. She had foreseen the work of the foul ones and had made two lists. Now she was sending it to him again.

Bernard Blake pushed his face close to the idiot who had just unwittingly saved him. "Fool. You have defined my destiny. Die like a coward for the morrow is mine." He began laughing wildly, hysterically, pounding on the bars and bringing the startled guard in seconds. Then he was gone, his footsteps not quite drowned by the laughter, echoing down the stone passageway until there was silence, and the lingering scent of lavender in the cell.

There was nothing he could do, so Martin lay down on his cot and thought. He thought about his mother, Uncle Antoine and the Chevalier. Madeleine came into his mind and he found he could think about her easily now without the pain he used to feel. He thought about François-Xavier and Toussaint and wondered how they were doing. Maybe they didn't even know what was happening to him. Maybe they were lying in their bunks this very second envying him. Then he thought about Father Blake and his vision of a noble destiny. Father Blake who was sick; who had behaved so strangely this very evening. Rejecting him and running out of the cell laughing about his destiny. Now that was not like Father Blake. Not at all. Unless of course that Father Blake had always been sick, and now he was just sicker.

~ ~ ~

Two things Father Blake had said came to Martin at that moment. Father had said that he, Martin, had given the girl a broken icon. He had, but he had told nobody that it was broken; it was a cause of his shame and he would never tell anyone that he had broken an icon. Not even Father Blake.

And the tribunal. Father said he could not testify because he knew that the members of the tribunal who had been here for several years disliked priests. But Niblett had only been here as long as he had. Father had lied to him. Twice. Martin's thoughts raced on. To know the icon was broken Father would have had to see it, and since the native girl had it, the only way Father could see it was if . . . Suddenly Martin knew it as if was written in stone on the floor of this very cell.

It was Father, the sick Father. Father Blake had killed the native girl because she had something to do with his destiny. Something that had gone wrong. So he killed her and then blamed Martin. Why? Why would he do that? Even to the point of encouraging him to die a martyr's death in the cause of their destiny. Father had hated him all the time and now he, Martin Goyette was dying for him. Worse yet, he had inadvertently aided him by providing him with information apparently important to his destiny.

The names in the Virgin. Father knew about them. They had to hold some significance. Lamar was special. But now she was dead and so would he be, soon. Martin also discovered there in the dark that he felt more sadness than anger over Father Blake. He was a very sick man. He should have noticed it earlier. Colleen had, and she had tried to warn him. But he had ignored her. Poor Father Blake; poor Martin Goyette. His thoughts turned to Colleen and it was only then that Martin Goyette cried, quietly to himself with his face facing the stone wall.

The Parramatta Road. East of the Bath Arms Hotel.
February 1, 1841. 1:00 AM

The bright light of the moon illuminated the road in front of him and Greg Mahony relished the cool feel of the sea breeze on his sweating back. He had been walking for an hour, one quarter the distance from Sydney to Parramatta. He'd be there well before morning and hopefully exhausted enough to sleep through the execution time of 9:00 AM He knew why he had decided to make the walk rather than spend the night in Sydney. He needed to do something; to work out the impotence of frustration.

Governor Gipps hadn't been able to see him until after 10:00 PM when he returned from a dinner with Bishop Bede Polding. The Governor had listened politely as Mahony presented his appeal for clemency, even alluding to the fact that he and the Bishop had already discussed the subject from that particular point of view.

Gipps would not – could not – commute the death sentence. Not after Myall Creek; not over the unanimous decision of a military tribunal; not when there was growing public outrage over the wanton disregard for aboriginal life. Justice had taken its course and now must be served. When Mahony had tried to point out the special nature of the case: the unreliability of the eyewitness and the absence of a body, Gipps had countered with a reference to Martin's virtual admission of guilt. When Mahony had tried to point out that it was guilt of a different kind that he had been admitting, he thought he saw a flicker of doubt in the Governor's eyes. So Mahony had decided to leave it at that, saying that if Gipps should decide after further deliberation to change his mind, commutation was still possible as late as 7:00 AM But then his hope died as suddenly as it had risen. Hardly possible, had said the Governor. The die was cast, his mind made up when he had authorized the construction of the scaffold the afternoon previously. Mahony was ushered to the door and to the warmth of a moonlit night. Then he had started walking.

The Parramatta River below the Orphanage for Girls
February 2, 1841. 1:30 AM

Bernard Blake slowly made his way down the path that led to the river. His head was throbbing terribly and the lights in front of his eyes were blinding him, even though it was dark. He held a lantern in his shaking hand. He had taken a long time to find the lantern. He knew he had to have it to read the writing on the paper. He had seen where Father Brennan had kept the lanterns many times before but this time he could not remember so he had fumbled in the dark at the presbytery until he had woken the priest. Father Brennan had tried to get him to go to bed; to rest, he had said. A doctor would be procured on the morrow. But he had pushed the old fool backwards and had demanded the lantern which was given to him by the frightened idiot. They'd all be frightened soon. And many would die. It had been so funny that he had laughed in the idiot's face until the imbecile fled.

Then he had forgotten where the orphanage was. There in the dark he had cursed the screaming demons for continuing to fight him on the road to his destiny. All was not lost. He would still win. The demons would lose, scream all they might; hiding the orphanage from him. But then he had remembered. It hurt to remember and he had to walk slowly through the dark, keeping the remembering with him. Then he had found it, looming out of the moonlight like a beacon to his destiny. He wanted to rest but he couldn't. Triumph was too close.

The barn smelled like filth but he ignored it and made his way to the place where the girl had dwelt. He thought he had thrown the icon on the cot, and his own wisdom told him that it would still be there. He entered her room, cursing the dark. His hand trembled as he tried to light the lantern. It took him a long while fighting the demons that were staying his hand. At last it was done and he raised the light above his head. He was right, of course. There it was. On the cot. The Maligned Mother with their destiny inside.

He clutched at it, losing his balance and falling forwards onto the cot where he lay panting, trying to get the strength to rise again. He pressed his lips to it and whispered his entreaty. The Maligned Mother answered him, for he found the strength to rise and stagger out from the confining dark to the open air. His steps took him to the river's edge. A thick log protruded from the water and he sank down on it. His fingers worked at the clay base. They were shaking so much he could scarcely hold her. At last the cavity appeared. He reached inside and found the paper. It was thin and crumbly as though it wanted to abandon its precious message to the night. So he tried to be careful.

And then it was free. He raised it to his eyes. But even in the bright moonlight it was useless. He needed the lantern. He put the lantern on the sandy bank and lay down beside it, planting his elbows in the sand so he could stay the trembling that the demons were forcing on him. He could see the words but they swam before his eyes. He brought the paper closer to his eyes and the light until a name emerged from the blurry dark.

SIGNY VIGELAND. His heart leapt and he cackled at the demons. He moved the paper up until his eyes found LAMAR just below Signy's name. He was slavering now, and he had to look away to refocus his eyes.

Bernard brought the light closer until it illuminated the darker strip below Lamar's name. There were letters there. Another name. It was faded worse than the others and even in the light he could not make it out. He shifted his elbows in the sand and turned so that his eyelids almost touched the yellowing paper. He followed the letters individually forming them with his lips. B E R N A. He almost choked on the spittle that gorged in his throat.

His eyes moved on until they encountered another letter, farther away than he had expected but another letter nonetheless. Squinting even more, he focussed on the first letter: B, and then the next: I, and the R. He knew it even then. The other three letters swam out to him, clutching him like they were drowning. O U S. But it was he who was drowning. He couldn't breathe.

BERNAD BIROUS. Bernard Birous. The Maligned Mother's ultimate choice. He got to his feet awkwardly and swayed towards the water. The pain in his head crested and he felt an explosion deep within him. He put his hands to his ears trying to quiet the noises but they wouldn't go away. Then suddenly they were quiet. Gone. And then he started to laugh. Louder and louder, the high-pitched frenzied sounds reaching across the water and upwards to the still leaves. The laughter had become hoarse, muted into a demented cackling by the time the two orphanage attendants reached him. He struggled against them but they led him away. And all the time he laughed.

7:00 AM

Greg Mahony stared at the bottle with bloodshot eyes. He couldn't sleep and even the whisky wouldn't help. He looked at the clock and kept drinking.

Colleen sat cross-legged in the guardroom staring at the bars in the window just above her head. Her hands were sore from tugging at them and her voice was hoarse from yelling at the sentry to let her out. Twice she had been caught trying to steal to the prison cells where she knew Martin was kept. Both times she had been caught and ejected by a kindly corporal who had finally lost his patience and had had her locked up in the lone cell in the guardhouse at the barracks gate. She had begged to be allowed to see Martin, but her pleas only seemed to firm the corporal's decision to keep her confined until after the execution.

Colleen sighed and wiped at her eyes. Then she got up, and reaching towards the bars, began prying at them with the long iron spike she always carried in her shoe to ward off ne'er-do-wells.

8:30 AM

The sunlight streamed into the cell and already Martin could feel its warmth. It was a good day to die. To see the blue sky; to feel the warmth in the air just before they put the hood on your head. He had eaten; had washed; had straightened his clothes and arranged his appearance as best he could. Father Blake had not returned and Martin had refused the services of the camp chaplain or even the priest in Parramatta they said they would send for. He didn't need them. They could tell him nothing. Whatever was out there was there regardless of any sanctimonious words. Martin Goyette was prepared.

He had decided just before the first rays of dawn that he would try to die bravely. That much he could do. It was the final battle. The one thing he could still win. He had lost everything. His mother, his brother, Madeleine. His comrades had deserted him; Father Blake had betrayed, then abandoned him. And the love of his life, Colleen, had rejected him. To cry any more would be pretend that things could get better. Death was an unknown, and dear God, it couldn't be worse than the misery he felt now. He had found fear around every corner. Without hope there was no fear. And so he had made his decision to die nobly, if only to not lose everything.

He heard them coming, the familiar sound of marching boots on stone and then they were outside his cell: four soldiers and an officer. The chaplain stood with them, clutching a bible and mouthing prayers. Manacles were placed about his wrists and he was led down the short corridor to the door which opened onto the courtyard, sunlight, and the scaffold.

Martin climbed the five steps, rigidly looking straight ahead, and then when he stood on the platform, up at the high blue sky. A lone bird circled above, wheeling freely in the air and Martin felt tears on his cheeks. He looked away and fixed his eyes on what looked like a loose stone in the top of the courtyard wall, and waited.

Someone asked him if he had any last words. He shook his head and then the black hood blocked out the stone and all light. Everything of this world gone except himself and the sound of the cicadas singing somewhere above. It seemed he stood there a long time, imagining the nod of the head that would send him plunging down.

~ ~ ~

The noises outside were garbled at first. Then the shouting became louder. A scuffling of running feet. The noise of a door bursting open and the shrill yell.

"Stop!"

Under the hood Martin could sense the confusion even as he tensed himself against the drop. Then he felt hands jerking at him, the hood being pulled from his head. He blinked in the sunlight trying to gather his thoughts. The smiling chaplain grabbed Martin's arm and turned him around to face the doorway to the courtyard. A sandy-haired man stood there, relief showing clearly on his ruddy face. Beside him, looking frightened and with the crow on her shoulder, was the native girl, Lamar.

The General Bourke Hotel, Parramatta, 3:00 PM

Pat Treacy took a long swig of beer and continued his story.

"I was away in the bush and when I comes home here she is. She just appeared. Her head was all smashed up and she was scratched all over. But she seemed all right otherwise. I tended to her for a week or more and when I read the Windsor paper, I knew it was her that they thought was dead. So I brought her in. We travelled all night. I thought we'd be too late. I'm just damned glad we wasn't."

Greg Mahony beamed and slapped Treacy on the back.

"That's sure one way to beat the hangman. Talk about cheating death. I knew he was innocent. I just couldn't figure out the tribunal."

"No, Mr. Mahony," said Martin. "You did your best. Really when you think about it, I did it to myself." He took his eyes from Colleen, who had her arms around him as if she would never let go, and looked at the two men opposite. "How can I ever thank you both enough? I feel as good about Lamar being alive as I do about cheating the hangman." He squeezed Colleen and smiled. "Well, almost." He looked at Treacy before continuing. "Where is she now, Mr. Treacy?"

"Gone. She just disappeared yesterday afternoon." Treacy looked wistful for a minute. "You know, I don't think she'll be back."

Mahony ordered two more drinks for himself and Treacy. "Now you two go. You've got friends in Longbottom who want to see you. And Mr. Neitch as

371

well. He's quite upset but—" Mahony caught himself but Martin hadn't appeared to have noticed, so he continued. "I think you'll get your job back. Now get out of here."

~ ~ ~

Outside in the hot sun behind the hotel where no one could see them, Martin and Colleen kissed until she could feel his hardness pressing against her. She giggled softly and nibbled at his neck. They held hands boldly all the way down to the ferry.

~ ~ ~

"Nice work getting him out of here before he asked about the priest," said Treacy.

"I didn't want to be the one who told him. He admired him so much."

"And now he's gone mad."

Mahony sipped his beer, remembering in the priest's haunted eyes the compelling aura of a man outside his own sanity.

"Yes," he replied simply.

Upper Colo River Area, February, 1841

The rain had stopped and Lamar picked her way silently through the sodden bushlands, avoiding the mud and all the time keeping the sun to her right. The pain in her head was not as bad as when it had made her seek out the blue-eyed one who had found her before. Now she was going back to the Dharug. The rains had come and kalabari would return. Kurikuta had heard them from the Dreamtime and had come herself, with the Ganabuda.

She climbed a large boulder and surveyed the wooded valley before her. The cliffs on the other side were high and craggy but she knew a way around them. Beyond were the Dharug. At the bottom of the valley a muddy stream wound its way around rocks and through the dim steep gorges. Lamar frowned when she saw the water. Would Kurikuta come to her there? There had been things of the Dreamtime that should have happened; things that Kurikuta had said. But it had not been as it should. Was it not yet time? Above her a rainbow dipped its way over the hills towards the Dharug, and, silhouetted against its coloured brilliance, Atha gave his cry as he flew before her. Lamar smiled and quickened her pace.

EPILOGUE

Anzio, August 6, 1858

The walled convent of St. Catherine of Genoa nestled among the olive groves not far from the town of Anzio south of Rome. Surrounded by cork oaks and Aleppo pines, the timeless seventeenth-century convent was a reminder of an age when the work of God held more sway over the minds of men. The forty-two Dominican nuns who lived there practised a way of life little changed from that of their forebears whose remains rested in the well-tended cemetery at the back of the convent. Few villagers had ever been inside the ivy covered walls and those who had told of the splendid lawns and flower gardens and the ornate stone benches where old men sat in the sun.

Three men did in fact sit in the sun but they were not old. Prematurely grey and stooped, they walked slowly and were usually attended by a nun who guided their steps. When they sat, they did so separately, not talking, heedless of the tame birds that pecked at their feet or of the limpid water ponds that reflected their white robes. Their eyes were blank, devoid of feeling or comprehension. Only the one on the bench in the shade, the one with the silver in his hair, moved his lips and he was talking to himself.

~ ~ ~

Bishop Thomas Rivarola left his carriage in Anzio and walked the two miles to the convent. He loved this part of the country and relished the opportunity to tramp it again, even if his heavy robes did not agree with the summer heat. As he strode along the narrow road he smelled the fragrance of the mastic bushes, and smiled. Yes, it was good to feel the air and smell the earth even if he really shouldn't be here. Not when this thing in France was unfolding. They said he was to go back immediately for further verification. Not that he needed any. He was convinced. However, orders were orders. But first was the matter of his old friend.

Rivarola tried to visit Bernard as often as possible. He knew the nuns were excellent with their three patients, all former Dominicans who needed close care and attention. He was aware, too, that Bernard didn't know him. However, Rivarola couldn't be sure that his talking didn't help; was not certain that behind those dull eyes that had once blazed with such passion, there was no understanding at all. So he went to St. Catherine's whenever he could get away from Rome, bringing food and sweets and lots of talk. He talked until the nuns came and took Bernard away. And all the time he talked the dull dark eyes looked straight at him, unblinking, seemingly unseeing.

Rivarola entered the convent grounds. It was such a peaceful place. The sun was bright and the scent of oleander heavy in the air. He was greeted by Sister Cecilia who led him into the garden to Bernard.

Rivarola hugged his old friend, feeling the thin shoulders and then the cold limp hand. He led Bernard to a bench in the sun talking as though Bernard were his closest confidant.

"Yes, Bernard, it's most amazing. I've seen nothing like it before. A peasant French girl from Lourdes. She's seen the Virgin. Nine times already. Always in the same place: in a grotto near the Gave de Pau River. The last time she appeared, a blind stonecutter bathed his eyes in the spring in the grotto and was cured.

"Remember that peasant girl from Calabria? Maria Balboni, I think, was her name. Well, this girl reminds me of her but is much frailer. Bernard, I've talked to her and I'm convinced. She's seen the Virgin all right."

Rivarola fumbled in his robe. "I've brought you something from Lourdes. A drawing of the girl seeing the Virgin. This girl's famous already. They gather at the grotto by the thousands hoping to see the Virgin talking to this child."

He placed the drawing on Bernard's lap. "See, there's the girl and that's the Virgin, and that's the spring she's standing in."

Rivarola noticed that Bernard seemed to be staring at the name on the top. Not only that, but he was trying to move a shaking finger to it. Rivarola laughed. "That's the girl's name. Bernardette Soubirous. Her first name's just like yours. I hadn't noticed that before."

Bernard turned to Rivarola. It was a moment Rivarola would never forget. For an instant, the old Bernard came back. Understanding flashed like fire and mockery in his eyes. Then it was gone. The drawing fell to the ground and Bernard yawned. Rivarola knew the sign and went to fetch Sister Cecilia.

When they came back Bernard was humming to himself. He must have accidentally stepped on his drawing, thought Rivarola. It was crushed, spoiled, ground into the earth, especially around the name. It wasn't recognizable any more.

Author's Afterword

The idea for this novel came during my research for a scholarly paper on the fifty-eight French Canadian Patriotes who were exiled to Sydney, Australia, for their part in the abortive uprising against the British in 1838. Martin is fictitious but those with whom he associated, as well as the principal actors in the rebellion, are not. Joseph Narcisse and Chevalier de Lorimier died on the scaffold as described. I based the accounts of the trials, the voyage on the *Buffalo* and the happenings at Longbottom Stockade on the diaries kept by three Patriotes.

Descriptions in the Australian section are as accurate as possible. While Lamar is fictitious, the Dhurag are not. I strove for authenticity and since I was born and raised near Parramatta I was able to identify with the places described in the narrative. George Gipps, Bede Polding, Henry Baddely and Emmanual Neitch were contemporary figures. The Bath Arms was a real hotel on the Parramatta Road near Burwood, and Neitch himself came from Genoa. The Parramatta Female Factory was a horrible reality.

While I took some licence with them, the scenes describing the visions of Reginald and Dominic were based on Catholic hagiographic accounts. However, almost all the characters in the European section of the narrative are fictitious except Cardinal Lambruschini and Bishop Ugolini. Naturally, all the errors and any misinterpretations of actual events reside squarely with me. And though I have written a work of fiction, it was surprising that in so doing, I found myself dealing with the same discretionary choices implicit in scholarly analysis.

Max Foran
Priddis, 2005

Author's Acknowledgements

My greatest thanks are to my daughter, Fiona, who inspired me to begin writing this novel and who encouraged me to continue when I was giving serious thought to letting it go. A special thanks to Marilyn Harker and Bob Dunn who read the manuscript as it was being written. Their positive support and suggestions meant a lot to me, and sustained my enthusiasm for a task that I discovered was much more daunting than I had anticipated. Thanks too to Carmen Moore, Gwen Chapman and Gail Anderson who liked the manuscript so much that they took it upon themselves to pursue possible avenues of publication. I appreciated the votes of confidence from my friends Gordon Fairhead, Fergus Hill, Wally Aebli, Tyler Trafford, Isobel Hogue, and Sandy Alvarez Toye, all of whom read the manuscript and thought I had written something for which I could be proud. Frank Giancarlo was there when I needed him. Brad Wojak did a fine job in rearranging the narrative to provide more cohesion and flow. Distinguished literary historian and colleague, George Melnyk, believed in the novel and promised to badger me until he saw it in print. Finally I would like to thank Lee Shedden for having the faith to bring *The Madonna List* to the public.

MAX FORAN is the author of a dozen books, including *The Chalk and the Easel: The Life and Work of Stanford Perrott; Trails and Trials: Markets and Land Use in the Canadian Cattle Industry; Roland Gissing: the People's Painter;* and *Calgary: Canada's Frontier Metropolis.* He is a professor in the University of Calgary's faculty of Communications and Culture, and lives near Calgary.